CLOUDY
WITH A
CHANCE
OF
MURDER

CLOUDY
WITH A
CHANCE
OF
MURDER

A DANIEL JACOBUS MYSTERY

GERALD ELIAS

LEVEL
BEST BOOKS

First published by Level Best Books 2021

This novel is entirely a work of fiction. The names, characters and incidents portrayed in it are the work of the author's imagination. Any resemblance to actual persons, living or dead, events or localities is entirely coincidental.

Gerald Elias asserts the moral right to be identified as the author of this work.

First edition

ISBN: 978-1-68512-025-2

Cover art by Level Best Designs

This book was professionally typeset on Reedsy.
Find out more at reedsy.com

Praise for the Daniel Jacobus Mystery Series

"Fans of ratiocination will be pleased with Utah concertmaster Elias' witty and acerbic debut."—*Kirkus Reviews*

"This richly plotted mystery will thrill music lovers, while those not so musically inclined will find it equally enjoyable."—*Publishers Weekly*

"A musical feast for mystery and music lovers."—*Library Journal* (starred review)

"...the twists and turns of his plotting will keep readers guessing. The real hook here, however, is the insider's view of the musical world..."—*Booklist*

"Brilliant and captivating on every level."—Starred review, *Booklist*

"Elias has a nose for creative detail and a refreshing impatience with pomposity. Indulge yourself in his artfulness."—*Kirkus Reviews*

"There's just one word for this book: bravo!"—Starred review, *Publisher's Weekly*

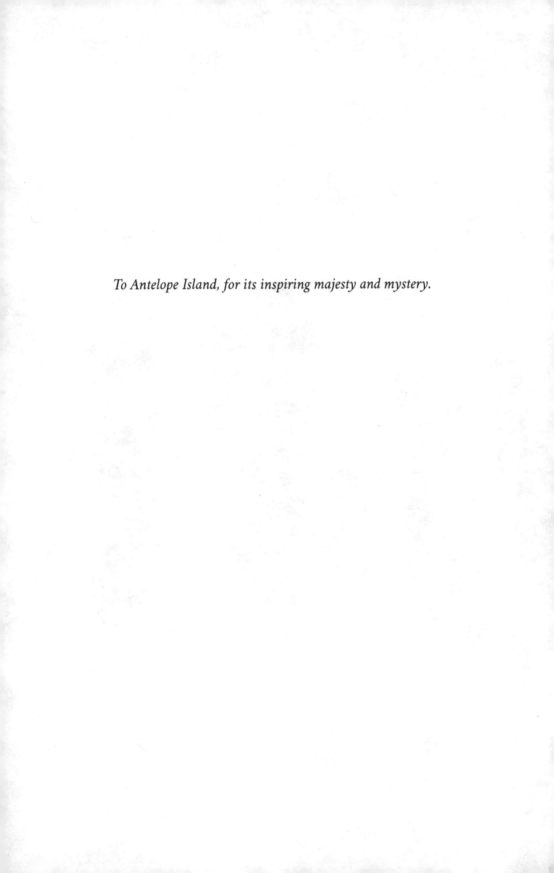

To Antelope Island, for its inspiring majesty and mystery.

Summer, from the *Four Seasons*
Sonnet written by Antonio Vivaldi for his
Violin Concerto in G Minor

Allegro non molto
Beneath the blazing sun's relentless heat
men and flocks are sweltering, pines are
scorched. We hear the cuckoo's voice; then
sweet songs of the turtle dove and finch are
heard.
Soft breezes stir the air….but threatening
north wind sweeps them suddenly aside. The
shepherd trembles, fearful of violent storm
and what may lie ahead.

Adagio e piano - Presto e forte
The fear of the furious thunder and lightning
saps the strength from the shepherd's tired
limbs as gnats and flies buzz furiously
around.

Presto
Alas, his worst fears were justified, as the
heavens roar and great hailstones beat down
upon the proudly standing corn.

Allegro non molto
Sotto dura staggion dal sole accesa langue
l'huom, langue 'l gregge, ed arde 'l pino,
Scioglie il cucco la voce, e tosto intesa canta
la tortorella e 'l gardellino.
Zeffiro dolce spira, ma contesa muove
Borea improviso al suo vicino;
E piange il Pastorel, perché sospesa teme
fiera borasca, e 'l suo destino.

Adagio e piano – Presto e forte
Toglie alle membra lasse il suo riposo il
timore de' lampi, e tuoni fieri
E de mosche, e mosconi il stuol furioso.

Presto
Ah che pur troppo i suo timor sono veri
tuona e fulmina il cielo grandinoso
Tronca il capo alle spiche e a' grani alteri.

i

Prologue

Utter chaos. Tons of wind-driven hail buckled the tent, trapping hundreds of concertgoers. The wind, oppressive, whirling, and wailing, mockingly imitated their moans. The storm, as severe as it was unforeseen, cut off electricity, blanketing the disastrous scene in pitch blackness.

A sudden blast of thunder jump-started the hailstorm back into unwelcome life. Yumi approached Sunny Flox, who, with Christian Bjørlund, was standing just outside the tent. An EMT ran up, pleading for assistance to extricate a group of Road Scholar senior citizens still ensnared under the flattened concert tent. *Are there injuries?* Yumi asked. *Impossible to tell. Probably. Have to get them to a safer place.* With her mobile phone's flashlight, Yumi illuminated enough space in front of her to begin the crawl back in.

"Oh, Jesus! I need help!"

It was Marcus Renfro's voice, cutting through the wind. He was somewhere in front of her, amidst the rubble, amidst the casualties. Exactly where was impossible to determine. Yumi feared for his safety. It was so dark.

"Help, here!" he called again, this time even louder. "It's Anita. She's had an accident. I think...I think she might be dead."

An accident? Yumi thought. *How is that possible? It doesn't make sense. I just spoke to her only moments ago. If Jacobus were here, he would say this was no accident. He would say something like, "Two and two is supposed to equal four, but this ain't four." No, this doesn't add up. In other words, Jacobus would say, "This was murder." If only he were here.*

Chapter One

Two Months Earlier

A crimson sun, too big to be real, dipped below the treetop canopy long before dusk, illuminating pastel, newborn foliage with a Maxfield Parrish glow, and casting long late-spring shadows onto the forest floor. Immediately after the ambulance, siren blaring, had rushed Daniel Jacobus to the hospital, unconscious and perhaps dying, Yumi Shinagawa sought solace in Jacobus's Berkshire woods, seeking reassurance, seeking within its comforting, stoic embrace the resolve to persevere if the unimaginable—that he wouldn't survive—became reality.

Was there ever a world before Daniel Jacobus? How could there be one without him? How would she, how could she, carry his torch? That would be her honor, her obligation, and also her burden. Since she began her studies with him when she was a teenager, a time that seemed a lifetime ago but in another way almost like yesterday, Jacobus had become more of a father to her than her biological father in Japan, who for so long had been remote in distance, in spirit, and now also in memory. A "salaryman," a traditional Japanese man of business, Mr. Shinagawa had dedicated his life to his company, spending mornings on the train, days in his office, and nights drinking expensive whiskey with his co-workers. He provided the income, for which she was grateful, but he had little time or room for paternal affection, for which she was not.

Jacobus had been her teacher, her mentor, her adviser. Her conscience.

He challenged her—that was the diplomatic way to put it. And the more he challenged her, the more she knew he loved her, because that was the measure of how much her success meant to him. He would tolerate mistakes—"Everyone makes them. Even me," he once confessed—but he would not accept lack of commitment or mental laziness, because that meant disrespect to the music. Oh, the hell to pay if he thought someone disrespected the music! If truth be told, Jacobus was an occasional pain in the ass. But she wouldn't dwell on that part. Not now.

The forest was cool in the shade, and moist, and a cushioning bed of humus muted her step like her violin's *sordino*. *Sotto voce*. Yes, she could understand why Jacobus loved his woods. Why they gave him such comfort. Of the sense of liberation from the constraints and stresses of life. Of the burdens of the three legs of the wobbly stool on which he had balanced his life's world-weariness: the childhood abuse he suffered at the hands of a notorious violin competition judge; his guilt, his irrational sense of responsibility for his parents' tragic fate in a German death camp while he safely fiddled as a student in the U.S.; and the sudden blindness with which he was stricken on the day of his concertmaster audition for the Boston Symphony, altering the trajectory of his life from performer to teacher. That was Daniel Jacobus's *weltschmerz*, as his parents would have said.

Though, amazingly, he won the audition, it was a Pyrrhic victory. In the end, even he realized that to be concertmaster of a major orchestra one needed to be able to see the conductor. *But so much the better for me*, Yumi thought, in a perverse sort of way. *Without his blindness, he would never have become my teacher.*

For just about anyone else, any one of those tragedies would have been life-shattering. But tragedy for Jacobus was as Mother Earth had been for Antaeus, a source of renewed strength. His dogged determination to endure had given Yumi strength. It made standing on a stage, performing even the most difficult concerto in front of thousands of judgmental listeners, seem like child's play. Familiarity with tragedy seemed only to have made Jacobus stronger, tougher, harder. *Seemed*, Yumi thought. *Seemed*. Underneath, she understood his vulnerability. His fragility. His sadness. His weariness.

2

And now he was at death's door. Her teacher, her hero, had attempted suicide. Antaeus had ultimately been subdued when Heracles lifted him off the ground and he lost contact with his mother, Earth, rendering him powerless. Heracles then crushed him. Would that be Jacobus's fate?

The blanket of silence the woods offered had been his solitude and his protection. Of course, for Jacobus, the silence was by no means silent. Not by any means. He would insist that what was called silence by others was in fact a symphony of sounds, and he took great delight in enumerating them. The show-off! Yumi had learned much from Jacobus about how to listen. Listening was the key to life, he maintained, whether it was to music or nature, the spoken word, or even random noise. When pestered sufficiently, he would explain, gruffly and with broad brushstrokes, that his success bringing criminals to justice was simply the result of listening to, and remembering what people said, how they said it, and in what context. It was when one listened and not just looked that one could gain understanding. The ears were much more important than the eyes.

"It's obvious that's what nature intended," he often said. "Ears are what's enabled humans to survive."

"Why do you say that?" she once naively asked. Only once.

"Because," he replied, "you can close your eyes. You can never close your ears. You are *always* hearing. But to listen, you have to use your brain. If you're listening, nothing can sneak up on you."

She learned to listen. From time to time, he would scoff and grudgingly accept that Yumi had learned a thing or two from him. And as she wandered through his woods, she smiled with the thought that he would be pleased that in the past ten minutes or so she had mentally cataloged a lengthening list of sounds. It included at least a half dozen birds: a robin, a house wren, two thrushes, a catbird, chickadees, the distant hollow report of a woodpecker. *What kind of woodpecker?* he would test her. And there were insects, not that she could distinguish them except for the bees, which she liked for their positive mission in the scheme of things, and the mosquitoes, which she didn't, and slapped at on her bare arms. Jacobus could tell one bee species from another by the qualities of their buzz. Or so he bragged. Yumi wasn't sure she believed that. And, as she skidded and slipped her way down the hill toward the stream, there, in the tree just above her, was the comic ratchet of a gray squirrel. Not too long until nut-gathering season began.

Then there were the background sounds rounding out the collage of faux silence. A light breeze that came and went, tickling the foliage, stirring it into life. An occasional car strumming along Route 41 which, as a tie to humanity, was comforting in its own way. The beep-beep-beep of a truck backing up somewhere distant, from the direction of Housatonic. Maybe it was the Millers' place, where they were adding on to their house, or the town road crew patching, finally, some late-winter potholes. And there was the ever-present white noise of the stream, which after a thunderstorm was a raging torrent, but which now, after two weeks without rain, was hardly more audible than her own breath. And, of course, there was the slosh of her footsteps in last year's leaves.

But as much as she had trained her ears to hear in the woods, Jacobus could hear twice as much. It seemed he could hear the sun rise and set. He could hear the trees grow. No wonder so many people underestimated him, simply because he didn't have sight. No wonder he was such a great musician. But now? How could the world continue to turn without Daniel Jacobus?

The toe of Yumi's hiking boot caught under the crook of a broken branch half-hidden in the leaves. She tripped, too busy listening to the sounds of the forest and not paying enough attention to what was right in front of her. Jacobus would no doubt have found a moral in that. A teaching moment. A reminder about the blind being able to see better than people with functional eyes. Or connecting to music: "Play it the way the composer wrote it before you start wandering off and get lost."

The branch over which she stumbled, landing on her hands and knees, was about four feet long, one end firmly lodged under a boulder, evidently broken off from one of the majestic ancient maples that towered over its vassals of ash, cherry, and pine. The branch, almost but not quite straight, was partially embedded in the thick, leafy humus. Time and insects had stripped it of some of its bark. Yumi, bruised only in her pride, got to her feet and dusted the leaves off her clothes and her hair. At first, she cursed at the branch with the same four-letter words she had learned from Jacobus, which made her feel much better. But then, considering the steepness of the hillside, she picked it up, tested its sturdiness, and used it to haul herself back up the hill. Her enemy had become her ally.

Returning to her red Camaro parked on Jacobus's pebbly driveway, Yumi was about to fling the stick, which had served its purpose admirably, back over the hillside whence it had come, but something prevented her. Something about the stick. It was almost as if the stick—this inanimate piece of wood—was sending her a message. As if it had purposely placed itself in her path so that she would inevitably find it. *That's ridiculous*, she thought. Nevertheless, she sat on the ground, her back against her car, and rested the stick on her lap, trying to understand its hold on her, examining it.

On one hand, the branch was crooked with obvious imperfections. On the other, it was strong and useful and durable, with its own crude beauty. Almost like a Janáček string quartet, where the inspiration is so earnest and heartfelt that the crudeness of his craftsmanship actually made it more beautiful than if it had been smoother, more polished. Or like a performance by the ninety-year-old Pablo Casals, whose technique was long past its prime, yet for its very fragility made his Bach Cello Suites even more sublime. Time-peeled bark—gray-black and hard on the outside, red-orange to a pale yellow on its inner layers—only partially covered the branch's underlying golden wood, blemished with worm holes and beetle tunnels, which in its own way complemented its personality. Character-building, Jacobus would have said. The branch was rough-hewn, inflexible. No. Inflexible was too negative a connotation. Stalwart was better. Steadfast. Unfaltering. It could be depended on, regardless of the circumstances. It had helped her climb the hill, hadn't it? And it could last forever, something she prayed for for Jacobus.

Tears came unbidden into Yumi's eyes. *This branch is Daniel Jacobus!* Not only in its characteristics, but also in its function. The stick had done for her what Jacobus had throughout her life. At first, when she was a student, she had thought Jacobus was blocking her path, just like the stick; an impediment, making life difficult, daring her to fall and to fail. Tripping her up. She gradually came to realize that it was intentional: Without saying so, he was telling her, "Look where you're going!" That it was up to her, not him, to understand how to reshape the impediment into a support, a tool to strengthen her, to enable her to make her way in an unforgiving world. It had been the most important lesson in her life—more important than how to play Vivaldi, Mozart, or even Bach—and he had taught that particular lesson without saying a word. Without articulating it. It was just who he was. His very being. The branch—a castoff of a maple that was a seedling at the same time Antonio Vivaldi's *Four Seasons* captivated Venice three hundred years earlier—was Daniel Jacobus, the musician whose own musical lineage could be traced back, unbroken, to Vivaldi's day. Yes, the branch was Jacobus. Yumi picked it up. In her hands, she sensed she held Jacobus's life in the balance.

She took the stick back to her Manhattan apartment and put it on her living room table. It would be her keepsake. Her talisman. Only a few days before, she had agreed to substitute for the Dutch violinist Edo Kuypers at the Antelope Island Music Festival in Utah. Some sort of medical emergency, they explained, that wouldn't permit him to leave Amsterdam. Of course, Yumi hoped he would recover from whatever his ailment was, but now she regretted having consented to step in. If Kuypers hadn't begged out, Yumi could have stayed by Jacobus's side until... Until whatever happened. But now, having agreed, it would be impossible to renege at this late date, especially as there were only nine musicians in the whole festival: the Kreutzer String Quartet, three other string players, the pianist Jamie Barov, and her. Besides, as an incentive they had offered, and she had accepted, the festival's invitation for her to replace Kuypers as guest soloist for Vivaldi's *Summer* from the *Four Seasons*. It would be so discourteous to back out now, at such a late date. Even though she was only three-quarters Japanese and hadn't lived in Japan since she was a teenager, her hardwired sense of obligation prevented her from even considering such an ill-mannered act.

Unable to sleep, Yumi returned to the living room and sat on her couch, staring first at the stick, then at the city lights sparkling in the night. She made a decision. She peeled off the remainder of the bark, breaking a fingernail or two as she scraped off the last, resistant bits. Definitely not something a violinist should do. Using a scissors, she tried unsuccessfully to clip off the dozen or so pointy nibs protruding along the branch. She had somewhat better luck with a box cutter, but it was the gardening hand pruner she had stashed away in a closet that did the trick. When she was done, she stood the stick up in the corner of her bedroom, said good night to it with a formal bow, and went to sleep. It had been a day filled with emotion, and worse, with uncertainty.

The next morning she called the hospital. There was still no word about Jacobus's condition. He was still in an artificially induced coma. Revived by a scalding shower and her morning cup of *genmaicha*, Japanese wheat tea, Yumi retrieved the branch. Ascertaining the area on it that would offer the most natural grip, she used a pruning saw to cut a few inches from each end, so that area would be at exactly the correct height for Jacobus to hold it. She really should be practicing all the music for the festival—there was so much repertoire she had to learn—but she could not escape her compulsion to finish her project of transforming the branch into a perfect walking stick. She found an old chisel in the same utility drawer as the box cutter and smoothed over the sharp edges from having sawn off the ends of the stick. Finally, she sanded it, at both ends and all along its length. It was now smoother, though its slight crookedness and some of its crusty exterior remained. That was an essential for Jacobus. Without the crusty exterior, without the imperfections, Jacobus wouldn't be Jacobus. And Yumi was convinced that as long as she continued to work on the walking stick, continued to hone its personality, Jacobus would continue to live.

The next day, Jacobus's condition still had not changed. What more could she do with the all-but-completed stick? Yumi took it to midtown Manhattan, to the studio of the internationally respected violinmaker and dealer, Boris Dedubian. She asked Dedubian to varnish the stick as if it were a great violin. She did not explain why. Over his long career, Dedubian had worked on dozens of Stradivaris and Guarneris worth millions of dollars so, not surprisingly, he was chagrined by such a request. He had never been asked to varnish a stick. But since Yumi was such a renowned violinist and—more to the point—a potential high-paying customer, Dedubian smilingly obliged. Yumi returned the next day. Dedubian had not only imbued the wood with a rich, glowing luster, he had managed to transform the characteristic imperfections in the wood into an esthetic enhancement, exactly what Yumi had hoped for. "You have a nice hard piece of maple," he had said. "It should last a hundred years." This brought tears to Yumi's eyes, partly because the stick was so beautiful and enduring, but more because it was finished, and she despaired.

Which is when she got the phone call. Jacobus had survived.

When Jacobus regained consciousness, he had no idea where he was. He thought he was dead, as had been his plan. He should have been dead, in any case. Why wasn't he? *Hell, maybe I am!* Jacobus thought. *But if this is death, it's the same as life. Sucks.*

It was so quiet. He went back to sleep, for how long he had no idea, and woke up again.

Music had been his only salvation, the only thing that had kept him sane. If he were now in heaven, unlikely as that was, considering his track record, there was only one word that was worthwhile for him to utter.

"Beethoven."

"No, it's me, Jake."

A familiar voice.

"Yumi! I was hoping for Beethoven, but you'll do. Where the hell am I? Are you dead, too?"

Yumi's laughter. *Was I funny?*

"No, Jake. Neither of us is dead. We're in your hospital room. But I'm happy to see that you're now not only alive but also awake."

Yumi's hand on his, her touch. Confirmation. *I guess I must be alive.* But the sound of her voice seemed so distant. Like an echo. Was she really there?

"Hospital room? I don't get it. I'm supposed to be dead. The kid brought me the poisonous mushroom, like I asked him. A false morel. *Gyromitra kill-my-tuchus* I think is the scientific name. They're lethal. What went wrong?"

"This is what I learned from the doctor. Everyone *thought* you'd eaten a false morel. But that kid was too considerate. He had a feeling you were up to something that wouldn't end well and he didn't have the heart to bring you a false morel. So he found you a real one. They're very expensive, you know. People love them. They're the Yo-Yo Ma of mushrooms."

"A false–false morel! Go figure. But...then why am I in the damned hospital?"

"They said because you ate it raw. That unless you cook morels, even real ones, they have toxins in them that can make you really sick. And if someone is allergic to it, which you seem to be, because you're pretty well covered with hives, it's no wonder they thought you might die. And the morel might have had some nasty bacteria from the soil on it, too, which couldn't have helped."

"That's all?"

"Since you asked, no. You seem to have washed the mushroom down with a whiskey chaser. They determined that when they pumped your stomach. They said you'll likely have some residual gastric distress, but that your heart is as strong as an ox."

"A congenial heart condition, eh?"

"I probably shouldn't say this, but it's so good to hear your silly jokes again. For a while I thought you might..."

"Die? Don't worry about me. I'm immoral. But what about—?"

"Sybil? She confessed. To everything. That's how much you scared her with your scheme. Setting the scene to make it look like it was Sybil who poisoned you. But I'll never forgive you for trying to kill yourself just to prove she was guilty."

"I thought it was pretty clever, myself. Kill two birds with one toadstool."

Jacobus was only partially satisfied with the result. The whole business, in which Sybil Baker-Hulme was merely the foulest of several foul protagonists, had disgusted him. Enough to want to be rid of a world in which notions of decency were spat upon. The sexual misconduct, the abuse of power. The murder. And at a music conservatory! Of all places, where the goal was teaching young people how to create beauty with their own hands, how had a music conservatory become a microcosm of a terminally ill world? What was happening to the classical music world? Was he wrong, and had it always been like that? Thinking back to his own childhood, he couldn't deny the only answer to that question was probably yes. Such great music, but such abhorrent behavior. The terrifying thought struck him that somehow those two such opposite forces might, paradoxically, be inextricably entwined. Interdependent. Wagner's misogyny and antisemitism were legendary, but who could deny the brilliance of his music? And he wasn't the only genius with a track record. The Renaissance composer, Gesualdo, murdered and chopped up his wife and her lover, and avoided prosecution only because he was a prince.

Why couldn't musicians argue over music and call it a day? Arguing is not a bad thing. Music arouses passions. That was its purpose. So arguments should be expected. Encouraged even. But murder? Jacobus hoped he would never live to see it again, but life had taught him that hope and expectations were two different—and for him, diverging—paths.

So, yes, Jacobus was gratified that his gambit had put a murderess behind bars, but he had truly hoped eating the mushroom would also have killed him in the process. How much longer did he have, anyway? He was an old fart. He had outlived his usefulness. Oh, how he would have gone out in a blaze of glory! His friends—few though they were—would have mourned him. Oh, the tears! But now? Now he was back to being an old, useless, blind hanger-on. Could he still play the violin? Maybe, a little. But why? And who cared anymore?

"I brought you a present," Yumi said.

She placed something in his right hand as he lay on his back in his hospital bed. He wrapped his fingers around it. *Hmm*. Roughly cylindrical. Definitely wood. Gnarly. He rotated his wrist to determine its weight, balance, and length. It banged against something metallic, which could have been his bedside table or some unfathomable piece of hospital equipment a few feet from it.

"Take a guess," she said.

"A stick!" he said with exaggerated enthusiasm. "You got me a stick! Just what I always wanted! Are you sure this isn't for Trotsky? He'll love it when I throw it for him to fetch. Or whack him over the head with it."

"You wouldn't do that, Jake. Would you?"

"Nah, it might break the stick. It wouldn't do any good, anyway. He wouldn't feel a thing."

"But, Jake, this isn't just any stick!" Yumi said. "It's your new walking stick. And I've named it, too!"

"Yeah? What?"

"Excalibur!"

"Excalibur?"

"Yes, that's the name of King Arthur's sword."

"I know damn well what the hell Excalibur is. Don't condescend."

"But I named it Excalibur because whoever wields it is the true king. It means you're the true king of violin teachers!"

Jacobus grumbled something incomprehensible while manipulating the stick in his hand, first as if he were a baton twirler, then as a pool shark.

"You don't like that name, Jake?"

"Far as I'm concerned, there hasn't been a king yet who shouldn't've been shortened by a head. Except maybe chicken à la."

He swung the stick as if he were an executioner and it was a scimitar, whacking it against the pole that held his IV bag.

"So, what would *you* like to name it?" Yumi asked.

From the sound of her voice, Jacobus gauged Yumi's distance from where he lay.

"Me? I would name it…Hocus."

"Hocus? Is that an Indian name? A chief or a warrior?"

"Guess again. Think. What does hocus go with?"

"Pocus?"

"You asked for it!"

Jacobus took the end of the stick, and with uncanny accuracy, poked Yumi right in the ribcage and let out a guffaw.

11

"Hocus! Hocus! Hocus!" Poke, poke, poke. "That's the name of my new stick! What do you think, Yumi? You like it? Hocus?"

"Maybe they really should have given you the other mushroom," she said and kissed him on the forehead.

Chapter Two

How had Jacobus been talked into it? For him to have been persuaded was as rare as steak tartare. How had they done that to him? The concert wasn't even going to be in a civilized place, like New York City or…he couldn't think of another civilized place on the spur of the moment…but was in the middle of the Great Salt Lake. In Utah.

It was Yumi's doing. And Nathaniel's, too. But it was Yumi who'd put Nathaniel up to it. Smart one, that fiddler, Kuypers, for backing out with a medical excuse. Maybe Kuypers had chosen to eat a mushroom, just like Jacobus had, to get out of having to go all the way to Utah to play some damn concert in the desert in the middle of a lake. Was Yumi humoring him, telling him how important it was for him to hear her perform? Could she really think that? She had her own career now, after all. A big-time *macher* in the music world. There had been a time, when she was his student, and even when she first started making her way up the ladder, when his advice might have meant something and she would have listened. Now that she was winning Grammys, playing concertos in Berlin and London and Salzburg, earning enough shekels to buy shiny red Camaros, Jacobus had a feeling she only pretended to listen to him. Which was fine. It was fine. Don't hurt an old man's feelings. Make him feel he's still important. Still relevant.

Jacobus's health improved, in fits and starts, like a beginning violin student learning to play vibrato. He had returned to his humble home in the Berkshires. But under the doctor's orders to take it easy—"One day at a time, Mr. Jacobus. One day at a time"—after a month he had become fidgety and, as a result, as was his tendency, grumpy. Only his absurdly affectionate hundred-pound bulldog, Trotsky, was unable to discern the depth of Jacobus's dour doldrums. So, in eloquent and endearing terms, Yumi told Jacobus how much it would mean to her—now that he was starting to feel better—if he and his best friend, Nathaniel Williams, went to Salt Lake City to attend two weeks of concerts at the Antelope Island Music Festival. She would be performing Antonio Vivaldi's virtuoso violin concerto in G Minor, *Summer*, from the *Four Seasons*.

A fine piece, Summer, Jacobus thought. *No surprise it was one of the world's most popular pieces of classical music. Smart to program it. Draws the crowds just like the flies Vivaldi imitates in the music.*

Jacobus was not reluctant to admit he liked Vivaldi...from the comfort of his living room couch. But why the hell travel two thousand miles to hear it? On the other hand, he loved Yumi like a daughter and believed her to be one of the great violinists of the day, not that there was much great talent to compare it to these days. Yes, her *Summer* would no doubt be a memorable performance. But...

"Nope. No way I'm going to Utah. Been there. Done that."

"Please, please, please!"

Then Nathaniel chimed in. The traitor!

"It'll be good for your convalescence, Jake. It'll do you good. Out there in the desert climate."

"Desert climate, eh? You know what desert climate is a euphemism for? T.D.H. Too damn hot."

"Oh, but it's a dry heat," Nathaniel said.

"Dry heat, my ass."

"Really, you don't feel it as much. No humidity, like here."

"Bullshit. So it'll be ninety-eight and feel like ninety-six. And what do you have against the Berkshires' ninety-percent humidity, anyway? The three H's: Hot, hazy, and home."

"There's a big barbecue after the last concert," Yumi said. "To celebrate. With ribs."

"So what?"

"And it's free."

That caught Jacobus's attention.

"Ribs? What else?"

"Fixins."

"Fixins? Like what fixins?"

"Baked beans. Corn on the cob. Coleslaw."

"Okra?"

"Sorry. No okra."

"Okay. I'll go."

"But there's no okra."

"I heard you the first time. I hate okra."

So Jacobus finally capitulated. He felt he had fought the good fight and, in fact, had extracted a major concession. He would go to a single concert: the one on the Friday evening of the festival's second and final weekend that included Yumi performing *Summer*.

The pressure brought to bear by his two closest friends, or as he was well aware, his *only* two friends, had eroded his resistance and ultimately proved to be too much for the old man. In the end, he had relented, though if he had known—if any of them had known—how catastrophically his jaundiced sentiments about the world of classical music would play out yet again, he would have given no ground. For the moment, he would go, though he vowed to have the word "cajole" expunged from the English language.

Yumi and Nathaniel took an early Sunday morning flight from JFK Airport. Nathaniel, whose bulk would have made it difficult for him to sit comfortably in the cramped economy section seats for the five-hour flight, graciously splurged for an upgrade to business class for both of them. As they boarded the plane, the phone in Yumi's back pocket vibrated. With her violin in one hand, her carry-on in the other, with her jeans more fashionably tight than unfashionably comfortable, and with a full planeload's worth of passengers in Zones 1, 2, and 3 testily crowded behind her, she chose not to check the message. Nor did she during the flight, either, other than to see it was from the ubiquitous Unknown Caller—no doubt trying to sell her yet another credit card—because she never could figure out if it was permitted to use a cellphone during flights and if so, whether it would actually work. Unlike her mentor, Daniel Jacobus, Yumi obeyed the rules as she understood them, whereas Jacobus believed a rule should be followed only if, upon breaking it, the result proved the rule was worth following. That philosophy, by definition, required all rules to be broken, at least once.

Arriving at the Salt Lake City International Airport before noon, Yumi and Nathaniel said goodbye to each other and went their separate ways. Nathaniel rented a car and drove into the city, where he had booked a room with two queen-size beds at the Waltz Rite Inn for the two weeks' duration of the festival. One bed was for him, the other would be for Jacobus when he arrived. To give him a fighting chance to get a decent night's sleep, he brought industrial-strength earplugs to block Jacobus's snoring. For someone with such acute hearing, Jacobus was deaf to his own leonine eruptions. Nathaniel had reserved tickets for all the concerts in advance and would pick Jacobus up at the airport for the second weekend of the festival when they would both go to hear Yumi perform her concerto.

By prior arrangement, Yumi was met at the baggage carousel by Joy D'Angelo, the assistant to Sunny Flox, the festival's artistic administrator. D'Angelo was short, cute, and a bit pudgy, with a friendly, little-girl face that Yumi thought should have had freckles (though they were not evident) and which was a little too hidden by long, curly auburn hair. She wore a new pair of inexpensive blue jeans and a beige Antelope Island Music Festival T-shirt with its logo of a line drawing of Frary Peak, the island's most prominent landmark. Both the jeans and the shirt were a half size too tight, exposing an inch of tummy that was probably not intended and didn't do her any favors.

The two women had never met, but as Yumi waited at baggage claim, D'Angelo recognized her immediately, as Yumi Shinagawa was a celebrated presence in the hallowed world of classical music. Yumi almost laughed out loud at the deferential tone with which D'Angelo introduced herself, as if Yumi were royalty, and when the suitcase rolled down the carousel, D'Angelo went to grab it for her. Yumi thanked her, but was content to

16

carry it herself, along with her violin. She had packed lightly, as usual, and was uncomfortable having anyone do anything for her that she could do herself. Probably another lesson she had learned from Jacobus. Other than her concert dress, the only outfits she had brought were lightweight, which she patted herself on the back for doing, because it was even hotter than she had remembered. "Dry heat, my ass!" Jacobus had said. The recollection made her smile.

It wasn't the first time Yumi had performed at the Antelope Island Music Festival. Years before, when she was a violinist in the New Magini String Quartet, she had appeared there with the noted pianist, Virgil Lavender. Even though there were some distinctly distasteful memories associated with that experience, she hadn't lost her love for the terrain itself. She had heard that the festival had struggled financially in recent years, but it now had a new CEO, a so-called turn-around expert, and apparently, it was again on more secure financial footing. Even if it wasn't, it wouldn't be the first time she would have performed with a paycheck in limbo. These smaller festivals were sometimes risky ventures, especially in some of the third world countries where she had appeared, but it came with the territory. Trying to find and develop a dependable ticket-buying audience and remunerative relationships with major donors were ongoing struggles, and she appreciated the efforts of those who believed in what they were doing, even if they weren't always successful. Besides, she loved to perform and if it didn't always fatten her checking account, so be it. She had more than enough money tucked away. And, of course, what she had was more valuable than a checking account. She had the music.

Joy D'Angelo, at the wheel of the festival's Ford Econoline van, slid her seat forward so her feet could reach the pedals. Yumi grasped the van's grab bar, pulled herself into the car, and landed uncomfortably on a seat belt buckle, which in turn jabbed her phone into her posterior, as if reminding her that she had neglected to check her messages. As they exited the airport, Yumi checked her voicemail and text messages. There had been several, from well-wishers and from Jacobus himself, who reminded her of details they both knew she knew about Vivaldi's music but who repeated it nevertheless, "so that you don't screw up." The last message, the one from Unknown Caller, was the one that gave her pause. It was as disturbing as it was succinct: "Don't go there."

She listened to it several times, close to her ear, as D'Angelo drove. A man's voice, but that's all she could tell. With only three words, so plainly spoken—almost too uninflected—and with the phone's mediocre sound quality and the car noise, it was impossible to tell if there was an accent. Maybe there was. But what could have been meant by *there*? Don't go *there*. The airport? The music festival? Was it metaphorical, as in: When you have dinner with your mother-in-law and she brings up politics, *don't go there*? And what if Yumi did understand what *there* referred to? Was it a warning intended to protect her? Or was it a threat to harm her?

She tried to be analytical, like Jacobus. To use her ears and her brain as he would. No doubt he would be able to narrow the mystery down to one or two plausible conclusions. She would call and ask him! He'd have the answer, for sure. But then she decided against that plan. If he felt she might be in trouble it would worry him that he was on the other side of the country. He would fret, and his health was still fragile. It wouldn't be fair. No, a call wouldn't do. And it was probably nothing to worry about, anyway. Some crank call. So she decided not to mention it, to Jacobus or to anyone else. And though she continued to wrap her mind around "Don't go there," none of her questions seemed answerable. In the end, she decided the only possible way forward was to be vigilant but undaunted.

Sunday traffic was light and they rapidly left the city behind, driving a half-hour north on I-15, past the refineries, then past endless Davis County suburbs. To make polite conversation, Yumi asked D'Angelo how she had come to her current job. D'Angelo explained that, like so many in the concert management field, she had started out as a music student hoping for an illustrious concert career. It was only after she graduated with a degree in violin performance and had subsequently taken a half dozen orchestra auditions without once progressing past the first round—forget about winning any of them—that she realized how intensely competitive a field it was. No one had told her that part. If only, she said. Regardless of talent or hard work, the opportunities to make a living as a performer were scarce. Once the costs of attending auditions—the airfares and hotel rooms, let alone the incalculable psychological burden of months of practice in preparation for unsuccessful ten-minute auditions—totally depleted her modest savings, D'Angelo made the wrenching but pragmatic decision to bail on her dream and adapt her musical skills and knowledge in a way that would at least keep her connected to a world she loved. And pay her rent.

They exited I-15 and turned west on Antelope Drive for another twenty minutes, driving past a sea of newly constructed housing developments and retail strip malls, built on land that had been, until recent years, orchards, farms, and ranches. A few miles from the Great Salt Lake, suburbia relaxed its encroaching tentacles, temporarily conceding its middle-class manifest destiny. Open fields, blind to their impending, inevitable fate, once again took over.

Yumi asked D'Angelo to tell her more about her job description...other than chauffeuring. It was the polite thing for Yumi to do. What she had done innumerable times over the years when total strangers generously ushered her from airports to hotels to concert halls to receptions and back again, whether it was in Boston, Basel, or Beijing. Even token conversation made the people doing all the grunt work feel that their volunteerism was valued and respected. Which it was. And that their lives as individuals were of sincere interest to the guest artist. Which they weren't. But it was courtesy, and courtesy was important to Yumi. It was part of her cultural DNA.

So she listened with half an ear to D'Angelo's responses while paying more attention, and deriving more satisfaction, from the majesty of the surrounding mountains and of the golden grassland rimming this eastern stretch of the Great Salt Lake's shore. *Mainly do whatever Sunny Flox asks me to do*, Yumi caught D'Angelo saying. Making sure the musicians had what they needed, helping set up music stands, keeping tabs on the stage staff and the EMTs, making sure the cabins are cleaned, being in charge of foodservice. A glorified gofer is what D'Angelo called herself. Yumi protested at the designation, but not too strenuously. After all, it was more or less true. It was the chauffeuring that took up most of D'Angelo's time, she said. A lot of trips to the airport, where she shuttled not only the musicians, but also groups of concertgoers who were arriving from out of town. It wasn't very exciting, D'Angelo said, but it was a way to meet some interesting people, and hopefully—between the networking and hard work—she would move up the administrative ladder. Maybe someday she would be a personnel manager for a major orchestra.

They stopped at the tollbooth, where D'Angelo showed her festival ID to avoid paying the nine-dollar entrance fee to another world. They then crossed the narrow five-mile causeway that was the only tether between the mainland and mountainous Antelope Island, a rough diamond rising out of the Great Salt Lake. The day was hot and clear, with the glare of the sun reflecting off the still water. Traffic was sparse and lazy. Arriving on the island proper at the end of the causeway, they turned left and wound their way south, ascending hilly terrain as they went. After a mile, at a fork in the road, they turned left again, hugging the island's eastern shore. From there, under a brilliant blue, cloudless sky, Yumi had a clear view across the lake's broad expanse. In the distance was Greater Salt Lake City's metropolitan area that they had left only an hour before. From this vantage point, the urban area, with its population of over a million, seemed puny and insignificant against the backdrop of the forested Wasatch Range, the western edge of the Rockies, immediately behind it. If they had taken a right turn back at the fork, a dirt road would have taken them to the barren campgrounds on the west side of the island, where the view was totally and eerily different: the vastness of the lake stretched all the way to waves of virtually uninhabited, treeless mountain ranges, starting with the Oquirrhs and then the Stansburys. It gave an overwhelming sense of isolation, as if one were a solitary colonist on another planet. Continuing south, they passed craggy Frary Peak on their right, rising two thousand feet above lake level.

Whoever first had the idea to have a music festival here was brilliant, Yumi thought. She relished the prospect of again roaming the austere natural setting that challenged her strength, her stamina, and her psyche, and which

20

stood in such stark contrast to the refinement of the music she would be performing. The rugged desert island, fifteen miles long and up to seven miles wide, was replete with coyotes, jackrabbits, bighorn sheep, and a herd of hundreds of American bison. It was that very contrast between high culture and unembellished wilderness that attracted Yumi to the festival. Whoever had left her the message "Don't go there," obviously had no idea that the threat or warning or whatever it was couldn't compete with the visceral hold the place had on her.

Not surprisingly, that combination of nature and music was the core of the festival's promotional strategy. With its proximity to the Salt Lake City metropolitan area, the administrators had focused their efforts on developing an enthusiastic local following of music and nature lovers who could easily commute to the concerts, an audience on which the festival depended for full houses and sustainable sponsorships. It was a well-recognized chicken-and-egg conundrum in the arts world: Without full houses, it was hard to make an effective pitch to get necessary funding from corporations, philanthropies, and public sources. Without the funding, it was an uphill battle to engage in effective marketing and promotion to get full houses. The Antelope Island Music Festival was no different in that regard from just about any other performing arts organization, at least in the United States. In countries like Germany, where everyone's taxes went in part to sustain the arts, they didn't have to worry about fundraising and PR. But success in the U.S. relied on an alchemy that only a small circle of enlightened administrators knew the magical formula to, and who were sometimes reluctant to share their secrets. It was Yumi's hope that this new CEO would be the Merlin the festival needed.

Yumi's sense of anticipation increased the closer they got to their destination. They were now less than a mile from the former Fielding Garr Ranch toward the southern tip of the island, the site of the festival performance venue, and where the musicians were housed and fed. Except for a handful of state park staff and a trickle of tent and RV campers on the northwest corner of the island, the festival participants were the island's only overnight occupants. Between 10 p.m. and 6 a.m. the island's toll gates were closed. No one could get in or out.

But while Yumi reveled in the otherworldly ecology of the lake and the austerity of a primeval, barren landscape, she was amused that some of her urban and urbane colleagues, so used to the around-the-clock bustle of city life, were made uneasy by their perceived sense of isolation. The eerie sensation that it was "too quiet." For Yumi, though, music and nature were inseparably joined at the hip. Weren't walks in the woods Beethoven's inspiration? And all those rivers immortalized by music: the Rhine, the Moldau, the beautiful blue Danube (even though it was brown long before Yumi first saw it when she performed in Vienna), and the "Old Man River," the Mississippi. And just look at the *Four Seasons* to understand the role nature plays in music!

D'Angelo pulled the festival van off the dirt road and into the ranch parking lot, now nearly empty, but which would be filled in a few days. Getting out of the air-conditioned car, Yumi was enveloped in a blanket of searing heat that sucked the air out of her. Though she had mentally prepared herself for hot weather, her knees almost buckled. Get used to it, she told herself.

"I'll walk you to your cabin," D'Angelo said. She pulled Yumi's suitcase from the back of the van and this time Yumi let her contend with it. She had her violin case to carry, and with the rocky path from the parking lot to the cabins, it wouldn't be possible to roll the bag. Still, she felt a pang of guilt allowing someone else to do the work for her.

"Am I the last to arrive?" she asked D'Angelo. There were still two days until the first rehearsal, and almost a week until the first concert. She was looking forward to having some time to explore—with or without her colleagues—before diving in to the intensity of two weeks of chamber music.

D'Angelo laughed.

"No way. Some of the musicians are here, but I've got to go back tomorrow for the rest. Jamie Barov's been here for days! He wanted to make sure the piano and harpsichord are both in good condition. You know how temperamental they can be, especially in this climate, and Jamie is very finicky about those things."

"I know. I've performed with him. He's a sweetheart, but he can be a real perfectionist. I'm happy he's here. How long has it been this hot?"

"It's been terrible. In the nineties for two weeks in a row. It went over a hundred three times! The upside is we get some really cool sheet lightning every evening. It makes you think it's going to rain, but it's been dry as a bone. I hope your instrument will be okay."

"Well, between you and me, I left my Guarneri at home. Old folks might like this heat, but it isn't the best thing for a three-hundred-year-old, four-million-dollar violin. I brought a really nice contemporary instrument I commissioned a few years ago. It does great in all kinds of weather. Solid, like ox," Yumi said with a laughable attempt at a Russian accent.

"That's good. I know that Mr. Bjørlund was a little worried."

"Christian worries about everything." Yumi laughed. "He and I have worked together before, in Europe. Speaking of which, Sunny has done a nice job putting together the programs for us this year," Yumi said.

"I think he's a genius," D'Angelo replied.

Yumi laughed again. "I'm not sure I'd go that far."

D'Angelo seemed embarrassed, and Yumi regretted having made light of the comment.

"Well, maybe not a genius," D'Angelo conceded. "But using just four musicians plus the quartet and Jamie, we've got so many different combinations. And the first week, to give everyone time to get used to things here, the programs are starting out pretty easy."

That was indeed the case, Yumi thought. The first week's programs included some charming eighteenth-century violin duos by Jean-Marie Leclair she would be playing with Dieter Waldstein, the first violinist of the Kreutzer String Quartet. Then there would be two snappy piano trios, one by Josef Haydn performed by Waldstein, Ingrid Goldman, cellist of the Kreutzer Quartet, and pianist Jamie Barov; and an early trio by Ludwig van Beethoven with Yumi, Barov, and Marcus Renfro, the other cellist. The Kreutzer Quartet would perform the poignant Schubert A Minor, and the four "independent" musicians—Christian Bjørlund and Yumi on violin, Hannah Carrington on viola, and Renfro—would do the Beethoven Op. 59, No. 3.

Even though those four musicians were not an established quartet, they were all headline stars in their own right and the Beethoven was a composition they had all performed elsewhere with others many times. It would be fun cobbling it together in one week!

The big ensemble piece for the first weekend, utilizing the combined forces of all the musicians, would be the *Holberg Suite* by the nineteenth-century Norwegian Edvard Grieg, a charming set of Baroque-style dances not nearly as difficult as they sounded. Audience pleasers for sure, but the repertoire for the entire program was both familiar and technically well within their comfort zones. Yes, Sunny Flox was a crafty artistic administrator, and Yumi was thankful for that.

"I look forward to seeing Sunny at dinner tonight," Yumi said.

"Except he's not here yet. He's in LA attending the annual arts admin conference and won't be back until Wednesday. But Anita's here."

"Anita Talbot? She's the new managing director, right?"

"Yes," D'Angelo said. "I just hope everyone gets along."

"Why shouldn't they?"

From the tone of D'Angelo's comment, Yumi had a feeling she would find out the answer soon enough.

They made their way past the big concert tent, affectionately nicknamed the Big Top, and the festival office. The musicians' cabins were not far down the hard-packed dirt path.

"I have to admit," D'Angelo said, "I'm one of your biggest fans. You've been such a role model for me."

"That's very kind of you to say," Yumi replied. Not that it would swell her head, but it wasn't the first time young violinists, especially women, expressed their gratitude to her. And Yumi was proud of the fact that her career was opening doors for others. She had Jacobus to thank for that. Though he had his faults, he couldn't care less whether someone was a man, woman, or kangaroo, as long as they could play in tune.

"I was wondering," D'Angelo continued. "Only if you had time. But I have my violin with me, and I thought... I know you're really busy, but, well, maybe if you could give me a lesson while you're here..."

The request was also not unexpected. Nor was it particularly unwelcome. It was flattery, in a way. Just about anywhere well-known musicians go to perform, there's some eager amateur or student, or even young professional, who would love the opportunity to have a one-on-one. Not only to learn something, but also to bask in the glow of the musician's celebrity. "Guess who I had a lesson with?" they would tell their envious friends. Inevitably, at the end of the lessons, they would say with a great degree of humility, "I know you must charge a fortune for lessons, and I'll pay you whatever your fee is," knowing that the usual response is, "Don't worry about it. You don't need to pay me anything." Followed by eternal thanks. Yumi had given such lessons more times than she could remember. Certainly more times than she could remember all the students' names. But it was in part her way—her obligation as she saw it—to pass along what she had learned from Jacobus, and what he had learned from the masters before him. Keep the cycle going. The only problem was, indeed, time. There was so much repertoire to rehearse in the next two weeks. And the little free time she had, she was hoping to indulge herself in the outdoors. But.

"Of course," Yumi said. "Let me just take a look at my schedule. I'm sure we can fit something in."

Before D'Angelo had a chance to thank her profusely, as custom dictated, they were intercepted by another woman walking briskly toward them. She was middle-aged and wiry with short hair, its incipient gray professionally disguised. In an off-white business suit and low heels, she seemed overdressed and out of place, considering the heat and the natural surroundings, and especially compared to Yumi, who was dressed in jeans, a white sleeveless, button-down blouse, dark sunglasses, and a sun visor on her forehead.

Yumi spoke first.

"Anita," she said and extended her free hand. "It's been way too long." Indeed, Yumi hadn't seen Talbot in years, when she was just beginning to learn the trade.

"Welcome to the Antelope Island Music Festival," Anita Talbot replied, shaking hands. Her grip was firm but stiff and dry. Formal. "Joy, make sure

Ms. Shinagawa gets everything she needs. Then see me in the office. You need to call the caterers before you go back to the airport."

"Okay, Anita."

"Anita," Yumi asked. "Could I pick up my rehearsal schedule at the office? Joy and I were just talking about scheduling a lesson, and—"

"There won't be time for any lesson," Anita said. "Besides, Joy has a contract and you have a contract, and neither of them provide for extracurricular activities. There's already more than enough work to do."

Yumi realized she had just inadvertently stepped in something foul-smelling, and might already have gotten D'Angelo placed onto a list of the same name. Not a good start. Indeed, the look on D'Angelo's face, a sudden bright red not the result of sunburn, suggested she was afraid she might even be fired. Maybe this wasn't the first time she had asked a guest artist for a freebie. Unlike Jacobus, however, Yumi would not try to punch her way out of a bad situation. Finesse and diplomacy were things she had learned from her childhood. Before Jacobus.

"Absolutely," Yumi said before D'Angelo had a chance to respond. "Joy, Anita's right. Sorry that I asked you if you'd want a lesson in your free time. Maybe after the festival we'll do something in the city. Let's go see my cabin."

Chapter Three

I t wasn't much to look at. D'Angelo had to yank open the door because it was stuck. Yumi took one glance inside and said, "Fine." D'Angelo hurriedly excused herself, still rattled by Talbot's edict. As she left to return to the office, Yumi said, "Don't worry, Joy. We'll figure out a time for a lesson." D'Angelo, who hadn't said a word after Talbot disciplined her, relaxed and began to apologize. Yumi interrupted her, convincing her it was no big deal. "Don't worry. That's how managers are," she said. "Sometimes they're just a pain in the ass." Yumi was, at times, still Jacobus's protégée.

"And one more thing," Yumi said, as if reminded by the comment she just made. "Joy, have any of the musicians mentioned anything to you about being discouraged from coming here?"

"Discouraged? What do you mean?"

"Oh, I'm not sure. But no one has said anything like that?"

"No. Why?"

Yumi had no desire to consider the issue any further.

"No reason. It's just such a beautiful spot. I can't imagine anyone not wanting to be here."

If Yumi hadn't been in a good mood, she would have described her cabin as so spartan and ramshackle that it approached being uninhabitable, but because she was happy to be there she entertained the words quaint, rustic, and cozy. Hastily cobbled together with planks—long since weathered—plywood, and nails in the festival's first year, the board-and-batten cabins were never intended to be particularly durable, long-lasting, or attractive. Over time, they had become noticeably rickety, baking in the summer heat, and

27

then—the other extreme—soaking up moisture in the icy winters. Having been unoccupied—except for rodents and spiders—since the year before, it was evident that the musty forces of nature had been at work on the cabin.

Furniture was sparse: a full-sized mattress and box spring with simple white linens and more blankets than she could imagine she would need; a folding chair of dubious strength; a simple wooden dresser with peeling dark veneer and with a clouded mirror appended to it and a candle in case the electricity went out; a portable clothing hanger; and a store-brand braided throw rug on the pine floor. To round out the décor, an inexpensive, framed Frederic Remington supermarket-quality print of a mounted cowboy rounding up a herd of cattle hung on a nail. It was not the lavish accommodation she and all the other musicians were accustomed to on their usual concert tours: plush hotels with their ergonomically designed beds and cushiony sofas, fully stocked minibars, high-speed internet, business centers, full-menu dining, twenty-four/seven room service, hot tubs, swimming pools, massage, and indoor exercise facilities. But then again, Antelope Island wasn't Paris, Vienna, or Lucerne, their customary haunts on the concert circuit. By no means. But at least the cabin had been cleaned.

And it had a functioning bathroom. That could not be said about the Big Top's outdoor backstage area, which only had a dozen or so Porta Potties, to be shared by the musicians and the audience alike. The "concert hall" itself was a massive white tent, shaped like a boiled egg sliced lengthwise and held up by poles, ropes, and steel cables, which accommodated up to four hundred people who sat in plastic folding chairs on a packed dirt floor. At one end of the tent was a temporary stage, wide and deep enough to fit the musicians plus the piano or harpsichord as the program dictated, and built two feet off the ground so that the back row of the audience was able to see the performers.

After sitting in a plane and car since dawn, Yumi was eager for some pre-dinner exercise. She slid her violin case under the bed where it would be out of sight and in the shade. She unpacked her bags, arranging her clothes in the dresser and on the hanger, and changed into a pair of gray running shorts, a pale yellow T-shirt, red baseball cap, sunglasses, and hiking boots. It was the template of the outfit which, except for concerts, she planned to wear daily. As it was her first day there, she would take it easy on her hike while getting acclimated to the island's altitude, forty-two-hundred feet at the shoreline. She applied sunscreen to her face, arms, and legs, and took along her water bottle to stay hydrated in the withering afternoon desert sun.

She walked south from the ranch grounds, along the rocky dirt track that served as both a hiking trail and a four-wheel-drive service vehicle road. After a half-mile or so she spotted someone approaching from the other direction, too far away for her to identify, but she could see he was African American. Within a hundred yards, Yumi recognized Marcus Renfro, the cellist with whom she would be performing. Renfro's complexion was much darker than Nathaniel's, a comparison that came to mind because they were the only two black cellists she knew. Nathaniel's skin was the color and transparency of her *genmaicha*, the brown rice tea she drank every morning at home. It was so light that when she had a suntan—like the one she fully anticipated she would end up with here on Antelope Island—added to her inherited Japanese skin tone, their color was almost identical. *So much for racial divisions based on color,* she thought, because Nathaniel's was much closer to hers than to Renfro's. Renfro was a dense black-brown, almost ebony, almost opaque, conspicuously dark in the context of the surrounding amber, tan, and pale gray-green of the island's dried grasses, sagebrush, and exposed rocky mass. *If Renfro's skin color matched anything she could compare it to on the island,* Yumi thought with amusement, *it was the grazing buffalo. But Renfro was much better looking, though maybe not to a female buffalo.*

He was wearing lightweight but expensive outdoor wear—a white, collared, short-sleeve knit shirt and crisp khaki shorts with lots of pockets. An Australian bush hat concealed the cornrows for which he was noted, as there weren't too many classical musicians with that hairstyle. A few years separating them in age—Yumi being the older of the two—they had previously collaborated from time to time at other festivals. Though he had lived in the Bay Area for many years, most of their work together had been in Europe. Renfro had been more of a Baroque specialist along with her soon-to-arrive colleague, the violinist Christian Bjørlund, before both men did a career pivot and moved into nineteenth- and twentieth-century repertoire.

Yumi waved. Renfro returned the gesture, calling back, "Hello, stranger!" He trotted up to her, where they initially shook hands but then, sloughing off the formality, gave each other a hug.

"Hot enough for you?" Renfro asked. Yumi laughed, not because the comment was particularly funny—it certainly wasn't original—but Renfro had a way of saying things that made people smile. You could see the kindness in his eyes. They began talking about the weather, then the music and the festival, at which point they parted company. Renfro, who had been out and about for hours, already had more sun than advisable. He headed back to the ranch while Yumi continued on her hike, picking up her pace while keeping a cautious eye on five representatives of the island's iconic bison herd, not far off the trail. Though the bison were familiar with humans in their vicinity and generally content to spend the days grazing on the hillsides, Yumi had been reminded on her previous visit to the island that they were nevertheless wild, unpredictable animals, and being the largest land mammals in North America, should be given a wide berth.

Yumi returned to her cabin an hour later to shower. The water pressure left much to be desired and the temperature was not nearly as steaming hot as she preferred, but she managed to scrub off the grit and dust that were part and parcel of the Antelope Island experience. Perspiration was a non-issue, as it tended to evaporate immediately into the desert air, where the humidity rarely exceeds ten percent. Unlike her youth in Japan, when a used bath towel would remain damp indefinitely because of the humidity, here her body was dry almost before she stepped out of the shower. Dressing in clean clothes, including long pants—since it could get chilly as soon as the sun went down—Yumi headed to the barn on the opposite side of the Big Top from the cabins, where a makeshift dining room had been set up for the musicians.

The barn was a reincarnation of the original mid-nineteenth-century structure built by settler Fielding Garr. It had undergone a series of evolutions, most recently its modest renovation by the state park administration as a multi-purpose space for the festival, while still functioning as a barn museum the rest of the year. In reality, it was more of a shed than a full-fledged barn, with the front exposed to the elements when the barn doors were fully slid open.

Yumi arrived to find those musicians who had already arrived at the festival, plus Joy D'Angelo and Anita Talbot, already seated for dinner. After cordial words of greeting all around, Yumi took a vacant seat on the bench, next to Marcus Renfro. Two folding tables had been placed end to end, with large bowls of food upon them, to be served family-style. The dinner, catered by a local food service company, was not nearly as appealing as her hike had been. Passing the bowls around, and spooned onto paper plates with plastic cutlery, an uneasy consensus was quickly arrived at: The food—a stew of some unidentifiable meat, vegetables overcooked by about a day, and a wilted salad almost as brown as green—was unequivocally bad. Worse than that, Yumi could not help but notice that some of the musicians' manners were shoddier than the grazing bison's. Scowling after one bite of stew, Dieter Waldstein spit it out—at least into a napkin—and groused, "What is this shit?"

Christian Bjørlund, the other violinist with whom Yumi would be performing that weekend, said, "Complaining already, Dieter? We're not here to eat. We're here to play music."

"Let's pray your playing has better taste than this slop." He said it with a smile, but unlike Renfro's benign humor, it was critical and hard-edged.

Whereas Bjørlund was tall, lanky, and blond, characteristically Danish, Waldstein was a head shorter, wiry, and compactly built. Though he was the oldest musician among them, Waldstein was still robust. Yumi suspected that when he reached old age he would be one of those men whose ears and nose grew disproportionately large, and sprouted tufts of hair from their respective orifices as well. With short-cropped hair, and a trim salt-and-pepper beard, now more salt than pepper, it appeared he could be a formidable opponent to Bjørlund if their evident animosity were ever to erupt further.

Yumi recalled Joy D'Angelo's words, "I just hope everyone gets along." Had Joy been aware of something unknown to Yumi? Had there been a conflict brewing before she had arrived? What Yumi did know about Bjørlund was his assertiveness, both on and off the stage. There was something about his eyes—were they a little closer together than most people's?—that gave Yumi the feeling that he was always sizing people up, even when he smiled. He also was known to seriously indulge in the unlikely sport—at least for musicians—of boxing. It was quite a contrast to his particular expertise in Baroque music of the seventeenth and early eighteenth centuries. Generally successful when he expanded his horizons into the quartet repertoire of the nineteenth and twentieth, Bjørlund still had his share of critics who believed he had not fully transitioned from the Baroque manner of playing. One of those critics, Dieter Waldstein, was obviously taking personal exception to their stylistic differences.

"Talk to Joy if you've got a problem with the food," Anita Talbot interjected, as if Waldstein's criticism had been aimed directly at her. "I've got a budget. Unlike music, there's nothing subjective about dollars and cents. If we show another annual deficit you can kiss this festival goodbye. So it's either the food or your fee. You want better food? Play for free."

At various times—and this was one of those times—Yumi wondered why people chose the professions they did; and once they made the choice, why they stayed if it made them so transparently bitter. Having become a veteran concert artist and having worked with just about everyone in the business, she was certainly aware of what was diplomatically referred to as "artistic temperament."

Musicians are passionate about music. That's wonderful. That's the way it should be. But couldn't one be passionate without becoming territorial or dogmatic? Without insulting one's colleagues? Artistic temperament was not a license to badger. Sometimes—more often than not, it seemed—the focus was more on ego and less on music. *If it's so important to be king of the hill,* she thought, *go climb Frary Peak.* Yet again she understood and sympathized with Jacobus's desire to part company from that world. A thought struck her: Could it have been Jacobus's voice on the phone, the voice that said, "Don't go there?" Something to ponder.

And the business end. Yes, arts organizations struggle financially. We all know that. That's a centuries-old tale. If there's an orchestra or festival that's *not* struggling, *that* would be the news! But one has a choice: Embrace the struggle or rail against it. Make it a welcome challenge—think of the greatness you're helping to create!—or bitch about how difficult life is and be miserable. Though Yumi had heard it all, she was disappointed, though not surprised, to hear the same song here. Here in this idyllic setting. But! She wasn't going to let it ruin her experience, either with the music or with nature. *Illegitimi non carborundum,* Jacobus always delighted in reminding her. *Don't let the bastards grind you down.* It made her smile, even as she choked down the tasteless, watery concoction labeled MIXED VEGETABLE MEDLEY.

Jamie Barov, famous for his tact and diplomacy almost as much as for his formidable pianistic skills, shoveled a grotesquely large chunk of stew into his mouth, and as he chewed on the tough meat, said with the thoughtfulness of James Beard, "You know, gang, I have to confess this might not be the best meat I've ever had. But it is certainly the worst." To which Marcus Renfro added, "Jamie, you think it could be that dead buffalo we saw last week?" The two comments broke the tension, with everyone then trying to outdo the others describing how bad the food was. Even Waldstein and Bjørlund retreated to civil behavior, regardless of what they might have felt behind their polite words. It uncomfortably reminded Yumi of the construction of the cheap chest of drawers in her cabin, a thin layer of peeling mahogany veneer covering over unsightly, pedestrian plywood.

By dinner's end, the air outside the barn had cooled in proportion to the tempers within. As soon as the sun set behind the Oquirrh Mountains to the west, the thermometer dropped. Atmospheric conditions were ripe for setting the sky alight with a continuous display of sheet lightning, the result of distant thunderstorms too far away for the thunder to be heard, and so dry that the rain evaporated before reaching the ground, the curious desert phenomenon called a virga. The musicians responded to the lightning with *oohs* and *ahs*, and even occasionally applauded nature's performance.

"We've had this every night," Joy D'Angelo said. "I hope we'll get some after the concert. Audiences love fireworks."

"And these are free," Anita Talbot added.

"Let's just hope the rain doesn't reach the ground," Renfro said.

Rehearsals began Monday morning with the repertoire for those musicians who had already arrived. While they worked, Joy D'Angelo picked up the remaining artists at the airport, so that the larger ensemble rehearsals could begin in earnest on Tuesday. Everyone understood how toxic the work environment could become if negativity prevailed, so after the initial tensions from the Sunday evening dinner a tacit but concerted effort was made to be tactful, polite, and sensitive, all the essentials when playing chamber music at the highest level. Yes, there were occasional glitches and disagreements during the rehearsals, but that was really the essence of music-making. That was, indeed, the only way to make things sound better.

Little by little, the musicians took delight in the change of scene from impersonal, big-city concertizing. Some, like Bjørlund and Cornelia Blum, the violist of the Kreutzer Quartet, took advantage of the island's hiking trails and natural beauty to refresh their spirits at the end of what had been a grueling concert season. Blum, who was also writing a book, used the outdoors for literary inspiration. Others—like Waldstein, who was not so interested in outdoor activities, and the Kreutzer's cellist, Ingrid Goldman, who claimed to be "heat intolerant"—opted to spend their free time reading in the picnic area adjacent to the tent and the cabins in the shadow of a stand of massive cottonwoods, which were among the few shade trees on the entire island. Jamie Barov, a fly-fishing enthusiast, was disappointed to discover the Great Salt Lake is three times saltier than the ocean, so there were no fish there to be angled. And though Antelope Island had a few dozen freshwater springs, there were no fish in them, either. Barov satisfied himself with tying flies, the tools and materials for which he had brought along with him to while away the little free time he had.

Yumi found Marcus Renfro to be her preferred hiking partner. She had a fondness for a fast pace and Renfro was the only one willing and able to match her stride, at the same time keeping her amused with his equally fast-paced banter. He also did remarkable imitations of the other musicians, especially the Europeans. His German and Danish accents were stereotypical and exaggerated, which made them even more entertaining.

Shortly after sunrise on Thursday morning, before the day's rehearsals began and before it got too hot, Yumi and Renfro were climbing to the top of Frary Peak, from which they could literally see for a hundred miles in all directions. Renfro reenacted some of the arguments that had occurred during the week's rehearsals:

"Dieter, I don't want you to take this the wrong way, but do you understand that you sound like shit, please?"

"Oh, Christian, forgive me. I appreciate your comment, but, you see, I was just trying to follow your example."

"If I may just say"—Renfro raised his voice an octave to sound like the intellectual cellist, Ingrid Goldman—"after reading Mendelssohn's biography, it's possible that he did want us to sound like shit. Don't you think so, Marcus?"

Renfro dropped his voice two octaves into a deep, resonant African American.

"Why, I don't rightly know, ma'am. It ain't my place to say."

Yumi had to stop in her tracks to catch her breath, partly from the climb but mostly because she was laughing so hard.

"Okay," she said. "Now do me."

"Do you? Really?"

"Yes. Do me."

"Here? Right now? The ground is so rocky."

Yumi gave him a shove in the chest. It was intended to be playful. At least half intended, anyway, but forceful enough for Renfro to stumble backwards on the slope. He grasped Yumi's outstretched wrist to avoid falling. He stabilized quickly, and released his grasp. It all happened in a few seconds.

"You know what I mean," Yumi said. "Impersonate me."

"Your wish is my command."

Renfro transformed his facial expression to a remarkable combination of benign and take-no-prisoners.

"That's me!" Yumi exclaimed. "How do you do that? Now, what do I say?"

"I think if we play it just a little slower, it will actually be stronger. As Mr. Jacobus says, 'Beethoven is better half fast than half-assed.'"

Yumi was taken aback. Renfro's inflection mirrored hers impeccably, with just the slightest tinge of a Japanese accent. After so many years in the U.S., her speech was almost as idiomatically American as a native. But it wasn't the accent that upset her. It was the content.

"Do I really talk about Jacobus often?"

"All the time."

That was disturbing. She thought she had long become her own musician, establishing her own artistic identity, free of—or rather, the combined result of all the teachers, artists, and experiences which had influenced her. Or so she had presumed. But now Renfro was suggesting that it was obvious to everyone she was still under Jacobus's sway. Well, maybe that was a good thing, though she didn't care for the thought that others might consider her more of an overachieving student than an artistic equal. Is that what they thought? Behind her back? Was their politeness to her simply an extension of the veneer that she perceived everywhere else? Both the hike and Renfro's humor had lost their luster.

"Let's go back," she said.

"Whatever you say."

With such diversity of ensembles and with such limited time constraints, it wasn't possible for every group to rehearse in the Big Top. The most pragmatic solution was for the large ensembles and those requiring piano or harpsichord to rehearse there. All the other smaller groups—duos, trios, and quartets—rehearsed in the cabins, the musicians lugging along their music stands and chairs.

Thus, after her Thursday morning hike with Renfro, Yumi knocked on Dieter Waldstein's cabin door to rehearse their Leclair duets. She looked forward to the collaboration. She was a fan of Leclair's music, particularly his famous Violin Sonata in D Major, and though she regretted that the reason for her being at the festival was the result of another musician's illness, she wanted to fully take advantage of the opportunity.

Waldstein gave her a peck on each cheek when she arrived, but after that cordial formality, Waldstein was all business. Notwithstanding the heat and surroundings, he was dressed in his "work" clothes: a red, sleeveless pullover vest over a button-down white shirt, four-in-hand necktie, and creased gray slacks. Though his cabin was identical to Yumi's, she had to admit Waldstein was even neater than she was.

Theoretically, there should have been ample room for the two of them to practice their duets, especially as they were standing, not needing chairs. But Yumi quickly discovered that Waldstein danced around so much while playing—which of course he couldn't do when they were seated while rehearsing string quartets—that Yumi felt she was being boxed into a corner. He seemed to be getting more exercise playing the violin than she had hiking up the mountain.

When Yumi was Jacobus's student, he had been critical of her for moving too much when she played, arguing that even without seeing—*especially* without seeing—he could detect variations in her tone quality that were inadvertent and distracting, as if someone were randomly adjusting the volume on a radio. She had countered by saying that freedom of motion allowed her to play more musically, but Jacobus was dismissive. "You want to float like a butterfly and sting like a bee?" he said. "Be Muhammad Ali. Be a boxer. You want to be a violinist, watch Heifetz, watch Oistrakh, watch Milstein, watch Zukerman, watch—"

"I get the message," Yumi had said. To convince her, Jacobus had her record the same music while standing still and then while moving around. When she heard both versions on his tape recorder, there was a perceptible difference. He was right, as usual.

As diplomatically as she could, she asked Waldstein, "Dieter, you have such a gorgeous tone, and this music is so straightforward, might it be possible just to let it speak for itself?"

Waldstein was taken aback. Heralded as one of the world's great chamber musicians, perhaps even more renowned than Yumi in that regard, his freedom of movement was one of his trademarks.

He explained, with the paternalism of a father to a child, that with their limited rehearsal time he felt that the best way to communicate his ideas—by which Yumi gathered he intended to mean his superior ideas—was by *showing* the gesture, rather than having to explain it verbally. It would save time, he hoped.

Yumi responded that since she had ears, she could easily hear his musical ideas. Having to see them was not only redundant but distracting.

"But if I stand still I'll sound like Bjørlund. You're not suggesting I play like him, are you?" he asked. "He plays like such a girl."

"Really!"

"Sometimes it sounds so thin. So...weak. Effeminate. I know it's very scholarly. No one disputes that. He's read all the books. You know what I mean."

"Certainly. And how do I sound? Like a girl?"

"No! Not at all! I hope you didn't misunderstand what I mean."

"Which is?"

"You are very strong. A strong musician. In all ways."

"Thank you."

"Yes, you play just like a man."

Yumi held her temper.

"So what you're saying, Dieter, is that Christian, a man, plays like a woman? And I'm a woman, but play like a man?"

"Exactly."

"Have you considered the possibility that Christian and I don't play either like a man or a woman, but are simply playing the music the way we think it should go?"

"You Americans hate stereotypes, yet there must be some truth to them, or they wouldn't exist. Don't you think?"

Yumi felt there was so much wrong with that statement, starting with the fact that she was not an American, that she felt she had no choice but to respond. Unfortunately, or fortunately, depending on what the outcome would have been, there was a knock on the door, and Sunny Flox, the mastermind of the festival's creative programming, entered.

"Hidey-ho, boys and girls," he said, poking his head in. "Just got back from LA and wanted to pop in and say hi. Delighted to be out of the big city and back in the fresh country air. Everything going well?"

"Just fine," Yumi said. Waldstein gave the faintest of nods, with what might have been interpreted as agreement.

Yumi looked at Flox, a tall imposing, man, not lacking in energy. One might have assumed a degree of athleticism from that. But there was an almost wilting softness around his edges that suggested he would have been more at home in a cushy urban office with lots of potted plants and soft lighting. Somehow, he seemed out of place in the rugged island environment, like foie gras on a truck stop menu. Part of it might have been the mellow echo of an accent from his boyhood Nashville home, where they'd called little Sidney Flox "Sunny" because of his disposition. The nickname stuck. No one called him Sidney except his mother.

Or the frameless granny glasses. Or simply that the number of hours he had spent indoors in his office, on the phone or computer, making deals with musicians and their agents and their managers, was what had given him that sallow, pasty complexion. Or his hair, wavy and well-managed but thinning, of a color that was neither this nor that.

He was known to be a tough bargainer with a soft touch that could fool you. He had certainly wrapped Yumi around his little finger when he had invited her to substitute for Kuypers. In retrospect, Yumi should have had the upper hand in the negotiation. After all, Flox would have been desperate to get someone good enough to fill Kuypers's shoes at the last minute. But Flox managed not only to hire her, but convinced her to agree to a fee which, at major festivals, would have been considered a pittance. And he made her feel good about it in the bargain!

Negotiations aside, Flox often asserted how much he loved everything about the festival, "from Elgar to the EMTs." And probably more than anyone else, he had been responsible for its growing success, both by his creative programming and being a networking virtuoso. He seemed to be on cordial terms with every musician in the world and had been able to cajole many of them into performing at the festival, rough-hewn as it was.

With their shoestring staff, he and Joy D'Angelo primarily, it was almost a miracle they had done as well as they had with audience development. Joy had told her that the big "cowboy" barbecue after the final concert had originally been her idea, and though Talbot panned it, Flox had endorsed it with the self-protective caveat that it was her responsibility to take care of the details. "You own it, you eat it," he had said. It had turned out that it was now going to be one of the festival's biggest draws, guaranteeing a full house for the final concert. Even if you weren't a classical music lover per se, how could you resist a cowboy cookout under the stars? Hadn't that been what had convinced Jacobus?

Yumi wondered how Flox's efforts meshed with Anita Talbot's responsibilities. She sensed that Talbot acknowledged Flox's success with a half-hidden sneer, and Yumi could understand why. Talbot's job was basically to raise money. And while, yes, it was great to have the best musicians and to have special audience events, all those things cost money. More and more of it. When Yumi had taken a peek at the annual financial statement of her own orchestra, Harmonium, she was perturbed to see the musicians simply listed as a single "fixed cost" item in the expense column, no different than Office Expense, Other Production, and Bad Debts. Regardless of the quality of their "product," for which it was impossible to calculate a dollar value, a music organization's managing director never took his or her eye off the bottom line.

In a way, the more successful Flox was at his job, the more difficult Talbot's became, because to hire the best musicians inevitably put pressure on the budget. Talbot liked to tell everyone within hearing distance that she managed with only a single, part-time grant writer working for her at this festival. That disclaimer put her in the best light if she succeeded and gave her an excuse if she didn't. Beyond the grant writing, it was up to her to do all the schmoozing with donors, and develop relationships with businesses, philanthropies, local politicos, and independently wealthy arts lovers. To be successful, she had to play the part to fit in with and impress her prospective clientele: keep herself looking fit and trim (and young, to the extent possible), dress fashionably, tastefully, and expensively on her own dime, keep a smile plastered on her face, and talk a good game. How do you convince donors that it's crucial for them to fork over five-, six-, and—please, God—seven-figure donations for chamber music concerts on a desert island? It was a constant juggling act, and not a job Yumi envied.

She had first met Talbot at the Sarasota Festival when Talbot was little more than the intern that Joy D'Angelo now was at Antelope Island. Unlike D'Angelo, Talbot had the drive and thick skin to move quickly up the ladder. But though Talbot had spent years honing her skills, strangely enough Yumi found that music did not resonate with Talbot, who seemed to have little empathy for musicians. Nor did she do much to disguise the impression that her time on Antelope Island was spent in purgatory, and the sooner she could escape to literally greener pastures, the better.

Flox and Talbot had what might be euphemistically called "a productive working relationship." To all who viewed their interactions, they didn't seem to care for each other in the least. Where Flox was soft and malleable, Talbot had edge. Where Flox was all about the personal touch and the folksy yarn, Talbot was about data-driven, corporate messaging. But they each had an equal stake in making the festival a success, if—especially in Talbot's case—for no other reason than moving up the corporate ladder. So each went about their jobs in their own way, and was disinclined to tread heavily on the other's turf. And Yumi was disinclined to pry.

"Peachy," Flox replied to Yumi and Waldstein. "I'll leave you lovebirds in peace and see how the others are doing."

After he left, Yumi and Waldstein reached a truce regarding musical and stage deportment matters: Of the two duos by Jean-Marie Leclair they were performing, Waldstein played the first violin part in one of them, Yumi in the other. Whoever played the first violin part would be the boss for that particular duo. The audience might be chagrined to see them doing a tango in one duo and then be reserved as chess players in the other, but it would give the audience something to wonder about as they listened, anyway. They shook hands on the deal.

By Thursday evening, though the musicians' food hadn't improved, the music-making certainly had. After a sumptuous dinner of defrosted fish

41

sticks and gelatinous macaroni and cheese, Yumi's group had its final pre-concert tent rehearsal of the energetic Beethoven string quartet, Op. 59, No. 3. It was a staple of every self-respecting chamber musician's repertoire. Yumi had performed it more often than any other when she was a member of the New Magini Quartet, so even though she had been a late substitution, with the familiarity of the repertoire and her consummate musical skills, it hadn't taken her long to fit into her new role. The other members of the ensemble—Christian Bjørlund, violist Hannah Carrington (the youngest of them, who had arrived on Wednesday), and Marcus Renfro—were not hesitant in expressing their approval and admiration for Yumi's ability to meld into their somewhat arcane style, which hearkened back to early nineteenth-century performance practice.

The main obstacle at the rehearsal was not the difficulty of the music or the playing of it, but rather the heat, which left everyone dehydrated, sapped their energy, and made it a challenge to concentrate and to play with the verve that the piece demanded. Because of the heat, at intermission they discussed concert dress, which traditionally and by contract required the men to wear white tuxedo jackets, black pants, and black bow ties and cummerbunds; and the women to wear long white dresses. On rare occasions, when it was hotter than usual, the men performed without jackets, but with the current sweltering conditions, there was general agreement that if the heatwave persisted they would need to go beyond that, perhaps the men playing without ties and the women in shorter skirts and a light top. But in order to do that they would need the approval of management, since the dress code was part of their signed contract.

Joy D'Angelo was in the tent, setting up chairs for the weekend concerts. Bjørlund beckoned her to the stage and told her to fetch Anita Talbot to discuss the dress issue. D'Angelo demurred, physically wincing upon hearing the word "fetch." One, especially an underling, does not "fetch" Anita Talbot. Yumi didn't care for the word, either. The only time she heard it was in the context of Jacobus throwing a stick for Trotsky to retrieve. "Fetch, you dumb beast!" he would shout.

Bjørlund must have perceived the slight. "What I meant was," he said, "to please ask her if she can spare a moment. At my request."

The quartet resumed their rehearsal of the Beethoven for only another half hour, at which point Marcus Renfro suggested that the potential of the performance's success would be enhanced if the rest of the evening could be spent relaxing rather than exhausting themselves. No one disagreed.

Anita Talbot, accompanied by Sunny Flox, arrived as Yumi was putting her violin into her case. Bjørlund explained the situation about the heat. Talbot's response was disappointing, if predictable.

"I just don't think it will look good without ties, Christian," she said. "If you want to play without jackets, okay. But ties stay on."

"But what if someone passes out?" Renfro asked. "I hear some guy in the Boston Symphony almost died from the heat playing at Tanglewood this summer. They had to take him to the hospital."

"I know all about it," Talbot retorted. "He was elderly. Besides, it's humid there. We're going to keep the ties on. It's what the audience wants, and what they want is what they're going to get."

"Anita, maybe we should ask the musicians in the Kreutzer Quartet about this," Flox said, ever the conciliator. "Dieter is a little older than the rest. Maybe it should be up to him." The shepherd tending his flock.

"That won't be necessary," Talbot said. "We've got a contract. You've all read it and agreed to it. It's summer in the desert. No surprise there. End of story. Ties stay on."

Talbot instructed Joy D'Angelo to finish setting up the chairs and then see her in her office for additional assignments. Talbot departed but Sunny Flox remained for a moment. Yumi saw him whisper something to Hannah Carrington before following Talbot out of the tent.

"What did he say?" Yumi asked.

"He said not to worry, that he'll fix it with Anita so that we can perform in more comfortable clothes."

"That's nice to hear."

"I suppose. But he also said something that sounded a little weird. Something about wanting to make up for not standing up to her over something else. Some other issue. And then he said, 'Forget I ever said

43

that.'"

Carrington made a gesture with upturned hands and hunched her shoulders as if to say, "Who knows what that was all about?"

With the rehearsal over, Yumi said good night and went to her cabin, totally spent from all the hiking and practicing and rehearsing. There was nothing to do on the island at night, so she stripped down into a white cotton nightie and slid into bed with a paperback mystery she had brought along for just such occasions. It was one of those forgettable whodunnits which, if you don't read the whole thing in one sitting you have to start all over again to remember who was who, and who did what to whom. After a few chapters, she couldn't keep her eyes open and resigned herself to having to begin again some other time. She turned out the lights, made herself as comfortable as she could in her squeaky bed, and listened intently to the music of Antelope Island's blissful silence.

Sometime thereafter—it was hard to tell how long she had lain there, half-asleep—there was a knock on the door. Maybe because it had been a stressful day, and maybe because in the mystery she had been reading there had been a luridly violent incident subsequent to a knock on a door, she was momentarily startled.

Why would someone be knocking at this hour? To steal her violin? That was her immediate thought. But, if they wanted to do that, couldn't they more easily have done it during the day while she was out hiking? And why would a thief knock in the first place? Maybe she had been living in a city too long. Maybe she had become so accustomed to living with the fear of crime over her shoulder that it had become second nature to suspect everything.

The cabin doors had no locks. But maybe a thief wouldn't have known that. Well, maybe daytime wouldn't have been easier to break in, after all, even if she hadn't been there. During daytime, an intruder could be seen. The absence of locks suddenly weighed on her. It was an issue that had given the musicians some pause, with their irreplaceable instruments, but Sunny had convinced them that the festival atmosphere was so wholesome and congenial that no one would ever consider stealing an instrument.

Still, the musicians had insisted that the festival guarantee the safety of their instruments while on Antelope Island by assuming any liability in case of damage or theft. Anita Talbot had finally, reluctantly acquiesced, though she complained that the additional insurance premium would put the festival out of business, which turned out to be a highly exaggerated claim. Fortunately, there had never been a problem. Yet.

But if not her violin, Yumi thought, *then what*? Why would someone be knocking at her door, and so quietly, in the middle of the night? What was nearby that she could grab if she had to defend herself? A few years before, she had been kidnapped and forcibly restrained by a demented opera singer. After that harrowing incident, she vowed it would never happen again, and she began self-defense lessons. So far, she had risen to a second-degree black belt in judo. That qualified her as an expert, but there was still a long way for her to go to become a tenth-degree master, her goal. Anyone who might want to harm her would be in for a surprise if they expected her only to be a sweet, innocent Japanese violinist, someone who "played like a woman." Still, it wouldn't hurt to have a weapon by her side.

"Who's there?" she asked.

She waited for the response, readying herself. *Don't go there*, entered her mind.

"Want some company?"

Yumi exhaled. A familiar voice. Marcus Renfro.

Yumi invited him in. Couldn't sleep, he said. Must be the heat, he said, though the night had cooled considerably. He had brought a bottle of cognac and the plastic cup from his bathroom which the festival had generously provided. Yumi went to her bathroom and returned with her cup after removing her toothbrush from it and rinsing it out. Renfro poured. After toasting each other, they chatted about the Beethoven trio and quartet they had been rehearsing, reprising previous performances, both memorable and disastrous, and about some of the upcoming concerts each of them had after the festival. Yumi had to get back to New York right away to begin the upcoming concert season with Harmonium. Renfro would be flying off to Nice to catch the tail end of the festival season there, performing mostly Baroque music with some old friends. Their talk was amiable, but Renfro, usually so garrulous and witty, was uncharacteristically laconic. During the week, Yumi had gotten used to him being the first one with some clever repartee. Tonight, however, he seemed simply tongue-tied. Their conversation felt forced, formal, lacking flow, moving in fits and starts with long, silent gaps, like a novice composer's string quartet. A sentence or two about the heat, then concert dress, then the food. Inconsequential and disjointed. He even had a hard time looking directly at her. Did she look that bad without her makeup?

To create some momentum to their conversation, Yumi asked Renfro if he knew that Nathaniel Williams was one of Yumi's dear friends. If Daniel Jacobus was her surrogate father, then Nathaniel was the favorite uncle. She was pleased when Renfro—who, like Williams, was one of a handful of professional African American cellists—waxed poetic about how, as a student, he had considered the older cellist a sort of role model. But then she was disappointed to hear Renfro had been dismayed when Williams went into another profession, that of being an expert consultant to insurance companies in the investigation of musical instrument theft and fraud. He felt Williams had thrown it all away just to make money. Having expressed that opinion, Renfro stopped abruptly, almost in midsentence, saying, "Well, maybe. I don't know," after which another extended silence commenced.

Half the bottle remained when their conversation reached a self-conscious, contemplative lull. Yumi understood very well why Renfro was there and felt sufficiently fortified by alcohol herself to pop the question.

"Are you done with the preamble?" she asked.

"Preamble? What do you mean?"

"So, are you going to take your pants off?"

Chapter Four

E ven with the best of intentions, by Friday morning—with the first concert that evening—the musicians' nerves had begun to fray from the inexorable heat, from the intensity of their work, and from jealousies both professional and personal, all of which were exacerbated by the primitive living conditions—at least by their cosmopolitan standards—on Antelope Island. The festival administration was a frequent target of musicians' irritability (especially Anita Talbot, who seemed to take particular pride in brandishing her badge of honor, a perpetual acerbic scowl). But there was nothing unusual about that. When it comes to musicians' gripes, managers typically tend to think they're overblown, and musicians think they're taken too lightly.

What was more troubling were the small skirmishes that had broken out within ensembles, between ensembles, and even with the eminently agreeable pianist, Jamie Barov. The simmering turmoil had started innocently enough, over a reasonable difference of opinion regarding tempos in the *Rigaudon* of Grieg's charmingly ingenuous *Holberg Suite*, which erupted into a heated argument between Waldstein and Bjørlund, the latter having been designated the concertmaster, or first chair, of that ensemble. Waldstein, the principal second violinist for the piece, thought Bjørlund was taking his solo much too fast: "Christian, showing off simply because you can is so unbecoming. It's a bit like…well, I won't say it in front of ladies."

Regardless of whatever truth there may have been to the criticism, it was not a constructive way to put it. And since the piece would be performed without a conductor, it was truly Bjørlund, as the concertmaster, who had the prerogative to decide the tempo, especially since it was his solo. At least that was Yumi's opinion. As concertmaster of Harmonium, when that orchestra occasionally performed without a conductor the other musicians actually counted upon her to be the de facto leader. Despite her best efforts to be a diplomatic intermediary, the animosity between Bjørlund and Waldstein from the initial dustup that had ignited with their disagreement about stew, and which had lain dormant throughout the week, lit up once again. Worse, their enmity had a ripple effect. Volatility among the musicians became as predictable as the evening sheet lightning.

Bjørlund, stung by Waldstein's criticism, declared a break in their rehearsal. Waldstein, incensed that he'd been made into a villain for what he felt was a valid criticism, stormed out of the Big Top. With the rehearsal at a temporary standstill, Yumi and Renfro followed at a safe distance shortly thereafter for some fresh air and to decompress. They spotted Waldstein facing the lake, puffing viciously on a cigarette, his back to them. There were some final details Yumi wanted to talk to him about in the Leclair duos, and after considering whether or not it was a good idea to approach him at that particular moment, concluded it might actually help him regain his equilibrium by rerouting his mind to more pleasant thoughts.

Unfortunately, while she was deciding, Bjørlund emerged from the Big Top, and with his naturally long stride accelerated by indignation, beat her to the punch. And "punch" wasn't that far off a description, as the two men's conversation quickly descended into a heated confrontation. Yumi and Renfro hastily debated whether they should intervene or just let the two antagonists try to work things out as adults. With more than a week to go in the festival, they decided that it would be in everyone's interest to try to coax the two violinists to make peace, and the sooner the better. As she and Renfro considered what words they would choose in order to accomplish that feat, Jamie Barov appeared from his practice room. Anita Talbot emerged from the festival office. They, too, had apparently heard the squabble, and as they were situated nearer to Waldstein and Bjørlund, Yumi and Renfro held back and watched.

They couldn't hear much of what was said in the huddle, but it was clear that Barov was having greater success than Talbot in dousing the flames. The only response Yumi heard to Talbot was Bjørlund yelling, "You are management. Stay out of this," whereas Barov, with a series of grotesquely sexually suggestive gesticulations, was able to bring a smile to Waldstein's face, then Bjørlund's. After several more minutes of additional de-escalation, Barov shook hands with each of the two men; and then, amazingly enough, Waldstein and Bjørlund shook hands with each other. Waldstein offered Bjørlund a cigarette. Bjørlund accepted. The conflagration had been successfully and miraculously been extinguished. Everyone looked happy. At least, happier. That is, everyone except Talbot, who looked more livid than either of the two men at the height of their pique. Yumi waved to Barov and Talbot as they parted from the violinists.

"I don't know what you said to them," Yumi called to Barov, "but whatever it was, bravo!"

With a smile, Barov said, "I had to do *something*! You can't have half the violin section killing each other! So I told them they were acting like a pair of bitches in heat."

Yumi laughed. "But that's not even what 'bitches in heat' means, is it?"

"Well, whatever. Doesn't much matter. That was the first thing that came into my head! But if they didn't get the message at first, giving them a graphic demonstration did the trick."

"We saw that," Renfro said. "Oscar material, Jamie." He gave Barov a thumbs-up. "And what did they say?"

"Oh, Dieter said, 'Well, if it isn't the pot calling the kettle black.' I guess I took one for the team there. We all had a good laugh. But I'm telling you," Barov continued, "all their hollering makes it absolutely impossible for me to practice, y'know? Sometimes you just want to put 'em out of their misery."

Unlike Yumi, who discovered freedom in her Camaro, Nathaniel, a New York City resident for decades, didn't enjoy driving and no longer owned a car. He arrived on Antelope Island in a rented Ford Taurus, hours in advance of the evening performance in order to beat the concert traffic. The festival had boasted a sellout and, because of the one-lane causeway, it was recommended that concertgoers arrive early with a picnic dinner to avoid being backed up halfway to the tollbooth. Yumi, aware that Nathaniel had time on his hands and an aversion to being out in the hot sun—or to any other discomfort, for that matter—invited him into her cabin for a rest. When he entered, he stared with a jaundiced eye at the single folding wooden chair of dubious strength. Rather than chancing it against his girth, which Jacobus had recently described as "corpulagenous," he sat on her bed while Yumi related all the gossip.

"My, my, my! Can you believe it?" he said. "And Bjørlund and Waldstein, of all people! They're such great musicians! What gets into people like that?"

"I know what you mean," Yumi replied. "I probably should have known better than to play in this festival, but you know Sunny. He's a snake charmer. He talked me into it. Jake warned me, and he was right. Playing quartets makes everyone *meshugenah*."

Jacobus had indeed warned Yumi. Yes, he had. Stay away from quartets, he'd told her. They never turn out well. He scolded her that she should have learned her lesson when she was second violin of the New Magini Quartet—before she got her job as concertmaster of Harmonium—which had almost ended with both of them being killed. "But no, you had to fill in for Kuypers," Jacobus had chided her on her last visit to his hospital bed, "who you don't even know, who just happened to call in sick. Call me cynical, but you think Kuypers might've decided in the end he'd rather tiptoe through the tulips in the Netherlands?"

And it wasn't as if Yumi was wanting for a gig, he argued. She already had a full-time, high-salaried job with Harmonium and this was her damn vacation. "Why don't you go drink some piña coladas on a beach in Jamaica," he suggested, "or better yet, make some piña coladas for me?" More and more, Yumi thought it could have been Jacobus who had left the cryptic message on her phone, "Don't go there." It would not be unlike him to be that abrupt and parsimonious with words. Jacobus did not understand why people so often acted contrary to their own self-interest, though Yumi had recently forced him to admit he had done so himself on many an occasion.

"Yeah? Give me an example," Jacobus challenged. "Just one!"

50

"Like when you ate a mushroom that was going to poison you to death simply to prove your point."

"Bah!"

"*Meshugenah* for sure," Nathaniel replied to Yumi's comment about quartets. "You can tell Jake all about it next week. I'll be picking him up at the airport and bringing him here next Friday afternoon, so there'll be plenty of opportunity before your performance for him to say 'I told you so.'"

"It won't take much." Yumi laughed.

"Surely," Nathaniel said, "they can't *all* be *meshugenah*."

"Marcus is pretty nice."

"Marcus Renfro? That's interesting to hear you say that. Between you and me, I don't trust him, if you want my honest opinion."

"Really? He told me he looked up to you. He called you one of his role models." Yumi noted how Nathaniel was now lounging on her bed, lying on his side with his hand on bent elbow, supporting his head. It was a posture not at all dissimilar to Renfro's, in the same place, just a day earlier. Under entirely different circumstances.

"Maybe that's what he told *you*," Nathaniel said. "It may be true there aren't too many African American cellists in the concert world, so in a way, it would be hard *not* to be his role model. But I've heard through the grapevine he's said some disdainful things about me for having left the profession. I'd say he seems a bit holier than thou, if you know what I mean, and I ain't even gonna say what I think of his musicianship."

Yumi laughed.

"You think I'm wrong?" Nathaniel asked.

"I don't know," Yumi said. "He seems like a nice enough guy to me."

The tent was brimmed with an audience, eagerly anticipating great music surrounded by nature. An extra buzz could be counted on for the opening concert of a festival, and tonight was no exception. When Yumi and Dieter Waldstein entered the tent through the flap held open by Joy D'Angelo and ascended the three steps to the stage, they were greeted with enthusiastic applause, some cheers, and even a few hoots and whistles. An American audience for sure, but a sincere one. As they bowed, Yumi spotted a few familiar faces from other festivals where she had performed. A couple, somewhat past middle age, waved at her. She didn't recognize them. Groupies, perhaps? Don't flatter yourself, she told herself. She smiled at them directly, just in case. They waved back. She had made them feel special, whoever they were.

She and Waldstein opened the program with the pair of duos by Jean-Marie Leclair. In two ways, it was a warm-up act for the bigger repertoire to come. As the first Antelope Island Music Festival concert of the season, it was a tasty appetizer before the main course. And, for Yumi and Dieter it literally was a warm-up, in that it enabled them to limber their fingers, hands, and arms with technically less challenging music, like a basketball player's shoot-around before the game starts. Not that they needed warming up otherwise. The temperature inside the tent was probably close to ninety. Thankfully, Sunny Flox had ultimately prevailed upon Anita Talbot to allow them to perform in less formal dress. Well, not actually prevailed if what Yumi had heard was correct. It was more that at the last minute Flox had granted them permission without Talbot's knowledge and now it was too late for Talbot to rescind it. There might be hell to pay at some point, but for the moment the ability to endure playing in such conditions was enhanced. No one was complaining.

That the music which began the program was not overly difficult did not make it any less appealing. Jean-Marie Leclair was a capable composer and a first-rate violin virtuoso in his day, so the craftiness of his music fit very comfortably in violinists' technical toolboxes. In other words, it sounded a lot more difficult than it really was. As a result, when Yumi and Waldstein finished their duos, they received a well-deserved and wholehearted ovation. The audience seemed to especially enjoy Waldstein's overt choreography when it was his turn to play first violin.

The duos were followed by a jaunty Josef Haydn piano trio, performed by Waldstein, Goldman, and Barov. Waldstein's demeanor expressed confidence and command; Goldman's, involvement and intensity; and

Barov's, playful joy. The music was full of the wit, humor, and lyricism of which Haydn was a master. After intermission, the newly-established quartet, with Yumi as the first violinist substituting for Edo Kuypers, performed the great audience pleaser, the Beethoven Quartet, Op. 59, No. 3, with its breathtaking, hurtling finale. And then, to finish off the evening with the kind of rousing send-off that Jacobus liked to call the Grand Kazatske, the merged ensemble performed the feel-good Grieg *Holberg Suite*, with Bjørlund as concertmaster, not-too-subtly taking his solo tempo even faster than at the rehearsal. "Take that, Waldstein!" it said.

Standing ovation! Yumi, with all the other musicians, exited through the flap in the side of the tent and returned to take a bow. Two bows. Three bows. All smiles. Everyone beaming.

After the concert, the musicians replaced their instruments in their cases, lying side by side on a folding table behind the tent. They exchanged the customary banal congratulations and pleasantries as they departed. Yumi breathed deeply, thankful to be out in the fresh night air after two hours inside the Big Top. As far as tents went, it was fine, but by the end of the performance, with the packed audience, it had become stifling and claustrophobic.

Regardless, the concert had been a success. It had been a fine way to open the festival. As Nathaniel rounded the corner of the tent, Yumi smiled and then waved, but before she could greet him she was intercepted by Joy D'Angelo. Yumi raised her right hand, palm forward, like a traffic cop, gesturing to Nathaniel to wait.

"Anita wants to see all the musicians in her office," D'Angelo said. "She's on the warpath."

"What about?" Yumi asked.

"Concert dress. I guess she was blindsided, so she's doubly pissed."

Yumi considered the consequences of her not attending the meeting.

"Tell Anita I'll be there soon. I have a special guest here I need to see."

"She'll be really angry."

"I can handle it."

"I mean she'll be really angry at me if not everyone is there."

"All right. Give me one minute."

D'Angelo went off to collect the other musicians. Yumi approached Nathaniel, his usual patient self.

"Hi, Nathaniel. Would you mind waiting a bit? The festival manager wants to see us."

"No problem. A while for traffic to clear, anyhow," he said. "It's worse than midtown at rush hour."

Yumi ran off to the office, where the musicians had already assembled. Anita Talbot, stood by her desk, arms folded. Sunny Flox, behind her, was pallid as leftover oatmeal. Though he was almost a head taller than Talbot, his posture was slumped, whereas Talbot was ramrod straight. The terms "spineless" and "backbone" as character descriptions were on display in living color. Talbot was every bit the dominatrix.

Talbot reminded the musicians what their contract said—as if they hadn't known—and that they were in violation for having disregarded the clearly stated dress code.

"What are you going to do?" Bjørlund asked. "Fire us?"

So typical of Bjørlund when he was agitated. So confrontational.

"Of course not. That's ridiculous. You think I would do anything to jeopardize this festival?"

"Then what, Anita?" Waldstein asked. His tone suggested he was taking on the role of the senior member of the musicians. The evenhanded mediator. "Dressing comfortably only helps us play better. Isn't that what it's supposed to be about? After all, we're here in the desert, not in Carnegie Hall."

There were mumbles of assent. A reasonable argument. But underneath, aside from the issue of concert dress, Yumi perceived a nuanced power struggle between him and the hotheaded Bjørlund.

"An infraction is an infraction," Talbot replied. "Slippery slope, Dieter. Slippery slope. You break one rule and where does it stop? Pretty soon you break them all. I'll be assessing fines in the morning."

Yumi noticed that Flox hadn't said a word.

The ensuing chorus of derision and objection did nothing to sway Talbot's edict. After further fruitless argument, the musicians threw up their hands in disgust, so close to being a synchronized gesture it was almost comical. The group dispersed in all directions. Yumi returned to the tent to find Nathaniel still waiting. She explained the cause of her delay.

Nathaniel laughed.

"Some things never change," he said. "Even in the most rinky-dink music organization—not that I'm saying this festival is rinky-dink—the boss always thinks he—"

"Or she—"

"Or she thinks they've got a monopoly on brains and dedication; that the musicians have to be strictly controlled or everything will fall apart. That's one reason why I left professional playing, and Jake ended up grateful he went blind before he got stuck playing in an orchestra for the rest of his life."

"Hey, Nathaniel, wait a second!" Yumi said, whose full-time job was as concertmaster of a symphony orchestra.

"Oops! Sorry!" Nathaniel said. "Got carried away."

Yumi laughed. Nathaniel had made a valid point. The predictability of musicians feeling oppressed by their management trying to wring the most music out of them for the least money came in a close third after death and taxes. But, she reminded herself, in the end, the musicians had the better of it, because they were the ones who got to play the music. Ah, the music!

"So, what did you think of the concert?" she asked.

"Sensational! I can't think of a single critical thing to say. Those duos were simply charming, I loved the Haydn, and the Beethoven was incredible—I can't believe how fast y'all played that last movement. And the Grieg. Well, Grieg is Grieg. It was fine. And after what you were telling me about the rehearsals, it was nice to see everyone getting along so well."

"You think so? I suppose you didn't notice that Christian and Dieter didn't say a word to each other."

"I missed that."

"Good. But FYI, they're no longer on speaking terms. Again."

Yumi and Nathaniel's conversation was interrupted by an unpleasant noise more associated with midtown rush hour than the quasi-wilderness of Antelope Island. It was the crunch of a car's front bumper engaging inhospitably with the rear bumper of the car in front of it. Followed by the angry honking of horns, the combined effect created an ugly disturbance within the island's tranquility, an angry tear in a silk tapestry.

"Uh-oh," Nathaniel said. "Sounds like I might be stuck here for a while."

"You and a few hundred other people. There's only one road out of here."

Yet another unpleasant noise followed a few minutes thereafter. This one was vocal.

"That would be Anita," Yumi said.

"The CEO?"

"The very one. And it sounds like the person she's chewing out is Jefferson Dance. He's the state park ranger."

The angry voices intensified as the argument became more heated and as the arguers walked closer to Yumi and Nathaniel.

"Anita, you want your music festival here, fine," they heard Dance say.

He was a tall man in a beige state park uniform and well-worn cowboy hat that was not part of the uniform. But his most distinctive feature was the patch over his left eye.

"Look, my men are cowboys first and foremost. What they're good at is riding horses and managing buffalo herds. And I've got some naturalists, and I've got some staff to take care of trails and campgrounds. But I don't have anyone trained to be traffic cops, and the state doesn't give me a cent out of their budget to provide security for you folks at the festival. So what do you propose I do?"

"That's really not my concern," Anita said. "But it is *your* responsibility. Look at the national parks. They've literally got millions of visitors and they seem to be able to manage."

"You think so? You ever wait in line for two hours to get into Arches?"

"That's not my point. My point is, they figure it out. We have a handful of cars here and we have gridlock."

Talbot and Dance passed Yumi and Nathaniel. Talbot ignored them. She might not even have noticed their presence. Dance put a finger to his hat and gave them a polite nod. Dance pressed his grievances about the state not providing the resources he needed as his voice faded into the night.

Yumi shrugged. "In conclusion, in general, a good time was had by all," she said, smiling.

"I suppose," Nathaniel said. "But I'm glad I'm not either one of 'em."

It was too lovely a night to go back to her cabin or to dwell upon unpleasantries, so until the traffic cleared, Yumi and Nathaniel found a bench overlooking the lake. It was hard to tell how many years the bench had been there. Its wooden slats were still solid but severely weathered and bleached by the sun. Its iron structure held the slats in place, but since the boards had shrunk as they dried, they had loosened around their screws, and voiced a clattering complaint when Yumi and especially Nathaniel sat down on them. In the distance, across the water's placid surface, the lights of Salt Lake City twinkled like lights on a Christmas tree.

"There's something about the atmosphere along the Wasatch Front at night that makes lights flicker," Yumi said. "It's magical. Don't you think?"

She derived a sense of comfort from nature's tranquil silence after the noisy grind of the departing traffic, and even from the music, as beautiful and meaningful as it had been. And from having Nathaniel Williams at her side. Over the years Nathaniel had been the Yin to Jacobus's Yang, a steadying, mellowing counter to Jacobus's edge. It had not ceased to be humorous to her whenever she saw the two together. Nathaniel, an African American, was a big man to begin with and, because he enjoyed food almost as much as the company that went along with it, had grown even larger, especially around the waist. Compare him to Jacobus, with his unruly mop of hair, thinned and grayed, and with his complexion pasty white except when it reddened while railing about one injustice or another, which was frequent. A head shorter than Nathaniel, Jacobus had shrunk with age whereas Nathaniel had grown, albeit horizontally, exaggerating their differences in stature.

Though physically and temperamentally so different, the bonds that sealed their friendship had nevertheless, if anything, deepened over time. That was one reason it meant so much to Yumi that both of them would be there for her performance of *Summer*.

"Yes, it is magical," Nathaniel said. "And that's why I brought you a little gift." He handed her a small volume he had tucked away in his jacket pocket.

"*Roughing It*, by Mark Twain," Yumi read. "Nathaniel, thank you so much!"

"It's a first edition, from 1872. He wrote it when he was traveling out west as a young man, when he was still Samuel Clemens, trying to strike it rich as a miner. He spent a couple days in Salt Lake City and talks all about the ruggedness of this part of the world. That's what made me think of you and your colleagues out here."

"I can understand why!"

"Here, read this paragraph," Nathaniel said and found a certain page. "I think you'll see what I mean. Is it too dark out?"

"No, I want to read it. I can use my phone light," Yumi said, and began to read, "'… in the edge of a level plain as broad as the state of Connecticut, crouching close to the ground under a curving wall of mighty mountains whose heads are hidden in the clouds, and whose shoulders bear relics of the snows of winter all the summer long. Seen from…these dizzy heights… Great Salt Lake City is toned down and diminished till it is suggestive of a child's toy village reposing under the majestic protection of the Chinese wall.'

"That's perfect," Yumi said. "What a beautiful description. It's just like what we're seeing right here, over a hundred years later. I can't wait to read the rest of it. Nathaniel, you're the best friend."

Yumi leaned against Nathaniel, who wrapped her in his substantial, avuncular arm, keeping her warm, further conversation unnecessary. The night had turned chilly, ironic after the musicians' argument with Talbot about the stifling heat. The whole week had been virtually cloudless, which made the days hotter, but it also made the nights cooler.

Long after the last car had left for the night, Nathaniel patted Yumi on the head and said, "You've had a long day. Time you got some shuteye, and I'd better be heading back to the city before I fall asleep at the wheel."

Yumi walked Nathaniel to his car and said goodnight. After he left, she took a detour on her way to her cabin. She tapped lightly on the door of another with her fingertips and smiled when Marcus Renfro invited her in.

Shortly thereafter, he expressed admiration for the tattoo on the small of her back, of a large black, white, and red dancing crane, wings spread, its long neck seductively bent. Tattoos were generally frowned upon in Japan. They were associated with the Yakuza, the Japanese Mafia, who were often heavily tattooed. But Yumi found the tattoos beautiful and the association with danger, even criminality, only added to her desire to have one. After all, when she was a teenager, hadn't she, along with her mother and grandmother, plotted to steal the infamous "Piccolino" Stradivarius violin from under the noses of armed guards at Carnegie Hall? And they would have been successful but for one man who uncovered their scheme. Daniel Jacobus. Ever since her tattoo three years earlier, designed by the famous artist, Takadano Baba, her crane had provided her with the good fortune and longevity, happiness, and peace for which it had become a revered Japanese symbol. And why shouldn't it continue to do so?

Chapter Five

"Yes, of course," Joy D'Angelo said in answer to Jamie Barov's question. "I'm going into the city anyway to drive Sunny to the airport. Yes, another meeting. Chicago."

It was the end of the first week. D'Angelo had been removing music stands from the stage after the Sunday concert. Barov was among a group of musicians eager to make arrangements to visit Salt Lake City the next day, the musicians' single free day before the end of the festival. Barov wanted to know if she could drive them all in the festival van.

The weekend's concerts were no less successful than Friday's opener, and there were no further mishaps with colliding automobiles. Yumi was looking forward to buying a new pair of hiking boots, as the ones she had had for years had started to come apart at the seams. Some of her colleagues wanted to go into the city simply for a change of pace—a momentary return to the urban environment with which they were more familiar and certainly more comfortable—to enjoy the local restaurants and pubs, to shop, or to visit old friends from the Utah Symphony or university music faculty.

Jamie Barov had accepted an invitation to the Steinway showroom, where he would be welcomed as a special guest to tickle the ivories on a recent shipment of new grand pianos. His imprimatur would go a long way to quickly reducing the inventory. After that he planned to race over to the outdoor retailers' convention for a fly-tying presentation. Ingrid Goldman made an appointment to go to the Peter Prier and Sons violin shop to have her cello's soundpost adjusted, as the instrument's transition to a dry climate had loosened it; and because the soundpost had loosened, it had shifted a good millimeter, the result of which compromised the instrument's resonance.

Yumi, waiting patiently until plans had been finalized and all the other musicians had wandered off, asked D'Angelo if she would like to have that lesson she'd requested before they departed for the city the next morning. D'Angelo was thrilled that Yumi had remembered, and said yes immediately. They agreed to meet in Joy's cabin first thing in the morning, far enough away from the office that Anita Talbot would not be able to hear them; or if she was able, Yumi could pretend it was just her practicing.

Later that night, in Renfro's cabin, Yumi shared the plan for the excursion, as he hadn't been among the group when it was discussed. His response was inexplicably tentative. He said it was a tempting proposition and he'd think about it, but that he might opt to remain on the island to practice for the upcoming week's concerts and maybe to take another hike. He might need some time to himself, he said.

That seems so unlike him, Yumi thought. He was generally such an extrovert who craved being part of the action, if not the very center of attention. The past two days, though, she had noticed a change. His behavior had become erratic, sporadically joking and then pouting. Withdrawn. The attempts at humor seemed forced and manufactured. Yumi was in the dark as to what it could be attributed.

With a reassuring wink, Renfro suggested that Yumi buy another bottle of cognac in town, since before Sunday night was over they would no doubt finish the one they had started. An effort to dispel her disappointment, perhaps? It was a sweet sentiment, but it was delivered as if by necessity rather than with enthusiasm. Not the kind of convincing performance for which she would pay for a high-priced ticket. Maybe she could change his tune.

Being awakened the next morning at dawn to the twirling song of the meadowlark certainly beat the blast of a Manhattan taxi. Yumi needed a long shower after a night of lovemaking, as exhausting as it had been spirited. She needed not only to cleanse her body—who said you don't sweat in the

61

desert?—but to clear her head as well. She was conflicted and perplexed. It had started as an enthusiastic, no-strings-attached celebration of a successful first week of festival concerts, a physical and emotional release. Enjoying each other's athletic bodies. Sex. And though his strong hands were fully engaged—wasn't there something special about a cellist's hands?—there had been moments when Renfro's mind seemed to be elsewhere, bafflingly distracted, regardless of her exertions. Moments when his motions were there, but not the desire. She had brought him back to the present while lying on her back, scissoring her legs around his waist and squeezed until he gasped.

"Is that something you learned in judo?" he asked, working up a smile.

"No. Not from judo. From experience," she replied and closed her eyes again.

Her attentions had been focused on Renfro's shallow breathing, not on external sounds of nature, when she heard it. She wouldn't even have been certain it was a pebble against the glass window except that Renfro, too, paused in mid-thrust. Her ears aroused, did she hear footsteps—quietly, cautiously—receding from outside the cabin?

"What was that?" she asked.

"What?"

"Didn't you hear it?"

"Uh-uh," he said. "I was enjoying myself too much."

"You didn't hear it?" she asked again.

"It's this island," he said. "It gets to you after a while. Maybe it was a buffalo."

He smiled at her again. Yumi tried to put the interruption out of her mind.

If it had only been that, maybe she would have forgotten about it. There was something uniquely peculiar about desert silence. It wasn't just the absence of sound. It wasn't just turning off your car radio. It was profound. Powerful. It was an active, dominating player. There were times in the desert when she would do the listening exercise that Jacobus had taught her and all she heard was...nothing. A blanket of silence, as if the world had come to a stop.

So, yes, maybe Marcus was right. Maybe the island had gotten to her. Except that later, he had put his hands around her throat. And squeezed. At first, she savored the eroticism, to be under his control. She pictured his dark fingers around her white throat. The playacting. The slightly dizzying sensation of restricted blood supply to the brain. It aroused her and she was about to climax, but then she looked into his eyes. There was something about his expression. The intensity. She sensed it wasn't so much about pleasure as something else. She wasn't frightened, even when his grip tightened. Breaking a chokehold was a simple judo maneuver. She could have him on his back and incapacitated in seconds if she wanted to. It was only when she attempted to speak his name and tell him he had reached her limit and no sound came out that she realized she might shortly lose consciousness. But at that moment he released his hold, blinked, and apologized if he had hurt or frightened her. He hadn't meant to. He hoped she enjoyed it, he said.

Refreshed, Yumi pulled back the plastic shower curtain and reached for the undersized, worn-out towel that hung on the plastic hook. She chided herself for having become far too spoiled with plush, Western-style bath towels. *Ah, Lucerne!* You could almost wear those towels. This one, in her cabin, was much more Japanese-style, almost thin as a handkerchief, though this one was from wear and tear and not from custom. She discarded the useless towel onto the floor and allowed five minutes for the desert air to finish the task.

As she waited, she looked in the mirror to inspect her neck. She felt where Marcus's hands had been, but there were no visible bruises. Nor was there a bruise to her ego when recalling how Renfro's mind appeared to have drifted. No, she was not in love with Marcus Renfro, and apparently, Marcus Renfro felt the same way about her. It was just a fling. Summer camp for adults. Chalk one up for experience. She could live with that.

But the pebble on the window? And the receding footsteps? She could not shake those away so easily. And then this morning, when she awoke, he was already dressed and pacing the floor. He informed her he would not be joining them in their jaunt into town. He would take a raincheck.

63

But the shower had cleared her head. She was determined to enjoy her day off and put any lingering dark thoughts behind her. Doubts and anxieties are so often magnified by night and by silence and by unfamiliar surroundings. How many times have we wrestled with the fear of imminent disaster, of demons in the night only to realize when the sun rose that it was the darkness alone that had fed our anxieties? That must be what it was. A pebble tossed on a window? How unlikely! It was a twig falling from a tree. Footsteps outside the cabin? A jackrabbit or a fox scurrying through the grass, no doubt. And to think there was any connection between those imaginary fears and a week-old prank phone call? A figment of her imagination.

She dressed in a spaghetti-strapped, grass green, cotton knit shift, hemmed two inches above the knees, and white low-cut sneakers. But first, she had to go through with the promised lesson with the D'Angelo girl. Scheduling convenience wasn't the only reason for the early-morning start. It was also the time when the gentle dawn breeze breathed refreshing, lake-cooled air over the island, before it was overtaken by the remorseless heat. It was a time of day when giving a one-off lesson would not feel as much of an imposition as it would otherwise.

Joy D'Angelo answered Yumi's knock on her cabin door, shoeless and dressed in jeans shorts and another Antelope Island Music Festival T-shirt. Yumi took a quick glance around the room. Clothes were scattered everywhere. Drawers open. Bed unmade. When Yumi was a child, space in her Japanese home was at a premium. Everything had to be put away or else there would be no floor space to walk. Futons were rolled up and stored. Floors were polished daily, not a major task as no one wore shoes inside a home. Everything had to be neat as a pin. It had been her English grandmother, Kate Padgett, who had "taught" her it wasn't a sin to be a little freer and easier with personal spaces. "You do know the maxim, dear Yumi, 'Cleanliness is next to godliness'?" *Obaasan* Kate would remind her granddaughter. "Of course you do. Well, my axiom is, 'Cleanliness is next to impossible.' Now go outside and play."

Yumi had always found it easier to concentrate when her practice room was spare and hoped D'Angelo's violin playing would not be as unkempt and disorganized as her room. Jacobus's house was a shambles, but that could be forgiven. It could be explained. Though a person with sight would have thought there was no rhyme or reason to where Jacobus let things lie year after year—on shelves, on counters, on tables, on the floor—he knew exactly where everything was, whether it was a book, record, or box of matches. Older things were on the bottom. Newly acquired things were on top. To have moved anything would have made it less organized. Those were his keys, apparently: an organized mind and a good memory. Yumi had yet to determine whether D'Angelo had either.

"Let's get started," Yumi said. "We don't want to keep everyone waiting for us." Indeed, the sooner they finished the lesson, the sooner she could begin to enjoy her half-day window of freedom. "What would you like to play?"

D'Angelo had been studying the Mozart Concerto in A Major. Would that be okay? That would be fine.

D'Angelo played the opening *Adagio*, followed by the exposition of the *Allegro aperto*. Yumi listened intently. Yes, the young lady had decent mechanical skills, certainly enough to play Mozart. There were technical challenges in Mozart that required careful practice, but no one could convincingly argue it was as demanding as Tchaikovsky or Brahms. So there was nothing wrong, per se, in D'Angelo's mechanics. What her playing lacked was a sense of the style, both in broad terms and the phrasing, of that particular concerto. Of personality. Yumi had studied the same concerto with Jacobus, and now she asked D'Angelo the same questions he had badgered her with when she was a teenager:

Do you know what *aperto* means, for instance? No, was D'Angelo's answer.

Do you know how old Mozart was when he wrote the concerto? Not really.

What his station in life was at the time? Uh-uh.

D'Angelo asked, "Why's that important?"

When Yumi had asked that question at her first lesson with Jacobus—it was with the *Devil's Trill* Sonata by Giuseppe Tartini—he had flown into a rage and almost kicked her out, then and there, and would have except that he owed a favor to Makoto Furukawa, his friend, and Yumi's first teacher. She would not be so harsh with D'Angelo. After all, this would be the only lesson she would give her and D'Angelo wasn't pursuing a career as a performer. It didn't matter as much.

"My former teacher, Daniel Jacobus, always challenged me to understand why I played something a certain way. I had to be able to defend what I was doing from first note to last. It took study. It took research. And of course, it took a lot of practice. Now let's start from the beginning and go over some details in the time we've got left."

D'Angelo then played it again, with modestly improved results. If expression was a window, then it had been opened a crack, but the playing was still tentative and too focused on playing correctly and not artistically. Yumi's pep talk needed a supplement.

"Joy, name some of your favorite violinists."

"Oh, I don't know. Perlman, Zukerman, Hahn, Heifetz (of course), Mutter—"

"You can stop there." Yumi laughed. "I want you to choose one of them. Any one. Then I want you to listen in your head to their sound. Then imagine you're that person and when you've got that in your head, start over again. Go ahead. Take your time."

D'Angelo closed her eyes, which Yumi took to mean she was concentrating. After a half-minute or so, she raised her instrument and began the Mozart yet again. The difference was, if not miraculous, noteworthy enough so that after a few minutes D'Angelo had to stop because she was laughing.

"What's so funny?" Yumi asked.

"It's just that I can't believe it!" D'Angelo said. "How did you do it?"

"I didn't do anything. *You* did it all. I just suggested you change your frame of reference from being a student to being an artist. Yes, we're all students, always—I'll be practicing the Bach sonatas until the day I die—but we're all also artists. That's why we play. That's who we are. So no matter what you're practicing, if you start out with the idea that *you* have something to communicate, that it's *your* music and not someone else's, your playing will improve more than any teacher can teach you."

When they were all done, when D'Angelo was putting her instrument away, she thanked Yumi for the umpteenth time for giving her a lesson that she would never forget. It made Yumi uncomfortable to be on the receiving end of so much gratitude and so she deflected the subject of the discussion, asking if D'Angelo had ever had lessons with any of the other musicians at the festival.

"Uh-huh. Last year I played for Mr. Bjørlund and Mr. Waldstein. They were so…different."

Yumi laughed.

"From me or each other?"

"Both, I'd say. Mr. Bjørlund was so academic. So intellectual. He knows all the étude books and all the pedagogical stuff, so he was able to tell me exactly all the things I should practice. He was great with technique, especially."

"And Mr. Waldstein?"

"Oh, he was more about freedom." D'Angelo laughed. "Freedom in the music. Moving freely with your body. How music has to flow. He talked all about feelings. Not so much *how* to play stuff, but *why* to do them."

Bjørlund and Waldstein. They say opposites attract, Yumi thought. *Maybe not in their case.*

"Interesting," Yumi said.

"Can I say one thing?" D'Angelo asked.

"Of course."

"Just that you're a lot nicer than either of them."

Yumi was tempted to ask what she meant by that because she perceived hidden innuendo, and decided she would rather not know, at least for the moment. Maybe she *was* simply nicer. Maybe that's all there was to it. But she also knew the way female students were treated by their male teachers far too often, and it made her cringe. The level of sexual misconduct in the classical music world had turned out to be far more rampant than the elegant stage presence would suggest. She had seen it. She had experienced it. Jacobus had gone to the extreme, almost killing himself to try to expose it.

And it wasn't only between teachers and students. Not by any means.

67

By conductors with women orchestra players. Not always women, either. Opera stars with young singers. Managers with artists. Anywhere there was an imbalance of power. Power. Maybe she was reading too much into D'Angelo's words. Yes, maybe she was over-analyzing a perfectly innocent comment.

But maybe she wasn't. Could it be that one of them, Bjørlund or Waldstein, was the one who tossed a pebble at Marcus's window? If so, why?

"Joy," Yumi asked, "did either Dieter or Christian ever discourage you from playing the violin? Did they ever say anything?"

"Not really *said* anything," D'Angelo responded. "But they both kind of hinted at it. Mr. Bjørlund especially. He's the one who actually suggested I think about management."

"Did he—or anyone else—ever say anything like, 'Don't go there'?"

"Not that I recall. But it's possible. Why?"

"Never mind. It's nothing. Let's go have some fun," she said.

On the drive from Antelope Island, Yumi tried to capture every nuance of whatever anyone said for any suggestion someone might have been complicit in either the window tapping or the phone call. But there was nothing. It was all just the usual chatter. She told herself she was becoming paranoid, appreciating even more the need for her temporary liberation, to be on her own after a cloistered week on the island. It had begun to feel like a penal colony.

Even with weekday traffic, it was only a one-hour drive to the airport to drop off Flox, and from there a mere fifteen minutes more into downtown. They disembarked at the main branch of the city library, a prominent, modernistic architectural landmark. With its curved, sloping exterior, everyone would be able to easily recognize it when it was time to reconvene for their return trip to the island. From the library, they went their separate ways.

Like the streets in Manhattan, Yumi's adopted city, Salt Lake City streets were laid out as a numbered grid. According to the tourist's map on her phone, the downtown shopping mall was five blocks away. But whereas the blocks in Manhattan were only about two hundred feet long, in Salt Lake they were six hundred sixty, if the Internet was to be believed, and the streets themselves almost as wide as Manhattan streets were long. Or so they seemed. It took Yumi a great deal longer to reach her destination than she anticipated; the stroll became more of a sprint, and with the sun fully risen, an increasingly uncomfortable one. Along the way, she waited for the light to change at the intersection of 200 South and 300 East. Among the few pedestrians willing to brave the heat, she had the uncomfortable sense that someone was following her. It wasn't rational, she knew, and attributed her unease to the series of minor but inexplicable events over the past week. She turned slowly, scanning the entire scene, but she didn't recognize anyone, nor did anyone seem to be paying her the least bit of attention.

Clearly, there was nothing to worry about. Chiding herself for imagining ghosts, she continued to the City Creek Mall where, to her relief, there was no shortage of outdoor-wear retailers in its air-conditioned comfort. After trying on hiking boots at five shops, she hit pay dirt at the sixth. Though the price tag was over two hundred dollars, Jacobus would be pleased she bought them on sale at a twenty percent discount.

With time on her hands, Yumi browsed around the shopping center. Tucked away on the second floor, a small boutique called Chic caught her eye. A headless red mannequin in the window, erotically posed, flaunted a white dress. She ran into the shop, tried on the dress, and bought it. Assuming Sunny Flox would be true to his word about more comfortable concert attire, it would be perfect for the sultry Big Top, and sultry in its own way. The dress was white—no change there—but strapless and knee-length for comfort; and lacy and form-fitting with a thigh-revealing side-slit for the visuals.

Success in hand, she began her return to the library. She took a different route, both for a new vantage of the city and also to evade whatever phantoms might have been following her, laughing at herself for her excess of caution.

Halfway back, she discovered a tiny ramen shop, and with it a yearning

69

for Japanese food that had been growing since leaving New York. Once inside, the aroma returned her to her childhood home on Kyushu, Japan's southern island. Visually, it wasn't so much that the decor looked Japanese. It was definitely contemporary Western-style, but it had the welcoming informality of a rustic Japanese *izakaya*. Each table, none of which could seat more than four, was different from the others, suggesting the furniture had been purchased at garage sales or secondhand stores. The same was true of plates and silverware. It made everyone feel welcome, especially the young people who were there, who undoubtedly had less disposable income for more expensive dining. The shop was also dimly lit and had a quiet but effective ceiling fan cooling everything off.

Suddenly ravenously hungry, she ordered a large bowl of ramen, choosing a soy-based broth, with extra pork slices, veggies, and boiled egg. The waitress who took her order was definitely Asian and probably Japanese, so Yumi took a stab and addressed her in their native language. The waitress asked, "Is that Japanese?" which gave Yumi second thoughts about the authenticity of the meal she was about to eat. She was relieved when it arrived, steaming hot. After a week of the food they had been served at the festival, anything would have tasted better, but this was as good as New York and a fraction of the price. And there was no line of waiting customers halfway down the block, either.

Yumi looked at her watch. As there was still plenty of time before she had to return to the library for the ride back to the island, she decided to catch up on some business while savoring the good food. Looking at her calendar, she began texting her New York students to arrange September lessons. There would be a lot of catching up to do after a summer off, during which some of her students had attended music festivals like Tanglewood and Aspen, while others stayed in the city with part-time jobs to help pay for their tuition. When the waitress arrived to remove her empty bowl, she wasn't ready either to finish her scheduling or endure the hot sun, and so ordered chilled *genmaicha* as a finishing touch to her leisurely lunch.

Absorbed in her planning, she recoiled at the sudden tap on her shoulder. It felt like an electric shock, arousing all the anxieties that had built up since

"Don't go there." Instinctively, she wheeled around, ready to confront her adversary.

It was only Franz Weiss, the second violinist of the Kreutzer Quartet and one of the quiet ones at the festival. He was a few inches taller than she was, making him about five-foot-nine, but excessively skinny. He was bald and wore glasses that made his eyes look too big; and his short-sleeve, white button-down shirt exposed his densely hairy arms and throat to ill effect. Yumi tried not to imagine what his back looked like.

Though she tried not to stereotype, she had pegged Weiss as having the ideal personality for a second violinist in a string quartet. A mixed compliment. While Weiss was a capable musician—more than capable, really—he was unassertive to the extreme. Willing to follow anyone else's ideas or style, he had little to offer in terms of creativity or originality. He fit in. That, he did superbly. But that was the extent of it.

"I hope I'm not interrupting," Weiss said.

"Hi, Franz. No, not at all. Well, I was just doing scheduling."

"Ah, scheduling! Our cross to bear. May I join you?" he asked. His eyes traveled to the second seat at her table.

"I'm leaving soon," Yumi said. Detecting an expression of being offended, or of being rejected, or of abject disappointment, but in any case, an expression he instantly suppressed, she added, "But sure. Have a seat."

"Thank you."

He pulled out the chair, which screeched on the cement floor.

"How did you know I was here?" she asked. It was such an out-of-the-way little place.

"I didn't," Weiss said. "I wanted a luncheon and was determined not to visit a Subway, Wendy's, or KFC."

Yumi laughed. Maybe Weiss was nicer than she thought, once you got to know him.

"But I'm glad you were," he added, with a smile that came and went so fast she wasn't even sure she had seen it. It caused Yumi to reassess her opinion once again.

They engaged in desultory conversation. Weiss was inquisitive. He asked her about her students. She talked about them briefly, mentioning the lesson she had given to Joy D'Angelo earlier that morning.

"Ah, the girl," Weiss said.

The waitress arrived and asked Weiss what he wanted to order. He said, "Whatever the young lady had."

The waitress took the order and left.

"May I say," Weiss said to Yumi, "I find you are very sexy."

Yumi placed her teacup, halfway to her lips, onto the table. "Sorry, Franz, but I have to leave now. Errands. See you."

Yumi left three ten-dollar bills on the table, twice as much as the lunch, plus tip, had cost. She grabbed her bag with her new purchases and left.

The sleaze! she thought. *You don't even know me! You've just ruined my day.*

Furious, she marched back toward the library—damn the heat—but then stopped short, remembering Marcus's request. She also remembered that Utah only allowed liquor sales at state-run stores. With time running short, she texted Uber to take her to the closest one near the corner of 300 South and 300 East. She quickly bought an expensive bottle of Courvoisier XO—that should cheer Marcus up. It had better!—and returned to the library just in time to meet her colleagues before a very nervous Joy D'Angelo, fearful of more strife with Anita Talbot, was about to leave without her.

Yumi waited to see where Weiss would sit in the three-row van, then took a seat as far away from him as possible. The ride back was livened by stories of the day in the big city, everyone chattering at the same time. But only one thing occupied Yumi's mind: Was Franz Weiss following me the whole time? If so, why? She shuddered when she considered the possible answers. Could it have been Weiss's voice on "Don't go there?" Again, why? Why? Why? Why?

Yumi heard Jamie Barov asking her what she had done in town. She blinked herself back into the present and answered, "Bought some shoes."

When they arrived back at the ranch, Yumi deposited her new boots and dress in her cabin—she had had enough hiking for the day—and carried the cognac, the hoped-for peace offering, to Renfro's cabin. There was no response when she knocked, so she took a peek inside. Though his cello was in, he wasn't. Disappointing. It probably meant he was out hiking. He could be anywhere on the island. There was no sense trying to find him. She left the bottle on his dresser with a note saying "See ya soon?" with a smiley face. She returned to her cabin and, why not, spent the next two hours getting her mind refocused by practicing for the week's concerts, fully expecting a knock on her door. But, disappointed a second time, there was none.

Nor was Renfro present when dinner was served. Yumi wasn't particularly hungry after her filling lunch, nor was the evening's menu—dried-up burgers on stale buns with defrosted French fries, glossily billed as Burger Night!—any more appealing than they had been all along. But it was Renfro's absence that was most responsible for sapping Yumi's appetite.

She began to worry. If you injured yourself out there, especially if you went off the trail, it was possible you wouldn't be found for days. And with the sun going down, it would get cold. And if you ran out of water...and if you encountered a bison or a rattlesnake...there were so many "and ifs." Though Anita Talbot had never exhibited much concern for the musicians' well-being, Yumi fretted whether she should nevertheless alert her to Renfro's absence or try finding him, herself. If it had been someone other than Marcus, she decided, she probably wouldn't have given it a second thought. It was, after all, their day off. Maybe he had gone to the other side of the island, where the campgrounds were, and met some campers for a cookout. He was good at making new friends. She had found that out pretty quickly, hadn't she? Or maybe he had gone up to the visitors' center, miles away, where they had interesting natural history exhibits from which he might now just be returning.

So in the end, Yumi decided to do nothing except go to her cabin. There really was nothing she *could* do. She undressed, got into bed, and opened up her mystery. After a few chapters, she realized she was so uneasy that she hadn't digested a thing about the book. She knew she wouldn't be able to sleep until she knew Renfro was back, so she got out of bed, put on her shorts and a T-shirt, and went to Renfro's cabin.

She knocked on the door.

"Yeah?"

Hearing his voice was a greater relief than she imagined it ought to be.

"It's me," Yumi said. "Want some company?"

"Not tonight. No."

Now, there was a punch in the gut! Not a moment of hesitation. Not even a reason given. What to do? What to say? She certainly wouldn't stoop so low as to reclaim her Courvoisier, as much as a finger of alcohol appealed to her at the moment. After considering her alternatives, she simply shook her head and returned to her cabin.

The shadow of negativity wasn't limited to Renfro. It seemed to have spread like a contagion. After their day off, Yumi had hoped the second week would begin on an upward trajectory, but instead, there seemed to be a downward spiral. Could it be because the programs were more difficult, at least in part? That, as a result, the setting on the intensity meter had been cranked up from comfortable to ultra? The Bartók Sixth String Quartet, the Berg Lyric Suite for string quartet, the Brahms B Major Piano Trio, Tchaikovsky's *Serenade for Strings*, the Mendelssohn Octet were all major compositions to be reckoned with. But no, that wasn't a likely explanation. It was a mere rationalization. After all, everyone there was a professional and more than capable. Yumi's concerto, Vivaldi's *Summer*, would be the easiest music to put together, and for that reason, she had offered to sacrifice much of her scheduled rehearsal time for the more challenging repertoire. But even that selfless gesture hadn't been sufficient to dispel the malaise. It was like trying to turn the tide using a bucket.

Renfro had become progressively and inexplicably more taciturn, resisting all of Yumi's efforts at conversation. Yumi even wondered whether he might be seeing one of the other women at the festival. She didn't think it likely, but the thought—please, not Joy D'Angelo!—lodged in her throat like a chicken bone. But then again, he didn't seem to be spending any time with anyone else, either. On those occasions she tried to engage him in dialogue, he found an excuse to go elsewhere, citing his need to practice or "work through some things." When she asked him matter-of-factly what he had done on their free day, he was equally evasive, saying that he'd "just wandered around for a while, nowhere in particular." And then told her she shouldn't be so prying, she wasn't his mother. Recalling their nights of passion together, Yumi had tersely responded, "I should hope not."

With the island's claustrophobia and the increasingly oppressive heat, as the musicians approached the end of the second week, Yumi was more than ready to put the festival in her rearview mirror. That feeling seemed to be one of the few instances of unanimity. The scuffles that were so common among great musicians when they rehearsed and which usually went by the boards became inflamed, like dry tinder, in which one spark could ignite an entire forest. That spark would be shortly forthcoming.

Chapter Six

"But it's my emotional support stick," Jacobus insisted. "FAA regulations."

"I'm sorry, sir," the JFK gate agent replied. "We don't have a designation for emotional support sticks. Our policy does not allow sticks of any kind on board."

"It's either my emotional support stick or my emotional support dog, and my emotional support dog is a monstrous bulldog, slobbers like a drooling idiot, and is not sufficiently compressible to fit in the overhead storage bin, so you'd be well advised to let me take my emotional support stick instead. Policy notwithstanding."

"Wait one moment, please."

The agent made a phone call, consulted with his superiors, and in the end allowed Jacobus to bring Hocus with him. He had left Trotsky back at his house in the Berkshires, anyway, along with his violin. Both were left in the able care of Emily Miller, his friend Roy's teenage granddaughter, who had agreed to house sit. She had also offered to house clean, as it was also much needed, but Jacobus declined because if she moved things around he'd have to relearn where everything was. Dirt and grime didn't offend him, regardless, since he couldn't see it. Another advantage of being blind. *How lucky can you get?* he thought once again. All those cleaning bills he never had to pay.

Jacobus, as a blind geriatric, was a member of a privileged category of airline passengers. Afforded the honor of being among the first to board a plane, he always booked an aisle seat in the rear of the cabin. This was

76

to enable him easy access to the lavatory without needing to navigate past a hundred pitying passengers who would no doubt be staring at him, and over whose thoughtless feet he might well trip. And these days, with his residual gastric distress, close proximity to the toilet was more than an idle convenience. Seat 34C fit the bill.

According to daily reports from Yumi and Nathaniel, the first weekend's concerts went splendidly. Jacobus couldn't decide whether the gushing superlatives were the truth or, in a devious ploy to ensure he would actually show up, merely sweet talk. Like the government briefings on "progress" in Afghanistan: "According to four-star Gen. Malarkey, Commander of the Whosie-Whats Division, 'Training of the Afghan armed forces is not yet complete, but we're making excellent progress.' " A little truth, Jacobus concluded, can be a dangerous thing. At least he wasn't going into a war zone.

Like Yumi, Jacobus usually packed lightly, partly out of habit and partly because he generally wore the same outfits, day in and day out, winter or summer, rain or shine. Three flannel shirts, all well broken in and rotated on a weekly basis, and an extra pair of corduroy pants. He had no idea what colors or patterns any of it was, colors and patterns having become useless concepts not worthy of his consideration. All he knew was what made him comfortable, and if anyone had a problem with that... Yumi, the sweetie, had bought him new flannel shirts after his house was burned to the ground, incinerating all his belongings. That was more than five years ago, yet already the new shirts were reaching their prime. They were making "excellent progress." He had made a slight concession to Nathaniel, who wanted him to look smart while attending Yumi's special summer concert. Nathaniel bought him a seersucker suit.

"Seersucker? You?" Yumi had to Jacobus said when she heard the news. She sounded pleasantly astonished. "That's just right for summer. You'll look great in seersucker!"

"As you would imagine," Jacobus replied, "how I look is of no importance to me. I told Nathaniel he's the seer-sucker for paying for it and I'm the unseer-sucker for wearing it."

"You and your blind jokes," Yumi said.

"Blind people are allowed to tell blind jokes. But don't ever let me see you telling one behind my back."

"What kind of jokes am I allowed to tell?"

"Deaf people jokes."

Because of the suit, he had to pack a larger suitcase than his usual carry-on, which required him to check it. But that was not an inconvenience, as he normally checked his bag anyway, rather than having to lug it through an airport and then rummage blindly for a vacant spot above the seats in the cabin. As he was traveling neither with a carry-on nor his violin, he felt entirely justified to take Hocus on board as his personal item, since it was indeed a personal item. Very personal, in fact.

With a five-hour flight ahead of him and a starched, squirmy biddy in 34B who was clearly uncomfortable sitting next to a blind person, Jacobus didn't bother to carry on a conversation, either civil or uncivil. That suited him just fine. Why waste his time bantering with a stranger who most likely had nothing interesting to say when he could be thinking deep thoughts about Bach, Beethoven, and Barbecue? His thoughts, though, gravitated to the daily calls he had received from Yumi. As the festival's second week of rehearsals progressed, it was perceptible to him, if not to her, that her reports had become less and less sanguine. It was apparent to Jacobus that her enthusiasm waned as the days went by. It amused him how Yumi always tried to maintain a positive front with him, because they both knew very well he couldn't be fooled.

It also concerned him. Something was troubling her, and Yumi was not one to be easily troubled. But, in order to keep her anxiety level down—she had enough to worry about, performing with a gaggle of prima donnas—he played along with her and reassured her that, yes, he would be there to hear her performance of *Summer*. Don't worry about me.

The plane landed ten minutes late at the Salt Lake City International Airport. The dame in 34B claimed she had a tight connection to Bozeman and so felt justified to climb all over him and knock his glasses off for the sole reason of being ahead of him on the exit line. So now, if his calculations were accurate, she would be the one-hundred-sixty-sixth person instead of one-hundred-sixty-seventh to disembark. *More power to ya, honey.* Jacobus took his time, not only because he was in no hurry, but because that made it easier to follow the masses through the terminal toward the baggage claim area rather than being trampled by them. Balancing himself with Hocus as he descended the escalator, Jacobus heard Nathaniel call his name from Carousel 4.

"How was your flight?" Nathaniel asked.

"Best granola bar I ever had."

"Well, at least you made it safe and sound."

"And I can't overstate how underjoyed I am to be here."

Though his flight had arrived, it soon became apparent his luggage hadn't. As the carousel circled and as the frequency of thudding, cascading roller bags diminished, so too did Jacobus's hopes that his suitcase would appear. Passengers collected their bags and the chatter around them dissipated. Eventually, the whir of the carousel thumped to a halt. There was no telling how long they'd have to wait for the bag, and the concert was scheduled to start at seven. There was still plenty of time, but knowing JFK's track record, one of the world's more chaotic airports, Jacobus's suitcase could have been sent to Timbuktu, where some lucky Tuareg would soon be sporting a new seersucker suit. Jacobus and Nathaniel began to discuss potential alternative strategies.

"Gentlemen, I couldn't help but overhear your conversation," someone said.

The voice was smooth, a little too smooth for Jacobus's liking. *Mormon missionary?* was his first thought. *What is this guy trying to sell?* Maybe he was being too judgmental. Still…

"Actually, you could have helped it," Jacobus said, his missing luggage having soured his mood. "All you would've had to do is go somewhere else."

"I think you'll be thankful I eavesdropped," the man continued, seemingly unruffled. "Let me introduce myself. I'm Sunny Flox, artistic administrator of the Antelope Island Music Festival. Just got in myself and it sounds like you have a bit of a logistical problem on your hands."

Flox offered to give them a lift to the island. His assistant, Joy D'Angelo, was picking him up and there was plenty of room in the company van. But what about the suitcase? Nathaniel asked. Could someone come back and get it? That would be so much trouble. Maybe it could be delivered to their hotel?

There was no one in baggage service able to answer that question. In fact, there was no one at all in baggage service. A decision was made. Nathaniel would wait at the airport for Jacobus's suitcase and then drive up in his rental car, but in the meantime, Jacobus would accompany Flox. Jacobus quickly agreed. He couldn't stand waiting, anyway. For anything. Never could.

What he couldn't know was that he was about to endure an hour-long travelogue about the Great Salt Lake, Antelope Island, and the history of the festival. What made it worse was that it was also unnecessary. Jacobus had been to this festival once before, and that occasion almost led to his demise. *Well, lightning won't strike twice*, Jacobus thought, but history was only the second reason he hadn't wanted to come, the first being he hadn't wanted to come.

"Antelope Island has been a spectacular setting for our festival," Flox said.

Already jetlagged, Jacobus tried to refrain from nodding off as Flox rambled on. The comfort of the van's air-conditioning and soundproofing didn't make staying awake any easier. *What the hell do I care about how mountainous the island is?* Jacobus thought. *How it's dotted with herds of free-roaming bison? How it's the migratory resting place of seventy-five zillion water birds, including the left-footed crapper and the ruby-nosed clamdipper?*

"You'll be interested to know, most of our audience is from the Salt Lake City area," Flox continued. "That gives us an ideal core. Almost all the others are out-of-towners. At first, they came mainly for the outdoor experience, but now a lot of them come primarily for the music. Seems we've turned a corner."

" '*Almost* all the others'?" Jacobus asked, who had a predisposition to being alert to flaws in logic, regardless of how tired or distracted he might be.

80

"What's left after the Utahns and out-of-towners? Coyotes?"

"Stragglers. We always get a few from the other side of the island. The tent campers and the RV aficionados. Not really the music they go for. It's the experience. Unique, really. After a while, the scenery can get to you. Bizarre, in a way. You can almost feel disembodied. Going to a concert is a break. A reconnection with humanity. I mean, sometimes the lake feels limitless, and gets calm as glass. Like a mirror. Snow-tipped peaks reflected in the water. Unworldly."

Tourism brochure aside, Jacobus thought, *doesn't this guy, Flox, get it that snow-tipped peaks don't matter to me? It's all black to me. It doesn't make a damn bit of difference to me whether I'm in the Garden of Eden or sitting on the can in my bathroom in the Berkshires.* Which reminded him. He better get to a bathroom soon.

"Can you step on it, honey?" he said to D'Angelo.

Another of the many advantages of being blind was that while wearing his dark glasses no one knew whether he was paying attention or was fast asleep. As Flox droned on, he was inclined to the latter.

"Did you know Utah's average summer temperature..." Jacobus didn't hear the end of the sentence.

He awoke when the car stopped at the tollbooth on the mainland side of the Antelope Island causeway.

Maybe Flox's voice got hoarse from yacking, but D'Angelo took over as they left the tollbooth and crossed the five-mile ribbon of a causeway that connected the mainland to their destination. The two of them, Flox and D'Angelo, were like a tag team. "The Great Salt Lake is a jewel in the desert," she intoned. "The largest body of saltwater in the western hemisphere. So salty, fish can't live in it. So shallow and flat-bedded that with the past year of record rainfall the lake's overall surface area had expanded almost fifty percent."

Salty, huh? he thought. *Well, maybe I can't see it,* he decided, *but what the hell?* Tired of being in one hermetically sealed cocoon after another since leaving the Berkshires, he rolled down the car window to get a feel for the area with his other senses. Hearing and smell, taste and touch. Senses he could depend on.

Blasting in on a current of searingly hot air, the pungent stink of saltwater and of decaying algae, brine shrimp, and brine flies assaulted Jacobus's olfactory lobes. He immediately rolled the window back up. So much for the great outdoors. Back in air-conditioned comfort, he surrendered himself to D'Angelo's tape-loop travelogue. A strategically reasonable concession, given the alternative.

"We're in the midst of a record heatwave," Flox said, taking the reins again.

"Really? How can you tell?" Jacobus replied.

"They say we might get a thunderstorm, though. One of these days. That should cool things off. You know, back in the eighties, the lake level was so high the causeway was covered. Totally submerged. Can you imagine that? For five years, you couldn't get onto the island."

I missed my chance, Jacobus thought.

The rhythmic bumps of the tires over the sectioned road surface matched Flox's verbal monotony. Their speed had accelerated gradually after they had passed through the tollbooth. Now they were cruising, and taking into account the quickened pace of the bumps, Jacobus guessed they were going about fifty miles per hour. Estimating they had been on the causeway for about five minutes, he figured they should be on the island any minute now. Not a moment too soon. After half-listening to all that talking, hearing some music would be music to his ears.

It was another fifteen minutes until Joy D'Angelo parked the car in the lot. Just up the hill from the Big Top, she said. Music emanated from below. As it was still a few hours before the concert, Jacobus gathered he was hearing a rehearsal in progress. Flox, needing to make some last-minute phone calls before the weekend, begged off. He instructed D'Angelo to accompany Jacobus. Walking gingerly on the descending, rocky trail toward the tent, poking his way forward with Hocus, Jacobus followed the strains of the first movement of the Octet in E-flat Major by Felix Mendelssohn, which he recalled would be on Sunday's program. Mendelssohn, a sixteen-year-old genius, damn him, when he composed it! Music bursting with the unrestrained exuberance of youth but with the hand of a mature master's craftsmanship. A perfect piece of music. *But I hope these guys have more rehearsals,* Jacobus thought, because the music was indeed bursting, but not with exuberance. Or perfection. Instead, there was an evident musical tug of war going on. One musician thinks it's too slow, another too fast, another too loud, another too soft. A meeting of the minds was as yet a distant goal. Passive aggression at its finest. Bad enough with one quartet, but with two of them combined? *Oy vey.*

D'Angelo, seeking out a shady spot behind the tent, told Jacobus there would soon be a hiatus in the rehearsal. She attempted to engage him in small talk to bide the time, but Jacobus had heard more than enough about the natural wonders of Antelope Island. Furthermore, he was constitutionally unable to concentrate on anything else when music was being played. Nor did he ever listen to music while doing something else. That would be ridiculous and an insult to the music. Can you imagine anything as absurd as listening to a Mozart string quartet while reading a book? Or while making dinner? If you had *Starry Night* on your wall would you watch "Antiques Roadshow" on the television?

The music stopped. Harsh words were exchanged inside the tent. Exactly what the words were Jacobus couldn't make out. But they were clearly adversarial. Had he said passive aggression? Take away the passive. Jacobus was vaguely aware that Joy D'Angelo had come to the end of some paragraph about audiences arriving.

"You probably have something more important to do than humor me, honey," he said. "I'll wait for Yumi here."

"Okay. It sounds like their break is just around the corner," she said.

"Yeah." Their break. Until the bell for their next round. Unless someone gets knocked out first.

Jacobus didn't have long to wait. Fortunately. D'Angelo had told him they were in the shade. But if this was shade, thank God they weren't out in the sun. At least a mild breeze had picked up. The music stopped. He waited.

"Jake! Hi!"

"Yumi." Jacobus received a hug and a peck on his unshaven cheek. Yumi told him he was looking much healthier now that his hives had disappeared, and other such niceties. He told her she smelled the same as always.

"Where's Nathaniel?" Yumi asked.

Jacobus explained about the delay with his luggage at the airport and said he expected Nathaniel to arrive soon.

"But I see you've brought Hocus with you."

"Never know when they'll need me to conduct, y'know?" he replied, swinging the stick perilously close to her head.

"I think we could have used you just now," she said. "Too many chiefs, not enough Indians."

"It's not politically correct to say stuff like that, you know," Jacobus said. "It's like with the Washington Redskins. By the way, did you hear that after all the bad press, they finally changed their name?"

"No! That's amazing!"

"Yeah, now they're the D.C. Redskins."

"You're incorrigible. Do you know that?"

"Would you have it any other way?"

"I guess not," Yumi said. "But I'm sure Anita would."

"Anita?"

"Our CEO. She'd probably fire me for saying something like that."

"Why? Is she a Redskins fan?"

"Between you and me, sometimes I wish she'd go to D.C., and stay. Sometimes she doesn't see the forest for the trees."

"Yumi, you've certainly become Americanized over the years. You're a veritable cliché factory. But what trees are you talking about?"

"She may be good at raising money, but I don't think she has much of an ear for music and she doesn't seem to like musicians very much. She's always harping on deportment, especially the superficial. She doesn't understand that when musicians argue with each other, that's part of the process. If you don't argue, something's missing."

"That rehearsal sounds like something more than a friendly difference of opinion."

"I suppose. It did get pretty heated."

"But it's a dry heat, right?" Jacobus said, never reluctant to rub it in.

Yumi swatted him on his behind.

"Harassment!" Jacobus shouted. "Where's Anita when I need her?"

"Very funny. But seriously, she sends us these memos telling us how we're supposed to 'comport' ourselves. Like we're children. And she doesn't have a sense of humor, either, like you do, anyway."

"Well, as I always say about management: Can't live with 'em. Can certainly live without 'em."

"Anita would send you a memo for saying that."

"No doubt."

Yumi and Jacobus whiled away the time a bit longer, but then Yumi said she had to run back to her cabin for some other music before intermission ended. Did Jacobus want to go with her and rest for a while?

"No, just point me in the direction of the nearest bathroom. My gastric distress came with me. Got a free companion ticket."

"They only have these Porta Potties here. Why don't you come and use my bathroom?"

"Nah. At the moment, the closer, the better."

As Yumi escorted Jacobus to the portable toilet, they discussed where they would meet Nathaniel when he arrived, and if time permitted, have a bite before the concert. If not, they would get together afterwards, before the two men returned to Salt Lake City. As soon as she departed for her cabin, Jacobus very cautiously felt his way up a step to the Porta Potty. Opening the door, the odor was immediately offensive, even to him. It made the lake's smelly brine seem like Chanel No. 5. It was so bad that he probed with Hocus to make sure he didn't step in anything he'd have to scrape off. Only the flies seemed to have found the commode a commodious sanctuary. He cringed as he sat down on the toilet, but then decided, what the hell, how much worse could it be than mine back home?

With little ventilation, it was sweltering inside the latrine and Jacobus regretted he hadn't accepted Yumi's offer. Regretted, but understood why. It was his inability to distinguish kindness from charity. Since his childhood, after he had been abused, after his parents were killed, and especially after he had gone blind, there had been so many times when he knew that the offer to help, however well-intentioned, was based on pity. And if there was one thing he detested even more than hip-hop and poetry slams, it was being pitied. People might think he was just a proud, stubborn old man, but the fact was… *Well, I guess I'm a proud, stubborn old man.* Declining any assistance whatsoever had become his instinctive, default response.

Another thing he couldn't do, as much as he was trying, was to force nature's pace. So as he sat there, waiting for his gastric distress to activate, he redirected his thoughts to the miracle of Mendelssohn. How this mere toddler—What was that? Someone banging on the outside of his latrine? Jacobus was about to shout out "Wait your goddamn turn" but silenced himself when he heard: "You spit in my face again, Waldstein, so help me, I'll kill you!"

A Danish accent. Christian Bjørlund.

Grunting, pulling, pushing, cursing. A real physical brawl. One didn't need to be fluent in German and Danish to understand that insults and obscenities were being hurled, and their tone was far from frivolous. As the scuffling intensified, as one or the other of them was slammed against it, the latrine rocked. Jacobus feared it could topple at any moment. He extended his arms outward, pressing against the side walls to brace himself as it teetered. With his pants lowered to his ankles, the next jolt against the latrine tilted it backwards. As his feet left the floor, his ass descended dangerously into the toilet bowl. He found himself stuck, even after the latrine stabilized. He did not envy his precarious situation, especially if the door were to swing open.

"Hey, assholes!" he shouted.

Startled, the two combatants fell silent. Jacobus, emboldened, determined to solidify the momentary uneasy truce.

"You hear the one about the old blind man stuck in a latrine?" he continued, as he attempted to extricate himself from the toilet bowl, like a cork out of a champagne bottle.

"No," Waldstein said. "I have not heard that."

"Things don't look good."

Another blind man joke, and a pretty stupid one, Jacobus thought. Though on second thought maybe not so bad, considering he'd made it up on the spur of the moment. At least he seemed to have diffused the situation, maybe by merely confusing them. He didn't hear any laughter, but there was no more audible rancor from the two combatants. He heard them walk off. Intermission over? Back to lovey-dovey music-making? It was a moral lesson for him, too. The next time someone offered him a favor, he would not look a gift horse in the mouth. Now, there was another addition to Yumi's growing collection of American clichés. With peace restored, Jacobus completed the task at hand.

Chapter Seven

It was a little before six-thirty, a half hour before the concert. Jacobus was listening with a critical ear to Yumi warming up backstage when Nathaniel phoned her.

Apologies, apologies. Jacobus's suitcase had not arrived and it was inevitable Nathaniel would miss at least the seven o'clock curtain time, if not the whole performance. *Ironic,* Jacobus thought, *since between Nathaniel and me, Nathaniel's the one who actually wanted to be here.*

"That's so upsetting," Yumi said. "I wanted to introduce him to all my colleagues. And thank him again for his gift."

"What gift?"

"A first edition of *Roughing It,* by Mark Twain."

"Probably got it gratis from one of those insurance claims he handled."

"Jake, you're such a cynic! It's a lovely gift. Did you know Mark Twain's real name was Samuel Clemens?"

"Samuel *Langford* Clemens to be exact."

"A lot of musicians used to have stage names, but I didn't realize Mark Twain—I mean Samuel Clemens—did."

"There are two theories why," Jacobus said. "The more well-known one is that 'Mark, twain' was the call Mississippi boatmen used in order to let the navigator know the depth of the river. Twain meant two, and referred to the depth of two fathoms, or twelve feet, which suggested dangerously shallow shoals for larger boats. Clemens might have thought it was an appropriate metaphor for his style of provocative satire. Maybe. Maybe not.

"The other theory is that when Clemens entered his favorite saloon in

San Francisco he would shout to the bartender, 'Mark twain,' meaning that the bartender should chalk up two drinks on Clemens's personal account. I like that theory, even if the first one is probably the true one."

"How do you know so much about Mark Twain?" Yumi asked.

"There are two theories. One is that I've been studying Mark Twain all my life."

"And the other?"

"I heard it on NPR last week."

Yumi whacked him on the butt.

"You hear that thunder?" Jacobus asked Yumi.

"You mean from me slapping you? Or is this a deaf people joke?"

"No, it's thunder. You don't hear it?"

"No."

"Well, I do. And I don't like the sound of it."

"It's probably a plane. The airport's not that far away. And I've got to go get ready for the concert," she said. "Behave yourself."

Jacobus left her to take his seat in the audience. Yumi, wearing the new concert dress she had bought at Chic, returned to warming up amongst her colleagues, practicing a last few G Minor scales to ready herself for *Summer*. There was a compartment in her violin case in which she kept her rosin, extra strings, a pencil, and a pair of good luck earrings made of pennies that one of her students made for her. She also stashed her phone there when she was in her concert dress. As she put on the earrings, the phone rang, reminding her she should turn it off before the concert started. It didn't bother her too much when people in the audience forgot to do that. Yes, it was annoying, but some of her colleagues would become apoplectic. Her phone's ring tone, the famous first four notes of Beethoven's Fifth Symphony, had amused her and her friends—"Isn't it adorable?"—when she downloaded it six months earlier, but now, with only moments before the concert, she found it irritating. She didn't have time for a conversation so she picked up the phone with the intent of turning it off, but when she looked at the screen and saw that it was from Unknown Caller, she decided to answer it.

The same voice as before. Uninflected. Matter-of-fact. This time, two words before disconnecting. "Leave. Now."

Yumi stared at the phone. She quickly looked around her. No one else was holding a phone. But there could have been time for someone to have put it down in the few moments she had been frozen in place. Could have been.

"Everything okay?" Franz Weiss asked as he passed her.

"Yes," Yumi said. "Why shouldn't it be?"

"Just checking. Sunny said we start in five minutes."

"Okay."

But clearly, things weren't okay. What was now clear was that "Don't go there" did refer to the festival and not the airport or some metaphorical reference. What was still *not* clear was whether it was a warning or a threat, but in either case, it was evident someone was telling her something was wrong. That she was in some kind of danger. "Leave. Now." Now, as in immediately? That's what it sounded like. It wasn't "Leave now," as in "hurry up." It was definite. "Leave. Now." Inflexible. But leave what? The tent? Leave the island? Was someone warning her to back out of the performance?

Could it have been Franz Weiss? Yes, he was a creep, but she had met much worse, and none of them had ever threatened her. And he hadn't bothered her all week, since they returned from Salt Lake City. She assumed he had gotten the message. But…

"Yumi!"

It was Joy D'Angelo, almost in tears.

"What's wrong?" Yumi asked.

"Anita found out!"

"Calm down, Joy," Yumi said. "What did she find out?"

"She found out that you gave me the lesson. She's on the warpath again. I think I'm going to get fired."

And maybe I will, too, Yumi thought. *Who gives a damn at this point?* But how had Anita found out? Yumi hadn't told anyone, and she was sure Joy hadn't, either. Weiss! Yes, she had told Franz Weiss about the lesson, at the ramen shop. That schmuck! He must have told Anita. But again. Why?

"Look, Joy," Yumi said. "I have to go play a concert now. I've got to be able to concentrate. You're a violinist. You understand how that works. So don't worry about this. I'll talk to Anita afterwards and we'll get it all straightened out. Okay? Just stop crying, please."

Yumi realized she was being harsh and tried to soften it by brushing D'Angelo's hair off her face with her hand.

"Okay," D'Angelo said. She attempted to smile, but what she managed to produce looked more like the beginnings of a carved Halloween pumpkin. "I've got to go take care of the hall lights."

Yumi was more frazzled than she could ever remember being. Jacobus had been with her just a minute before. Did she have time to run out to him to get his counsel? What would he say?

"Showtime, boys and girls!" Sunny Flox said, trotting past the musicians.

"*In bocca al lupo!*" he whispered to Yumi. "Go break a leg." He patted her on the shoulder, walked out to the stage, and began his introductory comments. There was no time to find Jacobus. She had no choice. She couldn't back out now. How could she, given the circumstances? She had been hired to save the day. She couldn't now ruin it for everyone. Especially over what was probably an idle threat by some disgruntled Baroque music fan! Yes, that's what it was. That's what it must be. Someone who had looked forward to Edo Kuypers and who didn't care for her style of playing.

To play or not to play? She made up her mind. She knew what Jacobus would say.

"Fuck 'em!" she said out loud, prompting startled glances from her colleagues, clustered there in the wings like a flock of brood hens.

Damn shame Nathaniel won't arrive for the beginning of the concert, Jacobus thought. Nathaniel was the sociable one, the one who attended concerts and lectures and enrolled in what were euphemistically called "continuing education" classes. Really just a way for old farts to postpone the inevitable, to avoid confronting their spiraling-down lives. Jacobus had no such fear. When you have Bach in your life, what was there to worry about? Why bother with basket-weaving and the impact of *Beowulf* on twentieth-century political thought when all you need is Bach's *St. Matthew Passion*? Even atheists, like him, should have no difficulty understanding that. He recalled the old ad campaign for Levy's rye bread: "You don't have to be Jewish to love Levy's." Well, you don't have to be Catholic to love the *St. Matthew Passion*.

So Jacobus was content in his isolation, or at least as content as his craggy, troubled soul would allow. He had no qualms about spending weeks, months even, alone in his Berkshire cottage, surrounded by his woods. He chuckled. In the nineteenth century, the term "Berkshire cottage" referred to the thirty-room mansions that New York's upper crust and Boston Brahmins built as their vacation retreats. The Shadowbrook mansion in Stockbridge was at one time the second-largest private residence in the country, and had a basement long enough for the rich little brats to have bicycle races in inclement weather. Jacobus's entire cottage could fit in Shadowbrook's kitchen, and for a blind man, smaller was better. Like his own house, Shadowbrook had been consumed by flames, which was about the only thing the two houses had in common. Once a house burns down, they're all pretty much the same. Like being dead. Ashes to ashes.

Unlike Shadowbrook, his house had been rebuilt, with the same design as the old one so he wouldn't end up walking into walls. And in his new house his sole desire, to sit in his living room and do nothing other than listen to music, hadn't changed. That, plus wandering through his eight acres of forest that buffered him from the rest of humanity, letting Trotsky carom through the woods to chase, but never catch, the squirrels. That was all he needed. Nathaniel, bless his heart, had been his connection to the rest of the world, like the causeway connecting Antelope Island to the mainland. Antelope Island, inhospitable and uninviting, set apart. Just like him. Except he didn't like dry heat.

How had it happened, he asked himself, considering his disinclination to attend concerts? Here he was, sitting on a crummy folding chair that his butt stuck to and which felt suspiciously like one chair leg was an inch shorter than the other three, under a massive tent with four hundred apparent sauna lovers, about to listen to a sweltering concert in his flannel shirt because his seersucker suit was hovering somewhere over Lower Slobovia. He had, so far, been buffeted about by the crowd, tripping over the feet of one concertgoer after another, until an usher—who unsuccessfully tried to pacify Jacobus by proudly proclaiming it was their biggest crowd ever—escorted him to his wobbly seat.

As he sat there, waiting for the concert to begin, he was already made unpleasantly aware of a mother unsuccessfully shushing her hyperactive kids just a few rows away. He tapped Hocus on the ground and fantasized what he'd like to do with it.

Why didn't he like to go to concerts? To put it succinctly: Carl Ditters von Dittersdorf. That was his buzzword whenever they asked him that question. And they always asked with one or more of the following connotations: What's wrong with you? How can you be such a snob? Are you too good for everyone else? Don't you feel the synergy of a live performance? Is it because you're blind and don't want people to feel sorry for you?

Whatever the innuendo, Jacobus's response was: Carl Ditters von Dittersdorf, and he'd let them figure out what he meant. Dittersdorf was a popular contemporary of Mozart whose name had the alliterative allure to make people laugh. But that was not the reason Jacobus referred to him. Rather, it was because his hundreds of compositions were so pedestrian that he was now only mentioned as a shorthand metaphor for mediocrity.

So, Mr. Jacobus, are you saying that contemporary composers are mediocre?

Guess again. Jacobus had long ago given up waiting even for the mediocrity of a modern-day Dittersdorf, let alone the greatness of a modern-day Beethoven. There was nothing new worth listening to, he felt, and those who claimed there was were either lying, had no taste, or were only comparing it to the trash composed last year. At the least, the very least, music should be a craft. A craft that required training and acquired skill, not some green college grad who felt not only an irrepressible need, but had the audacity to feel qualified, to "express himself" after two years of music theory. Banging on a kazoo with a stick while hopping on one leg? Popping balloons? Moaning into a trumpet? That's music?

Violinists had to study ten years, fifteen years, twenty years before being able to call themselves professionals. Before being able to even be considered for a job in an orchestra. Would you hire an electrician to wire your house who didn't know the first thing about volts, amps, and resistance? Would you take your car to a mechanic who didn't know how to open the hood? Where was the quality control? Where was the standard?

With few exceptions, that's what Jacobus thought of today's composers. There was something to be said for the Renaissance apprenticeship tradition. You worked your ass off for a master from the time you were a kid. You learned your trade from the ground up. Until and only when you could prove your skills could you graduate, and in order to do so, you had to produce a piece—a sculpture, painting, or composition—which proved you were worthy to be a master. The word for that: masterpiece. That's when you *began* to be a creative artist. Not a day before. Oh, for Offenbach!

Sitting there, in the tent, he felt his rage bubbling to the surface. But that was only one reason he rarely went to concerts anymore. Another was that he'd heard all the masterpieces, from Bach to Bartók, so many times that even *they* had begun to lose some of their luster. One of the essentials of a great piece of music is a composer's ability to first set up, then deceive, the listener's musical expectations. A sudden change of tempo or volume or key, an unsuspected modulation, a deceptive cadence, a new melody emerging from out of nowhere. There were so many ways to create mystery, to surprise. But how can you be surprised when you know what the surprise is in advance? "Honey, who should we invite for your surprise birthday party this year? Same as last year's? Same as next?"

And then all the mediocre performances! The so-called *artists* these days! They don't hold a candle to the giants of the twentieth century—at least in Jacobus's opinion—and in Jacobus's opinion, Jacobus's opinion was the only one that counted.

And the seats at concerts! They were so damn uncomfortable compared to his thoroughly broken-in Naugahyde couch, which, like stratified clay that preserved the imprint of billion-year-old trilobite fossils, had molded his prone body exquisitely into its vintage cushions.

And concerts these days started so damn late—or was it that he was getting tired earlier?—that he couldn't even stay awake until the fat lady *started* to sing.

And then there was the audience. That was the worst part, by far. Between these newfangled cellphones and the coughing and the candy unwrapping and the little brats whose parents somehow thought their delinquent children would be able to endure an hour and a half of Mahler, Jacobus sometimes wished he had a lethal weapon in his hands. Not that he'd have such a good aim with a gun. That's what had brought all this on. Those wild kids. He did have Hocus with him at his side. Just in case.

Jacobus had hoped that if there had been a silver lining to Nathaniel's absence, it would have been the welcome buffer of an empty seat next to him so that he could at least abhor the performance in peace. No such luck. Someone slipped into the seat at the last minute. Jacobus quickly ascertained it was a woman from the way she cleared her throat when he wiped his nose. What was that all about? Why shouldn't he be able to wipe his nose? When she tapped him on the shoulder and whispered in his ear, her voice confirmed her womanhood.

"Please use a handkerchief instead of your sleeve," she said.

"Lady, it's sweat, not snot," he insisted, holding out his sleeve for her inspection.

"Don't contradict," she said. "One doesn't sweat in dry heat."

"And who the hell does one think one is? Emily Post?" Jacobus asked.

"My name is Anita Talbot and I just so happen to be the managing director of this music festival."

So she was the one Yumi had told him about! Just his luck to be sitting next to her. Jacobus didn't care for the broad's tone of voice. If she wanted to be uppity, she picked the wrong playmate.

"That's so special," Jacobus said. "And I just so happen to be Yumi Shinagawa's former violin teacher and current mentor." That should put her in her place, he imagined, but Talbot just laughed.

"What's so funny?"

"You? Her teacher?" she said. And continued laughing.

So much for networking.

Sunny Flox quieted the audience and made a few perfunctory comments, yet another reason Jacobus didn't like going to concerts. *Just play the damn music.*

The concert began with the charming Tchaikovsky's *Serenade for Strings.* The majestic introductory *Andante non troppo* was followed by the playfully exuberant *Allegro moderato.* It started passably well—lovely music—though when you get eight musicians trying to blend their styles and play like a polished ensemble in only a few rehearsals, Jacobus thought, you've got a tough row to hoe. From the emergent egocentricity of their playing, he quickly sensed—even if no one else could—that the shelf life of "feel good" among the musicians had expired. After the first movement, violinist Christian Bjørlund started forcibly playing louder than Dieter Waldstein, who tried to make up for it by exaggerating his vibrato, for which his reputation was notorious to begin with. The dueling cellists, Marcus Renfro and Ingrid Goldman, took their cues from their higher-registered colleagues to bolster their own artistic profiles, out-crunching each other's bass lines with little regard for such esthetic subtleties as beauty or artistry. Too many chefs were spoiling the *bourée.*

The Tchaikovsky came and went. Jacobus hoped the same would be true of Talbot. To his dismay, she remained lodged in her seat. The audience loved the performance. *Let them. It's pretty music and the musicians are probably good-looking. What's not to like? Right?* The only thing Jacobus loved was that the temperature had dipped precipitously. He had stopped sweating, even though all the experts had repeatedly assured him he could not possibly have been sweating in the first place. Dry heat. His flannel shirt was now coming in handy, keeping him warm from the sudden evening chill, though he didn't care for the tone of the rumbling thunder, which he was sure everyone should be able to hear by now. The breeze had picked up considerably and he could hear the sides of the tent pop from compression and expansion, like a canvas bellows.

Yumi took the stage to begin her solo performance of *Summer.* She stood center stage, the other musicians seated in a semicircle around her. Of course, she was performing without music, which was good, because with the wind picking up it might have blown off the stand, even inside the tent.

Summer was the last piece before intermission, after which would be the Bartók String Quartet No. 6 and, closing the program, Berg's Lyric Suite. Jacobus had heard Yumi play *Summer* a million times. Hell, hadn't he taught her the damn thing, and hadn't she won a Grammy for her *Four Seasons* CD? But he'd never heard her perform *Summer* in summer, let alone with the weather reflecting the music's poetic sonnet: "Beneath the blazing sun's relentless heat men and flocks are sweltering, pines are scorched." Dry heat, my ass. Savvy programming for an outdoor summer festival, though Jacobus had always been puzzled by one line from Vivaldi's accompanying sonnet: "*Ah che pur troppo i suoi timor sono veri tuona e fulmina il cielo e grandioso tronca il capo alle spiche e a' grani alteri.*" "Alas, his worst fears were justified, as the heavens roar and great hailstones beat down upon the proudly standing corn." Hailstones in summer? *Bah.* Maybe in the eighteenth century, in Italy. Or just a bad translation.

To his surprise and disappointment, Yumi's performance was not as convincing as Jacobus had expected it would be. There was a tension in her sound that was unlike her. It reminded him of when she first studied with him so many years ago. Technically proficient, but with a steeliness that conveyed a sense of determination rather than of beauty. Vibrato, too much and too fast. He was not a purist by any means, but vibrato like that was out of place for Baroque music. The heavy indolence of the oppressive heat, usually expressed with extra weight on her bow changes, was all but overlooked. Then the fleeting thirty-second notes, portraying the music's north winds frightening the birds away, which she usually executed immaculately and precisely—as he had taught her—were rushed and not flawlessly in tune.

In the second movement, Vivaldi's dotted rhythms were traditionally played *sul ponticello*—directly over the bridge of the instruments—with intentional scratchiness creating an almost comical imitation of buzzing flies as the shepherd tries to rouse himself from his torpor before the storm hits. Tonight Yumi sounded distracted, not torpid.

Jacobus knew something was wrong. The audience might not realize it. Even the musicians might think it was just a bout of nerves. But not with Yumi. Nerves had never been an issue with her. Focus and confidence were her calling cards. Yes, there was something wrong. Maybe it was the weather? The sudden change. Barometric pressure. That kind of shit. He thought not.

It started in the last movement. The rain. Not just the rain in the music. The rain outside. Real rain. Wind-whipped, it began to lash the tent. Added to the rolling thunder, the cumulative noise made it increasingly difficult to hear the performance. *This is ridiculous,* Jacobus thought. *These damn outdoor concerts aren't worth a damn. If it's not some screw-up with the lighting or the amplification, it's the weather. There's always something you could depend on to go wrong.*

He was not alone in that judgment. The music, almost inaudible due to the mounting storm, came to an abrupt stop. Jacobus heard—barely—an announcement hollered from the direction of the stage. It was Flox again, with whose voice Jacobus had become all too familiar. But this time it wasn't a travelogue.

"Ladies and gentlemen, we're taking the musicians off the stage for the moment just until the storm passes, after which we'll resume. These things don't last long out here, folks. I promise. Thank you for your patience."

As if to put the lie to that statement, a defiant burst of hailstones bounced off the hard ground outside, their explosions crescendoing as the size and intensification of the hailstones increased.

"Jesus! Vivaldi was right!" Jacobus said with gleeful ambivalence. "There *is* hail in summer!"

It was at that moment, through the din, he detected another sound. The tent groaned. His acute ears picked up on the imminent disaster before anyone else's.

"Hit the deck, honey!" he said to Anita Talbot. Jacobus got down on his knees and began to crawl under his folding chair, making sure to take Hocus with him. Other than his violin, Hocus was his most prized possession, though he would never confess that to Yumi.

"What are you talking about?" Talbot said. "What are you doing? Sunny said to sit here."

It didn't take acute ears to hear the Big Top's central pillar snap like a gunshot.

The tent gave way. Confused cries and shouts mingled with the din of the gale and the pounding hail as ropes and poles surrendered to the sudden crush of tons of ice. Steel cables ripped their connecting carabiners from their grommets, clanging as they swayed like a hangman's nooses. The tent fabric, shifting ominously under the force of the ice and wind, flapped in protest. Perimeter tent supports fell like dominoes and tree branches cracked with the explosiveness of a Gatling gun. Jacobus heard the plaintive dissonance of harpsichord strings snapping as its wooden case splintered from the weight falling on top of it.

A few minutes was all it took for the Big Top to totally cave in, leaving it completely demolished. The roar of the storm made it impossible to gauge whether there were screams or stunned silence accompanying its implosion. The wind continued to howl, and rain and ice continued to pelt down. Jacobus, hunched under his flimsy chair, probed upward with Hocus. It didn't come close to being vertical before snagging on the tent ceiling. The musicians had been on a raised stage. Had Flox gotten them off in time? Where was Yumi?

Above the storm's pounding, injured and frightened people began to scream, calling out for rescue. The man who had been sitting next to him, who throughout the concert had been politely silent, was now repeating, "What the hell? What the hell?"

"You okay, lady?" he asked Talbot, having to shout.

"I'll manage," she yelled back. "Though I don't know how I'm going to get this dress clean."

"How do things look?"

"What? It's too noisy. I can't hear you."

Jacobus raised his voice as high as it would go.

"I said, how do things look?"

"We've lost electricity. Pitch black in here. You okay?"

"Peachy. Did the musicians get off the stage okay?"

"I believe so."

"Good. Did I mention how much I love outdoor concerts?"

That was the end of their conversation. Jacobus waited. He didn't know for what, but what was the alternative? More minutes passed.

There was a lull in the storm. Gradually, to Jacobus's ears, the concertgoers had become relatively calm, considering. A few soft sobs. Otherwise subdued. Or maybe just in a state of shock. Only the children who had been a nuisance before the concert started seemed to be having a good time. Jacobus heard one of the boys shout, "Ma, this is so cool!"

Jacobus heard EMTs on the scene begin to assist the stricken crowd. Some of the musicians, evidently having made it safely off the stage, were offering to help. Maybe such unlikely camaraderie was the result of the relief or the hope everyone felt that the worst had passed. Or, as in the aftermath of a tornado, an immediate kinship, a coming together of community, having equally shared and suffered a disaster. *Ironic,* Jacobus thought, *that sometimes the worst of catastrophes brought out the best in people. Oy, if that's what it takes.* One man called out, almost apologetically, "Sorry to bother someone, but I think I might've broken my arm."

It was a slow process. One by one they were rescued. Those concertgoers, hundreds of them, still waiting to be extricated from under the tent, became restive when the storm began to regain strength. Restive and maybe claustrophobic, too. *That was another advantage of being blind,* Jacobus thought. *Every space is more or less the same.*

A shifting in the collapsed tent, settling ever closer to the ground, was followed by a new eruption of screaming from one segment of trapped concertgoers. Icy water poured in through rents in the tent fabric.

"I'm choking," one woman moaned. "I can't breathe."

Well-intentioned but confused orders rang out. "We're getting to you!" "Be patient!" "Everything will be okay!" Who they were—festival staff, EMTs, or just Good Samaritans—was impossible to tell.

Jacobus, more or less pinned down and lying on the hard ground, tried convincing himself it really wasn't much less comfortable than his creaking bed at home, with that one spring protruding from the mattress and threatening to puncture his liver. Envying his massive bulldog, Trotsky, who was no doubt snoring on Jacobus's bed at that very moment, he made himself as comfortable as possible, expecting to wait for the long haul. His problem was that he was cold and wet and had begun to shiver. But still, he waited and wondered about Yumi. Whether she was safe. Why her performance had been filled with anxiety.

"Hey, Anita?" Jacobus said.

"Yes?"

"Where the hell'd you get this tent? A garage sale?"

"In a way. It's from Saudi Arabia. For a family wedding. Only used once before we got it."

"You get a good price?"

"Of course."

"A lot of hailstorms in the Arabian desert, you suppose?"

"Your sarcasm is noted. Your point being?"

"Jake, where are you?" It was Yumi calling him. More than calling. It was a desperate cry that somehow cleaved the relentless din and the crowd's clamor. Yet it might have been the most beautiful sound Jacobus had ever heard, putting his heart at ease. Yumi was safe.

"Yeah!" he said. "Over here."

"Are you okay?"

"No," he answered.

"What's wrong?"

"I'm lying in the mud with a fucking tent on top of me."

"Hey, bud," some guy shouted. "My wife doesn't need to hear that kind of language."

"It's all right," Yumi called back. "He's my teacher."

"So you really are her teacher!" Talbot said.

Jacobus felt Yumi's hand on his arm, comforting and restraining him at the same time.

"Are the musicians' instruments safe?" Talbot asked Yumi.

"Their instruments?" Yumi responded. Jacobus knew that Yumi would be

101

tempted to add, "Who the hell cares about the instruments? What about the musicians?" But she would be too polite to say that, especially considering the circumstances. "I think so," Yumi answered. "For the most part. It was a good thing Sunny got us off the stage because the tent pushed the harpsichord right through the floor. We could have been killed!"

"Sadly, you're right," Talbot said. "The harpsichord was insured, but the financial liability for all this is going to kill us."

"Can I help you up?" Yumi asked her.

Help her up? Jacobus thought. *How about step on her?*

"That's all right," Talbot said. "You take your former teacher…and current mentor. I can manage until the troops arrive. Assist the aged first."

On their hands and knees, over sodden packed earth, Yumi led the way through a maze of crumpled and overturned chairs and dangling tent cables and stricken humanity. Jacobus clasped her ankle in order to follow. The ground, usually dry and packed and hard as stone, had become slick and muddy. The mangled tent and furniture had carved out divots into which rivulets of melting ice flowed. Jacobus slid as much as he crawled.

"You know," Jacobus said, "this kinda reminds me of Woodstock."

"Woodstock!" Yumi replied. "I'm shocked. You went to Woodstock?"

"No."

"Then how are they alike?"

"I didn't want to go there. And I didn't want to come here."

They found the side of the tent and crawled under it.

"Well, I think we've made it safe and sound," Yumi said. She helped Jacobus to his feet. They still had the rain to contend with, which was quickly turning the dirt that covered their clothes into streaking mud. She waited patiently until he was able to straighten his back.

"And I'll get your clothes cleaned tomorrow," she said. "They'll be good as new. I don't know about my new dress, though."

Jacobus's teeth chattered. This was turning out to be more Vivaldi's *Winter* than *Summer*.

"Don't worry," he said, with effort. "Distressed flannel is the rage." Yumi, apprehensive that Jacobus could catch pneumonia standing outside in the cold rain, escorted him to her cabin, her arm around his shoulders. For once, he did not object. They stumbled forward through the storm along with dozens of others, like escapees from the misery of a forced labor camp. Jacobus halted.

"Hocus!" he said. "I left Hocus in the tent. I have to go back and get it."

Yumi, her voice conveying concern that Jacobus was becoming delirious, reassured him.

"Don't worry, Jake. After I put you into bed I'll go back and get it for you. I know where it is."

Jacobus resisted, and she had to tug him along. Once inside the cabin, she handed him towels to dry himself and ordered him to take off his wet clothes and get into bed and under the blankets. This time he did not protest. And now that they were alone, he was able to address the issue that was disturbing him more than anything else.

"Tell me what's wrong, Yumi," he said, shivering. "There's something that was bothering you. Before the storm."

"Why would you think that?" Yumi asked.

"Don't play games with me, Yumi. Shall we go over your performance note by note? You were distracted. You were worried. What aren't you telling me? Humor an old man, okay?"

She told him about the two phone calls, and about the inexplicable string of incidents in between, leaving out only what exactly she was doing in Renfro's cabin in the middle of the night when the pebble hit the window. She was reluctant to tell him about any of it before, she said, not wanting to bother him with it. But now, with the tent debacle and Jacobus ill again, it was the least of her concerns.

"I'll take care of you," she said, and he could hear her trying to hold back the tears.

"Don't worry about me. Nothing that a bad night's sleep won't cure."

"And don't worry about me, either," Yumi said. "They were probably just prank calls. Not a threat. See? I played the concert and I'm perfectly fine. Even with the tent collapsing."

"I still don't like it. From what you say, the calls sounded like threats. Both of them. Worse, I think the first one was made from somewhere else, but the second one came from right here."

"Why do you think that?"

"First of all, if the intent was to protect you, or to urge you to take certain actions for your safety, there was a critical word missing. 'Please.' 'Please don't go.' 'Please leave now.' You don't need to remind me that 'please' is a word I don't often use, because most of the time I find it unnecessarily cloying. But most people do use it, and when someone is trying to be persuasive in a positive way, to be helpful, 'please' will often be the key to the lock. Think about all the little brats who want their mothers to buy them a candy bar in the supermarket. 'Pleeeeeeeease?' You see? They're smart. They know what works. And the tone. You said the calls were impersonal, noncommittal. If someone was sincerely concerned they would express it. If the tone is flat, it's meant to do two things: be anonymous and be intimidating."

"Okay," Yumi said. "I can see that. But you also mentioned two different locations?"

"'Don't go there.' When you got that first call there was no context. Like you said. It could've meant the airport, or somewhere else, and it could've been metaphorical. But the second one made it clear the caller was in the neighborhood."

"Couldn't he have said 'leave now' from somewhere else?"

"More likely he would've said 'leave.' By saying 'leave *now*' I'm thinking he was fully aware that your performance was minutes away. It was an 'or else' kind of message. It was a threat, Yumi. And as much as a disaster the tent collapse was, it might have saved your life. You were vulnerable up there onstage. Exposed. The caller could have been someone in the audience. It could have been a musician backstage. You were able to walk away."

"But now I have to go back," she said.

"Why? You're safe here." Jacobus faked a cough, though after the first few it erupted into the real thing.

"Still, I need to go and help," Yumi said. "There are people trapped under the tent. Don't worry. If someone's trying to harm me, they've missed their chance. And now I'll be ready for them. I have a feeling I've dodged a bullet."

"That may be. But you're making a big assumption."

"What assumption?"

"That you're the only target."

Almost every day for the past week, they had been entertained by displays of nocturnal sheet lightning, not comprehending the slowly changing weather pattern and the clues that the brewing storm would finally erupt with a vengeance. Now, the Great Salt Lake was convulsed in a frenzy of anarchic whitecaps, illuminated by almost continuous bolts of lightning. In the dark, slipping on inches of packed ice as she returned to the tent, Yumi considered Jacobus's startling proposition, that she was not the only quarry in some sick person's sights. Whether that was true or not, none of it made any sense either way.

The scene around the ruined Big Top was no less chaotic than the waves. Some of the hundreds of concertgoers seeking shelter and guidance had found refuge under the barn's shed roof, crowding against ancient, rusty plows and worn leather saddles. An elderly couple, clearly dazed, wandered aimlessly in the rain and wind, asking, "Where are we supposed to go?" "Who's in charge?"

Apparently, no one was. Yumi coaxed everyone toward the barn and tried to provide reassurance that everything would be okay, but was far from certain she was convincing.

A sudden blast of thunder jump-started the hailstorm back into unwelcome life. Yumi approached Sunny Flox, who, with Christian Bjørlund, was standing by the side of the tent. An EMT ran up, pleading for assistance to extricate a group of Road Scholar senior citizens still ensnared under the flattened concert tent. *Are there injuries?* Yumi asked. *Impossible to tell. Probably. Have to get them to a safer place.* With her mobile phone's flashlight, Yumi illuminated enough space in front of her to begin the crawl back in.

"Oh, Jesus! I need help!"

It was Marcus Renfro's voice, cutting through the wind. He was somewhere in front of her, amidst the rubble, amidst the casualties. Exactly where was impossible to determine. Yumi feared for his safety. It was so dark.

"Help, here!" he called again, this time even louder. "It's Anita. She's had an accident. I think…I think she might be dead."

An accident? Yumi thought. *How is that possible? It doesn't make sense. I just spoke to her only moments ago. If Jacobus were here, he would say this was no accident. He would say something like, "Two and two is supposed to equal four, but this ain't four." No, this doesn't add up. In other words, Jacobus would say, "This was murder." If only he were here.*

Chapter Eight

Jacobus! He had been so weak when she helped him to her cabin. He could have pneumonia. She couldn't allow another person to die. He was the one who needed her now.

"I have to leave," she told the EMT, and rushed back to her cabin through the rain and mud. Holding onto the hope that maybe Anita was still alive, she wouldn't even mention to Jacobus what had happened. Marcus said she *might* be dead. Maybe he was wrong.

Yumi opened the door as inaudibly as possible, poked her head in, and was reassured to hear Jacobus snoring peacefully. She allowed herself just enough time for her eyes to adjust to the darkness to see that he was comfortable before closing the door and hurrying to her next destination.

Yumi found Sunny Flox on his cellphone in the festival office, a small rustic building behind what, until just a short time earlier, had been the Big Top. Originally a bunkhouse, the office had also previously served as a church and schoolhouse. At first an adobe two-story, gabled-roof structure, it was now faced with cinder blocks and painted white. It was now also leaking profusely. Amazingly, Flox was hardly disheveled, still in his trademark short-sleeve white shirt and red bow tie. He gestured for Yumi to wait while he spoke. He hung up shortly thereafter.

"Sorry," he said. "That was the state police. My phone battery's running down and the electricity's out, so I had to talk to them while I still could."

"Is it true about Anita?"

"I'm afraid so. She's gone. It's terrible. Something heavy evidently fell on her. One of the tent posts, maybe. They weigh a ton. The EMTs said her skull was fractured. I can't believe it, but if there's a good side to this, she's the only fatality. So far."

"But that can't be, Sunny! She was fine when Jake and I left her. I was there! We were talking to her and the tent was already down. I don't understand what could have happened to her in the few minutes after we left her."

"That's why I called the police, Yumi." He put his hands over his eyes as he talked. Frustrated. Tired. Blocking out the horror.

"What did they say? Are they on their way? People are losing it, Sunny. They're desperate."

"I wish. They can't. The police. I mean, they're not able to."

"Not able to what?" Yumi asked.

"Get here. The storm washed out a section of the causeway. The lake's higher than it's been in years and even before the storm they were worried about erosion. Antelope Island is cut off. We're cut off. There's no telling how long it's going to take to fix it. Days or even weeks, they said."

"Boats, Sunny! What about boats? It's a shallow lake."

"You've seen the waves! Boats have been warned off the water. As long as there's this gale and the gusts, they say the waves are too dangerous. The weathermen say this is a freak. The perfect storm. No telling when it will end. And before you ask, I tried convincing them to send a helicopter, but they wouldn't hear of it. No place to land. And the wind. Too damned unpredictable."

"Then, we're stuck here?" Yumi asked.

"It seems so. We're stranded. Everyone on Antelope Island is stranded. We've got overnight accommodations and provisions for staff and musicians, but what we're going to do for food, water, and shelter for hundreds of people..." His voice trailed off, but the implication was clear. The situation was dire and potentially catastrophic.

"What about all the food for the barbecue on Sunday?" Yumi asked. "We've got that. Don't we?"

"Joy scheduled delivery for tomorrow."

"I wonder what's happened to the rest of the people on the island," Yumi said. "Campers and hikers."

"What about them? They're not my responsibility. I've got enough—"

"I'm not saying they are. But they're trapped here, too. And so are the park rangers and staff. Any word from them?"

"I've contacted the head ranger."

"What's his name? Dance? Jefferson Dance?"

"You know him?" Flox asked.

"I've never met him. I just heard him and Anita arguing over that car accident last week."

"Oh, yeah. That. Well, I don't know what's keeping him. He was supposed to be here by now. What more can I do, Yumi? It could be that the road from their headquarters washed out, too. I just don't know. All I know is that Anita is dead. Okay?"

"I'm sorry," Yumi said. "This is all so terrible."

A sudden barrage of hail pelted the office roof, as if to reinforce Yumi's statement and rendering conversation impossible until it subsided.

"Where have they taken Anita?" she asked when her voice could again be heard.

"I had the EMTs carry her to her cabin."

Yumi considered the possibility there had been foul play, and apparently her face gave away her apprehension that a potential crime scene had been disturbed, because Flox threw up his hands.

"Well, I couldn't just leave her lying there for everyone else to trip over, could I? No one is that coldhearted! We'll just have to wait for the medical people or the police or who the hell knows to decide what to do. I just hope someone will get here soon. I mean, how long can she lie there before... I've tried contacting Herb to tell him—"

"Herb?"

"Anita's husband."

"They have kids?"

"A daughter in high school."

"My God."

"My God is right. But when I called there wasn't any answer, so what am I supposed to do, just leave a phone message saying your wife's been killed?

Shit, this is a nightmare."

Yumi had nothing more to contribute to the conversation. She needed to go back to Jacobus and tend to him. What had she done? Why had she insisted this old man, so soon after recovering from a brush with death, travel two thousand miles to a desert island just to hear her play a fifteen-minute concerto? Her ego must be out of whack. And now for him to suffer from this horror. Crawling on his hands and knees in the ice and mud. If anything happened to him, she would... She didn't know what she would do, but she knew she would do it.

"Sunny, could I borrow some of your clothes?" she asked.

Flox eyed her curiously.

"They're for Daniel Jacobus. He's soaked to the bone and his luggage was lost."

Flox told her to help herself. He had to get back to making calls. Yumi went to his cabin and rummaged through his closet and drawers, selecting pressed Oxford shirts and stylish pants, and did not hesitate to grab a few pairs of underwear and socks as well. Flox was bigger and taller than Jacobus, so the clothes' would be a little baggy. Relaxed fit, she would tell him. Jacobus, if he were able to see, wouldn't be caught dead in such dandified attire. But as he liked to say, Yumi reminded herself, it's one of the benefits of being blind.

One of Flox's dry-cleaned suits, hanging on the clothes rack, was covered with a plastic bag. Jacobus certainly didn't need a suit, but the plastic bag would come in handy. She removed the bag and placed the clothes in it to keep them dry. On her way out, she also took a gray Polar Fleece jacket off the coat hook and an Antelope Island Music Festival baseball cap from a small table next to the door. As she pocketed it, she saw an open notepad among the papers on the table. If the words hadn't been scrawled in capitals, underlined, and punctuated with several exclamation marks, she would not have noticed it. But notice it she did, and was left puzzling over its significance: "A PAIR OF BITCHES IN HEAT!!!"

It was a surreal mix. Reactions to the extreme conditions created by the storm ranged from silent stoicism to constant whining, accompanied by occasional shoving matches between the two points of view.

Among most of the throng—after the initial shock and confusion of the storm, the ravaged tent, and the death of Anita Talbot—the certainty that everyone would be stranded on the island indefinitely, even with its inherent hardships, created a sense of psychological equilibrium. Their immediate future was now a given and they had survived the worst. In effect, the question changed from "what's going to happen to us?" to "what can we do to get through this together?" which actually served to reduce the overall anxiety level.

There were those, on the other hand, who chafed at the situation, which was understandable if unhelpful. People who were cold, soaked to the bone, exhausted, and of course, people who were injured. There were complaints of lack of food, shelter, medical care, warmth, organization, information. "Why don't they tell us anything?" The correct answer to their complaints came in two parts: Because Anita Talbot was dead there was no one in charge, and since the likelihood of such a disaster had been so minuscule, preparation for such a turn of events had never even been envisioned, let alone planned. And though everyone knew those were the answers, and that at this point little could be done to change things, some people nevertheless were unwilling to accept it.

Some of those who were able got in their cars and drove off, storm or no storm, not realizing it would be impossible to get off the island. They would return, and they would be even more fractious than before.

The festival staff ushered all the remaining concertgoers into whatever relatively dry sheltered spaces were available, sequestering them in the barn, the offices, and some of the musicians' cabins. What food was available was set up on tables in the barn, warmed in chafing dishes with Sternos, and carefully doled out in modest quantities because no one knew how long it would have to last. Rain continued to fall, though with less ferocity. Blustery winds persisted.

Yumi herself was comforted to hear Jacobus still snoring long before she reached her cabin door. It brought a sorely needed smile to her careworn countenance, which, in the past hours, had become hardened with stress. His snoring reminded her of the buffalo that wandered the island's hillsides, grunting as they grazed.

"Keep your distance from the buffalo! They're wild animals, and even when not provoked have attacked humans." That was the default warning from the park rangers given to all newcomers, which the musicians—especially those who had never been to Antelope Island before—scrupulously heeded. Though it was difficult to imagine, Yumi reminded herself that to his enemies, Jacobus—this blind, infirm, snoring old man—could be a more formidable adversary than the buffalo were to an island visitor. But right now it was good to hear him sleeping, and she made sure to tread lightly so as not to wake him.

The sunlight, which until that afternoon had been the single, fixed, stark constant, had long been obscured by dark, swirling storm clouds. The transition into nightfall had been undetectable, and Yumi had no idea when day had become night. With the electricity out, everywhere there was darkness. "Earth was without form and void, and darkness was upon the face of the deep." Those were the biblical words describing *Chaos*, the starkly frightening opening of Haydn's oratorio, *Creation*, that Yumi had performed just two months earlier. Yes, if there was Chaos on earth, it felt like it now, here on Antelope Island. Darkness and nothingness. Darkness *was* nothingness. To be feared. Though not by Jacobus. Yet another advantage…
She felt for the door latch and delicately pressed down on it with her thumb.

"It's okay, Yumi," Jacobus said. "I'm awake."

Yumi entered her cabin, carrying the bagful of clothing. Jacobus was in bed with the covers pulled up over his head. She put the bag on the dresser, lit a candle, then began picking up his wet clothing scattered on the floor.

"How did you know it was me?" she asked.

"You tell me," he said from under the covers.

"Because if it were anyone else, anyone else would have knocked?"

"Obviously."

"What if I were a robber?"

"If you were a robber, when I said, 'It's okay, Yumi, I'm awake,' the robber wouldn't have said, 'How did you know it was me?'"

"That makes sense." She went about hanging his wet things on hooks in the bathroom. "I've got dry clothes for you. They may be a little big, but—"

"What's wrong, Yumi? What's worrying you?"

"Why should something be wrong?"

"Because you haven't asked me how I'm feeling yet. That's not like you. I'm sure you've been kicking yourself that you made a terrible mistake coaxing me—a poor, sick old man—to come all the way out here and get stuck in a natural disaster. But what's done is done, so we've gotten over that. Put it out of your mind. But it's clear something else is eating at your craw."

Yumi sat on the edge of the bed.

"Okay," she said. "You've got that right. But would you mind taking the blanket off your head so that I can see you when I talk to you?"

"Why? It's the same view for me either way."

"Still. It's easier talking to a person than to a lump under the blankets."

"Fair enough," Jacobus said. He pulled the blanket down to his neck. In the candlelight, Yumi was relieved to see that a color other than blue had returned to his cheeks.

She told him about Anita Talbot's death, breaking the news as gently as possible, then detailing the circumstances around it, and about her conversation with Flox and his presumptions about the cause of her demise. She didn't say a word about her own suspicions. Jacobus didn't say a word of his until she was finished.

"If what you say is accurate—and knowing you, I have no reason to doubt it—that was no accident," Jacobus said. "She's been murdered."

"There must be some other explanation, Jake. How could someone have killed Anita with everyone right there?"

"No, Yumi. No. That's where you're wrong. That was the perfect time and place for a murder. The circumstances were handed to him—or her—on a silver platter. The tent. The chaos. The injuries. It might not have been planned for that moment—it couldn't have been, obviously, because there was no way to know the apocalypse was about to descend—but the killer had Talbot in their sights and took full advantage of the opportunity."

"I don't know, Jake. That still sounds so speculative. I think we should wait until the medical people arrive. They'll be able to tell for sure whether it was an accident."

"So how many days will that be, Yumi? Two? Three? You just told me no one knows how long we'll be stuck here. You okay with having a killer on the loose until they come to make sure?"

"Maybe you have a point there, Jake."

Jacobus laughed. "Damned by faint praise, am I?" he said. "You're still not convinced."

"I'm just not as certain as you. But in any case, what do we do now?"

"First, maybe I should get dressed. If someone walked in, they might jump to conclusions seeing a handsome naked man in your bed."

Yumi handed Jacobus Flox's clothes and turned her back to him. While he dressed, she finally changed into dry clothes, herself. Why should she be timid about being naked in front of a blind man? Though Jacobus would no doubt have been shocked and disapproving had he been able to see her crane tattoo. She tossed her new, ruined concert dress into a corner. Nothing ventured, nothing gained.

She smiled. Marcus had been shy undressing in front of her, preferring lights out. Too bad. She would like to have seen more of him, considering how he felt in the darkness. Maybe next time. If there was to be one. That remained to be seen.

As they dressed, Yumi reviewed the string of strange and disturbing occurrences relating to Anita, each of which at the time seemed inconsequential, and some of which very well might be. For example, when Sunny had mentioned to Hannah Carrington about wanting to make up for not standing up to Anita over some other issue and then telling her to ignore that he said it. Or the volatility over the discussion about concert dress.

They discussed the ongoing confrontations between Dieter Waldstein and Christian Bjørlund, on and offstage, and Bjørlund's admonition to Anita Talbot to stay out of their argument. And, she recalled to Jacobus, Bjørlund was a trained, if amateur, boxer. Could he have had something to do with her death?

"Maybe," he said. "Maybe. Peripherally. But as much as string quartet musicians sometimes want to kill each other, they generally keep it within the family."

"Very funny."

"How do I look, by the way? Are you sure these clothes aren't meant for Nathaniel?" He was wearing a new, crisp pair of khakis and a blue Oxford shirt, both of which were two sizes too big for him. He had to pull the belt through to its last hole to prevent his pants from falling down. He felt like a Walmart doll in a gift-wrapped FAO Schwarz package. Yumi rolled up the shirtsleeves and pant cuffs to allow his hands and feet to show.

"There," she said. "Good as new. You could be a Ralph Lauren model."

"Don't insult me. In any event, it's hard to think why one of them would want to kill an administrator, even a bad administrator, which by the way is a redundancy. Professional musicians know very well that managers are going to try to squeeze as much as they can out of their talents, so for a musician to kill an administrator over a contract squabble, over money, would be to deny a colorful, time-honored ritual of musician-management relations. More likely, if it was a musician who killed her, it would be for personal, not professional reasons. To speak ill of the dead, she seems to have rubbed a lot of people the wrong way."

"Yourself included," Yumi added.

"I shouldn't be included," he said.

"Why not?"

"Because *most* people rub me the wrong way. We'll have to find out more about some of these relationships. Fortunately, it's not a full-size symphony orchestra we're dealing with. But as I've told you over and over—"

"Yes, I know, Jake. I should have stayed away from string quartets."

"Right."

"I'll listen to you from now on."

"Good. Call Nathaniel."

"Why?"

"Didn't you just said you'd listen to me from now on?"

"Jake, have I ever told you that sometimes you're not only incorrigible but a pain in the—"

"Many times. Music to my ears. I want you to call Nathaniel because it's highly likely we'll soon lose the ability to communicate with the outside world, and I want him to do whatever research he can about the Kreutzer Quartet, the other musicians, Anita Talbot, Sunny Flox, and the young gal, what's-her-name—"

"Joy. Joy D'Angelo."

"Yes, D'Angelo. Sometimes it's easy to underestimate the cute, cuddly ones. When Nathaniel's finally able to haul his sorry ass up here I want to be able to figure out this mess."

While Yumi made the call, Jacobus made an urgent trip to Yumi's bathroom, his progress slowed without the aid of his missing walking stick.

"Nathaniel says hello," Yumi said after Jacobus re-emerged. He found his way back to the bed and sat down on it.

"That's a good start. What else?"

"The story's been on all the local news stations what happened here. Well, most of what happened."

"How did they find out?"

"From Sunny's frantic calls to the authorities, I suppose. But so far they haven't said a word about Anita. Just about the Big Top caving in and that there were injuries. Nathaniel was shocked when I told him that it was more than that. I guess they don't want to say anything until they've notified next-of-kin."

"He's got my instructions about the background checks?"

"Yes. He'll look into those."

"Good. Anything else?"

"For what it's worth, your suitcase finally showed up. Your new suit is hanging up in what may one day be your room at the Waltz Rite Inn, where Nathaniel's eating pizza and watching the news on TV about the storm. He'll be here as soon as the causeway is open again."

"That's it?"

"Just one more thing. He said, 'Don't do anything Jake would do.'"

"Good advice. But speaking of things showing up, did you find Hocus for me?"

"Oh, Jake, I'm sorry! I was about to look for it when an EMT asked me to help some old folks, and then Marcus shouted out about Anita. So much was happening, I just didn't think about it. But I'm sure when the crew cleans up the Big Top, it'll be there. Don't worry, we'll get Hocus back for you."

"Well, it's just a stick," he said, trying to sound as if it didn't matter.

"I suppose," Yumi said. "But what should we do now?"

"As you said, we'll get it when they dismantle the tent."

"I didn't mean that. I meant, what do we do about Anita?"

"Give me a little context."

"Context?"

"Yeah, I was thinking about this situation while I was sitting on the can. I need to know more about how things have been here. What might've provoked one person to commit murder while surrounded by hundreds of onlookers. Pretty audacious. How could that've happened? Start from the beginning. I have a feeling we're going to have all the time in the world."

Yumi filled Jacobus in how, during the festival's first week, they had started out with some bumps in the road, some internal conflicts, but that there had been a growing sense of camaraderie, both as musicians and as human beings. How it gave real meaning to the word festival, being more than just a bunch of concerts that you got paid to perform. But then, the petty jealousies and power trips started resurfacing. Like a parallel to the weather, getting hotter and more…she couldn't really describe it…yes, intense. The weather became more intense. Unbearably so. Things had begun to spiral down from there. The fights between Bjørlund and Waldstein. Marcus's hot and cold behavior. Weiss's passive-aggressiveness. All bad enough, but nothing compared to the Big Top disaster this evening. And Anita's death.

When Yumi finished, Jacobus was silent. Had he fallen asleep again? She could never tell, with his dark glasses on.

He was silent because he was contemplating Vivaldi's sonnet to *Summer*. Upon reflection, it was striking that of all the *Four Seasons* concertos, summer seemed to be Vivaldi's least appealing season. In the U.S., everyone waits for summer. Fun in the sun! The great outdoors! Picnics and baseball! But for Vivaldi's Italians, summer was oppressive. In the sonnet, Vivaldi used the word fear three times, once in every movement: "fearful of violent storm," "fear of the furious thunder and lightning," "his worst fears were justified." Summer was cruel: "the blazing sun's relentless heat, men and flocks are sweltering, pines are scorched." "Threatening north wind." "The shepherd trembles." "The heavens roar and great hailstones beat down." Summer was not a time of joy. It was a time of lassitude and indolence at best, a time of peril and devastation at worst. Was Vivaldi prescient? Had he predicted these events? Or did he simply describe a condition of the relationship between man and nature that was universal and inevitable and led to death and destruction?

"Jake, are you awake?"

"No, I'm sleeping. You?"

Yumi had learned long ago which of Jacobus's comments she could ignore. This was one.

"So what's next?" she asked.

"I don't know. You've given me a lot of generalities. How about some specifics having to do with Anita?"

"Like Bjørlund threatening Waldstein when he said, 'So help me, I'll kill you'?"

"Like that. That's a start. Too bad he didn't say, 'So help me, I'll kill Anita.' What else?"

"I don't know." There didn't seem to be much else. "Christian did say, 'Management should stay out of it,' or something like that when he was arguing with Dieter."

"That sounds more like words of wisdom than a threat."

"I don't know then. Wait! Maybe there's something else. 'Like a pair of bitches in heat'?"

"Yumi, you offend my sensitive ears with such coarse language," Jacobus teased. "Have some of your female colleagues been getting on your nerves?"

"That's not what I meant," Yumi said. "It's something that Jamie Barov told Marcus and me that he said to Christian and Dieter to break up one of their arguments. Anita was there with them. It was funny at the time and seemed to do the trick. I had all but forgotten about it, but then I saw it written on Sunny's notepad in his cabin. You think that can just be a curious coincidence?"

If only Jacobus had Hocus in his hands. He had acquired a new habit to help him ruminate, tapping the stick up and down on the floor. Lightly. Not that it was a magic wand. He enjoyed the succulent sound of wood tapping on wood. The rhythmic repetition. It helped him think. There was something soothing, almost musical about it.

Maybe there was an esthetic reason, not just a technological one, why drums were the first manufactured musical instruments. Impossible to imagine what the first drum beats meant to the human species—the ability to manufacture sound! Until then, it had been a million years, give or take a few hundred thousand, of passively listening to the sounds of nature. Birds, animals, wind, waves, volcanoes. Breathing. You name it. But then, man learned to create his own sound, with his own rhythm! One of the greatest revolutionary breakthroughs in the entire evolution of humankind, as significant as the ability to make fire.

Since then, music had progressed. There was no question about that. As long as you listen to Mozart and ignore Manilow. But had humankind progressed morally? Not one iota, as far as Jacobus was concerned. Humankind was still bent on killing each other for the same damn reasons. Correct that: Back in the day, humans killed each other to survive. Now they killed each other for no reason at all. With Hocus, Jacobus could connect to his esthetic forebears, absorbing the stick's primitively natural resonance in a day and age when there were so many unnatural ones. These damned electronic devices. These—

"Jake? What do you think?"

"I'll tell you what I think. Curious coincidence, you asked. Curious? Very. Coincidence? Highly unlikely."

The candle on the dresser went out, leaving them in the dark.

Chapter Nine

The light on Flox's desktop computer, on reduced battery power, throbbed dimly.

"So what?" he said, answering Jacobus. It was clearly a rhetorical question, not intended to obtain additional information but rather to cut off the conversation, then and there.

Jacobus and Yumi had found him still at his desk. Navigating to the festival office in the dark had not been much easier for Yumi than for Jacobus, because though the electricity was out she decided not to use her phone flashlight, opting to conserve the battery. She had to rely on her sense of touch almost as much as he. Advantage, Jacobus. He was already a pro at it, but even for him, the going had been hazardous, as they traversed the ruins of the tent, with its ensnaring ropes, cables, and posts lying helter-skelter on the ground. Hand in hand, they probed forward, navigating around upended tables and chairs, slogging in mud that topped their shoes with every misplaced step, over and around downed branches that threatened to trip them. It would have been so much easier with Hocus. And they weren't the only wanderers, as they crisscrossed with bedraggled concertgoers, feeling their way to refuge, seeking companionship, or simply trying to regain a sense of normalcy by remaining active.

Jacobus was dressed in Flox's oversized clothing, with the festival baseball cap on his head and the Polar Fleece jacket collar pulled up against the wind and rain. His adopted outfit, though ill-fitting, was more presentable than what he usually wore. Given that everyone there was preoccupied with surviving the night, he need not have felt self-conscious with his out-of-character attire in any case. Nevertheless, he did. He pictured himself, to the best of his ability to picture anything, looking like a cartoonish, dandified fop.

So, when Flox's first comment upon their entering his office had been, "I see you've made yourself comfortable, Mr. Jacobus," Mr. Jacobus was put even more ill at ease. If Flox had realized what the repercussions were soon going to be for what was intended as an offhand comment, he wouldn't have said it.

Flox's office had deteriorated from the neatly efficient, organized workspace that it had so recently been. Documents, blown off the desk and shelves and strewn about, had taken on the new role of de facto paper towels, wicking the water that had leaked through the ceiling onto the floor. Flox's appearance was as scattered as the documents. His tie was off—a first for him in Yumi's recollection—and he continually pushed his hair back as if to keep it out of his eyes even though his receding hairline suggested there was little danger of that ever happening.

Flox was clearly nearing the end of his rope. He defensively reminded Jacobus and Yumi, more loudly than necessary, that he was, after all, only an *artistic* administrator, though neither Jacobus nor Yumi had questioned his credentials or his efforts. His job was to put together concert programs, he said. To hire guest artists. To chat up big donors, but even that was a stretch for his job description. He was *not* the executive director. He was *not* FEMA. He had *no* prior experience single-handedly managing natural disasters. He was *not* prepared to respond to concertgoers who demanded a refund, let alone those who threatened to call their lawyers as soon as they got home. And he certainly was *not* a murder investigator. He had *no* one to help him, and where his alleged assistant, Joy D'Angelo, had run off to was anyone's guess.

That's why, when Jacobus asked about "a pair of bitches in heat," Flox had responded, "So what? So Jamie Barov makes an innocent, good-natured remark to try to defuse a nasty situation. So Anita Talbot, who had the right to be PC in this day and age—okay, so she might have been a little hypersensitive and okay, so she may have been overly cautious when it came to liability, I'll concede that—so what, that Anita Talbot hears Jamie's comment and considers it offensive and reports it to me. So, I repeat, so what?"

Jacobus, forever reluctant to take yes for an answer, replied, "So, so, so. So, if it's so innocuous, so why did you write it down?"

"Because I had a pen and paper, that's why."

Jacobus said, "Mr. Flox, I commiserate with you. You're under a ton of stress. You've got a dead colleague and a washed-out music festival, and you're probably finding my questions beside the point in these difficult moments." His voice rose, "But let me just submit this to you: If you keep on fucking with me with sarcastic bullshit, you'll find the natural disaster you're having a hard time managing the least of your concerns. So let me ask you again. Why did you write it down?"

Jacobus hoped the shock treatment would produce the desired result. Sometimes it did. Sometimes it didn't. Not that he had anything against Flox. It was an approach he kept in his back pocket with students, but rarely drew upon. If he was a good teacher, browbeating shouldn't be necessary, and he believed he was a good teacher. But once in a while, when a student was exceptionally lazy, or would obfuscate, or outright lie, the nuclear option was the only one left. This time it worked. Flox responded almost before Jacobus finished asking the question.

"Okay, I'll tell you why. Because she wanted me, as artistic administrator, to report Jamie to the board, with the recommendation they not hire him again. That's why. Are you happy now?"

"Jamie Barov?" Yumi asked. She had agreed to let Jacobus do the talking, but she was stunned. "Why Jamie?"

Flox shrugged. The flippant gesture, inferring that he was simply the messenger, not his concern, infuriated her even more.

"Jamie is the best of all of them, Sunny! He was the peacemaker, and forget about being the best musician."

"Music wasn't the issue," Flox said. "Anita was concerned with how women are treated—aren't you?—and she found the phrase repugnant."

"But 'bitches in heat' aren't women!" Yumi said. "Bitches in heat are female

122

dogs! Dogs! And that's how the two *men* were behaving. It had nothing to do with women. Anita made a mountain out of a molehill. Not even a molehill. Word will get around if the festival censures him or drops him. You know that. You know how these rumors spread. People will ask why, and pretty soon they'll be making up stories that he's committed sexual misconduct. Presenters will start dropping him off their concert series. Musicians who don't know the truth will stop performing with him. She could have ruined his career like that."

"Well, I guess she won't," Flox said, beating Jacobus, who was about to say the same thing. Jacobus was also about to pose the question: If Barov was aware that Talbot had reported him, and considering the possible repercussions, could that have angered him enough to kill her? But Jacobus kept his own counsel for the moment, and instead he said, "Horses."

"What are you talking about, horses?" Flox said.

"What do you hear, Yumi?" Jacobus asked.

"I hear the wind," Yumi said. "It's whistling through the cracks. And I hear the waves. And pieces of tent flapping. And some people sloshing around in the mud. But not horses."

"Then use your nose."

"Brine. From the lake. What else?"

There was a knock at the office door. It was Joy D'Angelo, Flox's assistant.

"Not a horse," Yumi said. For once, Jacobus was wrong.

"Where have you been?" Flox asked, unwarranted irritation in his voice.

"Trying to get food to the masses to keep their minds off things."

"What do you want?"

"The cavalry has arrived," she said.

"Cavalry?" Flox asked.

"The park rangers. On horses."

A man with an eye patch strode in behind D'Angelo. Tall and wiry, he made D'Angelo seem even shorter than she was. Kept dry from the soaking rain by a broad-brimmed cowboy hat and a wool poncho over his brown park uniform, he seemed unperturbed by the storm.

"Jefferson," Flox said, "you're here. Finally. What took you so long?"

"And a good day to you, too, sir. Road from the ranger station's washed out. Had to turn back with the cars, so my men and I mounted up. Heard things were bad, and I see that bad might've been an understatement. We brought blankets, flashlights, backup generator, water, first aid. Whatever we could pack on the horses. We'll get some campfires going soon as the rain stops. That should settle folks down for now."

"Anything you can do to help me feed three hundred wet, angry music lovers is greatly appreciated."

"Who might these folks be?" the ranger asked. "Friends of yours?"

Flox introduced Jacobus and Yumi, explaining that she was a star performer and Jacobus her former teacher, but he did so somewhat brusquely, which suggested he would prefer they leave sooner rather than later.

"So, you're the park ranger?" Jacobus asked.

"Yes, sir. Jefferson Dance," Dance said. "Temporarily, anyway. I'm filling in for one of my compadres taking a well-deserved sabbatical in Las Vegas."

"Jefferson Dance, huh? Real Western do-si-do kind of name, Jefferson Dance."

"Yes, sir. Born and bred. Pleased to meet you."

"And what does one do as park ranger? Other than empty trashcans and make campfires?"

"Jake," Yumi intervened. "That's not polite."

"No offense taken, ma'am," Dance said. "Most folks don't know exactly what we do. Yes, we do empty trashcans and make campfires."

"See!" Jacobus said.

"That, and one or two other things. I'm in charge of a crew that manages the buffalo herd and naturalists who monitor bird and wildlife populations. We oversee and maintain the campgrounds, hiking trails, the visitor center, and marina. We enforce the rules and regulations for state park visitors. In fact, right now we've got a missing camper we're looking for. We—"

"I get the picture," Jacobus said.

"And may I say, Mr. Jacobus, I'm a bit of a music lover."

"Really? And what kind of music do you enjoy? Country-western? Jackie

Cash?"

"You mean Johnny Cash?"

"Whatever."

"Actually, my wife and I have season tickets to the Utah Symphony. They'll be starting up in two weeks with Beethoven Seventh. My favorite recording is Claudio Abbado and the Vienna Philharmonic. What's yours?"

Jacobus, rarely on the short end of a retort, had no response. Yumi, however, seemed to take great delight in the exchange.

"I think," she said, "that Jake goes more for Jackie Cash than Beethoven. Isn't that right, Jake?"

Jacobus, never willing to admit defeat, recovered sufficiently to at least deflect it.

"Sadly, my favorite conductors are all dead. Which reminds me—Flox, don't you think you should inform Jefferson here about our fatality?"

Dance's tone changed immediately. The levity was over.

"I hadn't heard about that," he said. "What's been going on?"

Flox explained.

"We'll need to take the body back to headquarters," Dance said. "It won't be pretty, but we've got a kitchen with a refrigerator room next to it. We'll put her there. Keep the backup generators going till the electricity kicks back in and then wait until law enforcement comes with the medical examiner."

"She was murdered," Jacobus said and explained why he thought so. Dance neither agreed nor disagreed with Jacobus's assessment. He said he wouldn't rule out anything, but that it wasn't within his current job description to investigate suspicious deaths.

"I'll leave some men here but I need to take most of them back with me."

"Is that really necessary?" Flox asked. "We need all the help we can get right here."

"I don't doubt that," Dance said. "But after the storm hit, we went and checked on the campgrounds. Everyone was okay in their RVs, but the tenters got beat down pretty nasty and like I mentioned, one of 'em's missing."

Flox continued to demur—what's a single camper who could be out on a hike compared to hundreds of people who are in dire need?—but Dance was politely firm. He wasn't "one of those law and order types," he asserted, but agreed there was a need to get the chaotic situation under control. He would leave a contingent of his crew with the festival. The others would take Anita Talbot back to headquarters and return to doing their jobs.

Dance was about to leave when the office door was slammed open so violently by Christian Bjørlund that it banged against the wall.

"Sunny, l demand to leave this island!" Bjørlund said, without preamble. "Immediately. My situation is unacceptable. Conditions here are insulting and degrading."

Jacobus recalled Yumi's description of Bjørlund as typically Scandinavian blond and blue-eyed, with a pugilistic bent. Judging from the crashing door and Bjørlund's tone of voice, in his mind's eye Jacobus struggled to erase an image of a red-faced, apoplectic Dane, bare-chested in boxing trunks and gloves.

"Fine," Flox said. "You want to leave? Here are the keys to my car. It's all yours."

Jacobus heard the jingle of metal hit the floor near the office entrance.

"I'll let you gentlemen work this out," Jefferson Dance said. "I've got work to do." Jacobus heard footsteps, then the door close.

"Just out of curiosity," Jacobus said to Bjørlund, "exactly why is it you're in such a rush to leave? Is it because you're all cold and wet? Or because the festival is kaput? Or because you and Herr Waldstein have a hard time making nice? Your little war over nuance? Or," and Jacobus gave it a dramatic pause, "does it perhaps have something to do with Anita Talbot's murder?"

"What are you talking about? She has died, I've been told. There was no murder!"

"We don't know anything for sure," Flox said. "Mr. Jacobus is just speculating."

"But it's food for thought, isn't it?" Jacobus said. "Christian here knows damn well no one can get off the island, but he comes in here all hot and bothered, making unreasonable demands, itching for a confrontation. It seems to me, maybe it's all a smokescreen. A deception. You didn't need to be deaf to hear him threatening to kill Waldstein. He's had training using his fists. If he and Talbot got into an argument, I'd say he's a pretty solid candidate."

There was silence.

"What's the problem?" Jacobus asked. "Case closed or not?"

"The problem," Flox said, "is that Christian was standing backstage with Yumi and me when the Big Top caved in. The whole time."

"That true?" Jacobus asked Yumi.

"As long as I was there, anyway," she replied. "Christian was still there when I went to fetch you from under the tent and take you to the cabin. But there was a lot of confusion, and there were those few minutes I was crawling underneath when I didn't know where anyone was, let alone Christian."

"He was with me, I can assure you," Flox added.

"Well, it was a theory. I was just testing it." Jacobus had eaten crow so many times he was getting used to the flavor. Still…

Bjørlund interrupted his thoughts.

"I've had enough of your ridiculous theories," he said to Jacobus. "And you, Sunny, will be hearing from my manager."

"Yes, I'm sure I will," Flox said to Bjørlund's back as he walked out.

"What would you like me to do now, Sunny?" Joy D'Angelo asked, clearly sounding anxious to depart. It seemed to rouse Flox back into the reality of the moment.

"Oh! I suppose with Anita gone I'm in charge now," Flox said. "That's a thought! Oh, I don't know. Why don't you go over to the barn and check out the food situation, like you said? Or help Dance. Or…oh, I don't know. You decide!"

"Okay," D'Angelo said. "Bye."

"Jake, that reminds me," Yumi said. "You haven't had a bite since you left New York. You must be starving."

"Why do you say that? I had a generous half-ounce bag of peanuts and a granola bar on the plane, though I'm not sure if civilized people would define that as food."

"Get yourself a late-night snack in the barn with everyone else who's been stranded," Flox said. "If you're not too late."

"Ribs and fixins, like I was promised? A feast for the marooned, huh? Well, if that ain't thought for food."

"In your dreams."

Chapter Ten

T he years had not totally liberated the barn at Garr Ranch of the odor of past bovine and ungulate habitation. It was, after all, a barn. At least that's what it was originally. Now it was a folk museum of old-time ranching and agriculture, exhibiting antique tractors and plows, pitchforks and saddles. The barn had not been designed or repurposed to mend the wounds, or feed and house hundreds of sodden, semi-traumatized people.

Rough-hewn floorboards and siding had been retained from the original structure to the extent possible to preserve its rustic character. As a result, the wind, which had hardly abated, whistled through gaps in the walls, adding yet another layer to everyone's discomfort and distress. Though the roof had been replaced many times over, water melting from the accumulated hail dripped to the hay-strewn floor like droplets from the canopy of a tropical rainforest. The tent, for all its state-of-the-art design, space-age technology, and steel cables, succumbed to forces of nature with which it was unfamiliar. But the barn, unlike the tent, had been built by folks who knew the land and the elements. For all its leaks and its discomfort and its cattle stink, it had been sturdy enough to withstand the wind and the weight of all those tons of ice. It had survived. That was something to be thankful for.

Yumi led Jacobus around puddles and persons to the food table in a far corner. Someone handed him a paper plate.

"Fill 'er up," Jacobus said. He held the plate out to the server, one of the festival staff.

"Here you go, bud!" the server said, with more enthusiasm than seemed warranted for the occasion.

Jacobus jiggled the plate.

"This doesn't feel very heavy," he said. "Are you sure you're not trying to pull a fast one on a blind man?"

"Sorry, bud, but since we don't know how long we'll be stuck here, those're the orders we got. A quarter cup each of creamed corn and baked beans. Take it or leave it."

"But I was promised ribs."

"If elephants could fly. There's no refrigeration here, so we only get our fresh food delivered the day of. All we've got now is this canned stuff. We do have some peanut packets and granola bars. Want one of those?"

"I'd rather have the elephant," Jacobus said.

"Sorry, we're out of elephants, too," the server joked. "No hard feelings, and I've gotta say: getting around the way you do, you're really adept."

"Just what the world needs," Jacobus mumbled. "Another dept."

He began to walk away, muttering but not arguing, plate in hand. The next person in line was the same mother with the four children who had been a reminder to Jacobus why he didn't go to concerts anymore. The server didn't get away with serving meager portions with the mother nearly as well as he had with Jacobus.

"Our pediatrician said my boys need nutrition," she demanded. "That includes proteins and complex carbohydrates. This is unacceptable."

The server began to explain, as he had to Jacobus, but his explanation was cut short.

"I bring my children to a concert," the mother said, "and first you let the tent fall on them. And then you let them starve? Can't you see they're traumatized?" Jacobus couldn't see, but he easily heard the boys whooping it up as they scampered around the barn. They didn't sound very traumatized to him.

The mother continued to make a scene and the server finally relented, heaping more upon the kids' plates than sanctioned, thinking it probably would solve the problem. Except it only made it worse, as the next several people in line observed the loosening of the rules and demanded their "fair share" as well.

The unwritten compact of cooperation was quickly beginning to unravel.

Jacobus felt a tug at his sleeve. He knew it was Yumi, because she did something like that every time he made a bad joke.

"What?" he complained. "Just because I said the world needs more depts? I'm an old man. I'm entitled."

"It's not that," Yumi said. "Make all the stupid jokes you want, but some of my colleagues and I are over in the corner and I thought you might want to talk to them. See what you can find out."

Yumi took Jacobus's hand and led him through milling erstwhile concert-goers and around rusty old farm equipment which, if not for finding safe haven in the museum would have ended up in the scrap heap.

"Get down off that tractor, Britten!" said the irate mother of the theoretically traumatized boys. "This minute! I'm going to count to three. One...two...I said—"

The boys came racing past Yumi and Jacobus, almost knocking him over. He didn't totally escape their hyperactivity, however. The puddle they jumped in—the one which Yumi had just guided Jacobus around—provided enough muddy spray to coat his left leg to the knee.

"If these weren't Flox's pants..." he said.

The musicians had gathered in the back, under the hayloft, where it was a little drier. Yumi introduced Jacobus to Hannah Carrington, the young violist, and Marcus Renfro. He had already met Christian Bjørlund.

"Where are the Kreutzer Quartet people?" Jacobus asked.

"They're all in Dieter's cabin at the moment," Bjørlund said. "Having an emergency meeting."

"Emergency?" Jacobus said. "What happened? Their music get wet?"

"If only," Bjørlund replied. "They have a concert in LA next week. It's the beginning of a tour for them, and they don't know if they'll have to cancel the whole tour if they can't get out of here on time."

"It's a lot of money," Carrington added.

"Money. Yes, money is important," Bjørlund said. "But all I can say is, thank

God all the musicians got out safely with their instruments. Another few minutes and who knows what could have happened? So let's be thankful."

"I agree," Carrington said.

"And we've decided to bury the hatchet with the Kreutzer," Bjørlund said to Jacobus. "Dieter and I shook hands."

"Well, I'm glad to hear it!" Yumi said. "It's so much better when everyone gets along, especially under these conditions."

"Yes, considering all that's happened today," Bjørlund said, "you know, with the tent and then Anita's terrible accident, we felt that arguments about musical interpretation were so petty."

"So ridiculous," Carrington said.

"And my behavior with Sunny," Bjørlund continued, preempting Jacobus's thoughts. "It was out of place, I admit. We shouldn't be complaining. We should be in mourning. For Anita."

"And for the festival," Carrington added.

"Well, that's very big of all of you," Jacobus said, as he spooned baked beans, now cold, into his mouth. When he was young, the word "beans," in the phrase "He's full of beans," was the polite way of saying, "He's full of shit," which is what he was convinced he was being handed by Bjørlund and Carrington. His understanding of human nature led him to believe that such sudden rapprochement was almost always only partly sincere, if at all. More likely it was a façade concealing an underlying conflict, like when an orchestra conductor complimented a musician at a rehearsal and the next day notified him he was fired.

Jacobus decided that other than to open his mouth to eat, he would keep it shut on the particular subject of sweet reconciliation until he knew more. Yes, the quartet brouhaha could wait, especially as it now seemed to be ancient history. But he'd still want to get Waldstein's side of the story. And then there was the ghoulish second violinist, Weiss, to talk to. Yumi's stalker. What might be his involvement? It all could be significant. It all could be meaningless. But there was a bigger issue foremost in his mind. Jacobus had also noted that Renfro hadn't yet said a word.

"Which one of you gents is Marcus Renfro?" Jacobus asked.

"That would be me," came a voice from among the group.

Did Jacobus detect a note of caution, of hesitation, even in those four single-syllable words?

"Pleasure to meet you," Renfro added. "Yumi's told me a lot about you."

"Nothing good, I hope."

"Everything good."

"Ah! Then my reputation exceeds me," Jacobus replied. "Tell me, Marcus, I understand you were the ill-fated person who discovered Anita Talbot dead. What can you tell us about that? How did that all happen?"

"What do you mean?"

"Just that Yumi and I had left her only minutes before, and she was fine, if a little disheveled. But I haven't been sheveled myself for well over three score and I've managed to survive. Any way to account for that, Marcus?"

"Not sure what you mean."

"I think it's pretty clear what I mean. She was under a chair next to me. Yumi and I spoke to her. She said she was okay. Then next thing we hear, you're calling for help because you think she's dead. Am I leaving something out?"

"They said something must have fallen on her."

"They said. They said. They said. Who said? All I know is the tent had long finished collapsing when we left her. What do you suppose could've fallen on her? A twenty-pound hailstone?"

The wind whistling through the barn and the hum of muted conversation among the crowd did little to dissipate the tension in Renfro's silence. Jacobus hoped the little gangsters who had sullied his pants kept their distance, at least until it broke.

"Look," Renfro finally said. "All I know is, I was helping people get out from underneath the tent. You can ask around. And then I saw Anita lying on the floor. I made my way over to her, around the mess of chairs and tent stuff, to help her up. And then I saw she wasn't moving. And that's when I called out."

"Was anyone with you to witness that?" Jacobus asked. "Did anyone else see what you saw?"

"I'm not sure what you're getting at, Mr. Jacobus," Carrington said. "Marcus is a valued colleague and we trust him implicitly. Don't we, Yumi?"

"Why, yes. We do. Of course, we do."

Jacobus heard a touch of ambivalence in Yumi's voice. Was it because she was surprised to be unexpectedly put on the spot? Or maybe she wasn't in total agreement. Did she have some doubt? Or maybe… Something else? Protecting Renfro? But why would she be doing that? Why protect?

Ah, maybe I can guess. Yes, whenever she talked about Renfro, "Marcus this. Marcus that," there was a je ne sais quoi softness in her inflection. Not always. But sometimes. Yes, I get it now.

"And you must be exhausted," Bjørlund said. "Like all of us. It has been a long, stressful day."

Jacobus thought the comment was addressed to him, and maybe it was, to shut him up, but Renfro's response beat him to the punch.

"The worst," Renfro said. "I'm wiped out. Nice meeting y'all."

"Yeah. Been a pleasure," Jacobus said. All he had wanted was information, to know what Renfro saw. To be able to picture the details in his mind's eye. He couldn't help it that he asked direct questions. He found Renfro's defensiveness disquieting. But maybe revealing. Maybe that was the very information he had been seeking.

With Renfro gone, talk gradually devolved to more mundane subjects: music—chamber music in particular—favorite composers, interpretations, remembered performances. Jacobus scraped the last remnants of corn and beans off his plate—he would have licked it had he not been in polite company—while listening to their disagreements. But it was a healthy, educated discussion with good-natured disagreement, as was musicians' typical wont. Jacobus gathered nothing from the conversation that would shed light on the cause of Talbot's death.

With the death of Anita Talbot looming in the background of everyone's mind, it occurred to Jacobus the barn's overall atmosphere was akin to the Jewish tradition of sitting shiva upon the death of a family member. One function of shiva was to remember the deceased in a positive way, but it was mainly to provide moral support to the survivor.

The first shiva he ever sat was when he was a kid in Germany, before he had given up practicing the religion, any religion. His Uncle Max suddenly died of a heart attack at the end of a long day in his dry-cleaning shop. Every day for a week, family members and friends streamed into the Jacobus household to regale Aunt Eva with stories about what a wonderful man Maxie had been. Some of the stories were even true.

Jacobus and his brother, Eli, spent most of the time at Uncle Max's shiva snatching food off the buffet table because, except for the Passover Seder, the food at a shiva was the best. All the women tried to outdo each other with the brisket and the kugel and the borscht. That's one thing that made sitting shiva different than being here in the barn—canned beans and corn, Jesus Christ!—but the feeling was indeed similar. Except they weren't mourning Uncle Max. They were mourning Anita Talbot. Rightly so, he supposed, in a way.

And Eli! Where, oh where, was his beloved older brother, Eli? Exterminated in the death camp with their parents? Why was there no record? They kept such good records, the devils. Had he survived? Was he lost? Jacobus had given up trying to find him. He had tracked down more than his share of murderers. Why had he been incapable of finding his own flesh and blood? Was that why he was obsessed with an insatiable need to discover the undiscoverable? Why should he care who killed Anita Talbot? Why not just leave it to the proper, if not always competent, authorities? Why? It was a question for which he had no ready answer.

"Don't you think so, Mr. Jacobus?"

It was Bjørlund talking to him.

"Eh?"

"Going from playing Corelli and Vivaldi to performing Brahms and Mendelssohn."

"Oh, yes. Sorry. Was having a hard time hearing with all this wind."

Bjørlund, in particular, had become garrulous. He talked about the unexpected challenges of "converting" from Baroque-style playing to open throttle, heart-on-the-sleeve chamber music of Brahms and Schumann; of the unexpected challenges of compromising one's ego and strongly held esthetic beliefs that must be made to be a successful chamber musician.

Jacobus had only recently come around to appreciating the unique quality of Baroque music played in the Baroque tradition on Baroque period instruments. When it started as a fad back in the sixties, playing in that manner meant playing out of tune with a tinny sound, with no vibrato, with a sea-sickening *wah-wah* on every long note, and with hyper-exaggerated tempos and dynamics. It seemed to be a refuge for musical zealots and castoffs and also-rans, refugees unsuccessful at making a living in the mainstream; and the sound they produced—no offense intended—kind of made him want to vomit, especially compared to the great violinists and cellists of the day. But over the years, the quality improved along with the scholarship, and musicians like Bjørlund and Renfro had brought respect and good taste to their niche market. Too bad, in a way, those two decided to jump centuries in their repertoire. Greener pastures, Jacobus guessed.

Carrington and Bjørlund, and Yumi, too, spoke of the extra-musical challenges of full-time chamber ensemble playing. Of the grind of being on the road for upwards of forty weeks a year, which made having a spouse and family next to impossible. And with the dizzying schedules, and eating in restaurants on the run, three meals a day for weeks, of simply maintaining a healthy diet and getting a precious bit of exercise. Of compromising on program repertoire to satisfy the predictably staid tastes of concert series presenters. Of being required to schmooze with well-meaning but self-aggrandizing groupies at post-concert receptions. Of recording companies more interested in error-free playing than in compelling music-making. Of managements and agents more interested in the bottom line than in music.

There was little for Jacobus to disagree with. For him, there was no music more transcendent, more sublime than Beethoven's late string quartets. But he also knew that to perform Opus 130 or 132 at a level Beethoven would have approved of took years of grueling, often contentious rehearsal, with endless arguments over the meaning of every note, every crescendo, every accent.

That was why Jacobus never had a quartet of his own, especially after he lost his sight, even though at one time he could have played every important violin part from memory, having either learned them at a young age or, after becoming blind, having listened to recordings so attentively with his unmatched aural acuity and impeccable memory. That was also why the tone of the conversation in which he was currently engaged seemed artificially benign.

There was one, very important, missing element in the discussion: the casualties. Of those who dedicated their lives to their art but, for one of many reasons were consumed by it. Destroyed by it. He had seen it all too often. He couldn't count the number of overwhelmed, unexceptional students whom he had counseled: "Don't worry. Not everyone was meant to be a musician. You're a smart kid. Be a doctor. Be a physicist. Even sell your soul and be a lawyer or investment banker. It's all a lot easier than being a musician and it pays a helluva lot more." At first, they would be downcast, disappointed that he had dashed their hopes of being famous concert artists. And though they might not have believed it if he told them, he had just enabled them to dodge a bullet. Sooner or later, they would realize that what he had given them by his brutal honesty was the opportunity for a successful, relatively normal life compared to one of endless struggle and frustration, backbiting, and unfulfilled dreams.

Another element to the conversation that was strikingly absent was the subject of the deceased. The opposite of shiva. It was as if they had put blinders on. Was it a defense mechanism or was it intentional?

The conversation had meandered from the subject of arts management to a discussion of which restaurants in Lucerne served the best schnitzel.

"How well did you all know Anita Talbot?" he asked.

The question brought an immediate hush. It might not have been the most sensitive question to ask, Jacobus told himself, nor might his timing have been impeccable. But if there was a killer out there, which he believed there to be, that person would still be stuck on the island with everyone else, in which case no one was safe. So, Jacobus decided to toss caution, and courtesy, to the wind. If they needed to talk about schnitzel they could do it on their own time and out of his presence. Besides, he was hungry and, oh, the thought of a tender Wiener schnitzel, breaded and fried in butter to golden perfection, and served with lemon, parsley, and maybe a few capers...

"Sorry if I'm being brusque, but I think Anita Talbot was murdered and sticking your heads in the sand isn't going to change that."

"Look here, Mr. Jacobus—" Bjørlund said.

"Sorry, Christian, but I have to agree with Jake," Yumi interrupted. "It's fine we're trying to pretend like everything's normal, but there's no law enforcement here at the moment and we don't know how long it will take for them to fix the causeway. That means there's really no one to investigate this if it is a murder, and it also means there's no one to provide us protection. I can vouch for Jake that the only thing he's interested in is getting to the bottom of this. For everyone's sake."

Carrington, still in her twenties, was the youngest musician at the festival. She had only recently entered the big time and hadn't yet developed a thick crust. From the lightness of her voice, Jacobus could feel the freshness of Carrington's youth. An optimism, perhaps, even given all that had transpired. He wondered what that voice would sound like in ten years. In twenty. When the blond ponytail he imagined her having started to fade to careworn gray and those bright blue, idealistic eyes developed crow's-feet wrinkles around them. Very few musicians retained that buoyancy their entire lives. Yumi still had it, God bless her. Not surprisingly, Carrington was the first to give in to Jacobus's dogged prodding.

"This was the first time I met Anita," she said. "She seemed okay to me. I guess. She hired me, so... I liked her. In a way. I mean, I guess I didn't dislike her."

"And you, Bjørlund?"

"I'm sorry, but I don't wish to speak ill of the dead," Bjørlund said.

"Give it a shot," Jacobus prompted.

"Well," Bjørlund sighed, "you know, we had encountered her at a few other music festivals. She's only been here at Antelope Island since last year. Before that, she was at Bozeman and before that, I think it was Ashland."

"That's a lot of moving around for a top administrator. Don't you think?"

"Maybe, yes. Maybe, no," Bjørlund said. "Some of these types become known for turning struggling festivals around before it's too late. They have a flair for restructuring boards, identifying new audiences, working with local politicians. Sometimes they initiate new strategic plans and capital campaigns. Reshuffle staff. You must know the drill, Mr. Jacobus. They have a reputation for being able to raise the necessary money. That's what it comes down to. Once they create enough positive spin and the world sees that the organization has returned to viability and is pointed in the right direction, they get a better job offer somewhere else and they're gone."

"You said, 'some of these types,'" Jacobus said. "But Talbot wasn't one of them? Is that it?"

"Why do you say that?"

"Because you also said, 'but I don't wish to speak ill of the dead.' Why 'but?' But what? So far, you've only spoken well of the dead. I'm guessing you don't believe she did such a crackerjack job in her previous positions? That there were other reasons she was riding the corporate merry-go-round?"

"She could be kind of critical," Carrington chimed in. "Sometimes."

"How so?" Jacobus asked. Smart kid. She'd waited for Bjørlund to start opening up, testing the waters, before jumping into the pond.

"She micromanaged when it just seemed so unimportant. She told me she thought I was wearing too much makeup for an outdoor festival. I mean, that wasn't even any of her business. Was it?"

Yumi related the story of Talbot reporting Jamie Barov's comment about two bitches in heat to Sunny Flox.

"Yes, that sounds like Anita," Bjørlund said. "She was one to take offense on behalf of others, even when there was no offense to be taken and there were no 'others.' Jamie made Dieter and me realize we were behaving childishly. That was all. But, you know, I think Anita was more concerned with the organization being sued than anything else."

Jacobus, recalling his own irritation over Anita's demand he use a handkerchief, put a chat with Jamie Barov on his to-do list. Barov would not have been pleased that Talbot had reported his innocent comment to Flox, especially as it had been effectively helpful. But that assumed Barov knew what Talbot had done. Establishing that would be step number one.

A sudden thought prompted him to ask, "And what about Flox? How did he feel about having a turnaround expert bossing him around?"

"I think that is hard to say," Bjørlund said. "What do you think, Yumi?"

"I can't really say, either," she replied, "since this was my first time working for Anita as a CEO. I got the feeling she and Sunny were like oil and water, but he's generally such an easy-going guy, I think he let her criticism just roll off his back."

"One time I saw them arguing," Carrington said. "Last week. I'm not sure what it was about because I couldn't hear. But Sunny was arguing back. That's for sure."

"Tell me about that," Jacobus said.

"They were walking on the path, from her office to his. I think it was last Wednesday. No, it was Thursday! I'm sure it was Thursday because we just finished rehearsing the Beethoven."

It sounded to Jacobus that Carrington reveled in sharing privileged information. To be center stage for a moment. And so young! One of musicians' cherished pastimes is spreading gossip. Maybe Carrington's information would come in handy, but what could it be worth, not being able to actually hear what passed between Talbot and Flox? What could one deduce from observing a heated argument but not hearing it? Certainly not lethal retribution. Hell, no. If that were admissible evidence, Jacobus would have been convicted fifty times over for the ones he'd been involved in. But still, could Flox have had a reason to resent Talbot—homing in on his hallowed Antelope Island turf, perhaps—that would cause him to strike out at her? But then again, how could he have done it if Yumi had been at his side when Talbot died?

Again, the conversation drifted, and again Jacobus let it. It was getting late.

Yumi said to Jacobus, "Aren't you getting tired, Jake?"

"Actually, I'm kind of enjoying this. This barn smells a lot like my old house. Though I could've gone for a little more food. Speaking of which, what's for dessert?"

Before Yumi could answer, a scream pierced the infernal, relentless wind.

A wraith in the night. What the hell was it? Where was it coming from?
"Help! Please help!"

Jacobus recognized the voice. It was that girl. Flox's assistant. Joy
D'Angelo.

Chapter Eleven

Jefferson Dance's skeleton crew, which had been loosely monitoring the crowd, ordered everyone in the barn to remain in place. Greatly outnumbered, they attempted to herd the suddenly restive crowd, skittish as a flock of sheep with a coyote on the prowl. Clutching Jacobus's hand, Yumi eluded Dance's men and ducked out the side of the barn. She dragged him along as quickly as she dared, Jacobus trusting that even in her haste she would lead him safely through the minefield of puddles and potholes and downed branches in the ravaged landscape. D'Angelo's cries persisted and, in the dark, they followed the trail of her voice.

She wasn't at the office. She was farther away down the path. Sunny Flox's cabin. Jacobus and Yumi were not the first ones to arrive. Not by any means. A small crowd had already congregated. D'Angelo was reduced to whimpering.

"Oh, my God!" Yumi said to Jacobus. "It's Sunny. He's dead."

Yumi described the scene in broad strokes. Flashlights illuminated the shambles of Flox's cabin with wandering tunnel-vision cylinders of wan, macabre light. There had been a struggle. His body was battered and sprawled sideways over his desk. He had been bludgeoned, broken bones horribly evident. Blood was everywhere.

"Who's here?" Jacobus asked.

"Just about everyone." Yumi started to rattle off the names. "One of Dance's men, I think. Dieter, Ingrid, Cornelia, Jamie—"

"Forget I asked. Who's *not* here?"

Yumi looked around.

"Well, Christian and Hannah. They must have gotten sequestered in the barn. And Franz Weiss, the second violinist. And Marcus."

"Renfro. Again," Jacobus said under his breath.

"I heard that, Jake. What do you mean, 'again'?"

"Renfro was next to Talbot when she died. Now he's MIA when we find Flox murdered. I'm not sure what I mean by again, but it is nevertheless again. And if there was any doubt Anita Talbot was killed, not by accident, but by intention—"

"You're grasping at straws, Jake. You're off base if you suspect Marcus. I'm going to go console Joy. You stay here and calm down."

"And find out what you can," Jacobus said. "I'll wait here and eavesdrop. I've lost my appetite, anyway."

As she left him, he called out, "And try to find Flox's 'bitches in heat' note."

A uniformed member of the park staff, young and inexperienced, attempted ineffectually to shunt the dozen or so gawkers clogging the cabin doorway out into the inhospitable elements. Though Jacobus stood amongst them, no one bothered him or even engaged him in conversation. *Funny how easy it is for blind people to become invisible to everyone else,* Jacobus thought. *They all carry on their own conversations with each other as if I'm not here. As if I can't hear. Can't see, so then can't hear? Makes no sense, but since when did humans make sense? Being invisible. Another benefit to being blind.* There were so many, he could hardly count them.

But he learned very little. Expressions of shock, horror. "How could this happen?" "Why?" "It's too horrible!" The usual. The one question that everyone seemed to be avoiding, though, maybe out of fear, was: Who did it? He did hear one onlooker suggest, almost smugly and with an artificially loud whisper, that a serial killer could be on the loose. Almost as if being the first bearer of potentially horrific news elevated his stature to that of an expert. "Hey, folks! Look at me! I'm a pundit!" As if they were in the midst of a TV drama, and it was somehow exciting. Asshole.

A tug at his sleeve.

"Yumi?"

"I have Joy with me," she said. "And something else."

143

Before Jacobus could ask whether it was Flox's note, Yumi said, "Don't ask. Just let's go outside."

He refrained from asking why the secrecy, but said okay and extended his hand. She grasped it and pulled him around a corner, presumably into the dark, where they would be out of sight from the gathering by the cabin. It was still raining and the wind was still swirling, so Jacobus assumed this was going to be important enough to risk pneumonia. Again.

"Okay," Yumi said. "We should be safe here. Joy, tell Mr. Jacobus what you told me."

It came out in small, choked sentences. Jacobus was uncommonly patient. It wasn't easy to piece the story together. It started when D'Angelo was in the office with Flox.

"Yes, we were there, too. Remember?" he said.

"Oh, yes. I'm sorry."

And after Jacobus and Yumi left, the phone rang, and Sunny saw that the caller was Christian Bjørlund's manager, Lawrence White. Flox asked Joy to talk to him because with so much on his plate already he didn't have the stomach to deal with a call during which he knew he would be yelled at. He said he was going to his cabin to pour himself a drink and get a little rest. He had been working so hard.

Sunny was right: White informed D'Angelo that Bjørlund was planning on suing the festival. Suing? For what? Joy had asked. For maltreatment and breach of contract. Joy hung up and reluctantly went to report the conversation to Flox. She knew he wouldn't want to hear the news about being sued, especially because that would have been something for Anita to handle, but she was just trying to do her job. She really was.

"And that's when I found him," she said. "It was so horrible...."

"I know, Joy," Yumi said. "And so unfair." Now was not the time to mention he had his faults. "So unfair."

Jacobus heard horses' hooves again. No mistaking this time. They were coming fast. The Lone Ranger again, no doubt. And it sounded like he brought a posse with him.

"Where the hell have you been?" Jacobus said as Dance approached Flox's

144

cabin. "You're out chasing your tail for some wandering camper while there's a murderer on the loose and look what happens."

"That's enough out of you," Dance said. "It may not be my job to be a cop here, but there's going to be some order around here. You included."

Straightforward enough for me, Jacobus thought.

Dance ordered his men to immediately clear the cabin of the dozen or so inside it even if they had to use force, and sequester them at the festival office. He would interview them one at a time, including Jacobus, Yumi, and Joy D'Angelo. One of Dance's men began taking photos of the carnage to hand over to law enforcement when and if they eventually arrived.

Dance feared that once word got out there had been another murder, the hundreds of people who had already been under enough duress would collectively snap and the situation would get out of control. He had his men order everyone who had been in the barn to stay there until further notice. If anyone got out of line, their names would be taken and reported to the authorities, subject to arrest, once they arrived.

"That's awfully draconian, don't you think?" Yumi said. "Couldn't that just make the situation worse?"

"What would you suggest, ma'am? Bingo?"

"No, Bach. What if you give them the stick, and I'll give them the carrot and play some music?"

"Not a bad idea," Dance said. "A little unaccompanied Bach could definitely help soothe the savage breast."

Yumi went off to get her violin, with instructions to be back in an hour for her interview with Jacobus.

Ten minutes later, Dance was sitting at the desk in Sunny Flox's office, and one by one he commenced questioning everyone who had been at the cabin when he arrived, demanding explanations of where they had been up to the moment D'Angelo had discovered Flox's body. One by one, Dance had his men cross-check and corroborate their alibis to the best of their ability. And one by one, he excused them. All of them. Yumi returned and reported that everyone in the barn, though reasonably upset, had not yet revolted.

"So now that you've narrowed it down, Dance," Jacobus said, at the end of his interview, "we know whoever did it was either a musician or a concertgoer who *wasn't* at Flox's cabin when you arrived."

"Mr. Jacobus, I'll ask you to mind your own business. Go back to your cabin, please. And stay there."

"But I don't have a goddamn cabin!" Jacobus argued. When he heard Dance slam his hand on the desk, he changed his tone. "Hey, I can't help it if I'm just a wandering minstrel."

"Then just do me a favor and wander off, if you don't mind."

Yumi offered Jacobus the use of her cabin to spend the night. She would stay with Joy in hers. Joy needed someone there with her, Yumi suggested, and Joy readily agreed. In fact, she begged Yumi. The thought of being alone, after what had happened to Anita and now Sunny—she couldn't get the sight of his mangled body out of her head—scared her to death.

"I just have one question, Dance," Jacobus said before they departed.

"Mr. Jacobus, have you ever heard the term gadfly?"

"Why? Do you have them on Antelope Island?"

"Never mind. What is it?"

"What if this camper that's gone missing was murdered, too?"

"Don't think that hasn't crossed my mind. That's one reason it's important we find him. Or her."

"You mean, you don't know if it's a goddamn man or woman?" Jacobus asked.

Yumi covered Jacobus's mouth with her hand.

"All I meant was," Jacobus, pulling her hand away and continuing in a less quarrelsome tone, "aren't you supposed to sign in or something when you go camping? One of those regulations? Not that I'd ever go camping."

"You're right, Mr. Jacobus," Dance said. "Everyone has to fill out a registration form. Name, number of nights, how many are in the party. But this person's registered name is Gene, so it could be either a man or a woman, meaning we have to keep our eyes out for anyone who looks like they're in distress. Even though the hail's stopped and the rain isn't so bad right now, with the wind still blowing like a banshee, he or she could be wandering around in the dark out in the elements. Hopefully, we won't find anyone face down in the lake. Hopefully, we'll find this Gene soon. In fact, before we leave here, we'll ask around. For all we know, Gene could have come to the concert. Good night, Mr. Jacobus. Thank you for your interest."

Yumi, her arm around Joy D'Angelo's quivering shoulders, led the way back to her cabin with Jacobus following in his former student's footsteps. *Ironic, in a way,* he thought. *It used to be the other way around.* When they arrived, she told him to make himself at home and said good night. She left him there and the two women set off for Joy's cabin.

Once the door closed behind him, Jacobus realized how exhausted he was. It had been a day from hell. A single day. He thought having to leave his cherished solitude in the Berkshires would be the worst of it. He'd go to Utah, join his friend Nathaniel where they'd go to a splendid concert performed by his protégée, and celebrate at the end of the weekend with a stomach-filling barbecue! What a hallucination that turned out to be, if a blind man may admit to hallucinating. In a single day, he had been in the vortex of a natural disaster and two murders. Under normal circumstances, the aggravation of his missing luggage and missing meals would have made him crotchety, but those were all but forgotten in the maelstrom.

Now he realized how much he had exerted himself, not only mentally but also physically; he could barely move his arms and legs in order to get into bed. Sitting on the edge of the mattress, it struck him with revulsion that he was wearing the clothes of a dead man. He tried not to, but he could smell Sunny Flox on his own skin. He undressed as hastily as his wearied bones would allow, and flung the clothes into a far corner where he wouldn't trip over them and—his dark sense of irony always tugging at him—kill himself. Having already familiarized himself with the simple floor plan, he had little difficulty feeling his way into the bathroom to do the usual ablutions. Reaching for a hand towel, he discovered Yumi had hung his own clothes up to dry. *So considerate,* Jacobus thought. *Where did she learn that from? Not from me.*

Jacobus groped his way back to bed and crumpled gratefully into it. As before, he pulled the blankets over his head, not that it was any more or less comfortable, but to block out the raging, evil wind that continued to rattle the window panes and whistle through its cracks. He might not exactly be Vivaldi's trembling shepherd, but he certainly commiserated with the poor schmuck. In another sense, which he admitted to himself was a childish conceit, by hiding under the blankets he wrapped himself in a metaphorical, protective cocoon, blocking out having to think about two murders. Why should it affect him? he argued. He barely knew, let alone cared about, those two people. Kid stuff. People get murdered every day. Why should he have to get involved? Let Dance deal with it. All Jacobus wanted to do was go to sleep.

There was a knock on the door.

"Jake, it's me," Yumi said.

"I know this tune. Come on in."

"I can only stay for a minute. I have to get back to Joy. She's in bad shape."

"Understood. Which means what you have to tell me is important. Like, what you meant by 'something else' outside Flox's office? As in, 'I have Joy with me. *And something else.'*"

"Right. It's what I found next to Sunny's body during all that confusion."

"You found the note?"

"No. I didn't see that."

"Then, the murder weapon, perhaps?" Good girl, my Yumi. Always keeping her eyes and ears open.

"It could be. In fact, it probably is."

"Maybe you should've just left it there," Jacobus said. "Or given it to Dance. It could get you in trouble, removing evidence from a crime scene. At least, that's what they say on *CSI: Miami.*"

"Actually, my concern was that it could get *you* in trouble."

"Me! Why me?"

"Because what I found next to Sunny was Hocus. That's why I took it."

His walking stick! How could it have gotten from the tent to Flox's office? Who had moved it from one murder scene to the other? The person who killed both Talbot and Flox, who else? Was it the murder weapon? It was still speculation, but Jacobus had little doubt that it was. But why? To frame him? That made no sense. No one would believe he was physically capable of either murder—which he wasn't. And besides, he could prove he wasn't anywhere close to either of the two victims when they were killed. So what was it all about? All he knew was that Yumi had taken a big risk to protect him. It could get her in trouble if anyone found out. He owed her one.

"I've got to get back to Joy," she said and handed Hocus back to Jacobus. He wasn't all that sure he wanted to handle it anymore, and as soon as she left he stood it in a far corner. Thoughts of burning it entered his head, but exited just as quickly. That would definitely throw suspicion upon him if he was caught doing that. What about fingerprints? If Dance put two and two together, couldn't fingerprints be incriminating? Nah, Dance is just a park ranger. What would he know about fingerprints? Besides, dozens of people could've handled that stick. And how are you going to pull fingerprints off a stick, anyway? Dumb questions such as those, which he knew he couldn't answer, were a symptom of exhaustion. They whirled through his mind until sleep temporarily put him out of his misery.

But ears never sleep. Hours later, in the midst of troubled dreams, even with his head covered by blankets, even with the howling wind, Jacobus's deft hearing did not miss perceiving the mechanical click of the cabin door's rustic latch—a sound as out of place as it was soft—slowly and quietly depressed. Instantly, he was fully awake and on high alert. *This better be Yumi,* he thought. *Maybe she forgot something. It could be Dance. Yeah, maybe it's Dance wanting to pester me about some inconsistency in my alibi. If it's not Yumi or Dance, I could be in deep shit.*

Hocus was too far away for Jacobus to grab if it came to protecting himself, though the idea of killing the killer with the same murder weapon had more than a dash of poetic justice. He remained motionless under his blanket.

It wasn't Yumi. Nor was it the murderous threat he was half expecting. It was a man's voice, not Dance's, just above a whisper.

"Want me to take my pants off?"

Jacobus almost laughed out loud from relief.

"Feeling frisky, are we, Marcus?" he replied.

"Mr. Jacobus!"

"You're sharp as a tack, lover boy. But sorry to disappoint you, I'm not in the mood tonight." Jacobus was unable to repress a wheezing laugh any longer.

He heard Renfro's steps beating a hasty retreat.

"Whoa there, young buck! Hold on a second," he said. "Since you're here, we need to chat."

Jacobus popped his head out from under the blankets. With wild wiry gray hair and with his opaque, glazed-over eyes, exposed without his dark glasses, he must have looked like a Jack-in-the-box from a child's most terrifying nightmare.

"What about?" Renfro asked.

"Just a few questions I've been asking myself for the past hours as I tried to block two murders from my mind and get some sorely needed rest."

"What questions?"

"For starters: Why it happened to be you who found Anita Talbot, suddenly dead? Or why this evening in the barn you were the first to leave our cozy klatch, so tired, you said, but were nowhere to be found when Flox's body was discovered in his cabin? And now you seem to have miraculously regained your *joie de vivre* and you're back here jonesin' for a little nooky! I must say, you've got chutzpah. And stamina."

"I already answered the first question. I was helping folks out of the Big Top and happened to see Anita. I didn't know she was dead. I just thought she needed some assistance. Besides, if I'd killed her I could've just walked away and no one would've been the wiser."

"Unless it was a pretense of innocence. Y'know, like the sobbing parents who call the police to report their kid is missing. Then the cops find the poor, dead kid in a ditch and the parents wail away, 'Who could've done this to our baby?' And a day later they confess. You wouldn't be the first."

"Mr. Jacobus, you go ahead and believe what you want to believe. Just because… Never mind."

"Just because what?" Jacobus asked.

"I said never mind. The answer to your second question," Renfro replied, "is that I was in my cabin. I had no idea Sunny was dead until that park ranger knocked on my door."

That response was a non sequitur. Just because Renfro says he was in his cabin when Flox was killed eliminates the possibility he was feigning innocence about Talbot? That made no sense at all. Where was this conversation leading? Nowhere fast. What Renfro had going for him was having Yumi in his corner. She was a good judge of character, generally anyway, and had obviously befriended this guy. More than befriend, it seemed! Jacobus's analytic skills were stymied by fatigue, at least for the moment. He couldn't put two cogent thoughts together. But if the phones were working in the morning he would call Nathaniel. There was something missing, to be sure.

"Okay, Marcus. Let's leave it at that. I'm just trying to figure things out. In the meantime, how about a little cuddle?"

"I think I'll take a raincheck, if you don't mind."

Renfro made a quick getaway, making Jacobus smile. Yumi and Renfro! Making music together, eh? Well, there were a few decent duets for violin and cello, but apparently they didn't need music. His smile was fleeting, as another thought took over his mental space.

"Just because…" That damned unfinished thought, choked off as if someone had gripped Renfro by the throat. He was jolted by another thought. Was the reason he assumed for Renfro's visit—that he had the hots for Yumi—the real one? Or was Renfro's plan something more sinister, and then he just played along with Jacobus's mirth upon being discovered? It kept Jacobus awake until a meadowlark—God only knew how the bird had managed to survive the storm—cheerily announced the new day had come. That's when Jacobus fell asleep.

Chapter Twelve

Jacobus was awakened by a gust of wind that not only rattled the cabin's windows, it also ushered in a foul odor, not of the lake's intense salty brine but of something distinctly worse. Visions of a pendular latrine danced in his head. The meadowlark was no longer singing. It must've fled. Smart bird. A knock on the door a few minutes later got him out of bed.

"Good morning, Jake," Yumi said, with exaggerated brightness.

"The answer is yes," Jacobus said.

"But you don't even know the question."

"Of course I do. I can smell the shit. Wake up and smell the ordure! That means the outhouses are overloaded beyond capacity, so now they need to use all the musicians' bathrooms to make do, as it were. And with your Pollyanna tone of voice, you're about to ask me: Would I mind getting dressed and get the hell out of here so they can come in and take a crap?"

"If you wouldn't mind."

"Not at all. It must be about seven o'clock anyway."

"How did you know?"

"Because that's when I get a caffeine headache if I haven't had any coffee, and mine is splitting."

It was fortunate Jacobus's own clothes had dried, because he would rather have gone naked than wear a dead man's outfit again, and he knew Yumi would be scandalized if he walked around naked. The one item of Flox's he did not eschew was the baseball cap, because if he spent a day under intense sun without one he would end up like its previous owner. Dead.

Jacobus followed his nose to the barn, appreciating on the way that the rain had stopped. They were served their meager breakfast, another small portion of baked beans and three Ritz crackers. Jacobus passed on the beans—suggesting that if they served something other than beans it might solve their latrine problem—and satisfied himself with a cup of camp coffee. With no electricity, water had been heated in a large pot over a campfire, into which coffee grounds had been stirred. After they settled to the bottom, the smoke-infused coffee was ladled out into cups. Jacobus took one sip, spit out the grounds that had remained obstinately afloat, and declared the coffee excellent.

The barn had served not only as the dining hall and triage center. It was also where many of the concertgoers had bedded down, having been provided with as many blankets as Jefferson Dance's park staff was able to muster. Some, who hadn't slept in the barn, spent the night on the floors of several of the musicians' cabins. But the majority had found shelter in their own cars in the parking lot, after shoveling the ice off of them.

Yumi had spent a difficult night with Joy D'Angelo in her cabin that seemed longer than the few hours that had actually passed. Whenever Yumi managed to fall asleep she was awakened by D'Angelo, crying out in fear every time she heard a sound outside the cabin, convinced that someone was going to come to harm her. It was perhaps an irrational fear, but not unjustified. There was a killer among them. In the end, Yumi gave up the prospect of sleep and spent the night comforting D'Angelo with soothing words and embraces.

When there was an early-morning knock on the door, D'Angelo ran into the bathroom, cowering, while Yumi answered it. It was Jefferson Dance, wanting to check on D'Angelo and let her know that he was now able to commit almost all of his men and most of his efforts on maintaining order and safety at the ranch. The missing camper, though a little the worse for wear, had returned to his tent. He hoped that information would provide some reassurance.

Coffee in hand, Jacobus needed to call Nathaniel, but the barn was not the right place. He did not want to discuss murder with all those potentially prying ears listening in. So Yumi and Jacobus made the call from the bench overlooking the lake where Nathaniel and Yumi had sat together so peacefully a week earlier. With the exception of the roiling waves, whose force was magnified by the lake's shallowness, it was a tranquil spot, one of the few at the moment. And, with the wind blowing into their faces from the lake toward the outhouses behind them, it sent the foul odor in the opposite direction from where they sat. A small comfort, perhaps, but a comfort nevertheless.

Though the rain had ceased, the wind hadn't conceded an inch, and Nathaniel reported that the persistent gale was forecast to continue indefinitely, making it too dangerous for boats or helicopters to access the island. The violent collision between the aggressive, moist airflow from the northwest and the pulverizing heat that had baked the region under an immovable blanket of high pressure were the conditions that had spawned a once-in-fifty-years storm, the meteorologists said.

Antelope Island hadn't been the only casualty. Wind gusts, compounding the effect of the suffocating blanket of ice, had toppled power lines and collapsed less sturdy structures for a hundred miles, over the entire Wasatch Mountain region from Ogden down to Provo. The damage had been extensive, and in Nathaniel's assessment, it didn't seem that Antelope Island, an essentially uninhabited semi-wilderness area, was a high priority in the cleanup in the storm's aftermath.

Jacobus had only managed to tell Nathaniel the basics, that in addition to Talbot being dead, Flox had now been murdered, when the connection began to break up. Jacobus rushed an updated list of names whose pasts he wanted Nathaniel to dig up and filter through a sieve. It was like panning for gold, except instead of nuggets of precious metal he anticipated the deposits would be toxic as lead. While Nathaniel went about his fact-finding, and as long as law enforcement authorities were thwarted in their ability to gain access to the island, Yumi and Jacobus would continue to probe on their own. To Jacobus, that seemed the only logical strategy.

"Backstory! Backstory!" Jacobus hollered into the phone.

"I heard you the first time," Nathaniel said. Then he was gone. The connection disappeared entirely into frustrating inaudibility.

He handed Yumi's phone back to her.

"Piece of shit died on me," he said. "Phones in the old days didn't die on you."

"Maybe," Yumi said. "But then again, in the old days there wouldn't have been any phone line here to begin with, and even if there was, you would've had to pay long-distance rates, so you probably wouldn't have made the call in the first place."

"Oh, yes I would have!"

"Really?"

"Of course. I would've called collect."

Though the presence of Jefferson Dance's full staff was intended to provide a heightened level of security, its unintended ancillary effect was to increase tension and anxiety. Dance's crew was everywhere, especially around Flox's cabin and the festival office, questioning everyone's whereabouts at the time the two murders took place. With so many people and so few resources, general confusion reigned. The only thing favoring the authorities' ability to maintain order, if it could be called that, was that no one was able to leave the island.

Schumann! Jacobus recognized it immediately. *Kreisleriana*, Robert Schumann's brilliant composition for solo piano that he had written in a manic four days! Though the sound of the piano barely cut through the blasted wind, the music brought the first smile to Jacobus's face since Yumi had started her performance of *Summer* the previous evening. The previous evening? A matter of hours. Jesus.

"Let's go!" Jacobus said. He tugged at Yumi's sleeve and pushed himself off the bench using Hocus for leverage. "Music! I need to hear some music."

For anyone watching Jacobus bang his walking stick on the ground, Hocus appeared to be a divining rod with the uncanny power to direct Jacobus to a reservoir, not of water but of music. They forged a path through tall grass, browned from drought but dripping wet from the storm. It led them to the piano shed, a small structure where the precious festival piano had been stored in semi-controlled conditions. Now, of course, in the absence of air-conditioning and with the abrupt increase of moisture, the atmospheric conditions had already thrown the piano out of tune. But for now, that was a minor consideration. There was music! And Jamie Barov was playing it, with a small crowd gathered outside—since there was no room inside—listening.

"Good morning, Mr. Jacobus!" Barov called out sunnily as he continued to play. "It's a beautiful day, don't you think?"

Jacobus didn't answer. The question was probably rhetorical, anyway, and furthermore, it made him uncomfortable to be singled out. Could that have been intentional? Some sort of deflection? Whatever, he was too enraptured with the music.

Robert Schumann was not Beethoven, but then again who was? Yet there was perhaps no greater *under*appreciated genius than Schumann. And what a tragic life! Whether he was manic-depressive, bipolar, clinically depressed, or suffered from some other unnamed, undiagnosed affliction—they called all those things "melancholia" in those days—no one knew for certain. But when Schumann was in his creative phase, he wrote his greatest compositions and at a frantic pace, faster than Jacobus could have written his own name (when he could still see). At other times, at the other extreme, for months on end, Schumann could not lift his hand in order to put pen to paper, could not utter a word, so immobilized was he from his depression. His final months ended in an insane asylum, diplomatically called a sanitorium.

That contrast, between blinding brilliance and absolute mental inertia, made Jacobus wonder about Barov's choice of music for the morning. In a way, it could be interpreted as a reflection of the events that had transpired since he had arrived on Antelope Island. First, the calm, then the violent storm with its attendant catastrophes. And now, again, a counterbalance? A sudden tranquility? Could Barov's choice mean something more, even if only subliminally? Whatever the motivation, the music had a calming effect on the listeners, distracting them from their troubles.

Barov continued chattering while he played, as if his hands had brains of their own. That was nothing unique for a musician, except that it was a damn lot easier for a pianist to talk while playing than for a violinist...or a flutist, for that matter!

"Folks, I have an idea!" Barov said as the music played on. He must have been addressing this to the general audience, and maybe Yumi as well. "What do you say we carry the piano to the barn and play some impromptu chamber music? Why should we let a perfectly good festival go to hell in a handbasket just over a measly rainstorm? What do you say?"

Everyone cheered. Even Jacobus thought it was a good idea. Even though Barov had conveniently avoided mentioning the deaths.

Yumi ran off to get her violin and a volume of Mozart sonatas for piano and violin she had brought to the festival to practice. In the meantime, Jacobus followed behind a levitated eight-foot Steinway grand piano, transported on the shoulders of a dozen celebrating men, like the groom at an Orthodox Jewish wedding. Even the black-and-white of the piano matched the image. A true labor of music love.

Sometimes musical spontaneity is a disaster. With the best of intentions, sight-reading musicians can lose their way in a rabbit hole of hyper-creativity trying to "make music," tearing apart the carefully constructed architecture of a composition by maximizing their spur-of-the-moment feelings. At other times sight-reading can be inspirational, when the joy of the music, of the collaboration, transcends the infinite number of bytes of detailed information that is exchanged between the composer and the re-creators. This was one of those occasions when it was the latter.

The audience could not have hoped for a more stimulating hour of music than Yumi Shinagawa and Jamie Barov sight-reading the Mozart sonatas in G Major, E Minor, and B-flat Major, after which they took a much deserved intermission. Not that anyone could forget what had happened the night before, but at least there was a sense that not all was evil in the world. On the other hand, like the character of Death in Saint-Saëns's tone poem, *Danse Macabre*, looks could be deceiving. The charming, elegant façade could conceal a decidedly wicked personality.

Jacobus waited long enough for the crowd to disperse sufficiently for him to approach the bench. The piano bench.

"Bravo, Barov!" Jacobus said. When Barov didn't respond, he added,

"What's wrong? Am I not the first person to have come up with that brilliantly clever anagram?"

"I'm afraid it doesn't quite rise to the level of Oscar Wilde, Mr. Jacobus. And yes, I've heard that one often. Too often, I'd say."

"Sorry."

"The games people play with names. Mozart even signed his name backwards at times—*Gnagflow Trazom*."

"The term is 'cancrizans,' if I remember correctly," Jacobus said. "Writing words and music backwards. 'Retrograde.' I suppose Mozart could have done it to hide his identity for some reason, but knowing Mozart, I suspect it was just for fun."

"Yes, and sometimes he would also anagramize his name. *Romatz*. He was like that. He liked games. You could say that Max Reger was the only composer whose last name wouldn't matter whether it was backwards or forwards. Just like his music. But I do appreciate your sentiment, regardless, especially coming from someone as highly esteemed as you."

"In this heat, more '*esteamed*' than esteemed. Say, Barov, if you've got a minute, I'd like to ask you a question."

"Sure. Go ahead."

Jacobus suggested they find a spot some distance from the barn because the question was of a more personal nature. Yumi begged off, saying she had to go check on Joy D'Angelo, who insisted on remaining barricaded in her cabin. As Barov and Jacobus walked, they discussed the genius of Schumann and Mozart, and Barov mentioned a recently published book that proposed the theory that one could become an expert on virtually anything if one simply dedicated ten thousand hours to the task. For Jacobus, that notion was as nonsensical as it was unprovable, and held no water when trying to understand the brilliance of those two composers. Mozart was a genius by the age of seven, and Jacobus himself had spent far more than ten thousand hours learning the Bach *Chaconne*, yet where had all that practice got him? It was more likely he'd regain his sight than be able to call himself an expert.

"What can I help you with?" Barov asked when Jacobus felt confident their voices would not be overheard. "No doubt this is about Anita and Sunny."

"No doubt. Maybe you can help me fill in the blanks. From what I've learned, there were certain things that tied Anita and Sunny together in life. They were in the same profession, they worked together, obviously. On the other hand, their personalities couldn't have been more different. You know what I mean. From what everyone tells me, Flox was cordial, diffident even. He liked people. Talbot was—how can I say this tactfully?—the opposite. But so far, the only thing that seems to tie them together in death—the only common denominator in their murders—is your offhand comment about two bitches in heat. What I want to know is, how you felt after you learned that Talbot had reported your comment to Flox."

"How I felt?" Barov asked. He sounded surprised.

"Yes, personally."

Barov laughed heartily.

"What's so funny?" Jacobus asked. "I'd like to know. Maybe it'll help me get Yumi to laugh at some of my jokes."

"I'm sorry," Barov said. "But, believe me, this is the first I've heard that Anita did that! I had no idea!"

"Yet you think it's funny?"

"Certainly. I mourn for her, of course. And for Sunny. But that is so typically Anita."

"How so?"

"She's had that history, you could say, of taking offense when there was no offense at all. Either intended or in substance. It was a harmless comment."

"Agreed. Except in this case," Jacobus said, "it might have been lethal."

Barov turned serious.

"Yes, I suppose. I suppose it could have been, if that was indeed the link. And poor Sunny! If his only fault was to have been the recipient of Anita's report. You mentioned that the only thing that ties their deaths together was my quip."

"Right."

"Let me make a slight correction. It's the only thing we know about *at this point in time*."

"Granted," Jacobus said. The man was quick on his feet. He had a brain.

Should that make him less suspicious, or more?

"So you want to know," Barov continued, "what do I make of the connection? I don't know. That's my truthful, if unhelpful, answer. What do *you* make of it?"

"Maestro!" An unfamiliar voice. Must be an audience member. One colleague would not call another one "maestro."

"Yes?" Barov asked.

"My wife says to ask if we could have more music from you and Miss Shinagawa. She wants to know if you can play the Pachelbel *Canon?*"

Barov gave Jacobus a subtle nudge in the side. These philistines, the nudge said.

"If only we'd brought the music!" Barov said to his new fan, sighing quite dramatically, as if it would have been his greatest pleasure, if only…. "But maybe some Brahms would do?"

"Okay, I suppose."

Barov excused himself and went off to find Yumi in order to satisfy not only the request, but also his own compulsion to perform, and even perhaps to escape Jacobus's further questioning. Jacobus meandered in the opposite direction, finding his way back to the old bench where he and Yumi had sat previously, because he had to think and he could not conceivably do so while listening to music.

Yes, he thought, *it's the internal satisfaction of playing music that drives the performer. Of holding the instrument. Of creating the vibrations. Though the word, satisfaction, does an injustice to the intensity of that feeling. The audience is important. Essential, obviously. Without an audience, there would be no performance. But the audience is ultimately no more than the performer's sounding board. His straight man. Creating the sound is everything. Orgasmic, if some of the onstage writhing currently in vogue is to be believed. If a great musician like Barov were to be deprived of that ultimate gratification by someone else's misguided intervention, could that drive him to distraction?* Jacobus thought it could.

The immediate question Jacobus asked himself was whether Barov's congeniality was an artful façade, under which brewed a pent-up anger at Talbot and Flox for laying the groundwork of an unfair formal complaint against him. He had denied knowing that Talbot had reported his comment to Flox, but who knew if Barov was telling the truth? With both of them dead, there was no way now to either prove or disprove it. Yumi had discovered Talbot's communique to Flox on his notepad. Why couldn't Barov have as well? And if he did know about it, what better way to deflect his involvement than to laugh it away? "Typical Anita." Maybe it was. Maybe it wasn't. Yumi had also told him that Barov said, "Sometimes you just want to put 'em out of their misery." Prophetic?

Jacobus was about to wipe his nose on his sleeve, but restrained himself in respect for the dead. Also, because he was distracted by the first graceful phrase of the Brahms A Major Sonata, *Allegro amabile*, spinning through the air. The recital had recommenced. *Amabile*, a rarely used musical term, meaning "charming, gracious, tender." What the world could use more of.

His thoughts were interrupted not only by the music, but also by a voice belonging to someone whose approach had caught him unawares. *Must be getting old and lazy. Getting? That happened long ago.*

"They play well together."

The accent was familiar, mildly tinged with the half-hidden haughtiness of a European intellectual. It didn't take Jacobus more than a moment to place it. Bjørlund.

"Jealous?" Jacobus asked.

"Of course! It's always better to be the performer than to be the bystander."

If that was intended to be a backhanded swipe at Jacobus, it was far too subtle for him to be troubled by it. And Bjørlund sounded far too chipper. It was out of joint with the current circumstances. But Jacobus would play along with it and see where it might get him.

"To be or not to be?" Jacobus replied. "The performer, that is."

"Ah, Hamlet. My tragic countryman. Well done, Mr. Jacobus," Bjørlund said. "The question of life and death, as we have here. Of murder most foul. And you're correct. For some, music is that important. That critical. Yes, such terrible business this has been. I couldn't sleep a wink all last night."

"Too many roommates, eh?" Jacobus asked.

"So to speak. I donated my cabin to our damp visitors, exiled from my own Elsinore."

"Ha! Never a borrower nor a landlord be!" Jacobus said.

"Yes, Polonius had a point. But those soggy music lovers had it the worst, trapped under that tent. Would you believe I ended up sleeping in Waldstein's cabin?"

Jacobus laughed, imagining the two adversaries grappling over who got the sheet.

"Strange bedfellows," he said. "Alas, poor Dieter. He knew you."

"Strange bedfellows, indeed. Weiss and Barov as well."

"So they all knew you. What about the girls?"

"Yumi was with the D'Angelo girl. Hannah and Cornelia slept in Ingrid's cabin. It's like your American-style summer camps. Bunks, you call them?"

More like bunk, Jacobus thought, considering Bjørlund's forced jovial tone.

"I understand Marcus is a big guy," Jacobus said. "Must have been pretty cozy, all five of you piled into one crummy little bed." *Too bad Yumi wasn't part of the conversation right now*, he thought. *She'd poke me in the ribs good.*

"Chamber music is very intimate," Bjørlund responded, "but perhaps not *that* intimate. And it wasn't that bad. Marcus was elsewhere."

"Elsewhere?"

"Somewhere. I don't know."

After another few minutes of an unproductive, desultory tête-à-tête, Jacobus brought the conversation around once again to that intriguing little detail Yumi had accidentally uncovered on Flox's notepad. The little detail that did not make sense in the present context. Yet.

Yumi and Barov were playing the second movement of the Brahms, *Andante tranquillo*, in the distance. What could be more lovely than that? More innocent? Jacobus asked himself. Could people kill each other over music? Did they?

"When Jamie scolded you and Waldstein for acting like two bitches in heat," Jacobus said, "you couldn't have appreciated that. Am I right?"

"I'm afraid you are wrong, Mr. Jacobus. If someone *else* had said that, like Anita for example, we probably would have attacked her, too, in the same manner we were attacking each other. But the way Jamie said it, and with his smile, you knew it was well-intended. It made it hard for us not to laugh at ourselves. And once you laugh at yourself, it's hard to be angry at someone else. Don't you think?"

I do think. Don't I?

"*Cogito. Ergo interrogo,*" Jacobus said.

"Excuse me?"

"I think. Therefore, I ask: Don't you think it made Barov angry when he found out Anita reported Barov's comment to Flox?"

"She did that?" Bjørlund said.

He sounded genuinely surprised at the thought, no longer sporting the Hans Christian Andersen, happily-ever-after tone of voice he had pasted on. On the other hand, good musicians have the ability to express multilayered levels of every emotion under the sun through their instruments even though they might not feel it themselves. Why not through their voice, too? If one practiced enough...

"Apparently so," Jacobus said.

"I wouldn't think that of Jamie," Bjørlund said. "First of all, it assumes Jamie had knowledge Anita had done such a horrible thing. Do we know this for a fact?"

"We don't."

"See! And even if he had known, to be angry enough to kill her and then Sunny? Not Jamie. That is simple fantasy."

That seemed to be the consensus. But. He could be wrong. There was a possible alternative ending here. An "or." Was it possible Bjørlund insisted upon Barov's innocence in order to take suspicion away from himself? To protect oneself by pretending to protect another theoretical suspect? Jacobus chastised himself for such convoluted thinking. He could tie himself into knots more intractable than a Reger fugue. Bjørlund had used the verbs "think" and "know." Conjecture versus fact. So much *think, think, think.* Jacobus needed to *know, know, know.* But what was there to know and how would he find it? There was only one more thread left to follow.

"You still going to sue the festival, Bjørlund?"

"You seem to know everything, Mr. Jacobus," Bjørlund said, sounding genuinely surprised once again.

"Not everything. By no means, not everything. Yet. But you were pretty peeved when you were yelling at Flox in the office last evening and then the call from, what was his name, your agent?"

"Lawrence White. And he's not my agent. He's my manager."

"Sorry. How could I have made such a blunder? In any event, the important thing is, he threatened to sue the festival. No ifs, ands, or buts. You must've been pretty angry to get hold of your manager and have him call pronto like that. What was it you said about your treatment? 'Degrading'? 'Insulting'? Must have made you angry. Angry enough to kill someone, maybe? How much was Lawrence shooting for? One million? Two million—"

"It was a mistake."

"A mistake? You mean your manager called the wrong festival?"

"Don't be ludicrous. As I said in the barn, I had behaved irrationally. Once I had a chance to calm down and saw that we were all in the same predicament, that nothing could be done about it, I called Lawrence back to tell him to forget about the threat, but I wasn't able to get hold of him because of the phone problems. I didn't even know it had gone as far as it did until you just told me.

"And think about this, Mr. Jacobus, because you are such a logical thinker. If I had wanted to sue the festival, why would I have turned around and killed the golden goose?"

Well, I've laid another egg, Jacobus thought. *And it isn't golden. Bjørlund had a point.* Baffled and frustrated, he decided it was time to go back to the barn and listen to Brahms. It was already the final movement, *Allegro grazioso*, and if there was anything that could put him back into a good mood, or at least get his mind off of murder, it was that.

Bjørlund asked Jacobus if he needed someone to accompany him to the barn, but Jacobus had no desire for Bjørlund's continued company. There was something he didn't care for in Bjørlund's character. Something subtly deceitful. Something rotten in Denmark. Withholding, perhaps. Maybe there was nothing to it. Hardly enough to accuse someone of murder. Maybe the reason he felt the way he did about Bjørlund was that he didn't care for the violinist's playing. That he wasn't convinced with Bjørlund's Baroque-style Beethoven. It was too narrow. Too reedy. Maybe Bjørlund was a perfectly fine individual. It was so hard to separate the man from the musician. So hard, with the ability of music to weave a glowing cape around a cancerous soul. Like the beguiling sirens of Greek mythology, luring the innocents to their doom with their enchanting song.

Jacobus had found that out the hard way, years ago, in his lethal confrontation with the conductor Vaclav Herza, a consummate maestro but whose evil was as powerful as his musicianship. Bjørlund was not that, for sure, in any sense. But who was he, really? And for that matter, Jacobus asked himself, who is anyone? Really? Jacobus was starting to think that the older he got, the more indecisive (though no less judgmental) he was becoming. Did that mean he was acquiring greater wisdom, gaining the ability to weigh all sides of an issue with disinterested equanimity? Or was he simply becoming vacillating and doddering?

When they parted ways—Bjørlund to his practice, Jacobus to the barn—Jacobus attempted to conjure a quip derived from "Get thee to a nunnery," but his good humor had dried up and he couldn't think of an appropriate word that rhymed with nunnery, so he merely grunted a sound that was not a word at all to indicate their conversation was over.

It was slow going for Jacobus. The puddles from the day before had all but evaporated, but the pounding from the storm's wrath had left the ground strewn with branches torn from the grove of venerable cottonwoods surrounding the ranch. Tapping his way forward with Hocus, Jacobus poked the ground, flicking off his walking stick's distant relatives to avoid tripping, but before arriving at the barn, the Brahms had already reached its gentle conclusion. After the applause, Barov continued the recital with a solo piano piece by Scriabin, a composer whose talent Jacobus acknowledged but whose music he never enjoyed listening to. He changed direction.

When Jacobus was sitting on the bench, facing the lake, the prevailing wind had been in his face, from the east. Walking toward the barn it was on his back. Jacobus turned again, keeping the wind on his left cheek, because it had been on his right earlier in the morning when Yumi had escorted him from the cabin to breakfast. His direction should eventually lead him to Flox's cabin, which had been sixty-seven steps after Yumi's. But with all the crap on the ground, the number of steps would increase. How could he keep track of—

"Care for some company?"

"Yumi."

She laced her right arm through his left, carrying her violin case in her other hand. As they walked, she guided him only when he began to veer off course. Otherwise, she let him lead. She knew from experience he would have it no other way.

"What do you think Brahms was like?" Jacobus asked. "As a person."

"If he was anything like the A Major Sonata, I'm sure he was a very nice person."

"It's my understanding he could be a real curmudgeon," Jacobus said.

"So what? You're a real curmudgeon, too, but you're also a very nice person. At least in my opinion." She kissed him on the cheek, which he wiped off.

"What was that all about?" he asked.

"I just wanted to see you be a curmudgeon," she said, laughing.

Their mood became much more somber as they approached Flox's cabin. Jefferson Dance was there. Whether he had been there the entire day or had come and gone and returned again, Jacobus didn't know. But he was glad to find him, because to talk to Dance was the reason he wanted to go to the cabin.

"What do you think of Brahms, Dance?" Jacobus asked. He could care less what Dance's answer was. He only asked to stroke his ego, to loosen him up for tougher questions later.

"Is this a trick question to find out if I've heard of Brahms?" Dance asked.

"You've already established your bona fides. I'm serious."

"I'd say Brahms was a first-rate craftsman with second-rate sentiment."

"That's a little harsh," Yumi said. "Don't you think?"

"Second-rate, you mean? Not intended. After Beethoven and Mozart, I'd say second-rate's a pretty ringing endorsement."

Jacobus was impressed with Dance's straightforward perceptiveness, especially since in his initial estimation, Dance was not much more than a glorified cowboy. But he wasn't interested enough to pay much attention to the ensuing debate between Dance and Yumi over what defined second-rate, and waited until the discussion ended in stalemate.

"You learn anything more about what went on here?" Jacobus asked.

Dance sighed.

"I've seen my share of tangles before—goes with the territory—but I've always left charge of a murder scene to others and don't much care for it. From what it looks like, I'd say whoever killed Flox also killed Talbot, and that person was an amateur. More than that I'd have a hard time with."

"The first part—that it was the same person who killed them both—seems clear to me," Jacobus said. "But why amateur? With Talbot, he picked his moment and did it even while there were people around."

"That's a puzzle, certainly. But I'd still say amateur because of what happened to Flox. It looks like someone tried to strangle him, but was unable to, and so he swung at Flox with something, and I say swung because of all the damage in the cabin. He swung a lot, meaning he was inefficient, and the weapon was something hard—something like your walking stick."

"I have an alibi!" Jacobus said.

Dance laughed for the first time in Jacobus's recollection.

"Don't worry, Mr. Jacobus," Dance said. "You're not on any suspect list. But it was definitely a hard object, judging from the wounds and broken bones. On the other hand, I don't think the perpetrator was particularly strong, since it took an inordinate number of blows to kill him. Maybe it was a woman."

"I have an alibi, too!" Yumi said.

"Don't trust her!" Jacobus said. "She has a black belt in judo."

"Only second degree, though," Yumi amended.

"Whatever," said Jacobus.

"And that's been my problem," Dance said.

"You don't know the color of your belt?" Jacobus asked.

"I wish it was only that. My problem is, everyone's got an alibi. My men have questioned virtually all the folks who were at the concert last night. Everyone's been so cooperative, I almost feel guilty interviewing them. They've been through enough misery. But there are so many of them and so few of us, and as I mentioned, they're not trained investigators. And on top of that, we've got to take care of everyone until we can get some outside help. Just about run out of food. Not to mention we're getting low on water, both for here and for the folks in the campground."

"The showers seem to have worked well enough," Jacobus said.

"I'm talking about potable water. I hope you didn't drink the water from the shower."

That's all I need, Jacobus thought. *Dancing another jig with gastric distress.*

"And the natives are getting restless?" Jacobus asked, returning to the subject at hand.

"That sort of reference isn't much appreciated in these parts, Mr. Jacobus. But the answer is yes. Though we're doing the best we can, taking care of folks who're all hungry and tired, and some who're injured. But in the meantime, who knows who might've slipped through the cracks?"

"With so many the people here," Yumi said, "don't you think someone would've heard Sunny? Especially with such a struggle?"

"You'd think. But I've got a theory why no one did. With the storm still blowing through, you couldn't hardly hear yourself think, and with everyone huddled in the barn, Flox's cries might not have been able to cut through all the noise."

"But D'Angelo did," Jacobus said, trying to poke holes.

"D'Angelo didn't hear Flox," Dance reminded Jacobus. "She saw him."

Jacobus discovered that there was an idea bubbling around in his brain. Unbidden. It was hard to even call it an idea, it was so vague at first. Beginning as a mild sensation, gradually it gained momentum and solidity, crystallizing into a perception and finally a cogent thought, and at some point in the future, maybe it would turn into a plan. It had gathered its own traction, as most of his interesting thoughts seemed to. About to congratulate himself for his keen analytical power, he reminded himself that in the ten seconds it had taken to conceive this thought, Mozart would have plotted out an entire symphony. A good lesson in humility. Nevertheless, Jacobus sought to capture his idea and, consolidating it even as he talked, found a spot for it in the corner of his brain labeled "to be continued," reminding himself to talk to Yumi after parting from Dance.

"Hmm. Could be," Jacobus said. "Or…"

"Or what?"

"I've got a second theory. Or at least a variation on your theme."

"Let's have it."

"That Flox knew his killer. Meaning the first blow, whatever it was, was close in. It surprised and then subdued him, but didn't kill him. At first, he wouldn't have been inclined to call out, and then it would've been too late. He wouldn't have had time. Same with Talbot. That's what the two attacks had in common. Both Talbot and Flox knew who their killer was."

"A sucker punch?"

"As it were."

"If Jake is right," Yumi said, "then it would probably mean that…"

"Exactly," Jacobus said, finishing her thought. "It would probably mean that the killer is someone associated with the festival."

"A musician," Dance said.

"That's not exactly what I said, but probably."

"A disturbing thought," Dance said. "But that would certainly narrow down our work."

"Though let me remind you that you said you're not trained to do this kind of investigation."

"Did I?" Dance paused, and Jacobus wondered why. "Well, you don't need to rub it in."

"Not intending to," Jacobus said. "Except that you told us everyone had alibis."

"So far as we know. Why?"

"Well, might there not be a few people who don't?"

"Give me a for instance, if you don't mind."

"Little Miss Woe-Is-Me, Joy D'Angelo, for example. Jamie Barov, for another—"

"Not Jamie!" Yumi said.

"And last but not least, your cozy friend, Marcus Renfro."

"Jake!"

Chapter Thirteen

Yumi waited until they had parted company with Dance and had returned to her cabin. Jacobus knew what was about to come down the pike because she didn't say a word until they arrived and she closed the door behind them. She didn't actually close the door. To be precise, she slammed it.

"How dare you accuse these people of murder? They're my colleagues! They're the people I work with! They're—"

"I've done no such thing!" Jacobus shouted back. "All I've said, Yumi, is that they don't have alibis. For example, Won't-you-be-my-neighbor Barov wasn't with us in the barn when Flox was killed. Teary D'Angelo was the one who *claims* to have found Flox dead. And worst is Marcus Amorous, who not only just happened to find Anita Talbot dead, he also just happened to wander off from our group in the barn a scant half hour before the hue and cry went out that Flox had been beaten to death."

"But those three are the nicest people in the whole group," Yumi said. "Christian and Dieter and Franz Weiss, they're the nasty ones. But even with them, it's just impossible any one of them did such horrible things."

"Not quite impossible. Unlikely, but not impossible. In fact, it has to be possible, it *must* be possible, because there are two dead people and the only thing that's impossible is that they killed themselves."

"I suppose."

"And it's going to be up to you to figure out if they're all telling the truth."

"Me? Up to me? What are you talking about?"

"Not just you. You and Felix Mendelssohn."

171

Jacobus explained his plan, the one that had popped into his head while talking with Dance. His thinking was that if any of the festival group was indeed the murderer, they would be on guard if there was a whiff they were being scrutinized. So Jacobus proposed doing the opposite: Create a scenario as if everything was copasetic. Since the impromptu recital that Yumi and Barov performed earlier had been such a big hit with the audience, Jacobus argued, get the whole group together for a feel-good reading of the Mendelssohn Octet, which was already on the docket for performance. See if anyone acts out of character. See if anyone shows their hand.

"That sounds like a ridiculous idea to me," Yumi said. "Let's say, hypothetically, one of them truly was involved, what would there be about playing the Mendelssohn Octet that was going to get them to act out of character?"

"That's where you come in, Yumi. You need to get the ball rolling by acting out of character yourself."

"How, for example?"

"Be a prima donna," he said. "Put on airs. Play your opposite. Provoke the others. Give them a dose of 'an attitude.' "

"You mean, you want me to be a bitch in heat?"

Jacobus laughed.

"I don't know about the heat. But a bitch, one way or the other."

"I don't know if I'm able do that, Jake, in or out of heat."

"You'll be fine. All you have to do is pretend you're me."

"That might work. You'd certainly be the right role model. But, still. I play the violin. I'm not an actor."

"Don't act, then. Just think about what other musicians do and say at rehearsals that drive you nuts and make you want to kill them, and then all you have to do is repeat it. Blather, rinse, repeat."

"Still, Jake, it's horrible to think one of my colleagues is a murderer."

"Sure it is. I agree. It's horrible, and chances are none of them are. But if this is a way we can determine that, so much the better. And if one of them shows his hand, the good news is that it lifts the veil of suspicion from everyone else."

"No, Jake," Yumi said, after a pause. "I'm still not buying this. This is the weirdest scheme you've ever had. I think it's a total waste of time."

"Yumi, I admit I'm grasping at straws," Jacobus persisted. "But we've got no resources here. It could be that I'm wrong and that all of your colleagues are totally innocent. But," he reminded Yumi, "until we know who was behind the killings, everyone could be in danger. Including you."

"Okay, Jake, I'll do it, but did I just hear you admit you might be wrong?"

"I must have misspoken."

They discussed logistics. Yumi brought up the fact that the octet is written for eight string players, but does not include piano. What should they do with Barov? And what about Joy?

Jacobus acknowledged that complication, but was gratified it was Yumi who thought of it, because it meant that Yumi was onboard, and that was the main thing. In the end, they determined to seat Barov and D'Angelo in the audience on either side of Jacobus, where he could keep tabs on them. As far as plans went, it wasn't nearly as ingenious as it seemed when it first popped into his brain. It was like all those times woke up in the middle of the night with what at the moment seemed the most ravishing melody ever conceived, but when in the morning he recalled it, it was drivel, even more banal than the jingles on the TV commercials for local credit unions and discount furniture stores. This was how his current plan felt now. It was unlikely it would amount to anything, but until they were able to regain contact with Nathaniel, it was the best Jacobus could come up with. At least his ulterior motive for the plan would be realized: He would get to hear the Mendelssohn Octet, which was inevitably a joy.

Organizing a concert on the hoof was conceptually easy, but logistically challenging. As Yumi had discovered over the years, scheduling a simple string quartet rehearsal often required the combined sleight-of-hand of a Las Vegas magician with the diplomatic nuance of a United Nations ambassador. For each additional musician, the difficulty seemed to increase exponentially.

First, they had to track down the seven other musicians for the octet, not counting Barov and D'Angelo. Without the use of cellphones, this seemingly simple task took over an hour. Dieter Waldstein, Ingrid Goldman, and Cornelia Blum were the easiest to find, as they spent much of their time reading and writing. The others were scattered about the festival grounds. Renfro, who had become emotionally remote over the past week, was physically remote as well. Yumi discovered him wandering the Frary Peak slope just north of the ranch, and even after she caught his attention by waving her arms like a flagman on an aircraft carrier, he continued in the opposite direction. She jogged up the hill after him.

"What are you doing up here?" she asked, winded, with her hands on her thighs, when she caught up to him.

"Just walking. Wanted to get away. Why?"

Yumi proposed to him, as she had proposed to all the others, that they collaborate on the Mendelssohn, explaining how much the audience had enjoyed her performance of the Mozart and Brahms sonatas with Barov. How it helped everyone regain their equilibrium under such trying circumstances.

At first Renfro balked, claiming, not without justification, that reading through the Mendelssohn was a damn sight more difficult than the sonatas. For one, eight players versus two. Secondly, not all of the eight players had become comfortably familiar with each other's playing style. Three, the Mendelssohn's split-second precision required a lot of rehearsal, and so far, the ones they had hadn't gone particularly well. Chances were they would muck it up and the audience would not be pleased.

Even though Yumi believed Renfro had overstated his case, she acknowledged all the difficulties. But, notwithstanding Renfro's dogged resistance, she persevered, quietly insistent. Not the right moment to be the bitch, she told herself. And not the right moment to question his fickle behavior. At least not yet.

So she cajoled, for the time being: It's so much fun. Everyone loves the energy of that piece, even if it's not perfect. And under the current conditions, no one expects perfection anyway. And, don't forget, they had started to rehearse it before the Friday storm. The audience will appreciate the effort and the good intentions even if the actual performance is rough around the edges. It'll take their mind offs of everyone's troubles. She also mentioned, understated but underlined, that everyone else had agreed to do it, so it would only be Renfro holding back the entire enterprise. He wouldn't want to be the one to do that, would he? (What Yumi didn't mention was that she had used the same argument with everyone, only substituting one name for another.) Renfro finally agreed, though no less reluctantly than Yumi had initially agreed to Jacobus's scheme. They began their return to the ranch. With the wind gradually dying down, the heat was returning, and they slackened their pace to conserve energy.

Arriving back at the ranch, Yumi and Renfro gathered with the other musicians at the festival office. They discussed when they should begin their informal performance. Yumi pressed for as soon as possible, while both the idea and the weather were still fresh, and before the former cooled and the latter heated. After unnecessarily prolonged debate, during which everyone seemed to feel a need to append one superfluous consideration after another, it was agreed. They would begin in an hour, part of that time devoted to "advertising" the event by spreading the word among the widely scattered concertgoers, and then to practice their individual parts in whatever remaining few minutes were available.

Jacobus, who had remained in Yumi's cabin to rest, think, and go to the bathroom, finalized his stratagem upon hearing the autumnal lilt of a Chopin nocturne floating in from the direction of the barn. Barov. He couldn't help himself. He couldn't stop playing the piano. Jacobus admired that. Music oozing out of every pore. He decided he would first garner Barov's enthusiastic approbation for the octet performance, which he expected would be forthcoming. Next he would enlist the cheerful Barov to convince the mournful Joy D'Angelo, who had doggedly remained holed-up in her cabin, to join the festivities. Jacobus found it ironic that he had taken upon himself the unnatural burden of being the jolly, lighthearted one while assigning Yumi the opposite role. *We'll see which one of us is the better con artist,* he thought.

He had taken only a few steps when he heard someone approach him from behind, walking at a much faster pace than he.

"Mr. Jacobus."

"Ah, Dance. I figured it was you."

"How so?"

"The length of the stride gave me an estimate of height, so I knew it was a tall person. And the fast pace suggested it was you."

"Why do you say that?"

"Who else, coming from the direction of Flox's cabin, would have as much appreciation for Chopin?"

"A musician, maybe?"

"Bah! Not to sound harsh, but most working musicians would prefer brunch to Bruch. And anyway, I believe they're powwowing over at the office at this very moment."

There was a crash. The music came to a sudden halt. Jacobus started.

"What the hell?" Jacobus asked. What catastrophe were they about to endure now?

"It's all right," Dance said. "It's just the park crew demolishing the Big Top. My orders."

"You'd think they could've waited until the music was over," Jacobus grumbled.

"Most people don't have the same appreciation for music that you and I have."

"Clearly."

"And it's a big clean-up. That tent was the size of half a football field. Not an easy job to remove it. It's for everyone's safety."

There was no way the impromptu concert could proceed with the hollow clatter of wood and metal debris being heaved into piles, and the repetitive mechanical screeching of a winch, powered by a rumbling generator, hoisting who knew what to relocate who knew where. Jacobus shook his head in dismay, imagining what this place, this island, must have been like a hundred years ago, two hundred. Before machines. Before people. Before noise! A place with quiet. With tranquility. With peace. What had humans done to this place? To every place? Between then and now, what had the world become? Suddenly very tired, Jacobus wished he was back in his woods in the Berkshires. The solitude. Where humanity would leave him alone. Where there was silence. Yes, if there was one thing more beautiful than music, it was silence.

"Well, I guess there's a moratorium on Chopin for now," Dance said.

Jacobus informed Dance about the plans for the Mendelssohn Octet and convinced him to tell his workers to take a break when that performance started. He invited Dance to attend, but did not explain the method of his madness other than that the performance was intended to be a creative effort at crowd control. He guessed that would be an objective Dance would endorse, and he was correct.

No sooner had he parted company with Dance than his path was crossed by Jamie Barov, returning to his cabin after being forced to abandon his Chopin due to the commotion caused by the tent's ongoing demolition. Jacobus told Barov about the Mendelssohn and was successful in his effort to enlist Barov's support to bring Joy D'Angelo along.

Jacobus knocked on her cabin door, but he had to announce their names before D'Angelo would open it, and even then she did so cautiously. At first, she refused their invitation to attend the concert, claiming she did not want to leave her cabin "at this point in time." But Barov pleaded. "I need to sit next to someone who's better looking than Mr. Jacobus here," he said. The ice began to thaw when D'Angelo admitted she had never heard the Mendelssohn Octet, signaling she was ready to be persuaded. Barov masterfully exploited the chink in her armor, not only getting D'Angelo to agree to join them, but eliciting a welcome insuppressible smile along with it. Jacobus had a hard time believing either one of them could be a murderer. But then again, he had a hard time believing anyone could be a murderer.

Jacobus did not like sitting in the front row for a concert. The noise bothered him. Not the audience noise. The stage noise. In order to produce a sound that projects in a large concert hall, musicians often generate a perceptible level of non-musical grit. Flutists inhaling, violinists scraping, pianists pumping pedals, and conductors grunting. To Jacobus's sensitive ears, the turning of the musicians' pages was like an ocean wave breaking on the rocks.

The farther back one sits, the less the extraneous noises are audible. Go back too far, though, and unless you're in an excellent hall, the sound of the ensemble becomes as nondescript as a cheap blended Scotch, losing much of each instrument's individual clarity. So Jacobus usually split the difference, choosing to sit a little more than halfway back. But because on this occasion he was more concerned with the musicians' non-musical interaction than on the subtleties of the acoustics, he sat in the front row. Besides, they were in a barn reconfigured into an impromptu performing space. It didn't make a hell of a difference where he sat. The acoustics would be, at best, pretty lousy.

What chairs hadn't been destroyed in the wreck of the Big Top were set up facing the back of the open-faced barn. With the barn doors open to keep the warming air circulating, it was almost more of a shed than an enclosed structure. Those who were late arriving went without the luxury of a chair and either sat on the rough wood floor or, if they were too old or too stout to bend their knees, they stood. The musicians set themselves up against the back wall so that they had a surface for their sound to bounce off. It also protected them, and their instruments, in the event of another sudden deluge. Jacobus, with Barov and D'Angelo on either side of him, sat in the middle of the front row.

Though Jacobus was not anticipating a polished performance, one plus for the musicians was that even with eight instruments continuously intertwining in seemingly infinite combinations, Mendelssohn was able to mold each of the parts to fit exquisitely within the confines of each individual instrument, meaning that to the listener it sounded harder than it really was. Considering how much the crowd had appreciated the Mozart and Brahms sonatas, any reasonable reading of the gifted teenager's masterpiece would go over extremely well.

If it ever started, that is. Jacobus listened to the ensemble warming up in front of him. Two violas, two cellos, and one...two...three violins. Only three? Yes. Listening intently, he only heard three violinists. Someone missing? He listened even more carefully. He was sure. There were only three.

Ah! The one violinist he did not hear was the one with whose sound he was intimately familiar. Yumi. At first he was alarmed and was about to get up and look for her. Could she be in trouble? How could that be, with all the musicians who were possible murderers either onstage or sitting beside him? But then he understood and relaxed. Yumi was playing her role. She had worked with enough prima donnas. Now she was going to be one.

"Your protégée seems to be late," Barov whispered to him.

"Really!" Jacobus said. "I had no idea. I can't imagine what's holding her up. I'm sure she'll show up...sooner or later."

It was later. The audience, let alone the musicians, had already started to become impatient, having to wait, close-packed, in uncomfortable, warming conditions, when Yumi sauntered in.

"I'm *so* sorry to be late," she announced loudly. "I just had to take a nap and somehow my crazy alarm didn't go off. Thank you all for being so patient. Let's play some music!"

The musicians tuned quickly, obviously and reasonably eager to get started on what everyone expected to be a nonstop run-through of the piece. After less than a minute, however, Yumi stopped playing and waved her bow in the air.

"Is there a problem?" It was the voice of Dieter Waldstein.

"It just doesn't sound right," Yumi said. "Could you and Christian try to blend your sounds a little better?"

Waldstein began to dispute the criticism, but Cornelia Blum, the violist in the Kreutzer Quartet, interceded, familiar with Waldstein's propensity for being long-winded.

"Dieter," she said. "Forget about it. Let's just start over."

Blum had been one of the softer-spoken musicians in the group. Violists were often like that, Jacobus reflected. Caught in the middle register of the music, they were the glue that brought the top and bottom voices together. And, they were also often caught in the crossfire of the arguments between them. Jacobus liked to think of violists as music's diplomats, smoothing out hurt feelings and rough phrases with soothing words and golden tones. Were people with that type of personality innately attracted to the viola, or did playing the viola mellow out whoever played it? It was an interesting question, but probably an unanswerable one. Did it provide Jacobus with insight into the murderer's psychological profile (assuming it was a musician)? Perhaps. Perhaps not. But it was certainly something to chew on.

But for Blum to make such a comment—"Forget about it. Let's just start over."—was notable for its undercurrent of exasperation, and though subtle, for its definitiveness. It was reminiscent, in fact, to the tone of "Don't go there." Might it be possible that the phone calls to Yumi with the ominous messages had not been a man's voice? It gave him something more to consider.

Blum's comment signaled two things to Jacobus that were much more certain: that some of the musicians had second thoughts about the idea of playing the octet in public before it was adequately rehearsed; and that Yumi was winning an Oscar for her acting. He only hoped the musicians would forgive her once they found out she was doing it upon his explicit instructions.

"Great idea," Yumi said to Blum. "I was going to say the same thing."

"But this time," Blum cautioned, "let us not stop, please."

They began again, and this time they managed to play at least two minutes before Yumi said, "I'm sorry to stop again, guys. I know we said we wouldn't, but…"

"What is it this time?" Christian Bjørlund asked. "Dieter and I are blending. Are we not?"

"It's not that, Chris," Yumi said. "I know everyone's trying really hard. But—I'm not sure how to say this, so I'll just be frank—it's just not up to my standards."

Was it Jacobus's imagination or did the audience stop breathing? Even the wind seemed to stop blowing. If there is one thing all musicians agree upon, it is the avoidance of criticism in public. It is anathema. In baseball—Jacobus's favorite sport, which he listened to religiously on the radio—if a batter argues balls and strikes with the umpire, it's okay as long as the batter doesn't turn his head. But once he turns around, and his criticism becomes public, he's tossed right out of the game. You don't show up an umpire.

And you don't show up another musician. Anything goes as long as it is kept backstage, as the brutal confrontations between Waldstein and Bjørlund had so recently demonstrated. But in front of an audience—who are led to believe that musicians are next in line for sainthood—all punches, including verbal ones, are pulled. Decorum, civility, politeness rule the day, the way Congress behaved before the current era.

It perpetuated two illusions: that the musicians' ideals are as selfless, as lofty, and as pristine as the music they're playing; and that their performance is beyond mortal reproach. If there's absolutely no way of circumventing criticism of a colleague in public, it is so carefully couched that it comes out sounding like a compliment: "I absolutely loved how you phrased that. How about we do it like that all the time?" Or at worst: "Should we try to match your sound there, or do you want to match us?" For Yumi to have made the comment—"it's just not up to my standards"—was the flip side of telling the public that the other musicians were inferior. She had shattered the illusion.

The other musicians, however stunned and embarrassed, were still restrained by the tried-and-true dictates of professional decorum. They responded with comments dressed up to sound polite, couched in soft verbiage, but through which the knife edge could be felt. The only voice Jacobus hadn't yet heard was Renfro's, which was curious, because Yumi had mentioned that he, among all the players, was most like Barov in having the conciliatory voice, in being able to turn the tide in a positive direction.

It was Barov who whispered in Jacobus's left ear, "My, aren't we being catty today!" And into his right ear, D'Angelo whispered, "Yumi saved my life last night. What's happened to her?"

Yumi said, "Okay, guys. Let's try it just one more time. And I *promise* not to stop again."

This time they played for less than ten seconds when Yumi stopped.

"I'm sorry," she said, somber as a veterinarian telling an old dog's master that the fateful, dreaded moment had arrived. "I think we just need to move

181

on to the second movement."

"What are you doing, Yumi?"

It was Bjørlund.

"What do you mean?" she asked.

"You're being so disrespectful. Why?"

"I just want it to sound good. That's all."

"There are ways to do that and ways not to do that. You're being disrespectful."

"Am I? I don't think so."

"Ask anyone. If Edo were here, he never would have behaved like that."

"That's enough," Renfro said. He said it with, for him, unlikely harshness. It wasn't loud. It was softer, in fact, than the raised voices that preceded it. Yet it was chilling in its finality.

"Yes," Dieter Waldstein, said, after a pause. "He is right. It is enough. More than enough."

Interesting, Jacobus thought. *Interesting and disturbing at the same time.* The force of Renfro's tone in his defense of Yumi. Like a warrior standing in front of his general, bearing the brunt of the attack, sacrificing himself.

On second thought, was that really Renfro's intent? Could it be that Renfro simply found the entire exchange distasteful? Adults acting like little brats in front of people who adored them? Either interpretation seemed reasonable. Another curious possibility: "If Edo were here..." Edo, what was his last name? Kuypers. Yes, Edo Kuypers was the guy Yumi was subbing for. The guy with the medical emergency. It clearly sounded as if Bjørlund had some history with him. Some positive history. He evidently held this Kuypers in higher regard than Yumi, at least for the moment. Perhaps worth doing some digging. "If Edo were here..."

"You can dress these musicians up, but you just can't take them anywhere," Jamie Barov whispered into Jacobus's ear as the onstage row continued.

"Tell me about Bjørlund and Edo," Jacobus said.

"Edo Kuypers?"

"How many violinists named Edo do you know?"

"Only that there's not much to tell. He was supposed to be here and play *Summer*. He apparently got sick and begged off. Yumi filled his spot admirably. At least until fifteen minutes ago. I guess he and Christian and Marcus were friends."

"Marcus, too?"

"Yes, all three. They were all Baroque musicians at one point, until Marcus and Christian saw the light—i.e., a bigger paycheck—by expanding their repertoire. What Edo's been up to I don't really know. I haven't kept up. I don't travel much in Baroque circles. It's a different world. I suppose it's possible, likely even, they played in some festivals here and there back in the day."

If only Nathaniel were here, Jacobus thought. *Or even his phone.* He wanted to get hold of this Kuypers and find out what seemed to be eating at his former colleagues.

Chapter Fourteen

Consistent with Jacobus's hypothesis, Cornelia Blum stepped up to assume the role of senior diplomat. It reaffirmed his admittedly generalized notion of violists as the mediators in the musical animal kingdom. She delivered an announcement to the audience, apologizing profusely for the unseemly behavior of her colleagues and regretting that the performance they had hoped to entertain them with would sadly now not take place.

"How well do you know this violist, Blum?" Jacobus asked Barov, before he, too, dispersed. Jacobus liked the way she played, but this was the first time he'd heard her speak. "She's got a nice, round mezzo, like her viola sound. Big gal, like her viola?" Jacobus asked.

"Actually, she's quite svelte, though men who are attracted to women would likely say she is 'fine-figured.' And she's very, very bright. She's an author, too."

"Really! I've got some good viola jokes for her."

"Don't we all. No, right now she's writing sort of a memoir about all the festivals she's played in over the years."

A memoir. Maybe Nathaniel's background checks wouldn't be quite so necessary.

"A tell-all?" Jacobus asked, hopefully. "Yellow journalism, purple prose, black humor, whitewash, well read?"

"Colorful, no doubt. You should ask her yourself."

"I just might."

Barov excused himself to return to his cabin and fly-tying. "Fish can't argue with me," he said. D'Angelo, on his other side, offered Jacobus assistance to wherever he was going, which he declined. As Blum spoke, calm and conciliatory, Jacobus heard the musicians rise from their seats and remove themselves from the stage, their words indecipherable but, from their tone, distinctly sullen and resentful.

Jacobus prepared to leave until he heard Yumi call, "Marcus! Wait!" There was no response from Renfro, at least any that he could hear. Why did she say that with such urgency? To thank him for standing up for her? Or to find out something more about the situation between Kuypers and Bjørlund? Knowing Yumi, it could be either. Or both. *Or,* he thought now, *a third possibility. Between Kuypers and Renfro.*

Cornelia Blum's public apology did not mollify everyone. Rumbles of muted dissatisfaction snaked through the audience like a distant subway, including a few distinct boos. From the unflattering comments that accompanied them it was evident they were primarily directed toward Yumi. *How quickly they forget,* Jacobus thought. *Just a few hours before, they were shouting bravo for her Brahms and Mozart.* The situation was turning ugly.

"I also have an announcement." A voice behind Jacobus ascended over the growling. Jefferson Dance. The crowd quieted.

"Some good news for a change, folks. I've heard from our friends at Hill Air Force Base in Ogden. It seems they have an aptitude for building things on the quick. They're jury-rigging a temporary pontoon bridge as we speak. The causeway should be functional by the end of the day, at least for emergency vehicles."

At the flip of that switch, the audience had something to look forward to of greater import than a mere chamber music performance. Anger turned to celebration and the aborted concert was forgotten, if not by the musicians, at least by the audience. They would be able to go home soon and relate to their loved ones the tale of their Robinson Crusoe weekend in full-color detail. How they endured untold hardship. The wind. The rain. The hail. The annihilated tent. And last but not least, the deaths. That would be the part of the narrative, the inside scoop, that everyone would want to hear about. It was horrible! Let me tell you all about it! *Survivor: Antelope Island*.

Jacobus was no less relieved than anyone else that he'd soon be able to get the hell off the island, but at the same time, he was disturbed by the fact that it would also ease the way for the murderer to get the hell off the island. And once everyone had flown the coop, catching him—whoever it was—would be that much more difficult. Almost impossible.

He felt a tap on his shoulder.

"I'm not sure what you were up to with that stunt you had the young lady pull," Dance said, "but you came very close to causing a situation for which I would have held you directly responsible."

Jacobus would typically have objected forcefully to such an indictment. But on this occasion he did not, because not only was it worth his while to maintain Dance as an ally, he had to acknowledge that Dance was right. He had put a lot of people, especially Yumi, in a very poor light, all for a wildly concocted scheme with no definite outcome in mind.

"*Mea culpa*," Jacobus said. "With extra *mea*. It won't happen again. Promise. Scout's honor. But I've got a question for you. How did you know someone was coming to fix the causeway? I thought all the communications were down."

"Desperate times call for desperate measures, Mr. Jacobus."

Dance explained that, given the deteriorating circumstances, he either had to take an extraordinary chance or, if he did nothing, risk a dire situation becoming a calamitous one. Without bothering to consult its owner, he took the liberty of requisitioning one of the private outboard motorboats moored at the marina at the top of the island, and asked his staff for a volunteer.

One of his men, an ex-Air Force Special Operations officer with three tours of duty in the Middle East under his belt, stepped up. He motored in to Willard Bay on the mainland and managed to contact the air force base. It had not been a crossing Dance would have recommended to anyone who had a sensitive stomach or wasn't competent to operate a small craft on treacherous waters. The commanders at the base were receptive to the urgent request of one of their own, and had the equipment and the manpower to get the job done.

"Sometimes these military folks like to show off what they can do," Dance said. "Good PR for their recruiting."

Dance added that though he expected law enforcement would gain access soon, he would relax only when they arrived and took over the situation, especially dealing with the two corpses on ice at the ranger station.

"I must say, Dance, you've earned your merit badge the past couple of days."

Dance just chuckled.

"I'll take that as a compliment, Mr. Jacobus. But please don't cause me any further trouble."

By the time Dance went off to oversee the final dismantling of the festival tent, Yumi's voice had, like those of all the other musicians, evaporated into thin air. Jacobus's inclination was to return to Yumi's cabin and wait to hear more about her follow-up conversation with Renfro, if indeed it ever occurred. But then he decided he wanted to talk to Cornelia Blum, and after asking more people than he had wished to in order to find her, was pointed in the direction of her cabin. He knocked on her door.

Jacobus didn't understand what people had against body odor. Well, he did understand, but he didn't agree with it. The way a person smelled—or the way they covered it up with the vast array of socially acceptable scents and fragrances: soaps, lotions, perfumes, colognes, and deodorants—was, to a blind man, one of the many important indicators of who they were. It was as important as what someone looked like to a person with sight. How could one judge a person's character if they wore a bag over their head? Well, he supposed he could, in a way, with such a person. But there was so much Jacobus could tell from body odor, from their hygiene to their philosophy of life. Whether they had garlic for dinner, whether they had just run a marathon, whether they were telling the truth at an interview, or whether they had just slept with someone. What a shame that Madison Avenue had decided that the world needed to be ashamed of how it smelled.

Cornelia Blum seemed not to be ashamed of her personal scent, or at least Jacobus had concluded as much when she opened the door and invited him in. There was a healthy pungency radiating from her, as if she had savored her week in the desert heat and had absorbed its earthy scents into her flesh. She clearly was not embarrassed and was perhaps even overtly proud of how she smelled. The memoir she was writing, Jacobus concluded from her body odor, would be straightforward and truthful, not unlike her viola playing.

"I hate to disappoint you, Mr. Jacobus, but I'm getting ready for a tramp," she said when she answered the door. "A good, long, exhausting tramp, or hike as you say. After that fiasco of a 'concert,' I need to vent my frustrations so that I don't injure someone."

"I understand," Jacobus said. "I won't keep you long. Tell me about this book you're writing."

"My book! So much for secrets. Oh, well. It's nothing profound. I thought it would be interesting for the general reader to get an inside view of what it's like for a professional musician who tours a lot," Blum replied. "All they ever see are the musicians sitting on stage with our fancy costumes, but they have no idea what goes on behind the scenes. And to show how music can bring people together, though you wouldn't have guessed that would be possible after today. I want to give them a taste, based on my experiences. So it's part memoir, part travelogue, part history."

"Do you name names?"

"Sometimes, but only when it's positive. I have no intention of creating scandal, like some other authors, if that's what you mean."

"Though I'm sure you could if you wanted to."

Blum laughed. It was soft but rich and thoughtful, consistent with the way she smelled.

"Oh, yes. And if there had been a question about what the climax would be, it is here, now, on Antelope Island. This disaster. And these killings. I'm not sure how I'm going to deal with that in the book."

"Deal with it?"

"Yes, you know, about my colleagues. What if one of them did it? Everyone is so suspicious of one another now. And the way Yumi behaved with the Mendelssohn! I could not understand it. It was so unlike her. I thought, what is going on? This is crazy. Does she have something to hide?"

"Don't worry about Yumi. There was a reason for her behavior, and it was my fault. And I will explain it to you once everything's been sorted out. I wouldn't want you to get the story wrong in your book."

"Okay, it won't be published for at least another year, anyway, so whenever you're ready."

"But I would like to know—if you're at liberty to tell me—about any connections between the musicians here with Talbot and Flox at previous festivals."

"Connections?"

"When and where. What the circumstances were. Whether there were any arguments. Strained relationships, if you will."

"In other words, the stories I am going to *exclude* in my book?"

"Precisely. You know, the dirty linen that musicians smell every day but never wash in public." Jacobus knew what was coming next, that Blum would object. So he quickly added, "And, of course, it will all remain confidential."

After an hour, Blum had still not departed for her hike. Jacobus's problem was not that he had no new leads. It was, as he had feared, that he had too many. No wonder Blum raised her verbal eyebrows when he had asked about connections. Everyone had performed with one another over the years. Everyone had crossed paths with Anita Talbot and Sunny Flox. No one had liked the former. Everyone had liked the latter. That level of unanimity, almost unheard of when it came to opinions about the music, was par for the course when it came to evaluating the administrators, partly because when word got around about what Mr. or Ms. So-and-So did to one of their colleagues, it could infect the general psyche like a virulent virus.

"And now, Mr. Jacobus, I must leave for my tramp, before it gets too hot again. I hope I haven't wasted your time."

Yumi was still not at her cabin. There was not much else for Jacobus to do, other than wait, which aggravated him because he felt guilty. That she returned shortly thereafter was a reprieve from his bout of self-incrimination.

"Well," Yumi said, "I hope you learned something. You better have."

She sounded distant, impersonal. He already regretted what he had made her do. And for what? He wanted to apologize, but couldn't think of the right words.

"Other than you're a damn good actress?" he said. "Nothing, damn it."

"I learned something," she said. "I learned that you were wrong about Marcus. I hope you heard him defending me."

Jacobus conceded the point.

"Yumi, I..."

She must have sensed his remorse, a sentiment he rarely felt, let alone expressed. Her tone softened. She began to make an effort to soothe an old man's bruised self-esteem, unexpectedly fragile. The latent confrontation ebbed even before it ignited. They discussed. He probed. She responded.

"Yumi," Jacobus asked when he felt he was back on firm ground, "do you know anything about any affairs Dieter Waldstein might have had in the past?"

"No, and I'm not going to find out, either."

So much for reconciliation.

"I was just—"

"You've already talked me into being a bitch, and you saw how that turned out. I'm certainly not going to let you talk me into being a—"

"Of course not. I was just wondering..."

"What were you wondering?"

"Well, maybe whether he and Talbot... Or he and Talbot and Flox... The three of them?"

"Jake, sometimes you shock me. Either you have a sick mind, a lurid imagination, or your libido is on overdrive."

"All three, no doubt. And you can probably add senility to the list. But is it possible?"

"Possible? I suppose so. Anything's possible. It's also possible you and Nathaniel—"

"What are you talking about?" Jacobus bellowed.

"See? Just sayin'. But so what? And as I said, I'm not going there. End of story."

She's right, Jacobus thought. The only thing his questions proved was that he was as confounded as ever. Anyone could be the murderer. And no one could be the murderer. Yet, a murderer there was. Here. And now.

There are those who believed Jacobus had almost supernatural powers of observation. But in the ensuing silence, as Jacobus tried to dig himself out of his latest hole, questioning even his most elementary powers of reasoning, there was nothing supernatural about his hearing the unmistakable sounds of an engine and the skidding grind of tires on the potholed dirt road. A car had just pulled up outside. Any idiot would have heard that. On the other hand, not any idiot would have been able to conclude from the precise characteristics of such mundane sounds, as Jacobus could, that trouble was brewing.

First of all, the car came to an abrupt halt, suggesting the driver was in a hurry. But then, curiously, there was an extended period of thirty seconds or so before a car door opened, at which time not one, but a pair of doors opened. Obviously, the car had two occupants and they had had a discussion before exiting it. A conference, perhaps? To determine a plan of action? Then, the two doors were closed quietly, as if they did not want their arrival to be noticed. *How ridiculous is that?* Jacobus thought after they had driven up with such fanfare. So, the riders were attempting to be careful, but were not particularly judicious in their efforts. Finally, two pairs of footsteps: the first pair, lumbering with long, slow strides; the second, following, with quick, light steps. A man in front, bigger and older than a smaller, more agile woman following. That seemed likely. Both pairs of footsteps stopped just outside the cabin door.

All told, and taking into account Dance's announcement of the imminent road repair, Jacobus anticipated that the pair at the door had to be among the first to have crossed the causeway. Who would that be? The police, of course, who would be investigating the murders of Anita Talbot and Sunny Flox. What bothered him, though, was their overly cautious approach to Yumi's cabin. That could only mean one thing. Trouble.

So, when Yumi answered the knock on the door, Jacobus was not surprised whom she greeted.

"Ms. Shinagawa?" A man's voice. Slow and husky.

"Yes."

"I'm Detective Vern Gettelman. This is Officer Leona Guzman. Utah Highway Patrol."

So far, no surprise. No doubt, Dance had informed them of the fuss with which Jacobus had pestered Dance over potential suspects. Jacobus now expected they would want to question him directly. To hear his thoughts. He was ready. It was their next statement that surprised him.

"Ms. Shinagawa, we'd like to ask you to come with us."

"Me? Why?"

"We've got a few questions to ask you regarding the deaths of Anita Talbot and Sidney Flox."

The police designated both the festival office and Flox's cabin as crime scenes and off limits to the public. Detective Gettelman set up his interview room in the windowless piano shed, one of the few available spaces that afforded both visual and aural privacy. It had been constructed only to store the piano and harpsichord. Given those instruments' sensitivity to heat and humidity (or the absence thereof), the piano shed had been built with greater care towards insulation and climate control than for the musicians' cabins. Even though the piano was still in the barn and the remnants of the harpsichord were a pile of splinters buried somewhere under the Big Top, the room was cramped. It was an unorthodox space for interviews, but considering the circumstances, it was the best they could do.

People were slowly permitted to leave Antelope Island, but the process was painfully methodical and time-consuming. There were two reasons for that. The first was that before anyone could leave, they were interviewed by one of the half dozen law enforcement officials who set up a checkpoint at the parking lot exit, and were required to provide their contact information if further questioning was necessary. The second was that the military pontoon bridge that had been hurriedly built to reconnect the two fingers of the breached causeway was single-laned and temporary. Fifteen miles per hour, not fifty, was the maximum permitted speed.

Both Gettelman and Guzman wore police uniforms that were tight fitting, but in all likelihood for two different reasons. Vern Gettelman, red-cheeked, with short and curly, graying hair, was about to burst out of his uniform. He gave the appearance of a former college football player who had given up on the exercise but not on the fried chicken. He was seated in a folding chair that was all but obscured by his bulk, his stubby hands folded between spread knees with ankles crossed. Leona Guzman was a young Hispanic woman, a head shorter than Gettelman, with long, black hair tied into a bun at the back of her head. She stood in the corner, behind Gettelman and off to his right. Unlike Gettelman's uniform, hers seemed intentionally shrink-wrapped to highlight her figure. In another setting, like a disco bar, the tight fit might have been appropriate. She didn't look like the type of person who would consider a career in police work to be her dream job, except, perhaps, in a TV drama.

"We just have a few routine questions for you," Gettelman said.

Yumi was more than willing to be cooperative. Nevertheless, it made her unexpectedly uneasy the way he said "routine questions." It wasn't the first time she'd had to talk to law enforcement over the years—Jacobus had gotten them both into enough hot water—but there was something about Gettelman's tone that her instincts told her to be wary of.

"I'm happy to help however I can," Yumi said.

"Thank you. We appreciate that. Please tell us what you remember of your movements from the moment last night that the tent collapsed until Sidney Flox's body was discovered."

The look on Yumi's face must have been what prompted Gettelman to say, "I know that's a lot, but we need to construct a coordinated picture, and considering how long it's going to take to allow everyone to leave the island, well, frankly we've got plenty of time."

Yumi spent close to the next half hour describing in as much detail as she could recall how she had been on stage performing *Summer* when the storm hit; how the musicians then left the stage at Flox's instructions; how, after the tent collapsed she helped people crawl out from underneath, including Daniel Jacobus; how she had helped him to her cabin and returned to assist others. That was when Marcus Renfro had shouted that he thought Anita was dead. After that, she went to Flox's office and then to his cabin to get dry clothes for Jacobus. She returned to her cabin. From there, she and Jacobus made another trip to Flox's office, where they'd encountered Joy D'Angelo, Christian Bjørlund, and Jefferson Dance. From there, she and Jacobus went to the barn, where they had their meager dinner and conversed with some of the other musicians. It was at that time they heard Joy D'Angelo's cries. They raced over to discover that Flox had been killed. Yumi hoped the excess of detail she provided would bore Gettelman and Guzman to tears and in doing so, they would thank her and let her go quickly.

"You certainly have a good memory." Those were the first words Guzman had spoken since Yumi had arrived. Her voice was lightly inflected with a Hispanic accent, high-pitched and youthful, almost like a high school student. It was birdlike and musical. But Yumi resented the tone of the comment. It almost sounded like an accusation.

"I'm a concert violinist," she replied. "I've been memorizing concertos since I was six years old. I'm trained to have a good memory."

Gettelman ignored the exchange.

"So I just have a few questions to fill in the blanks and then we can excuse you," he said. He sounded bored.

"Go ahead."

"First, from the time you crawled out from under the tent with Mr. Jacobus until you went back under, ostensibly to help others, to your knowledge had anyone else talked to Ms. Talbot?"

"I have no idea," Yumi said. "Since I was going to and from my cabin to tend to Jake—Mr. Jacobus."

"So it's possible, theoretically, that in that time, no one spoke to Ms. Talbot."

"Theoretically, yes, that's true."

"In which case, it could have been you and Mr. Jacobus who were the last ones to see her alive."

"That's possible."

"That being the case, Ms. Shinagawa, isn't it also possible that you were the first ones to see her dead?"

Yumi's body tensed from the shock at the direction these "routine" questions were taking. Yet her internal discipline enabled her not to show it. At least, that was her intent. Gettelman was clearly trying to egg her on, to provoke her into an emotional denial. To coerce her into a false confession? Would he sink that low? She wasn't going to play that game.

"If she hadn't still been alive, that would have indeed been possible," she said.

"Well, thank you for your candor, Ms. Shinagawa. That's all I need."

Yumi was relieved, but somewhat bewildered.

"May I go now?" she asked.

"Certainly," Gettelman said.

"May I ask a question?" Guzman asked.

"Would that be okay with you?" Gettelman asked Yumi. Why was he asking her for her permission for a fellow officer to ask a question? As Jacobus would say, there was something not kosher about this.

"That's not up to me," Yumi said.

"Just trying to be…you know…accommodating."

Or the good cop, bad cop ploy. Yumi thought that was just for TV shows. She didn't say anything.

"Very well," Gettelman said. "What's your question, Guzman?"

"Just a little detail. Does Mr. Jacobus have his walking stick?"

Easy question.

"Yes. Thank you." Interview ended?

Not quite.

"How did Mr. Jacobus get his walking stick back?"

"What do you mean, get it back?" Yumi asked, suddenly seeing a little detail turning into very large nightmare.

"What I mean is: It was there when the first decedent was discovered. That has been confirmed."

"By whom?"

"That has been confirmed." Guzman's little girl voice was starting to become shrill, abrasive. Was it really changing, or simply Yumi's perception of it? "But then it went missing. That has also been confirmed. Then it was seen next to the second decedent. That has also been confirmed. Then it went missing yet again. And then Mr. Jacobus seems to have it again."

Guzman stopped abruptly, an accelerating train suddenly slamming on the emergency brakes.

As she had not been asked a question, Yumi determined she would not be the first to break the silence. Also, she didn't have an answer that wouldn't incriminate her and Jacobus.

"You mentioned"—this time it was Gettelman—"that you and Mr. Jacobus were with colleagues when D'Angelo called out for help."

"That's right," Yumi said. Was he letting her off the hook? This was a little too easy.

"That's been confirmed, Guzman? Hasn't it?" Was he making fun of his subordinate? Mocking her? Did this hint at animosity between them, or was this a well-honed schtick?

"Yes. It has been confirmed."

Another silence.

"So, is that all?" Yumi asked.

"Not for me," Guzman said. "Because we understand that when Ms. D'Angelo called out, the park staff told everyone to stay there. But you and Mr. Jacobus disobeyed their orders and went directly to the second decedent's cabin. Why?"

"Because it was clear Joy was distressed. We wanted to help."

"Could the real reason be so you could retrieve Mr. Jacobus's walking stick?"

"Why is that so important?" Yumi realized immediately that was the wrong question. That had been the trap all along.

"Because," Guzman said, "we believe that was the weapon that was used to kill both decedents. And removing evidence, especially a murder weapon, from a crime scene is a serious crime in itself."

Yumi noted that Guzman hadn't said it had been confirmed that she had been seen retrieving the walking stick from Flox's cabin.

"I don't know how Mr. Jacobus got his walking stick back, if that's what you want to know," Yumi said. She hoped she would not regret having lied.

"Look," she continued, "there's a killer on the loose here, and from the way you're asking these questions about Jacobus's walking stick I get the feeling you think one of us might have done it. May I remind you that we were with our colleagues and about a hundred other people in the barn when Joy cried out that Sunny had been killed? Or would you prefer I refer to him as the second decedent?" *I probably shouldn't have said that*, she thought, *but they goaded me into it.*

Gettelman played the role of peacemaker.

"No one's accusing you of anything, Ms. Shinagawa. We're just trying to get to the bottom of this. The truth. As you say, there's a murderer out there. Don't forget that we just arrived here and there's a big mess we have to contend with.

"I wish I had as good a memory as you do, Ms. Shinagawa, but do I remember correctly that you and Mr. Jacobus went to see the second...Mr. Flox in his office, that you were the last ones there with him after Ranger Dance, Miss D'Angelo, and Mr....How do you pronounce his name?"

"Bjørlund?"

"Yes, that's it. That's a tricky one. After they all left, and from there went to the barn where people were eating?"

"That's right."

"And that it was from there, sometime later, when you were conversing with your colleagues, that you heard Ms. D'Angelo cry out?"

"Correct. That's why it couldn't—"

"Well, the problem we have with that—and I think this is what Officer Guzman might have been trying to get at—is that from the time you left Mr. Flox's office to the time Ms. D'Angelo cried out, we haven't been able to find anyone who can say they saw anyone else go into his office or into his cabin. So, theoretically, you could have been the last ones to see him alive. Or conversely..."

"The first ones to see him dead," Guzman said.

After yet another silence, this one very long—at least it seemed so to Yumi—Gettelman slapped his hands on his thighs and stood up.

"Boy, this chair is uncomfortable," he said. "I think my butt fell asleep. Okay, Ms. Shinagawa. You can go now. Thank you for your cooperation. But please tell Mr. Jacobus he has to turn in the stick to us. It is evidence. You wouldn't want *him* to get into trouble. Would you?"

Chapter Fifteen

"Forget it!" Jacobus said.

"But, why not, Jake? Why shouldn't we just give them the walking stick?" Yumi asked. "I know I lied about it and I know it means a lot to you, but—"

There were two reasons. The first was that the stick did mean a lot to him. But if he admitted that, she would think that he was getting soft in his old age, eroding his crusty persona that had been the bedrock of their relationship. *You don't want to see an old man cry, do you?*

The second reason was the more immediate one, anyway.

"Because," he said, "if they start thinking that you or I were involved in Talbot or Flox's murder—which apparently they have—they'll figure out a way to turn random, superfluous information into so-called evidence. Like fingerprints or DNA or matching the bruise marks on the decedents' craniums to bumps on the stick. I know those cops. Once they have a murder weapon in their hands they'll start drooling like Trotsky with a bone and arrest the first person they can lay their hands on. Us."

"That sounds pretty far-fetched, even for you, Jake," Yumi answered. "If there's one fingerprint on Hocus, there will be a million. I don't think they'd be able to get anything from that. And if there was DNA on it, it would've been all washed off in the rain. We were standing out there with Joy for a long time."

"You're right. It is far-fetched."

"So you agree to return it?"

"By no means! Because as we've learned from past experience, sometimes the truth *is* far-fetched. Cops have never discounted the unlikely. They even seem to thrive on it, especially when they can't figure out the likely."

"So what do you propose we do? Stonewall? That's just going to put us under the microscope even more."

"This is what we're going to do," Jacobus said. "We're not going to give them Hocus. We're going to give them Pocus."

"Pocus?"

"Go make another stick and I'll take it back to those two G-men, Gettelman and Guzman. They've never seen Hocus. They won't know the difference."

"Where am I going to get another walking stick?"

"Maybe off the ground? As in one of the many I've almost broken my neck tripping over since yesterday?"

"I suppose I could. Where will I get the tools?"

"How about from Barov?" Jacobus asked. "With his fly-fishing gear. Maybe he's got a saw and crap like that."

"But didn't you say you suspected Jamie?"

"So what? I suspect everybody. And asking him for the tools wouldn't change that calculation. It could only be a help."

Barov, as proprietary of his fly-fishing gear as he was of his pianos, was cooperative if not enthusiastic. He expressed incredulity that anyone would think a fly-tying kit would have a knife with which to prune a stick, but he did have a scaling knife, not for fly-tying but for the fish he would not be catching in the Great Salt Lake, that he was willing to lend. An hour or so later, Yumi had crafted what seemed to be a reasonable Hocus facsimile. Jacobus, having decided it would be best to go alone, knocked on the door of the piano storage room.

Someone opened it. Jacobus shuffled in with baby steps, arms outstretched like that same baby waiting for his mother to pull a sweater over his head. His left hand—the one not holding the newly crafted walking stick—came in contact, as if unintentionally, with a face at approximately his same height. One gentle, tangential swipe: smooth cheek, fine nose, full lips. He smelled the lipstick, recently applied. The young lady. Guzman.

"Detective Gettelman?" Jacobus asked, helplessly. "Are you Detective

Gettelman?"

"I'm Officer Guzman. You're Mr. Jacobus?"

"Last time I looked, ha-ha," he said. "If you know what I mean."

Guzman didn't laugh.

"Please come in, Mr. Jacobus." Gettelman's voice.

Jacobus heard a footfall from even farther away. There was a fourth person in the room. That was unanticipated.

Gettelman offered his seat to Jacobus, who pretended to almost miss it as he sat down, and had to be rescued from falling to the floor by both Gettelman and Guzman, each grabbing one of his arms and lifting him into the chair.

"What brings you here, Mr. Jacobus?" said the fourth person.

Dance! He should have guessed Dance would be there. He quickly calculated the risks and decided to throw caution to the wind.

Once seated, Jacobus said, "Uh, Detective Gettelman, I have an apology to make. Yes. Apology." He explained how he had made Yumi promise not to tell anyone that she had removed his walking stick from Flox's cabin. Because of how much it meant to him. It had been a gift from a dear, recently departed friend—"They've been dropping like flies lately, my friends have"—and relinquishing it would cause him more heartache than he thought he could bear.

"Is it really necessary for you to take this from me?" he asked the police officers. "I don't want to impede your investigation, but..." His words, mumbled and trailing off, feigned imminent senility.

"I wish it were otherwise, Mr. Jacobus," Gettelman said, "but your walking stick might be crucial evidence. We strongly believe it was the weapon that killed both the first and second decedents."

"Oh, my God!"

"If you hand it over voluntarily," Guzman said, "things will go much easier on Ms. Shinagawa. And you, too, for that matter."

"I suppose," Jacobus said, and rolled his tongue around the inside of his mouth as if he had loose dentures about to fall out, "the important thing is to find whatever evil person did this..." Again, he drifted off.

"So, are you going to give us the walking stick," Guzman asked, "or not?" Jacobus was evidently making her impatient, as he had hoped. She would lose her objectivity.

"Oh, yes! Yes! Yes! Yes!" He held out the stick. Guzman took it from him—no doubt wearing gloves—with a little too much eagerness. As if she were worried he'd change his mind and not let go of it. Jacobus extended both arms, as if a kidnapper had just snatched his baby.

"We'll take good care of it," Gettelman said.

"Um… Will I get it back…soon?" Jacobus sniffed once or twice, removed a handkerchief from his back pocket, and blew his nose.

"Someday. Perhaps," Gettelman said. "Thank you for stepping up to the plate."

"I just have one request," Jacobus said. "One request. May I? Could someone please help me back to my cabin? If it's not too much trouble. Without my walking stick, I don't know if—"

"Of course."

Gettelman ordered Guzman to assist Jacobus.

His arm linked with Guzman's, Jacobus shuffled toward Yumi's cabin. He managed to lose his footing repeatedly and it seemed an eternity before they arrived. *It must be driving Guzman crazy,* he thought. Upon delivering him to the cabin door, Jacobus smelled coffee inside. If Guzman smelled it, she didn't acknowledge it. Instead, she said, "It might be a good idea for someone to make you a new walking stick, Mr. Jacobus."

That was even better luck than Jacobus had counted on. Now, he wouldn't even have to hide Hocus. Hocus would be the replacement for the replacement.

"What a wonderful idea, young lady," he said to Guzman. "Thank you for your thoughtfulness."

His strategy, with one serious question mark, seemed to have succeeded, though he could have ruined it when he almost burst out laughing when Guzman had placed exaggerated emphasis on the adverb, "If you hand it over *voluntarily.*" What were they going to do, wrestle him to the ground? Have him bound and gagged?

The question mark, obviously, was Dance. After asking why Jacobus was there, Dance had remained ominously silent. Unlike Gettelman and Guzman, Dance had seen him with Hocus. But he hadn't intervened at Jacobus's subterfuge. Jacobus hoped his silence, whatever the intent, would continue.

Jacobus entered Yumi's cabin.

"Nathaniel! You're a sight for sore eyes, or so the saying goes."

"How did you know I was here, Jake?" Nathaniel asked. "It was supposed to be a surprise."

"Not difficult. One, we know the causeway repairs were underway. Two, I knew you'd be anxious to bring us the information you've researched, and that after the cops you'd find a way to be the first across. And, three, I smelled the coffee! Better than that swill they were serving. Who else would've thought to bring good coffee other than my bosom buddy. Right?"

Yumi handed him a cup.

"Mmm. Ambrosia," Jacobus said, slurping it down. "So, what have you got for us?"

It was a very happy reunion, the three of them. Nathaniel sat side by side with Jacobus on Yumi's bed so that he wouldn't have to sit in the rickety chair, which Yumi took. Even for Jacobus, with his predilection for seclusion, having a trusted friend suddenly reinserted into what had become a hellish new normal revived his spirits far more than he would have expected. Along with the coffee, Nathaniel had also brought Jacobus some clean clothes, unaware that Yumi had requisitioned Flox's for him. He hadn't brought the new seersucker suit, however, which was still hanging in the closet at their room at the Waltz Rite Inn.

"Someday you'll wear it, Jake," Nathaniel said.

"At my funeral. Maybe. Just don't let me know."

Nathaniel told Jacobus and Yumi all he had learned about the backstories of the members of the Kreutzer String Quartet, the other four musicians—excluding Yumi—and festival staff. He had scoured websites, press releases, news articles, social media—anything and everything he could find online and by phone.

Christian Bjørlund had recently published a book on Baroque string-playing technique. "It's selling like hotcakes," Nathaniel said.

"Are you serious?" Jacobus asked.

"No. Just joking."

Dieter Waldstein was in the process of divorcing his wife who, rumor had it, had been having an extramarital affair with their housepainter whenever Waldstein went on tour, which was almost all the time.

"Never trust a German painter," Jacobus said.

Franz Weiss, the Kreutzer's second violinist, had recently lost an audition for the Berlin Philharmonic, placing second to a twenty-one-year-old conservatory student who had never played in an orchestra but whose technique had been described as "otherworldly."

"Maybe that's why everyone says he's hardly said a word since he got here," Jacobus offered.

"Or maybe it's just that he's an asshole," Yumi said.

"Oooooh!" Nathaniel said. "I'm bettin' there's a story there! I'm gonna have to hear all about that one."

"Even so," Jacobus said, "with his experience, that must be hard to take, losing an audition to a kid."

"But what does that have to do with killing people?" Yumi asked.

"Probably nothing."

Ingrid Goldman had recently joined the Green Party and had been arrested protesting climate change inaction at a rally in Berlin. Cornelia Blum, in addition to being a budding author, was vegan and had just separated from her female partner, a paleo, over the burning issue of diet and nutrition. Hannah Carrington, still in her twenties, was experiencing her first bout of tendinitis and, believing the cause could be the new viola she had bought, was now seeking a smaller instrument. Marcus Renfro had just released a double CD of the Bach cello suites, played first on a Baroque instrument in the style of the period, then on a borrowed, million-dollar Matteo Gofriller cello set up in the modern fashion and performed in a more contemporary style.

"I suppose that's selling like hotcakes, too," Jacobus said.

"Actually, yes. It's nominated for a Grammy."

That left Jamie Barov among the musicians. He had recently toured with Yo-Yo Ma as part of the Silk Roads project, performing not only classical music but traditional music from the more exotic regions of central and east Asia. Like Ma, he seemed to revel in the dual role of musician and goodwill ambassador.

"What about cutie pie, Joy D'Angelo?"

"Jake," Yumi said, "why can't you be more respectful?"

"Ha!" Jacobus said. "I heard something like that said to you recently!"

"Yes, but don't forget, I was *trying* to be a bitch."

"Well, I guess I'm just a natural."

"One of you can explain that to me later," Nathaniel said. "Or maybe it would be better to forget about it. In any event, Miss D'Angelo is the daughter of two Utah freelance musicians. She had a normal upbringing—"

"Hey, wait a second!" Jacobus interrupted.

"What's wrong?"

"If she's the child of two musicians, how could she have a normal upbringing?"

"Very funny. As I was saying, she had a normal upbringing. After she got her degree, she auditioned several places but gave up. Looks like she saw how difficult it was for her parents to make ends meet, and she needed a job. Hence, the move to administration. Can't say I blame her."

Much of what Nathaniel had found out, Yumi already knew from her prior interactions with the musicians over the years, and so was at least able to confirm the information. However, none of it suggested anything that might help Jacobus put the pieces of the puzzle together. None of it appeared to relate to Talbot and Flox's murders.

Their leads were as cold as the coffee had become.

"What about Anita and Sunny themselves," Yumi asked. "Did you find out anything about their pasts?"

"Nothing that would make anyone want to kill either one of them, let alone both," Nathaniel said. "Being in their positions as concert managers, they had their share of scuffles with agents and artists, but nothing out of the ordinary that I could find. At least in relation to the folks who have been out here. This business about 'bitches in heat' seems the worst of their shenanigans.

"Is it possible that Sunny killed Anita," Nathaniel continued, "and then someone else killed Sunny? For revenge, maybe? They didn't seem to like each other very much."

"That's been the damn problem!" Jacobus erupted. "People who don't like each other very much! That's normal! Especially in *this* business! Nobody likes each other very much! Why can't they do us a favor and outright hate each other? If they hated each other maybe we'd have something to go on!"

"Another cup of coffee?" Nathaniel asked.

Outburst over.

"Sure. Black, no sugar," Jacobus said. He took a deep breath. "What about the Kreutzer Quartet musicians?"

"They're Germans," Nathaniel said. "They probably like milk and sugar with theirs."

"Thank you. You're a wonderful help. But look, they've been here in past years. They've worked with both Talbot and Flox. Could they've had a bone to pick? As a group, maybe?"

"Not that I know of. Maybe we should just ask them."

"That's an idea."

"But we better do it fast," Nathaniel said.

"Why?" Yumi asked.

"Because everyone's packing their bags. With the causeway open again, folks are starting to leave."

Folks leaving jogged Jacobus's memory. There was one person who had already left, in a manner of speaking.

"You do that," he said, "but first, could you make a call for me? If your phone's working."

"It is," Nathaniel said. "And they've got the electricity up and running, too."

"Miracle of miracles. What I want you to do is give Edo Kuypers a call."

"Edo Kuypers? Why Edo?" Yumi asked.

"Because when you had your little skirmish in the barn, Bjørlund said, 'If Edo were here, he never would have behaved like that.' And Renfro responded, 'That's enough.'"

"Yes, Marcus was defending me," Yumi said. And from her tone, Jacobus gathered that Yumi was now defending Renfro. "It was very kind of him, given the way I was behaving."

"Maybe," Jacobus said. "Maybe not. Maybe the real reason was that he didn't want Bjørlund talking about Edo Kuypers, so he said, 'That's enough.'"

"But why?"

"I don't know. That's what I want to find out."

"You still think Marcus could be a murderer?" Yumi asked. "I find that hard to believe, Jake. Both about him and about you."

"It does seem pretty speculative," Nathaniel said. "Awfully thin to me, Jake. I wouldn't bet on it."

"I'm not saying that he is or he isn't, damn it! I'm keeping an open mind. It's just that Renfro and Bjørlund and Kuypers seem to have had a history. All I'm asking is, call Kuypers and let's find out what he has to say about it. See if there's anything to it."

"I don't even have Edo's phone number," Yumi said.

"But I'm sure Miss D'Angelo does."

The banging inside alarmed them as they approached D'Angelo's cabin. It sounded like a mortal struggle. Yumi ran to the door and yanked it open. The room was a shambles. But it wasn't because of the storm or of a brawl. D'Angelo, tears streaming down, was in the middle of the room, flinging her clothes and belongings in every direction. Her cabin had been unkempt the first time Yumi had been there. Now it appeared as much a disaster area as the collapsed Big Top.

"I don't know what I'm doing!" she cried. "They're all ordering me around. All of them! Do this! Do that! Dieter says, 'Carry my bags!' Ingrid says, 'Clean my room!' I don't know where to start. It's just too much. I can't stand it!"

Jacobus was about to give her a lecture on growing up, but Yumi placed her hand on his arm. It was a signal with which he had become familiar: *Keep your damn mouth shut. Let me handle it.*

"Nathaniel, why don't you take Jake for some more coffee?" *Interesting that she should ask Nathaniel,* Jacobus thought. *She truly doesn't want me to open my mouth.*

The two men left the cabin, but Jacobus signaled to Nathaniel that he wanted to stay outside the walls and listen in.

"Joy, let me help you straighten up," he heard Yumi say.

There was no response from D'Angelo. Presumably, she did not object.

"You know," Yumi continued. "you can think of this as your big chance."

"What are you talking about?" D'Angelo asked. "This is the worst day of my life."

"I know it seems that way and you're in a tough position. But how about you look at it this way: Anita and Sunny are gone, and there's only one person here who can take their place right now. You! So, now you're in charge. You're the boss. You've wanted a career as an arts administrator, right?"

"Yes, but—"

"No 'but.' This is your moment, Joy. A moment you can take advantage of. It's such a terrible situation in so many ways, but if there's anything good that can come of these tragedies, it's that it's opened up this incredible door for you. If you step up now, you'll get noticed. I'm sure of it."

"But what am I supposed to do?"

"I think the first thing you can do is clean up your room and notify all the musicians for them to come to you, right here. Don't ask them. Inform them. Tell them you'll work with them to organize their departures. You have to get them to the airport, don't you? Work on their flight schedules. Find out where they can be contacted so you can send them their fees, maybe. Musicians are always more than willing to talk about having their checks sent to them! Do all the things you do normally, but the only difference is, this time it's you making the decisions, not someone ordering you around."

"I can't do this!"

"Oy!" Jacobus said, outside.

"Shush your mouth!" Nathaniel whispered.

"Of course you can," Yumi said to D'Angelo. "Don't you remember our lesson?"

"You mean about doing research?"

"I mean about not thinking of yourself as a student, but as an artist. Same thing here. You're not an intern anymore. You're the CEO. Just imagine yourself as the CEO, okay? And we'll be there to help you because we'd like to talk to them, too. Okay?"

"I suppose. Okay."

"Great! You can do it, Joy! I know you can!"

Yumi gave her a hug. When she was halfway out the door, she turned and asked, "Oh, just one thing. Do you happen to have Edo Kuypers's phone number?"

"Sure."

She found Jacobus and Nathaniel waiting for her.

Jacobus said, "That was masterful. Who did you learn that from?"

"Sometimes you learn things on your own," Yumi said.

Chapter Sixteen

Back in Yumi's cabin, Nathaniel made the call to Amsterdam. He put the phone on speaker. A man answered.

"Edo Kuypers?" he asked.

"No, I'm Andreas. His flatmate. Edo isn't in."

"Give me the phone," Jacobus said. Nathaniel handed it to him.

"Not like that," Nathaniel whispered to Jacobus. "Turn it around. Now, upside down. There."

"When's Kuypers getting back?" Jacobus asked without preamble.

There was a pause.

"I don't know. Who is this?"

"We're from the music festival. Just checking on him. His medical emergency. Where did he go?"

Another pause. It was a pattern that Jacobus quickly got used to.

"I don't know that, either. I am not my brother's keeper."

"Thank you for the clarification. How long's he been gone?"

"He left last Sunday, I think."

"That's a long time. Are you worried?"

"Why should I be?"

"Just in case you were Kuypers' keeper."

"Edo comes and he goes."

"How long have you been flatmates?"

"Two years. Two and a half." For some reason, Andreas felt a need to add, "But we're not gay, if that's what you're thinking. It's to afford the rent. Amsterdam is expensive."

"Not as much as this call," Jacobus said.

"The call's free," Nathaniel whispered. "Times have changed."

Jacobus ignored him.

"Are you a musician, too?" he asked Andreas.

"Oh, God, no! I'm a server at a coffeehouse."

"No wonder he sounds high," Yumi whispered to the others. "Inhaling everyone's fumes."

"All right," Jacobus said to Andreas. "Call us when Kuypers gets back, okay? You got that?"

Andreas got it. Jacobus hung up.

"Why the hell didn't you get any background on Kuypers?" Jacobus asked Nathaniel.

"You didn't ask me to. That's why. You asked me to find out about people at the festival. Not everyone they've ever known."

"Let's not argue," Yumi said. "We've had enough of that. Why don't we just ask Christian and Marcus what their connection to Edo is?"

"Because one of them—whether you want to believe it or not—might be a killer," Jacobus replied. He raised his hand. *Cease and desist!* "Like you said, don't argue! I don't think we want to put ourselves in the awkward position of being the next on someone's list."

"You keep saying that," Yumi replied, "but I still can't believe that either of them could do anything like that."

"But, do you admit there are strange coincidences here?"

"Maybe."

"Aha! Tell me why you concede 'maybe.'"

"Maybe if Kuypers disappeared—and I'm not saying he really disappeared—but if he disappeared last Sunday... It was Sunday night when Marcus started acting so erratically. I know that because it was on Monday when I went into the city."

"Now you're using your head," Jacobus said. "You're saying they might have been in touch with each other?"

"I'm not saying anything. Just that maybe it's interesting. That's all."

"So what do we do?" Jacobus asked.

"Here's what we can do," Nathaniel said. "There's a Baroque music festival that's been going on in Amsterdam for years, called Let's Go Dutch. I wouldn't be surprised if Kuypers, Renfro, and Bjørlund played there together one time or another, when Renfro and Bjørlund were still doing that stuff. I can give the festival a call," Nathaniel said. "And it's free, too."

"Kiss my ass," Jacobus said.

The phone was once again placed on speaker. A Let's Go Dutch receptionist answered. Nathaniel explained that they were from the Antelope Island Music Festival and apologized for calling at such a late hour, but it was important. The receptionist connected them with the cellphone of Carl Swietan, the festival's personnel manager, who had already left for the night.

"Yes," Swietan said, "they all played here. But not for several years."

"Because they decided to no longer go for Baroque?" Jacobus asked.

"Are you making a joke, sir?"

"Probably not."

"To answer your question, then. Yes and no. For Bjørlund and Renfro, yes. We were sad to see them go. They were—"

"But not Kuypers?" Jacobus asked, impatient.

"That was another situation, I'm afraid. Edo, you see, we had to let go."

"Fired, you mean?"

"We don't like to use the word. I believe that is the word you use in America. Yes, okay. Fired."

"And why was he fired?"

"Did you not say you were from the Antelope Island Music Festival?" Swietan asked.

"Yeah. So what?"

"I understand both Christian and Marcus are performing there. I think you should be able to get the answer to that easily enough from them. Good day. Or I should say, good night, as it is getting quite late."

Nathaniel asked if they could call back if they should need him again, to which Swietan grudgingly acceded, if it was absolutely necessary. He then hung up, leaving Jacobus, Yumi, and Nathaniel with more questions and still no answers. The main question was, what could Kuypers tell them about Renfro and Bjørlund that they seemed intent on keeping secret? The secondary question was, with Kuypers unavailable, how would they find that out? It was possible he could lend much-needed insight. Without it, they were just treading water. And how long can you tread water? Sooner or later, you either sink or someone scoops you up. In the eyes of the cops, who viewed them as prime suspects, if Jacobus and Yumi didn't make progress soon, they would be sinking like lead weights.

As Dance had said, desperate times call for desperate measures. Jacobus decided to throw caution to the wind once again. He needed another chat with Cornelia Blum for some more background, after which he would confront Bjørlund and Renfro with what he knew. Yumi and Nathaniel would see what else they could glean from the others, using Joy D'Angelo, newly anointed CEO, as their cover. They would circle back to Yumi's cabin ASAP, hopefully before everyone had a chance to abscond.

"Tell me about Edo Kuypers, Ms. Blum," Jacobus said. "It sounded like Christian Bjørlund had a high opinion of him. And maybe, Marcus Renfro, too?"

"Please call me Cornelia. You're right about that. They all performed together at any number of music festivals. That was when Christian and Marcus were still primarily Baroque musicians. I, myself, have never played with him, as I'm not a Baroque person. It's quite a particular style of playing and it's hard to make the transition more than once."

"Do you have any idea what Kuypers's medical emergency was, Cornelia?"

"I can't say. However, for the past few years I understand he's suffered from bouts of depression."

"Is that why he had to back out of this festival?"

"I don't know. It's certainly possible. It would be a shame. He is a fine violinist."

"Do you know if he ever worked for Talbot or Flox?"

"I doubt it. They're in such different circles."

On the other hand, the Kreutzer String Quartet had had the most frequent contact with Talbot and Flox, which stood to reason as they had been an intact ensemble for almost two decades and were top-billed at festivals around the world. Jacobus didn't want to get sidetracked, but since he didn't know which track he should be on, he asked about the quartet. Blum was not reluctant to state that Dieter Waldstein, as their first violinist and spokesperson when not accompanied on tour by their manager—which was most of the time—had had occasional run-ins with Talbot.

"As you've seen, Mr. Jacobus, *most* of the time Dieter has a slow fuse, and he is really a gentleman in rehearsal *most* of the time. But when he ignites he can become quite incendiary."

"Yes, I'm well aware of that," Jacobus said, recalling his harrowing escapade in the latrine. "How incendiary?"

"If you mean, enough to kill someone? No, I am fairly certain of that. There was no reason. With Talbot, the arguments were trivial: starting times for concerts, stage deportment, attending those silly post-concert receptions. Things of that sort. Dieter has had his affairs, but everyone knows that."

"Everyone?"

"He's what is sometimes referred to as 'a ladies' man.' Dieter can be very charming, so they say, when he finds a particular specimen he is attracted to."

"You don't agree."

"I'm not the kind of lady a ladies' man would be interested in."

"I see. What about Talbot? Was she a specimen he might have turned on the charm for?"

"It's possible. There were rumors. But I don't indulge in rumors and I never pursued the thread. My colleagues' personal lives are their own, and I make it a rule never to intrude."

"What about Franz Weiss?"

"What about him?"

Jacobus related the story of Yumi had told him about her unpleasant experience with Weiss in the ramen restaurant.

"That would be like Franz," Blum said. "But, really, he is harmless. He wouldn't say boo to a manager, let alone beat them to death. Of everyone in the quartet, Franz is the one who keeps to himself. He comes to work, does his job, and goes home. He says very little and plays very well. He is the ideal second violinist."

Jacobus raised his hands in surrender. He had run out of questions.

"Well, thank you for your time, Cornelia."

"It was a pleasure to talk to you, Mr. Jacobus. I'm sorry I couldn't be of more help."

"No problem. No problem."

"In fact, may I ask: What would you think if I interviewed you for my book? You've got quite a compelling story. Yumi has been telling me."

"Thanks, but no thanks."

"Why not? It could make you famous."

"Because, from the way you smell, I expect you'd want me to tell you the truth. And if I told the truth, no one would buy your book."

Blum laughed.

"Have it your way, Mr. Jacobus. I think you've probably made a wise decision."

"By the way, what's the name of your book going to be?" Jacobus asked.

"I haven't decided yet. But being out here in the desert with all this wildness, I'm thinking of calling it *Symphonies and Scorpions*. What do you think?"

"Catchy. You think it will sell?"

"Unlike here, in Germany they like to read nonfiction, so first I write it in German, and hopefully it will sell. Then we will see. Who knows? Maybe then English. But if there is an audio version, I will let you know."

"*Viel glück*," Jacobus said.

"*Vielen Danke*," Blum replied. "I am impressed. You speak German very well, without an accent."

"*Bitte schön*. But I have to say German's a language I've spent my whole lifetime trying to forget. No offense."

"Tell me about you and Edo Kuypers," Jacobus said to Christian Bjørlund, interrupting his packing.

"I really don't have time for this, Mr. Jacobus."

"What's the hurry?"

"Joy has told everyone to assemble in her cabin in fifteen minutes if we want to get paid. She requires our contact information so she can send us our checks. Then she will organize the motor pool to the airport."

She's getting the hang of it, Jacobus thought.

"I wouldn't want to stand in the way of a musician getting paid," Jacobus replied, "so let's make it short."

Fortunately for Jacobus, Bjørlund was a fastidious shirt folder.

"Well, what is there to tell? Edo and I were colleagues for many years. It began when we went to the Royal Conservatory at The Hague as students. We both tutored privately with Anner Bylsma, though not at the same time. He taught us to play Baroque music the right way."

The innuendo was that Jacobus had not taught Yumi "the right way." Jacobus chose to ignore the slight. *Musicians would make great assassins*, he thought. *Maybe they were.*

"Our paths crossed and recrossed," Bjørlund continued. "But then they diverged. I moved on and so did Edo."

"Moved on? That's a curious way of putting it. More like 'fired' is what I've heard about Edo."

"Oh, you mean the incident at the Let's Go Dutch festival! Why didn't you say so?"

"Don't prevaricate, Bjørlund. It makes my hair curl. What went on?"

"I wish I knew, to be very honest. All I know is that there was a quarrel between Edo and Marcus. The next day, Edo was gone. I suppose that's why Marcus took exception to me bringing up Edo's name at the Mendelssohn abortion earlier today."

"If they had this big fight, wouldn't it have been uncomfortable for the two of them to be working together here?"

"Musicians fight all the time, Mr. Jacobus. As you've seen, and no doubt experienced yourself. And look at Dieter and me. But that was as bad as it gets. If every fight led to musicians refusing to work with each other, there would be no more music."

"You've got a point there, Bjørlund."

"Now, if you don't mind, I must finish packing. The sooner I leave this island, the better."

"You've got another point there."

Jacobus's next stop: Renfro. He, too, was hurriedly packing.

"Okay, Marcus. I'll make it quick. Fill in the gaps for me. You and Edo Kuypers had a fight a few years ago at the Let's Go Dutch festival. He got fired. I need to know what happened and what it has to do with what's been going on here, if anything."

"It was nothing," Renfro said.

"'It was nothing'? That means it was something," Jacobus said. "Come on. Spit it out."

"It was nothing."

"Don't be dense, Renfro. How many times will we have to repeat ourselves until you give me an answer? Because all I have to do is notify my pal, Detective Gettelman, that you're concealing information in a murder investigation, and he'll make sure your colleagues will be on their way to the airport without you, and then you can tell him 'it was nothing.'"

"All right," Renfro said. "All right. Little Dutch Boy."

"Ah! A riddle! Let me guess. Thumb in the dike—causeway repair?"

"Not close."

"Okay. I'll play the game. Kuypers is Dutch."

"You're getting warm."

"Kuypers is the Little Dutch Boy?" Jacobus asked.

"So to speak," Renfro said.

"So to speak. So to speak. Speak! Speak to me about what this is about, damn it!"

"Okay. But just calm down. As you know, Edo, like Christian and me, started our careers as Baroque musicians. Some years ago we were performing the complete *concerti grossi* by Pieter Hellendaal at the early music festival in Amsterdam, Let's Go Dutch. After one particular rehearsal, Edo and I got into this friendly discussion about bow technique. You know it's much different with Baroque bows—"

"I don't need the lecture, young man," Jacobus said. It was not difficult for him to understand how Renfro, Bjørlund, and it now seemed, Kuypers, could grate on each other.

"Sorry. In any event, the discussion goes back and forth, back and forth. It's never-ending, you know, because no one knows for sure how they played back then. But at one point, I get a little pissed off and I call Edo the Little Dutch Boy. Not a big deal, right? It's all very playful. Edo says back to me, 'Okay, if I'm the Little Dutch Boy, that makes you an Uncle Tom.' And then he rolls his eyes, like in the old minstrel shows. Not PC, to be sure, but it was not in public and we both think it's funny. We were good friends and we both had a good laugh."

"But someone else might not have thought it was funny," Jacobus said. "Is that what you're getting at?"

"I don't know. I guess so. All I know is there was this meeting and the next day Edo was fired. That's the truth."

"But there's one thing that doesn't make sense, Renfro. What I want to know is, why didn't you try to help him? After all, if *you* weren't offended by being called an Uncle Tom, why should anyone else be?"

"That's just it! I did! I did! I would never do anything to get Edo in trouble. We were colleagues. We were friends. I went to the administration and told them it was all in fun. That we were just joking. But they said what our intent was didn't matter. That the public perception would be negative. That the public would demand they do something to show they wouldn't tolerate racism against people of a different skin color."

Skin color! Jacobus thought. *What the hell was skin color? If only all humans were blind, how much better off the world would be. Except they'd find some other equally nonsensical excuse to kill each other. Religion was a biggie. Race and religion. World War II in a nutshell. That's why my parents, along with six million others of my ancestry and how many more of their never-to-be-born descendants, were no longer walking the earth. And what had ever happened to my dear brother, Eli, lost somewhere in the Holocaust? I've never known and probably never will.*

"What?" Jacobus asked. His mind had drifted and he hadn't been paying attention. He must be getting senile.

"I said, I thought it was ridiculous, and I've never gone back to Let's Go Dutch."

"Bjørlund, too?"

"I don't think so."

"Why didn't you tell us all this in the beginning?"

Jacobus felt as if he had the opposite ends of a chain in his hands, but without any of the connecting links.

"I can't tell you. I just can't."

The day before, Renfro had said "just because..." and then clammed up and refused to elaborate. Jacobus wasn't going to let this happen again.

"Okay," he said. "Let's play twenty questions, shall we? You said the Dutch Boy episode happened a few years ago, right?"

"Yes."

"Does that have anything to do with Kuypers being hired here?"

"Yes."

"And then unhired?"

"He wasn't unhired. He got sick."

"If he got sick, where is he? In a hospital? He sure hasn't been at home with his buddy, Andreas."

"I don't know."

"You don't know, or you're not going to tell us?"

"All I'll say is that I had nothing to do with their deaths. You have to take my word. And now I've got to go."

"Yeah, I know. Ms. D'Angelo is cracking the whip."

"Whatever you say."

Damn.

Jacobus returned to Yumi's cabin. Though he was agitated and preoccupied he really should have been paying more attention. He sat down on the bed only to find Nathaniel's face, and not the mattress, under his butt.

"What a way to wake up," Nathaniel said. "Next time remind me to sleep standing up."

"Just be thankful I didn't fart," Jacobus said. "Get me back on the phone with Carl Swietan."

"Sorry to be calling so late again," Jacobus said to Swietan. "Look, we did as you suggested. We know about the argument between Renfro and Kuypers." He related what he had found out from Bjørlund and Renfro, and toyed with mentioning that his questions were in regard to a double homicide. He decided not to, as it might result in Swietan clamming up like Renfro had or insisting on a lawyer. "And we know that the day after the argument, Kuypers was fired. The connection seems obvious, but we'd like you to confirm it."

"Very well. Word about the Little Dutch Boy and Uncle Tom exchange was brought to our attention, as everything becomes known among musicians, sooner or later. Usually sooner." Swietan was getting a little too smug for Jacobus's taste, but he held his fire. "We, the administration of Let's Go Dutch, held an emergency meeting and decided we didn't want bad publicity. We were struggling financially, we were trying to broaden our audience—"

"Broken record," Jacobus interrupted. "Nothing new here. Tell me something new, Swietan."

"So, we made a big public statement how we want to be inclusive and how we take racially offensive comments very seriously. Et cetera, et cetera. You know how institutions must protect themselves these days. To make a long story short, sadly, Edo was let go. It wasn't my personal decision, of course, but it was for the good of the organization."

"Of course." The corporate line. Who cares about the individual? The right or the wrong? The ability to make a living and provide for one's family? "And what about Kuypers? How did he take it?"

"Not well, I'm sorry to say. It wasn't our intention, but after our problem with him, other organizations were reluctant to hire him. Poor Edo dropped off the radar, so to speak."

Yet he was hired for the Antelope Island Music Festival. And then withdrew because of illness? Something was rotten in Holland, too.

220

"End of story?"

"End of story. Yes, from our point of view."

Jacobus was about to end the call. Sudden connection. Not quite end of story. Little Dutch Boy. Uncle Tom. Bitches in heat. Put them out of their misery. Marcus Renfro. Christian Bjørlund. Edo Kuypers. Now he would take a stab. If he was right, the loose, scattered links would start to form a chain.

"I know it's after midnight for you, Swietan," Jacobus said. "I do appreciate your cooperation. Sincerely. I'll send you a vase of tulips when this is all over."

"So we are finished?"

"Not quite. Just one more question, then I'll let you get back to your coffee shop."

"That's where I happen to be right now."

Ah, those Dutch. You gotta love 'em, Jacobus thought.

"More power to ya," Jacobus said. "Here's my question. You said it was brought to the festival's attention that Kuypers had called Renfro an Uncle Tom."

"That is not a question."

"Very perceptive, Carl. I'll rephrase it: Who was it that brought it to the festival's attention?"

"That's easy to answer. It was Anita."

The missing link.

"Anita Talbot?" Just to be sure.

Swietan laughed.

"There is only one Anita in this business. We administrators are always poaching each other's festivals, trolling for new talent or big names. Looking for new angles. She is going to be one of the best, mark my words. Sometimes I think visiting these festivals is really so we can get free vacations, but she takes these things seriously."

"Thank you for your valuable insight."

Swietan apparently couldn't tell whether Jacobus was being sarcastic or not—he was—and after an uncomfortable but thankfully brief silence, hung up.

Jacobus now had the motive he had been seeking for Marcus Renfro to have murdered Anita Talbot. He played out the sequence: Years ago, in Amsterdam, Talbot either overhears—or, better yet, is made aware of secondhand—the Uncle Tom, rolling-eyes exchange between Renfro and Kuypers. As was her inclination, she assumes the worst possible connotation and informs the Let's Go Dutch administration, arguing that Kuypers is undoubtedly a racist. It shouldn't be tolerated. The result: Kuypers is summarily fired. Perhaps it even throws Kuypers into a bout of depression that Blum had mentioned.

Renfro, his friend and colleague, is guilt-ridden. He even feels a sense of responsibility, though he knows it isn't his fault. Anger, too, no doubt. And now, years later, Talbot pulls the same vicious, misinformed stunt with Barov and his innocuous "bitches in heat" comment. Renfro witnesses it and knows she's passed it along to Flox, just as she had passed along the poisonous message to Let's Go Dutch. It infuriates Renfro to see contorted history repeating itself once again. He snaps, and kills Talbot, taking advantage of the tent disaster to disguise his actions, claiming that he found her dead. It all fits. But what about Flox? Why the rage against *him*? That's the only link that's still loose, dangling out there.

Time to visit little Joy D'Angelo again. He had memorized the path to her cabin and couldn't have gotten there faster if he could see.

He opened the door and walked in without knocking. She was alone.

"Yumi's not here, Mr. Jacobus," D'Angelo said. "She went off with everyone else. I think Detective Gettelman wanted to talk to her some more. He didn't seem very happy."

Alarm bells went off in his head. It was more important than ever that he solve this puzzle fast. Apparently, D'Angelo did not notice Jacobus's distress.

"I love Yumi!" D'Angelo continued. "She's changed my life. You must love her, too."

"We get along," Jacobus said. "But I'm not looking for her. I'm looking for you."

"Me? What can I do for you? I'm really busy getting all the musicians back

222

to the airport."

"I'll cut to the chase. What don't I know yet about Kuypers coming here, honey? Tell me. Tell me everything you know, and start with how he got hired."

He heard D'Angelo get out of her chair and start pacing the room.

"If I tell you everything, will it get me in trouble?"

"Not nearly as much as if you don't. But why are you asking me? You're the boss, right?"

"Well, okay then. I'm not sure if I know everything but here's what I do know. Mr. Kuypers getting hired was a bit of luck for us. Well, at the time we thought so, but it didn't turn out that way, did it? He was actually hired to replace another violinist, Leslie Hsu, who's performed here a lot in the past. Mr. Bjørlund recommended her, in fact. She had once been his student."

"What happened to her?"

"She has a boyfriend, and she just became pregnant and decided it would be better for the baby to stay home in New York. It's probably a good thing, considering."

Jacobus laughed.

"Is that funny?" D'Angelo asked.

"Just your choice of words: 'Became pregnant.' As if she woke up one morning and voilà! Pregnant! The Immaculate Conception. The act of becoming. Not really an act at all, is it? 'Becoming' is too passive."

"I'm not following you."

"One does not 'become' a musician, for example. One works one's ass off. One practices. Studies. Listens. Imitates even. Everything *but* becomes. One does not 'become' pregnant just as one does not 'become' a musician. One actively engages in a highly charged physical and emotional activity, whether it's making music or making love."

"That may be," D'Angelo said. "I got some of that from Ms. Shinagawa, and I guess she learned it from you, but I don't see what point you're making."

Nor did Jacobus. At first, at least, but he knew there was a connection there somewhere. What he did assuredly feel was rage. But over what? Certainly not the pregnancy of a woman whom he'd never heard of. Something about

Kuypers's story? Yes, there was something about it he was missing. The rage was there, regardless. Was it the sense he had that Kuypers had somehow been victimized? Or become a victim?

Victimhood disturbed him deeply. Everyone claimed to be a victim these days. Smokers still suing the tobacco companies a half century after everyone knew goddamn well cigarettes will kill you. "You tricked me! I'm a victim! You owe me!" Bullshit. Jacobus suddenly realized he was about to go off the deep end, thinking about his own *tsuris* more than the Kuypers connection, which was unhelpful. He put victimhood and the passivity of "becoming" in the back of his mind, where it belonged.

"Never mind," he said. "Go on."

"So we were in a bind for violinists," D'Angelo continued. "We had a long list, but no one we wanted was available. Marcus recommended Mr. Kuypers, and so Sunny decided, why not give Edo another chance?"

"That's what Sunny said? 'Another chance'?"

"Yes. Those were his words. 'Another chance.'"

Which meant only one thing: that Flox must have been aware of the history.

"What do you know about Let's Go Dutch?" Jacobus asked.

"I've heard of that. It's a Baroque festival in Amsterdam."

"Anything else about it?"

"I don't know. Is that important?"

"Never mind. Then what?"

"Then, when Anita found out Sunny had hired Mr. Kuypers, she ordered him to cancel his contract."

"So it wasn't Anita who unhired Kuypers?"

"No, it was Sunny. I was there. He didn't want to, but he did."

Jacobus recalled Yumi telling him the cryptic comment Flox had made to Hannah Carrington. That he wanted to make up for not standing up to Anita Talbot over something. And then saying, "Forget I ever said that."

"Why?" Jacobus asked D'Angelo. "What reason did they give Kuypers?"

"I don't know. They never told me. They argued about it. But then they came up with the story that he was sick, which is what they told everyone,

224

because otherwise the musicians would have objected. I guess Mr. Kuypers could have sued.

"I was really upset. You shouldn't do things like that. The medical issue was just a cover-up. I didn't think it was right, but that's when they hired Ms. Shinagawa. So I guess something good came of it in the end."

"But it was Flox who actually fired Kuypers? After hiring him?"

"Yes. Like I said."

"Couldn't it be possible," Jacobus postulated, wanting to be certain, "there's another possible scenario? That when Kuypers saw that Anita was running the show, he was the one who decided to make up an excuse to get out of coming here? That he'd rather forgo the paycheck than work for her?"

"I suppose that's possible, too. But why would he do that?"

Jacobus had forgotten that D'Angelo didn't know about Talbot getting Kuypers fired at Let's Go Dutch, and wanted to keep that under his hat for the time being, so he dissembled.

He improvised. "Because, as you know, Talbot wasn't the easiest person to work with."

"Don't we all know that! And, you know, that's possible, too, because he told Marcus that he wasn't really sick."

"He, being Flox? Is that what Flox told Marcus about Kuypers?"

"No, that's what Mr. Kuypers told Marcus about Mr. Kuypers."

"Are you telling me Kuypers spoke to Renfro?" Jacobus asked.

"Yes."

"When? How?"

"By phone. Last week. Marcus told me. They were friends, he said."

"Honey, you don't know how helpful you've been."

"I have? Oh. Well. Thanks."

And it's possible what you've told me has nothing to do with two murders, but I have a feeling we've just poked a hornet's nest.

Chapter Seventeen

J acobus returned to Yumi's cabin. She wasn't there, which added to his unease. What he had not expressed to D'Angelo were his misgivings about Renfro. His growing certainty that he had killed Talbot and Flox. Jacobus had now established three intersections between Renfro and the deaths of Talbot and Flox: One, Renfro had discovered Talbot's body, or so he claimed; two, he had awkwardly and perhaps conveniently absented himself shortly before Flox was killed; three, Jacobus had now learned that Renfro was the friend of Edo Kuypers, whom both Talbot and Flox had disgraced. Talbot had done so on two occasions, when she got him fired from the Amsterdam festival, and when she had his contract canceled here.

Could it be that Talbot's gross misinterpretation of Barov's "bitches in heat" comment triggered Renfro's pent-up rage? Enough to seek retribution? It would be understandable. It fit. Barov had saved the day when he artfully disarmed Bjørlund and Waldstein. Talbot, recalling Yumi's description, had been livid. If Talbot's actions were to have resulted in a black mark on Barov's career, as it definitely had on Kuypers's—and who's to say it couldn't—is it possible that Renfro took extreme measures to make sure that wouldn't happen?

These thoughts, and darker ones still, plagued Jacobus while he waited for Yumi. If his qualms amounted to something more than the idle fears of a guilt-ridden old man who had calculatedly put the well-being of one of the few people he truly cared about into potential jeopardy, could Yumi now be in danger?

He had rarely felt such personal turmoil, and not for himself, but for her.

The peril he had put her in with that outlandish plan for her to act like a prima donna. After that debacle of a concert, he heard her seek out Renfro. What if Renfro had been as angry with her as he had been at Talbot and Flox? Who knows what he might have done to her? And now. Where was he now? And where was she? He sat on the side of Yumi's bed and waited with greater anxiety than when he was in his hospital bed, with his own life hanging in the balance.

His face in his hands, he also reflected upon his own prejudices. Was he unfairly condemning Renfro in part because he was African American? As much as he condemned racism, could he absolutely deny that racial prejudice had influenced his own thought process? Even though he couldn't see him?

But Nathaniel was black, damn it! And wasn't Nathaniel his closest friend, as much of a brother as Eli had been? And the business about Uncle Tom and the rolling eyes. It was offensive to him, regardless that it was done in jest.

So Jacobus *believed* his assessment of Renfro was not racist, but did he *know* it for sure? As Jacobus always reminded his students, there's a big difference between *thinking* you know something and *knowing* you know it. When you're performing the Brahms concerto and you only *think* you know it, that's when you're in real trouble.

Jacobus discovered that he had been gripping Hocus for he didn't know how long, and so tightly that both of his hands were stiff and painful. Hocus, the murder weapon! The one that Marcus Renfro snatched up and with which he smashed Anita Talbot's head in, claiming she had died by some accident. Then the stick went missing because Renfro took it with him and killed Flox with it. His work done, he left it by the body, incriminating both Yumi and him, intentionally or not. *Damn it!* Jacobus thought. *I'm not a racist. Renfro is a killer.*

Jacobus almost had to pry his fingers open to release his grip. This plain stick that Yumi had given him. She had named it Excalibur and he had made a joke of it. *How we wish we could do things over,* Jacobus thought. *How we wish. But of course we can't. Life goes on. Life isn't always fair.* He was about to amend that to life is *never* fair when the cabin door opened.

"Jake, are you in here?"

"Yumi."

He heard the light switched on.

"We were looking all over for you!" she said. "Are you okay?"

"Never better," he said. "Who's 'we'?"

"Marcus and I. We're both here."

"Yumi, I think—"

"Don't worry. We've sorted things out."

"What have you sorted?"

"Well, it turns out that Marcus knew Edo from when they played—"

"Yeah, he and I have had a lengthy chat about the unlikely friendship between Uncle Tom and the Little Dutch Boy."

Yumi said, "Jake, I believe him. Can't you see how Anita's reaction to Jamie's 'bitches in heat' comment would get Marcus upset? It would make *anyone* upset. It doesn't mean he killed her."

"I don't see anything, literally or figuratively. Because I still want to know three things: How Marcus happened to be the one to discover Talbot dead only minutes after we spoke to her, where he was when Flox was murdered, and how Hocus got from Point A to Point B."

"I've explained those things, Mr. Jacobus, and if I didn't respect Yumi so much—"

"Well, there are explanations and there are explanations, and yours is far from sufficient."

"Jake!" Yumi said. "You're being unfair."

"Am I?"

Jacobus stood up, and banged Hocus on the floor with each assertion:

"Well, someone please tell me where I'm wrong: Some years ago, Anita Talbot gets Edo Kuypers in hot water over an innocuous comment she totally misconstrues."

Bang went the stick. "Edo Kuypers gets fired."

Bang again. "So far, so good?"

"So far," Renfro said.

"Thank you. Now, fast-forward a few years. Talbot gets everyone's friend, Jamie Barov, in hot water over an innocuous comment she totally misconstrues yet again."

Bang. "Will Barov get fired? Who knows? But here's the nub. Here's what you don't know, Yumi. Edo Kuypers did not withdraw from this festival for medical reasons."

Bang. "Let me repeat, Edo Kuypers did not withdraw from this festival for medical reasons."

Bang. Bang.

"He didn't?" Yumi asked.

"No. Talbot fires Edo Kuypers before he even gets here! 'Let bygones be bygones' was apparently not in her lexicon. Then, shortly after she reports Barov's 'bitches in heat' comment to Sunny Flox, who scribbles it down on a notepad, she finds herself dead. And *shazam!*"

Bang. "Sunny Flox, too, soon finds himself dead!"

Bang. "And among all the musicians in the world, only one of them happens to be on the scene both in Amsterdam and Antelope. And who may that be? None other than Edo's buddy, Marcus Renfro."

Bang.

"But that's not true!" Renfro said.

"Really! You mean to suggest you weren't in Amsterdam and you're not here on this godforsaken island?"

"No. That's not what I'm saying. What I'm saying is that you're wrong that it was Anita who fired Edo. It wasn't Anita. It was Sunny!"

Well, well, well, thought Jacobus. *Well done.* Even though he already learned this from Joy D'Angelo, he had just gained valuable insight hearing it straight from the horse's mouth. Even in his old age, Jacobus gave himself credit for being passably good at jigsaw puzzles. Using his fingertips as eyes, he had worked his way up to thousand-piece puzzles, linking the pieces together by feel. Remembering where he had set each one down. He relished the sense of triumph to finish a jigsaw puzzle faster than Nathaniel. Now, with this human puzzle, he was putting it all together. Piece by piece. Fitting them into place.

"You're sure of that?" Jacobus asked. "That it was Flox and not Talbot who fired Kuypers?"

"Yes," Renfro insisted. "That's a fact."

Jacobus approached Renfro as closely as he dared. So close that he could hear Renfro's accelerated breathing, through the nose with mouth closed.

"So how is it, young man," Jacobus asked, "you happen to know that to be a fact?"

Sometimes, the power of silence is appreciated the most when it is sudden and unintended. We're surrounded by sound, Jacobus thought, *constantly battered by it. It's inescapable. Sometimes the sounds are desirable, soul-filling: music, for example. Or nature. Yes, nature.*

The sounds of his woods in the Berkshires came to mind. How he wished he was there now. But even in the silence of his woods, there was sound. He had tried to show that to Yumi, a dutiful student in that regard, though she had been so rigorously trained in the practice of human-generated musical sound that she had almost discounted the notion of nature's music as an equally rewarding stimulus.

In a way, the absence of sound is like the absence of love. The longer we have either, sound and love, the more we expect it to be the norm, and the more we take it for granted. Suddenly remove it, and we are shocked. Bereft. Though in Jacobus's life there were long periods during which he and love were distant relatives, and the absence of love was not sudden. It came and went. He had gotten used to it. With silence, it went even further. It was the opposite. He relished it, sometimes even more than music. Absolute silence. When he died, would there be a moment of silence for him? That would not be inappropriate. The only thing better, perhaps, would be a moment of Mozart. But in general, for him, silence was peace.

Except for now. The silence after his question, "So how is it, young man, you happen to know that to be a fact?" was abrupt and ragged, like a burlap sack ripped through with a dull knife. How can the absence of sound sometimes be sublimely beautiful and sometimes hideously ugly? Jacobus asked himself. He would have to ponder that sometime, but what he knew for sure was that he wasn't going to be the one to break this one.

Jacobus waited. Yumi waited. Renfro waited, but Renfro was the weakest of the three.

"What do you mean?" he asked.

"I'd gathered it was Talbot who uninvited your friend here," Jacobus said. "Now you're telling me it was Flox who did the dastardly deed. Please explain how you know that."

"I wasn't the only one in Amsterdam. Christian was there, too. Why don't you ask him?"

"You're saying you think Christian could've killed Talbot and Flox?"

"I'm not saying anything, except it's no more likely I did than he did."

"You're wrong there, pal, because Christian was with Flox when Talbot was killed and was with us in the barn when Flox was killed. So the ball is still in your court, Marcus."

"Talk about racist comments," Renfro said.

"That's not racist, Marcus," Yumi intervened quietly, "any more than bitches in heat is sexist."

Ah! She was finally starting to see the light.

"And I'll ignore it, Marcus," Jacobus said, "because you know that's bullshit and you're just attempting to change the subject."

"I really don't care."

"No doubt. And I suppose you didn't care that after Edo got trashed in Amsterdam he got retrashed here. I guess I'm wrong. I would've thought you'd be pretty mad at what happened to your friend. Mad enough to kill? I don't know. Maybe. You hear crazier things."

"Think what you want. I didn't kill anybody."

"You know, Marcus," Jacobus said, "you're really a lousy liar. This is what I think. I think you tried to give Edo a break—make amends—and helped get him hired here. God bless you. Pennies in heaven. But then he gets fired before he even arrives. Medical emergency, they tell everyone. But who would know the real reason? Talbot: Yes. Flox: Yes. But they wouldn't want anyone to know that. So someone else must have known. Who else would know? D'Angelo: Yes, but she swore she didn't tell anyone. Kuypers: Obviously. Kuypers, Kuypers, Kuypers. So, what I think is that you were in communication with your buddy, Edo, who told you the whole tragic, sordid saga that he had just been fired again. That must've really pissed you off. And then to rub salt in the wound, Talbot and Flox go after Barov in the same infantile way they did with Edo. That was one step too far, as far as you were concerned. They crossed the red line. Can't say I totally blame you, Renfro. You know, these managers."

"Believe what you want. I didn't kill Anita, and I didn't kill Sunny. That's all I'm going to say."

Yet another silence. This one not electric. This one bloated and foundering.

Things happened suddenly.

The cabin door opened.

"Anyone home?" It was Nathaniel.

Renfro shoved Jacobus, who fell heavily to the ground, his head narrowly missing the corner of the bed. As Yumi and Nathaniel ran to Jacobus's aid, Renfro bolted out the door, slamming the door shut behind him.

"Let him go," Jacobus said. "Let the cops catch him."

Yumi and Nathaniel helped Jacobus to the side of the bed and waited for him to regain his breath. A multi-leveled silence. Jacobus was dazed and his left shoulder throbbed but, other than humanity, he did not think anything was permanently broken.

Yumi put her arm around him.

"What do you think now?" Jacobus asked her.

"I'm in shock, to tell you the truth. I couldn't believe Marcus would do anything like kill someone, especially in cold blood. I thought this was just another of your crazy hunches. But then I started remembering how erratic his behavior got last week."

"Tell me about it."

She explained how, when she went into the city, he had been so upbeat and buoyant, but how, by the time she returned in the evening, his mood had changed radically. Even without their amorous liaison—which Jacobus clearly now knew about—Renfro's behavior was equally baffling and disconcerting. Given that it was Marcus who had initiated their night of lovemaking, it was more so. It must all have been a sick ruse. Jacobus had finally found the answer. There seemed little doubt.

"What should we do now?" Yumi asked.

"Let the cops know, I guess," Jacobus replied. "Unless you want to make a citizen's arrest."

Nathaniel offered to dial Detective Gettelman's number, but before he did, there was a knock at the door. Jacobus assumed it wouldn't be Renfro, and he was right. It was Jefferson Dance.

"Dance, you're just the person we're looking for," Jacobus said.

"I'm not so sure about that, Mr. Jacobus. You see, I come bearing grave tidings. Law enforcement asked me to accompany you and Ms. Shinagawa to the office. They're going to be taking the two of you in for questioning."

"What the hell are you talking about? We know who killed Talbot and Flox, and I can assure you it wasn't us."

"I'm not saying I think you did it, but I've got no choice in the matter. I'm bound to do what they ask, so you'll have to explain that to them. As a state park ranger, even as a temporary one, I do have the authority to arrest you, though I'd rather not. So, can you just make this a little less difficult than it already is and come quietly? I'm not big on using force, but if it comes to it..."

Nathaniel said, "Let's just go with him, Jake. It'll all get sorted out, and as you said, Renfro's not about to get away."

With all the hoopla over the past hours, Jacobus had paid scant attention to the weather. Without his being aware, the wind had abated and the temperature had climbed. He realized he was once again excessively hot. It was as if the storm had existed only in his imagination. If only the horror it had swept in had been equally ephemeral, but that was still very much with them and very real.

It infuriated Jacobus that he and Yumi might be falsely charged with murder when the real killer, Renfro, would remain at liberty. At best, it would require all his power of persuasion to get them out of their predicament. Yet, at that moment he saw no alternative.

"All right. What the hell."

Dance led the way along the cleared path, with Yumi and Jacobus, arm in arm, behind him. Nathaniel followed. With the sun out again, the ground had dried up fast in the heat-driven wind.

"It's getting too damn hot again, Dance," Jacobus said. Prodding his way forward with Hocus, the ground was almost as rock hard as it was before the storm. "How do you stand it? What is it? One, two-o'clock?"

"It's actually closer to seven, Mr. Jacobus. That's about when the temperature reaches its maximum out here. Latitude and longitude thing. Angle of the sun and all that."

Jacobus could hardly believe that an entire day had almost passed. Between the change in time zones, all the commotion, and the "latitude and longitude thing," he had lost his sense of time, an ability he had always prided himself on. Soon, all the musicians and concertgoers would be gone from the island. Almost certainly, Renfro would be among them. And where would he and Yumi be? Interrogated like common criminals.

"Why exactly are we suspects?" Yumi asked, who sounded almost more irate than Jacobus. She had not only been deceived by a murderer, she had shared her bed with him. And now she was being accused of the very crimes he had committed. The only reason she kept her voice down was that they were overtaken by some annoying little kids whooping it up, and by clusters of jabbering concertgoers, elated that they had finally been rescued and overjoyed at the prospect that they would soon be off the island and on their way to a good meal.

"You're not suspects, technically," Dance said. "Just what they like to call persons of interest. Mainly it's because they haven't figured out a motive why you'd do such a thing. If they had one, you'd be suspects for real. I'd say Detective Gettelman is more interested in why you and Mr. Jacobus pulled a fast one on them."

"What do you mean?" Jacobus asked, as if he were innocent. As if he had no idea what Dance meant.

"The stunt you pulled. That walking stick you gave them."

"I was just doing my civic duty." Dance couldn't restrain a chuckle, even in such a somber moment.

"Like heck it was. That wasn't your cane. That was chicanery."

"How do you figure?"

"That stick was cottonwood. They hardly grow in New England and the wood is soft. It would make a lousy walking stick. The stick you gave them looked suspiciously like the branches knocked off the trees in the storm Friday night. I'd guess you found it just lying there on the ground. That would make it two varieties of lying. It took them a while, but Guzman finally figured out the stick you surrendered to them couldn't've been whittled more than a day or two ago. So they're curious why you might be hiding a murder weapon. I can't say that they don't have a point."

"Why do you think Jake would do something dishonest like that?" Yumi asked.

"Maybe because he thought the cops would misconstrue things," Dance replied. "Maybe he thought the real stick would get the two of you into more hot water."

"If it was true that Jake gave him a fake stick," Yumi asked, "and I'm not saying it is, how long did you suspect that?"

Dance snickered again, as if recalling the punchline to an old joke. "Immediately, actually, especially when he pulled that helpless blind-man act. It was a good thing I was standing behind those two, because if they'd seen my face it might've given the whole show away. And don't forget, I'd seen Mr. Jacobus with the real stick. It's a beauty. I'm guessing maple, nice and solid. He really pulled the wool over their eyes. They're not bad cops. They just haven't spent enough time outdoors, is all."

"Yumi! Yumi!" Joy D'Angelo's voice. Out of breath. Running towards them.

"Oh, hi Joy," Yumi said. "We're a little busy now."

"Won't take a sec. I'm just arranging rides back to Salt Lake City for everyone and wanted to know when you and Mr. Jacobus want to go."

"I'll be driving them," Nathaniel said. "I've got a car here. No need to worry."

"Okay, then. Thanks. That makes life easier! Mr. Dance, there was a camper I gave a ride to from the airport. Do you know if he might need a lift back?"

"What's his name?"

"A Mr. Collier."

"You mean Callier?"

"Could be. He didn't write it down. He just said it. I thought it was Collier. I guess because Collier is such a common name I thought that's what it was."

"I'm pretty sure it was Callier," Dance said. "Least that's what he wrote down on his campsite registration."

"I suppose," D'Angelo said. "He did have an accent. I suppose it could've been Callier."

"I'll be checking on him," Dance said. "His bicycle was in bad shape. I'm pretty sure he'll need that lift."

"Mr. Collier had a bicycle, too, so you're probably right."

"Callier or Collier!" Yumi interrupted, in a much louder voice than was usual for her. "Frankly, I'm tired of this conversation. We're about to be arrested for two murders we didn't commit and you're debating whether it's an *a* or an *o*? What the hell difference does it make?"

"Maybe it does," Jacobus said, in a much quieter voice than was usual for him. "Dance, didn't you say his first name was Gene?"

"You've got a good memory, Mr. Jacobus. Yes. Gene. Gene M. Callier."

When Daniel Jacobus was a child, he wanted to be Beethoven. Not be *like* Beethoven. Actually *be* Beethoven. The seven-year-old would brush up his hair in an unruly tousle, wear ill-fitting old clothes, and put on boorish and gruff airs. His brother, Eli, suggested, "Why don't you be Mozart? You wouldn't be nearly as obnoxious."

Whenever little Daniel would whine about having to practice or do his music theory homework when his friends were playing soccer outside, his mother, Esther, would tell him, "So you want to be Beethoven? Think like Beethoven!" The way she said it wasn't strident or loud. It had the tone of "I'm just reminding you what you told me you wanted, Daniel." With young Jacobus's capricious personality, she had to repeat it often, so much so that it almost became a family mantra. Now, whenever Jacobus listened to any music by Beethoven, after the first note he would hear his mother's loving, patient, quietly insistent voice: "You want to be Beethoven? Think like Beethoven!"

Beethoven had been his hero for as long as he could remember. He listened to the symphonies and all the chamber music from the cradle. Dozens of compositions. That was no exaggeration. His father would play the brittle old 78s on their Gramophone with the big acoustical horn, changing the scratchy discs every seven minutes.

But it wasn't only the music that profoundly influenced little Daniel. It was also the process by which Beethoven produced his masterpieces. That was the true inspiration. Beethoven carried around a little music notation notebook wherever he went—for his famous strolls in the Vienna Woods, to the inns and taverns that he frequented. Whenever he had a musical idea, he would write it down, without regard to how or where it would end up. It could ultimately be part of a concerto, a trio, a song, a mass. It didn't matter at the moment. Nor did it matter whether the ideas were of high quality. It could end up in the trash. It could be as minuscule as a few notes, or it could be a melody or a fragment of a melody. Often the scribbled ideas were indecipherable to anyone but him, and quite often they were mundane and more pedestrian than most of his less esteemed contemporaries. If he had incorporated them intact and performed them as originally written, chances were today no one would have ever heard of Ludwig van Beethoven.

But what Beethoven did was rewrite, rework, reconfigure. Scratch this out, add this, move this around. Over time and with relentless revision, his ideas began to take shape, getting incrementally better over time. All of that was well and good, except then something extraordinary, something miraculous, took place.

Between the next-to-last step and the final step, Beethoven's mind took a leap across a vast intellectual chasm, a chasm where every other composer's mind stopped and accepted the tried and true. It was a moment when all possibilities, all permutations, all theoretical connections suddenly locked into place, and Beethoven knew: This is how it must be! *"Es muß sein!"* is what he wrote in the score of his final string quartet. And what "must be" was unlike anything anyone else could have conceived of, or come close to achieving before or since. That's why Jacobus scoffed at recent attempts to reconstruct Beethoven's scattered notations for an unfinished tenth symphony. No computer or human brain could understand a farthing how Beethoven's mind worked. It was imbecilic. It was outrageous, because it put blinders on what everyone knew about Beethoven's greatness: His mind worked unlike any other human being's. If the reconstituted tenth symphony were ever performed, Jacobus promised himself to blow up the concert hall.

Of course, Jacobus never believed he could reach the lofty conclusions Beethoven realized on a regular basis. That would require an egotism even beyond Wagner's, a composer who put only Beethoven on a higher pedestal than himself. But he could heed his mother's advice: "You want to be Beethoven? Think like Beethoven!" And he did so not only in music, but also in order to solve problems. Since he arrived in Antelope Island, the problems had become more complex, more intractable, seemingly by the minute. As he thought about solutions, he rearranged all the pieces, all the possibilities. He had gone off on tangents, coming up with bizarre, unprovable scenarios. Little by little he had made progress. But the progress was unacceptably slow and incremental. Two steps forward, three steps backward. There had been too many variables, too many loose ends.

That is until Dance had said Gene M. Callier. Not Collier. In that moment, in his blindness, he saw everything, just as Beethoven, in his deafness, heard everything. Everything essential coalesced, down to every little detail, like Robert Schumann's manic depression, Baroque music, and the games Mozart played. But mostly, *Roughing It*, by Mark Twain. *Yes, especially that. Thank you, Nathaniel, for giving Yumi such a precious gift. I'd asked you for backstories, and that was the one I needed but hadn't even realized it. Until now.*

Everything extraneous fell by the wayside. It didn't matter that haughty Christian Bjørlund liked to box. It didn't matter that the roach, Franz Weiss, was a closet skirt-chaser. It didn't matter that Mr. Helpful, Jamie Barov, was too pleasant to be real. It didn't even matter that Joy D'Angelo and Marcus Renfro's alibis were as shaky as a bowl of Jell-O in an earthquake. None of that mattered. The only thing that mattered was that there was a camper named Gene M. Callier. Thank you, Mama, for nagging me to think like Beethoven.

"Dance," Jacobus said, "do me a favor."

"If I can."

"Go to Gettelman and Guzman and tell them you didn't find us. Tell them we're at the White Rock campground and they should be there in about two hours. They can have a nice dinner first. "

"But—"

"Trust me, Dance. Just this once. Please!"

It was such a rare occasion for Jacobus to use the word, "please," that everyone took note of its significance.

"Okay," Dance said, "I'll trust you. Seeing as you said please." He went on ahead.

Jacobus explained his plan to Yumi.

"So go find Renfro," he concluded. "Tell him all is forgiven. With my sincere apologies. That I understand everything."

"Is that it? 'All is forgiven?' 'I understand everything?'"

"That's enough for now. Just bring him to the campground the way I said."

Jacobus said to D'Angelo, "Joy, dear, drive me to White Rock Campground. Have I ever told you you're going to make a great CEO?"

His conclusion had to be right—it was the only possibility—but it was so implausible that Jacobus needed confirmation. He asked Nathaniel to make one final call to Amsterdam.

"Yes, Andreas," Jacobus said. "I understand I am bothering you. Yes, I know. You've explained to me you are not your brother's keeper. It's just a quick question."

"What do you want?"

"Has Kuypers returned yet?"

"No. He has not. Will that be all?"

"Last question, after which you'll never again be troubled by the pleasure of my company. Is his violin still there?"

"Yes, it is. Good-bye."

Chapter Eighteen

Huddled in his cramped, sweltering tent, he was startled when the tapping on the top of it began. Even though the tent was buffeted like a flag by the wind, he could hear it. Persistent, probing, rhythmic tapping. Not threatening. Disinterested. But because it wasn't threatening, it was all the more alarming for being monotonous and inexplicable. He looked up and saw something being poked down onto the top of the tent, like someone pressing a finger into an inflated balloon, except he was on the inside of the balloon. Unable to see through the density of the tightly woven tent fabric, he couldn't tell whether it was an animal or some device. A bear? A raccoon? He did not know the wildlife on this island, but he had heard stories.

It was unfathomable. First, the poking was at the top, then little by little it spiraled down and around his circular tent. Slow. Systematic. It couldn't be an animal. But what was it? The poking stopped as suddenly as it had started, but then there was a scratching noise dragging in the dirt, just outside, followed by a tap against the tent. This happened over and over until whatever was doing it made a complete circumnavigation of the entire base of the tent. It was almost as if someone was taking a physical X-ray of the tent.

What should he do? Ignore it? The last thing he wanted was to bring attention to himself. He wanted to avoid trouble like the plague. Trouble? He wanted to avoid any contact whatsoever with anyone, or anything, until he had escaped.

Or should he call out, and ask what was going on? This silent poking was so strange. What did it mean? What did it have to do with him?

"Mr. Callier? That you in there?"

Ah. One of the park rangers. Though the voice was unfamiliar.

"Yes."

"I'm a blind man," said the voice, "and seem to have lost my bearings. Wondering if you could give me some help."

A blind man. On Antelope Island. Curious. But innocent enough. Harmless.

He felt so trapped. At first, he thought his compact, two-person tent, and everything inside it had been irreversibly ruined. He would have gotten a smaller tent, but they laughed and convinced him that with the quantity of supplies he'd bought, if he had a one-person tent he'd have to sleep on his cooler.

They also said the tent was guaranteed to be waterproof and perhaps it was. But it hadn't been hail-proof. He had been gone when the storm hit. The storm almost killed him and when he had managed to find his way back, in the dark, the tent was flattened, almost undetectable under the layer of ice. He had dug it out with his bare, freezing hands, and had managed with great difficulty to re-erect it, its pole skeleton, constructed with "space-age" technology, having buckled but not broken under the weight of the ice.

It had brought small comfort to be inside the tent once again. Indeed, it was almost worse. Everything—his clothes, his gear, his food—was waterlogged and frozen, even though only a few hours before the storm it had been hot and dry as an oven. He had shivered, and not only from the cold and damp, but also from fear and exhaustion.

Like many of his countrymen, he had learned to cycle almost before he could walk. There were close to a million bicycles in Amsterdam, more than the number of inhabitants. Cycling was not simply a leisure activity, or for one's health, or even for sport. Cycling was a principal mode of transportation. People cycled to their jobs, their schools, their markets. In the Netherlands, he could cycle for a hundred miles and not be winded.

But this had been different. This was unanticipated. The altitude. From being six feet below sea level in Amsterdam to over four thousand feet above, here. He had been unprepared for that swing. Just walking had winded him at first. And the incline! Climbing the two-thousand-foot mountain even without the thin air would have been a struggle for him. The rental agency told him he needed a mountain bike, with the fatter tires and all those gears, but he had never ridden one of those before. He had grown up riding the Omafiets, *"Grandma bike," with* a step-through frame, upright position, mudguards, and a skirt guard. It was what everyone rode. In his childhood, he had a single-speed, and later, when he could afford it, a three-speed. All of his bicycles had coaster brakes, where you pedal backwards to engage the rear brake, rather than hand brakes. He never needed anything more demanding. Most Dutch bicycles were upright or "sit-up" style – with taller frames than typical bicycles, providing good visibility and comfort. On a flat surface.

So he did not heed the rental agency's advice and instead rented a bicycle that was as close to his experience as he could find. That turned out to be a terrible decision, as had most of his decisions since the disaster. He had severely underestimated the necessity of multiple gears while going over the mountain, and the narrow tires threw his bicycle off balance every time they dropped in a pothole or bounced against a rock in the mountain path, which was every few feet. He couldn't count the number of times he crashed, landing on the hard ground, a sharp rock, or even the thorny grass, wearing little protective gear. Yes, he had biking gloves, but no helmet. Who wore helmets except Americans? Nor had he brought enough water to traverse the mountain, miscalculating the length of time the ride would take, expecting it to be only an hour or so, given the horizontal distance. "As the crow flies," the Americans say. He was no crow. The ride had almost killed him even before he narrowly out-sprinted an irate bison he had disturbed. He had become dehydrated and the sun scorched his exposed skin to an unnatural, dangerous red. By the time he reached the ridge, he had almost given up. But when he'd looked down and seen his destination, his determination was renewed.

He did not think it would have been possible, but the way back, during the storm, had been worse. The hail, so powerful it had dented his bicycle's frame, had battered his head and shoulders, leaving him cut and bruised. Gusts of wind literally blew him and his bicycle off the ground. He had lost the trail in the darkness and wandered about the mountainside for hours, searching for the pass.

He finally found his way back to the west side of the island and his campground, only to discover his tent in shambles. If he hadn't immediately reassembled it, he would have died from exposure. With whatever little strength he still had, he battled the incessant wind that frustrated his efforts to pitch the tent. The rain fly got caught in a sudden gust and blew off into the lake, irretrievable, and he had

had to place heavy rocks inside the tent to prevent it, too, from following the rain fly, but at last, he was able to restore the minimal shelter he needed to survive. He lay exhausted throughout the night, his body bruised and broken, chilled to the bone yet feverish, on a sodden sleeping bag, wishing he were dead.

The park ranger had stopped by at dawn. He called to him from outside the tent, which was still shivering from the force of the wind.

"Mr. Callier?"

"Yes?"

"I saw the bike outside your tent and just wanted to check to make sure you were back, safe and sound," he said.

"Yes. Thank you. I am fine."

"Glad to hear that. That was quite a night. You gave us a little scare when we couldn't find you."

"I am fine."

"Good. Well, have a nice day."

He needed to leave. Immediately. As soon as the ranger's footsteps disappeared, he emerged from the tent, debating whether to break it down, pack it with his other belongings, and attach it to the back of his bicycle. Or throw it in the Dumpster at the edge of the campground. He needed to leave no trace.

Or should he simply leave everything in place? If he did that, no one would be suspicious. They would assume he was still on the island, which was good. Afflicted by indecision, he changed his mind, back and forth, finally deciding to leave most of his things there, simply because it was less weight on his damaged bicycle and he'd need all his remaining strength to get off the island.

He emerged from the tent. Everything was steel gray. Everything. A roiling, opaque soup of low clouds filled the sky, dwarfing ten-thousand-foot peaks on the horizon. The entire, limitless lake was in constant motion, whitecaps slashing at the shore. Tall dry grass covering the mountains bowed and swayed like a chorus in the wind. All of it gray. It was as unnatural a world as he could imagine, and he was thankful he soon would be rid of it.

The rain had abated, but the easterly wind was proving to be a relentless, depressing adversary, hindering his escape. He would have to ride into it. He mounted his bicycle in excruciating pain. Every muscle rebelled. Yet he knew *he had no choice, and anyway, it was a mere few miles to the causeway and the way was only modestly hilly. Up one rise on the dirt road, a left turn, and it was downhill from there. He could do it.*

Most of the so-called campers were in their monstrous American recreational vehicles, as big as houses, insulating those inside from the natural world. Like mice in cages. What kind of recreation was that? And those who had tented through the night, like him? They had suffered and were preoccupied with salvaging what they could of their ruined gear. So no one paid him the least bit of attention, and that was good.

Buffeted by the wind, he slowly pedaled toward his destination. Toward freedom. Freedom delayed but freedom nevertheless. Yes, it was the thought of freedom that kept him pedaling. Left, then right, then left, then right. He kept his mind focused to give himself the will, the strength to keep going. His life had been ruined, ruined many times over, and since there was no way to go back in time, the only way to change history was to change the future. And that he had done.

He had coasted downhill with ease, on the paved road. He had overcome the worst that man and nature could throw at him. It had almost killed him, but he had prevailed. His speed increased without even having to pedal, and the breeze in his face cooled and dried him. It was now all so effortless that he laughed out loud as he rounded the bend, descending to the causeway.

There was no traffic in either direction. This was perfect! If he had prayed, he couldn't have asked for more. The water on each side of the causeway was choppy, splashing over the road surface, as bad as the North Sea during a gale, but that was of no concern to him.

Bristling with adrenaline, he picked up speed. Freedom was straight ahead of him. The finish line, the tollbooth, was just a few miles ahead. It was unpreventable. He had won. Faster he rode, sprinting like Johan van der Velde at the Tour de France. Just get to the finish line along this ribbon of road. Like an arrow about to find its mark.

Why was there was nothing underneath his bicycle?

The roadway was gone! He was in the air, jettisoned like that insane American motorcyclist, Evel Knievel. He pedaled ineffectually, floating absurdly in nothingness, for an infinite moment. Then gravity crashed him into the water, landing on rocks just under the surface. He was stunned, not only from the shock and the impact, but also from incredulity. What had happened? He couldn't understand. Waves pushed and pulled at him and repulsive saltwater stung his eyes and invaded his throat and lungs. He blindly reached for a boulder, slipped, reached again, and held on, resisting a growing temptation to just let go and be done with it.

Hanging on for minutes, vomiting lake water, his wits and strength slowly returned. Looking up, he slowly clambered up the earthworks that provided the causeway's underpinnings and crawled back on to the road surface. It was then he saw what had happened, dashing his hopes as painfully as his body had been dashed. A section of the causeway—a hundred meters, two hundred, who could tell?—had been washed out by the storm. There was no way he would be able to traverse that gap.

He looked down into the water to find his bicycle. It was under the water and had caught on a rough outcropping of rock, one slowly rotating wheel protruding above the surface. Between waves' crests, the rest of the bicycle reappeared, visually distorted by the water, teasing like a mirage. It was mangled beyond repair. He was trapped.

He sat at the edge of the cloven road, mentally and physically numb, for how long? He had no idea. Facing north, he stared at the vast expanse of the tormented lake. In the distance were the mountains above Promontory Point, motionless and uncaring.

He didn't move when a woman in a uniform slowly drove up in a pickup, stopped, and asked him what he was doing. Don't you realize it's dangerous to be out here, the woman asked? That the roadway could continue to weaken and give way? He shrugged.

"Are you staying at the campground?" the woman asked.

"Yes. White Rock. Why?"

"Get in the truck. I'll give you a lift back there. You've walked a heck of a long way."

Fifteen minutes later he was back at his tent. It had dried out, at least. He crawled in and went to sleep, exhausted, for the rest of the afternoon.

And now, this blind man had been tapping. Tapping and poking. It shouldn't be

245

difficult to get rid of him.

"Yes," he said to the blind man. It could arouse suspicion if he were uncivil. "I can give you some help. Wait there. I'll come out."

"Actually, I was wondering if I could come in. I think it's starting to rain again. Crazy weather."

He didn't hear any rain, and the last thing he wanted was a visitor, but could he say no to a blind man? Or was it really a blind man? It could be someone telling a lie. He would find out soon enough.

"Okay," he said. "Wait." And on his knees—since the tent wasn't high enough for him to stand—he crawled to the tent door, unzipped the semicircular entrance, and returned back to the far end.

The stranger was already on his own hands and knees, ready to enter. It was clear that he was not only blind, but old, with gray, wild hair, and heavily lined, unshaven cheeks. And he was wearing old winter clothing. In this heat! Inside the tent, it was even worse. The old man wouldn't be able to stand it for more than a few minutes.

As soon as he had unzipped the entrance, the man crawled in, and as he did so he saw with horror that the blind man carried the stick in his hand. The stick! How had he gotten it? What could this mean?

The blind man sat with legs crossed, yoga-style, just inside the entrance to the tent. He seemed unperturbed, absolutely calm. There was no need to panic.

"I don't know how they can stand it, sitting like this in Japan," the blind man said. "After five minutes, I can't feel my legs anymore, but maybe that's good because for the first five minutes they hurt like hell. Can you imagine doing a two-hour dinner like this, sitting on the floor? I tried it once and they had to carry me out of the room. Give me a good old chair any day of the week."

"How did you know my name?"

"It's on the tag outside your tent, on the post. Isn't it?"

"You said you were blind."

"You're quick on the draw, Mr. Callier. You're absolutely right. It was that ranger, Mr. Dance, who told me. Nice guy, Dance."

"Yes, he looked for me...."

"Looked for you? When did he look for you?"

"*Recently. Never mind. That's not important.*"

"*Right. Not important. By the way, does my walking stick look familiar to you by any chance?*"

"*It's a walking stick. They all look very much the same.*"

"*I suppose. This one was custom-made for me. I thought it might be a little different, but how would I know, right? I have a name for it. Hocus.*"

"*Hocus? What is that? Latin?*"

The blind man laughed.

"*Sounds like it. Doesn't it? Nah. Hocus is short for hocus-pocus. Have you ever heard that term?*"

"*It's a children's word, isn't it? Something to do with magic?*"

"*I suppose it could be, yeah. One definition I found for hocus-pocus is 'deception or trickery. Meaningless talk or activity, often designed to draw attention away from and disguise what is actually happening.' What do you think of that definition?*"

"*I suppose it is as good as any other. But as you can tell, it's very hot in this tent. What is it that you want?*"

"*Oh, sorry! I got carried away. First, I've got some good news. Mr. Dance asked me to spread the word, to tell folks that it looks like the causeway's been repaired. We'll finally be able to get the hell out of here.*"

That was good news, indeed. It was evening. He could be across by dark. Maybe that was too optimistic. Maybe wait until after dark. That might be safer. But even without his bicycle he could walk across the causeway, or get a ride from someone. That would be easy enough. No one would turn him down with all his gear. On second thought, he would just leave it all here. He had no further use for it.

"*Thank you for letting me know. Is there anything else?*"

"*Just one thing:* 'Toglie alle membra lasse il suo riposo il timore de' lampi, e tuoni fieri.'"

What? Who is this blind man? Quoting the sonnet from Vivaldi's Summer! My concerto! And the very words that confound me: "The fear of the furious thunder and lightning saps the strength from the shepherd's tired limbs."

"*That's kind of how I feel,*" *the blind man said.* "*That storm and all. Makes me* farblunget. *How about you?"*

He would not offer a response. He must be hallucinating with this blind man in front of him. He can't be real.

"Cat got your tongue, Mr. Callier? That's fine. But you might want to ask Ranger Dance what's happened to your bicycle. It seems to be missing. I hope no one stole it."

How does this man know such things? Who is he?

"Why would you think I have a bicycle? Did he tell you?"

"He didn't have to. The way I see it—pardon the expression—that's the only way you could've made it over the mountain to the festival and back. I don't think you would've risked biking along the road because with all the traffic you would have been spotted. Going over the mountain on foot, though, would've taken way too long for your plans. And since the roads were out after the storm, a car wouldn't have been possible. That leaves a bike or a horse. Bike seemed much more likely. A horse is so cowboy. Don't you think?"

"I don't know what you're talking about."

"You don't, Little Dutch Boy?"

This was unbelievable. He needed to rid himself of this blind man.

"Please leave. It's getting too hot in here."

"But it's only dry heat!" The blind man cackled.

"Nevertheless, I think our discussion is over."

"I don't think so, Mr. Kuypers."

He knows my name!

He was speechless. He had to escape. But the entrance was blocked by this man sitting in his way. He might have to use force, even against an old, blind man.

"Mr. Kuypers? Are you still here?"

"Yes."

"Can I ask you one more question, please?"

He was too dumbfounded to object. The blind man seemed to know almost everything.

"What is it?"

"Only where you might be hiding the knife?"

Oh, my God. He does know everything. *He had it hidden under his sleeping* bag. It hadn't moved since he returned from the festival. No one knew about the knife. Absolutely no one. But how? How was it possible? It was not possible.

The blind man didn't wait for an answer, but continued.

"You're probably wondering right now, how can this old blind man know so much about you and what you've done. So I'll tell you what if you agree to tell me why. Is that a deal?"

He couldn't answer. He was in a state of shock.

"Hey, Edo! You hear me? Is it a deal?"

"Yes, yes. Tell me what you know. What you think you know."

"Good. Thank you for that. Let me start out by telling you my name. It's Daniel Jacobus."

"Jacobus. Yes, Jacobus. I've heard that name. You're Shinagawa's old teacher."

"See, we're off to a good start. You're exactly right. I'm the old teacher of the young lady who substituted for you here at the festival. The young lady to whom Unknown Caller made two threatening phone calls: 'Don't go there.' 'Leave. Now.' The unknown caller is now known. It is known as you."

"You have no way to prove that."

"And I know all about the unfortunate story of the Little Dutch Boy and Uncle Tom and of the nasty recourse taken by Anita Talbot, reporting your innocent comment at the Let's Go Dutch festival. That single, asshole decision by them turned your life upside down. But when they hired you again for the Antelope Island festival, you thought to yourself, Edo, maybe my luck has changed. Maybe I can resume my career. But then, before you even get here, Sunny Flox, at Talbot's behest, unhires you. And to top things off, your friend, Marcus Renfro, calls you in Amsterdam and reports that history was repeating itself when Jamie Barov said that Christian Bjørlund and Dieter Waldstein were behaving like two bitches in heat.

That would have been last Saturday. When you heard that Barov was going to be blackballed for that comment, that was the straw that broke the camel's back. You decided you had to act. So you packed your bags and hightailed it all the way here, bent on revenge. Rather than make yourself visible at the festival, you decide to set up shop here at the campground, make a lightning strike over the mountainside, and return here to your tent. A clean hit, as they say on the cop *shows. What you didn't count on was the storm. That created a real challenge. It must have been excruciating getting back over the mountain in that storm. But then again, you're Dutch. The Dutch are a practical, persevering people, and bikes are as familiar to you Dutch as Big Macs are to Americans. But the storm also created an unexpected opportunity, didn't it?"*

"Why do you say that?"

"Because your original plan was to kill Talbot and Flox by stabbing them to death. Once you had made your way to the tent you waited for the ideal moment and situation. But here's the thing: With stabbing, there would have been no question it was murder. With the storm collapsing the Big Top and with Talbot stuck under it, you had a sudden inspiration! You could make it look like an accident. Grab whatever weapon was handy and kill her with it. And we both know what the weapon is, don't we?"

"The stick."

"Yes. My stick! Bad luck on your part, because when I saw that it had also been used to bludgeon Flox, it got me very angry. For one, I don't like being set up. Second, it was something Ms. Shinagawa made for me, and it pissed me off that it was being used for ulterior, evil purposes. So, Edo, now it's your turn."

"First, answer me one more thing."

"Go ahead."

"How do you know about the knife? Nobody knows that. I told no one."

"Just a matter of putting two and two together. It starts with me being familiar with your reputation as a fine Baroque violinist. I've even listened to some of your recordings, and even though I think you could work on your tone, I've found them to be very musical and stylistically representative.

"So, when after determining that it was unlikely any of the musicians (except for your defender, Marcus Renfro) or concertgoers could have been Talbot and Flox's murderer, that left either the state park personnel or the campers. I arbitrarily ruled out the personnel, and though that might have been rash it seemed more likely that the murderer was someone who would want to come and go quickly. So that left the campers. The difficulty was, Renfro had given me every reason to believe it was him, and so I forgot about the campers.

"That is until Dance told me a Callier, not a Collier, was tenting at the

campground. *When he told me that, all of a sudden my bells and whistles went off so loud I almost went deaf, if you can believe it. First, because Gene M. Callier had been the so-called 'lost' camper, and second, because of the middle initial, M. It just seemed strange that someone would use their middle initial signing up for a tent site, especially appended to what was already an unusual name, Callier.*

"So I started asking myself. Could this be a pseudonym? Maybe I started thinking that way because Yumi had been given a book by Mark Twain, aka Samuel Clemens. As a music scholar yourself, you would no doubt be aware of the pseudonyms and nicknames composers have occasionally come up with over the centuries. Some were meant to disguise their identities: George Gershwin was born Jacob Gershowitz. Aaron Copland was Aaron Kaplan. Some were meant to be clever: the Brit, Philip Heseltine, called himself Peter Warlock. Or descriptive: Schubert was nicknamed Schwammerl, little mushroom, because he was short and dumpy. The most famous is of course Mozart, who was baptized Johannes Chrysostomus Wolfgangus Theophilus Mozart. 'Theophilus' is Greek for 'loved by God', but little Wolfgang preferred the Latin 'Amadeus' that we know and love.

Once I started down that path, I asked myself, could it be that the unusual name, Callier, was an anagram? Not such a big mental leap. Click, click: Callier—Leclair, the great Baroque violinist of the eighteenth century. And Gene M. is a corruption of Jean-Marie. That was very clever of you, if I say so myself, but entirely predictable. And it gave you away. You should've chosen someone from the twentieth century, like Szymanowski. That would've had me climbing up the walls."

It was astounding. And though he already knew the answer, he asked anyway, to be sure.

"But you knew about the knife! As I said, I told no one."

"Well, I've always told my students to read their music history. It makes the music so much more interesting and gives them that much more potential for their interpretations to be creative. Don't you agree? As you and I know perfectly well, Jean-Marie Leclair came to an unseemly end. October twenty-third, 1764, if my memory serves me. Three vicious stab wounds to the gut while standing in the vestibule of his ratty apartment. Assassinated. Found in a pool of blood. Some say his estranged wife. Some say the gardener. Some say his nephew. For a variety of

reasons. No one was ever caught. What was generally agreed upon was that the motive was revenge.

I concluded that as you had taken Leclair's name to pursue your machinations, you would also adopt his method. History repeating itself, except of course, in reverse. You were Leclair. So you must have had a knife with you. Certainly, someone with your intelligence and cunning couldn't be expected to go off to kill someone without having a weapon. That would have been asinine. A gun would have been problematic in so many ways, and a heavy weapon would've been a pain to schlep over the mountain. Yep. I'm sure there was going to be a knife. But then you had the better idea. The stick. Bravo for your improvisation."

If it was true that the causeway was repaired, the only remaining obstacle for him was this blind man sitting in his path, holding his accursed stick like a flagpole between his legs. It was so hot. This old man could not last forever. He was reassured when he felt for the knife under his sleeping bag and found it to be in the exact position he had left it.

"Mr. Jacobus, somehow you have understood everything. I am amazed. But there are parts of the story that I now wish you to hear."

"Yes, that's part of our bargain. I'm all ears...so to speak."

"Very well. You know that I was unfairly dismissed from Let's Go Dutch."

"Yes. Then and now, Edo. Then and now."

"Then and now? What do you mean?"

"Then, Let's Go Dutch. Now, Antelope Island Music Festival. But it's what happened to you between then and now that interests me. After you were fired the first time. Pissed off, were you? You know, people react differently to adversity. Some let it roll off them and move on, or even get stronger."

Or just push adversity into a corner and build a bitter brick wall around it with broken glass on top, *Jacobus thought. That's how he felt about his own response to misfortune. Though Yumi would have a higher opinion of him than that. Tell him how noble and heroic he was under his crusty exterior, but what did she know? What did she really know about him? All he had done was manage to survive. And if not for her, and Nathaniel, and music—*

"That is easy enough to say, Mr. Jacobus. You judge me how you want to. After I was fired, my career—my life—went into a tailspin. But it wasn't my fault.

After Anita's complaint, word got around. No one wanted to hear the whole story. Not that it would have mattered. I started being blackballed. And the more that people stopped hiring me and musicians stopped performing with me, the more depressing my situation became. It started a downward spiral. I became a pariah. I couldn't handle it and you may know, we Dutch, we like to drink a little. And for years, we've had the cannabis bars. All legal. Gradually I became an alcoholic. Yes, I admit it. And every day, I visited the so-called coffee shops where I smoked and was high all the time in order to prevent being so low. I lost my friends and my colleagues, and then there was the divorce from Renata, my wife, that was ugly, and separation from my children. I dropped off the face of the music world entirely. The more I was ostracized, the more I became depressed, and the more I realized it was all about nothing and it was not my fault! Do you understand this, Mr. Jacobus?"

Jacobus had heard this song before. On one hand, there had been Robert Schumann. The severe depression. The manic creativity. It broke Jacobus's heart, and when he understood who Gene M. Callier really was, it was partly because he had been reminded by hearing Schumann's Kreisleriana. But Kuypers was far different from Schumann. Schumann's soul never faltered. Even in his worst times, he never made excuses. With Kuypers and others like him, it's always someone else's fault. Someone else to blame. The reality is, life's not fair. Whether you think it's God's will or the roll of the dice, no one set the world up to be fair. It's like with auditions. He constantly reminded his students of that fact. Only one person wins an audition. Everyone but that one person has to deal with losing. If you're going to dwell on it, whine about it, complain about it, cry in your beer, that's no one else's problem. That's your problem. Move on.

"Poor Edo," Jacobus said. "That's tough. To get fired over some innocent remark. Typical management assholes, wouldn't you agree?"

"The worst," Kuypers agreed. "They ruined my life unfairly."

"I didn't say that. Yes, they fired you. But it wasn't them who ruined your life. It was you who ruined your life. And then you extinguished two lives because you couldn't admit it to yourself. Isn't that more like it, Edo?"

The heat was unbearable. Kuypers wrapped his hand around the hilt of his knife. He didn't want to use it, but it was becoming evident that Jacobus was not *convinced of the unfairness of it all.*

"*Oh, the injustice!*" *Jacobus railed.* "*You make an innocent little remark—Uncle Tom—and poof, your life is ruined. Ruined! How can people be so unfair? Right? But think for a minute, Edo. If you think* you *were treated unfairly, that doesn't compare to Sunny Flox.*"

"*He deserved it. Just like Talbot.*"

"*Oh, no, Edo! That's where you're wrong. Hate to break this to you, but Sunny Flox did not want to unhire you. He was forced to by Anita Talbot.*"

"*That's not true.*"

"*Ah, but it is true. So you might have been deprived of a job unfairly, Edo, but you deprived someone of his life. Unfairly. Sunny Flox did not deserve to die.*"

He couldn't take much more of this. These accusations. All this blind man, Jacobus, did was twist the truth. He will soon feel the twist of the knife.

"*And if I may add,*" *Jacobus said,* "*think about the millions of people to whom your misunderstood innocent little quip referred.*"

"*What do you mean?*"

"*Look at the broader issue here, Edo. Who are we referring to when we talk about Uncle Tom? It's not about a single person named Thomas. We're talking about centuries of slavery, servitude, and all the racism that's still part and parcel of our fine way of life. So, yes, Edo, they were wrong to fire you for your comment. I am in absolute agreement with you there. But please don't talk to me about unfairness. There have been too many people throughout history, mine included, that have a stronger claim to unfairness than you do. But we don't go around killing people over it.*

"*Not only that,*" *Jacobus continued,* "*you put your friend, your true friend, Marcus Renfro, in real jeopardy. He knew you were there at the concert even though he didn't mean for you to come. He didn't intend for you to come. He saw you kill Talbot in the Big Top and knew you killed Flox in his cabin, but he kept his mouth shut. You know why? To protect you! Because he understood the unfairness of your firing in Amsterdam and the unfairness of your unhiring here on little old Antelope Island. He was willing to let you go free and risk taking the rap himself because he's a far more compassionate soul than I am. But what he wasn't good at was pretending. His mood changed faster than the weather here,* and there had to be a reason for it. And the reason was you! He was going to take the fall for you, and you would have let him. How noble of you!"

This man does not understand anything, Kuypers thought. He assaults me with no mercy. He is like the others.

"Mr. Jacobus," Kuypers said, continuing to talk as he lifted his knife silently from underneath the sleeping bag. "It seems we are at a turning point. Yes, yes, yes. So I did what I had to do. I don't know how you found out, but it is the truth. I killed the two of them. They deserved it and we can talk and talk all day, but it is getting too hot in here from all your hot air. So I have to ask you a question—" at which moment he lunged at Jacobus with his knife.

Jacobus, whose plan all along had been to goad Kuypers into revealing himself, had anticipated the attack would come at some point. When he heard Kuypers put an unnatural emphasis on the word "question," he readied himself. He knew that Kuypers was seated in an uncomfortable, constricted position and could not stand up, as he had ascertained from the height of the tent from when he had probed it. He also knew he would have sufficient space to reorient Hocus straight forward, like a lance. With Kuypers moving forward, Jacobus jabbed him with all his strength just below the sternum, knocking the wind out of him. The next instant he clubbed Kuypers on the side of his head, stunning him.

Kuypers, dazed, fell back. He moaned but did not lose consciousness. Jacobus could have killed him, then and there, with a few more blows to the skull, just as Kuypers had killed Talbot and Flox. He was tempted to kill Kuypers, not so much because Kuypers was a murderer, but because of the phone calls to Yumi: "Don't go there." "Leave. Now." Because although the initial intent of those calls might have merely been to disrupt the festival by frightening Yumi—Kuypers's innocent stand-in—Jacobus was convinced that Yumi would have been third on Kuypers's killing spree had not the storm intervened and created chaos. The threat to Yumi's life was something real, something Jacobus could simply not abide. Jacobus was not uncomfortable with the justice of revenge. Kuypers was writhing in pain in front of him. Should he kill Kuypers? No, killing people was for barbarians. He would let Kuypers suffer a worse fate.

Jacobus, who had not moved from his seated position, took the end of his stick and plunged it down rapidly—here, there, everywhere—as if he were churning *butter, until it came in solid contact with Kuypers's ankle. Kuypers cried out. Concluding he would not be able to get past this mad blind man, Kuypers instead slashed at the back of the tent with his knife, rending a ragged opening. Kuypers was out and running as fast as his hobbled ankle would allow.*

Jacobus, though pleased with having subdued an armed opponent and forced him to turn tail, didn't believe his victory was all that extraordinary. Having taken his time to carefully gauge the tent's dimensions, he had determined that Kuypers's ability to maneuver inside the tent was severely restricted from side to side. Sitting in the entrance of the tent, he knew Kuypers could only come forward. It also meant that Kuypers's ability to elude his trusty staff was so limited that Jacobus didn't have to have a particularly good aim to find his target. And having a long staff compared to Kuypers's short knife was a distinct advantage. Also, Jacobus had come to the conclusion that Kuypers, in the end, was a coward. So Jacobus gave himself credit for being adept, as the food server in the barn had said. But nothing more.

Nevertheless, he was out of breath from the exertion, and his shoulder was killing him from when Renfro had knocked him down, but he wasn't so spent that he couldn't wheeze out a laugh. He had hoped that Kuypers would have seen there was no hope and have given himself up. But at least Jacobus had elicited a confession. Kuypers might have thought he had escaped, but Jacobus had planned for that contingency, too. There was only one direction for Kuypers to run, unless of course, he ran into the lake, which was not likely. The most difficult thing for Jacobus now to do was unfold his legs—stiff and sore—and crawl out of the damn tent. After that, he'd have ample time to meet up with the others.

"Edo, old boy. Sorry to say, I have a feeling your fun's just begun."

Chapter Nineteen

From her vantage point, Yumi could see the treeless campground nestled against the shore of the lake. The storm clouds had dispersed, leaving the sun, which had begun to set over the western mountains, to turn the sky, the water, and the land a heartless bronze. When the figure emerged from the tent, it was too small to determine whether it was Jake or Kuypers. But when it started to run, there was no doubt which one it was. But where was Jake's signal—waving Hocus from the tent—to confirm that he was all right? She waited. Ten, twenty, thirty seconds, holding her breath, her hand shielding her eyes from the setting sun. Should she forget about the damn plan and race down to the tent? Let the murderer go free in order to save the most important person in the world to her?

Yumi stood in the middle of the dirt road, stationed where Dance said Kuypers would have to go when he fled toward the causeway and freedom. Jacobus had agreed with his assessment. Renfro was at Yumi's side, also according to Jacobus's plan.

Kuypers dashed along the road. Though there was still plenty of daylight for him to see his way forward, the lay of the land would prevent him from seeing her and Renfro until he turned the corner. As far as Kuypers knew, freedom was still within reach, even if he had to run for it.

How much longer could Yumi wait for Jacobus's signal? It was taking too long.

At first, the road paralleled the lake. The pounding waves had calmed and the tall dried grasses and brush that covered the rocky terrain swayed, clicking in intimate conversation. Otherwise, except for the fugitive, the

257

primordial landscape was still. After a few hundred yards the road on which Kuypers ran turned inland and began an uphill ascent. As he made the turn he finally saw them. His pace slackened. He was already winded, anyway, and he was limping.

No doubt, he would assume Marcus was there to help, Jacobus had reasoned. All part of the plan. First, Jacobus would get Kuypers rattled and make him realize there was no way out. If he didn't succeed in getting Kuypers to surrender outright, he predicted Kuypers would try to convince his old friend and Yumi, as he had unsuccessfully tried to convince Jacobus, how unfairly he had been treated, with the hope they would let him go, maybe even drive him to the causeway. After all, they were all musicians! Musicians understand each other! We're all brothers, right? Kuypers would do his best to sway them, but failing, he would ultimately give himself up. He had no choice.

There was the signal from Jake! He had crawled out of the tent and swung Hocus over his head like a victory banner. Hocus, the magic stick. The stick from Jacobus's woods that had brought him back to life. Yumi relaxed and focused her attention on Kuypers.

Kuypers, his eyes questioning, slowed to a walk and then stopped altogether, just a few feet in front of them. He still held his knife in his right hand. Panting from exertion and panic, he seemed uncertain what to do next. Yumi knew that she had been the one who had taken Kuypers's place at the festival, and in his current mental state, she was probably the last person he wanted to see standing in his way. She also understood that he might trust Marcus, which is why, by prior agreement, Renfro stepped forward.

This was the one part of the plan Yumi was uncomfortable with, arguing that Kuypers would be unstable and unpredictable, and that, since she had no personal relationship to Kuypers, she was better equipped to think and respond rationally and quickly in the event of an attack. Renfro insisted that it was his responsibility to make amends for allowing Kuypers to have "done what he had done"—Renfro hadn't even been able to use the words "kill" or "murder"—and wanted the opportunity to convince Kuypers to surrender without further incident.

"Edo," Renfro said, quietly and calmly, maximizing his persuasive skills. "I did the best I could. I didn't want this to happen. Any of it. I even hoped you wouldn't get caught. I hoped no one would have gotten caught. But, Edo, you killed people and they know everything. It's all over. Put down your knife and give yourself up."

Kuypers inched even closer. Yumi didn't say a word or move a muscle. If Marcus couldn't convince him to surrender, certainly she wouldn't be able to.

On the way to the island, Renfro had explained everything to Yumi. Once he started, the dam broke and it all gushed out. Renfro and Kuypers had not only been friends. They had been like brothers. Even more than brothers. Renfro confessed to Yumi that for a time they had been lovers.

"You did the best you could?" Kuypers said to Renfro. "Marcus, you did nothing! You promised me you would help me escape."

"How, Edo? How could I have helped you escape? There was no way off this island! For any of us!"

Renfro moved closer to Kuypers. Yumi held her position, watching Kuypers's eyes intently for any sign of change, preparing herself to act.

She now understood what was behind Renfro's erratic behavior. He had lobbied hard for Kuypers to be hired at the Antelope Island Music Festival and was elated when Kuypers was given the chance to resurrect his life when the opportunity arose. But then, when Talbot ordered Flox to cancel the engagement, Renfro was as heartbroken as Kuypers must have been.

But Renfro's big mistake had been when he called Kuypers to tell him Talbot and Flox were about to do the same thing to Jamie Barov that they had done to him. It had infuriated Kuypers, snapping him out of years-long lethargy into an obsession for retribution. He told Renfro he was coming to the island.

"You told them I was coming," Kuypers said to Renfro.

"No, Edo. I didn't tell anyone you were here. Even when I saw you at the concert...saw what you did to Anita, I didn't tell them. They all thought you were still in Amsterdam. Edo, you shouldn't have come here. I told you not to. I kept your secret. What else could I do?"

Once Kuypers had reached the island, he and Renfro had met in secret on the day Yumi had gone into Salt Lake City with the other musicians. Kuypers didn't divulge specifically what his intentions were, but Renfro suspected that it was to somehow confront Anita Talbot. That's what accounted for his own behavior, he admitted. He apologized to Yumi.

"I'm so sorry how I treated you," he said. "No excuse. But knowing he was here and not knowing what was going to happen...I was torn up inside."

"Why didn't you tell me?" Yumi had asked on their way to the campground to confront Kuypers. "You know you could trust me. Why didn't you tell anyone?"

"I should have. I know I should have. I just couldn't."

"And even after he killed two people, Marcus? How could you have not done anything?"

"I know. I didn't want him to get away with it. I hoped he'd get caught. I just didn't want to be the one to do it."

Yumi tried to be understanding. But she was not sure she could be forgiving.

Kuypers was now as close to Renfro as Yumi was. Mere steps away.

"Edo," Renfro said. "My friend." His hands spread from his sides, he took another step forward. That was his mistake. Kuypers rushed at him, screaming, with his knife poised.

Yumi leaped at Renfro from behind and to the side, rolling into him with her shoulder to knock him off his feet and away from the attack. But before the two of them hit the ground, Kuypers viciously slashed at Renfro, etching a diagonal red line across Renfro's chest. Renfro, with a gaze of disbelief that his friend would attack him, fell to the ground. Yumi, already on one knee, rose to step in front of the wounded Renfro to confront Kuypers.

Kuypers raised his knife above his head, preparing to strike down on the left side of Yumi's neck. It was the attack she anticipated, which called for a simple *naname-tsuki* response. With her left hand, she grasped the top of Kuypers's wrist as it came down. At the same time, she stepped back to avoid the thrust and turned ninety degrees to her right, pulling Kuypers around in a semicircle in front of her. She then applied pressure to the top of his wrist with her right hand, the only possible result of which threw him down onto his back. Once on the ground, she maintained her grip on his wrist and applied pressure with her right knee against his side. She then slid her right hand under his right arm to engage his wrist. At that point, she had several options, including breaking his wrist, breaking his elbow, or pressing the point of his knife into his neck, killing him. She chose none of those options. Instead, she disarmed him, removing the knife from his immobilized hand, taking special care—as she was a musician—not to cut her fingers on the blade. The entire maneuver took less than five seconds.

She had been taught in judo to show respect for one's opponent and tried to make it sound sincere, but she wasn't sure she succeeded when she said softly into his ear, "It was an honor replacing you as the Vivaldi soloist." It came out sounding more like a snarl.

Yumi rushed back to tend to Renfro, lying on his back, his hand covering his bleeding chest. Kneeling at his side, she was puzzled that his eyes seemed to be gazing not into hers, but behind her. Was he going into shock?

"Marcus, are you okay?"

"Look out."

Yumi turned around to see Edo Kuypers holding a very large boulder above his head, clearly prepared to slam it down onto hers. But before he could, a rope appeared around Kuypers's torso. The rope was quickly tightened and winched up to his armpits. Kuypers was lifted off the ground, forcing him to drop the boulder harmlessly to the ground.

Yumi's eyes followed the rope ten yards behind Renfro to a black-and-white spotted horse with a man sitting on it.

"Mr. Dance!"

Jefferson Dance touched his fingers to the brim of his cowboy hat.

"Ma'am."

Kuypers, like an ensnared snake, writhed to free himself from the lasso around him.

"Excuse me a minute, ma'am," Dance said. He backed his horse up a few steps, which tightened the lasso even more, and dragged Kuypers backwards, his heels etching tracks in the dust. Dance then had the horse, tossing its mane, take a step forward, suddenly slackening the rope so that Kuypers, off-balance, found himself flat on his back. Dance trotted his horse up to Kuypers, prone on the ground, and instructed the horse to place a front hoof, gentle but suggestive, on Kuypers's chest. Kuypers understood the message and stopped struggling.

Dance dismounted and handed the reins to Yumi.

"Seems you know how to take care of yourself, Miss Shinagawa. If you wouldn't mind keeping an eye on Mr. Callier here, whose name I guess isn't Callier, I'll tend to your friend. I think I'll be able to patch up his wound okay till we get him to a doc. I've seen a lot worse."

Yumi looked at Kuypers lying on his back on the ground. Bruised and covered in dust, seemingly defeated, he supported himself with his elbows. When Dance's horse whinnied, Kuypers made a sudden move, as if he was considering the possibility of getting up and running away. Yumi saw that his left ankle, the one he was limping on, was swollen. She stepped on it, applying all her weight. She wouldn't break it, but it would discourage Kuypers from considering any further ambitions, either with a boulder or with tossing a pebble at a cabin window.

"Tell me, Edo," she said. "First it was Anita. Then it was Sunny. Who was next on your list? Was it me?"

"I don't know what you're talking about," Kuypers said.

Yumi reapplied the pressure on his ankle. Kuypers gasped. With a smile she tried to conceal—and with more satisfaction than her upbringing would have deemed appropriate—she said to him, "Leave now, Edo? *Hmm?* Don't go there."

The wail of a police siren, yet one more unnatural intrusion on the surreal scene, emerged from the distance, getting closer.

"Sounds like Detective Gettelman and Officer Guzman will be here any minute," Dance called to Yumi.

Gettelman and Guzman! What if they totally misconstrue the whole thing? Yumi thought, with a jolt. *What if they still think I was involved in the murders and that Kuypers had been my next potential victim? How will I explain my way out of that?*

Dance must have seen the concern on her face.

"No worries," he said. "I'll let our friends make the arrest. But you can count on me to be what the lawyers call a darn good witness. We'll get this all sorted out. You're good as gold. And here comes Mr. Jacobus, himself, with his walking stick. The original one."

Chapter Twenty

J oy D'Angelo dropped off Jacobus, Yumi, and Nathaniel at Ticklin' Ribs, on the outskirts of Salt Lake City. Before she drove off, she handed Cornelia Blum's business card to Jacobus.

"She asked me to give this to you," D'Angelo said. "She said she wants to talk to you about co-writing *Symphonies and Scorpions*, the book she's working on. Especially the part about the previous two weeks."

"Only if I star in the film," Jacobus said and put the card in his back pocket.

Marcus Renfro, with Jefferson Dance at the wheel of his pickup truck, joined them shortly thereafter. Dance was treating his new friends to a meal at his favorite barbecue joint. The lunch hour crowd was loud and expectant, the line already snaking outside the restaurant for the best smoked meats in town.

Dance had been correct that Renfro's knife wound was superficial, though the scar would be a permanent reminder to him to be careful in his choice of friendships. He was bandaged around his chest, but otherwise intact. Yumi and Renfro had said their private good-byes to each other the night before, in his cabin. Tenderly, but carefully. She voiced concern over his wound. He voiced approval of her tattoo.

Before leaving Antelope Island, Renfro had an interview with Detective Gettelman and Officer Guzman. They had valid questions about Renfro's role in protecting Kuypers and in withholding information that could have expedited Kuypers's apprehension. But with Jefferson Dance backing him up, the interrogation proved exculpatory enough to receive permission to return to his home in the Bay Area. Once there, Renfro would recuperate for a week before embarking on his festival in Nice. Only Guzman had expressed serious reservations, which were alleviated once Renfro agreed to testify against his former friend.

There were no questions about Kuypers's role. He had been expeditiously arrested, booked, and jailed, and had an appointment with a local public defender.

D'Angelo wasn't able to join them for lunch because she had a meeting in Salt Lake City with the Antelope Island Music Festival board of trustees. Still reeling from the multiple disasters, the board had quickly appointed D'Angelo acting CEO after she confidently assured them she could handle the legal, financial, and media fallout. At the meeting, she would give them a PowerPoint presentation with the outlines of a plan to move forward, and hoped that by the end of the meeting her designation would be changed from acting to interim. The board would, of course, initiate a national search for permanent replacements for Anita Talbot and Sunny Flox, and though D'Angelo would certainly throw her hat into the ring, she was already making inquiries for administrative openings with other, more established festivals. It could prove to be an effective bargaining chip, she told Yumi, with a wink.

Once inside Ticklin' Ribs, Jacobus, Yumi, Nathaniel, Dance, and Renfro waited impatiently until there was an unoccupied table for five. The East Coasters had four hours before their flight to JFK.

They sat around a circular table covered by a plastic red-and-white checkered tablecloth. Jacobus, dressed in his seersucker suit for the occasion, was intoxicated by the aroma of smoking meats. Yet to have a full meal since leaving his home in Massachusetts, he ordered a full slab of ribs with extra sauce (the restaurant's homemade spicy variety) and sides of coleslaw, red beans and rice, and hushpuppies. And a sweet iced tea to wash it down. Nathaniel insisted Jacobus wear a bib over his suit. The dry cleaning costs could be formidable.

"Are you really going to eat all that?" Yumi asked.

"My eyes are smaller than my stomach," Jacobus said.

"You and your blind jokes. But what about your gastric distress?"

"There are times one must make sacrifices. Besides, Dance is paying."

While waiting for their order, they did a postmortem of the weekend, connecting the final dots in the bizarre series of events. The only (minor) bombshell was offered by Jefferson Dance.

"To tell you the truth," he said, "I was suspicious of the man whose name I thought was Callier even before you were."

"How so?" Jacobus asked.

Before he answered, a few of the customers came by, tapping Dance on the shoulder and saying hello and telling him what a great job he'd done for them at some point in the past.

Dance tipped his hat and returned the greetings.

"What was that all about?" Jacobus asked once the acquaintances walked away.

"Just some investigative work I did for a few folks a while back," he said.

"I thought you said you weren't a cop?"

"I'm not. Exactly. But I've done a thing or two."

He left it at that.

"Anyway, it was the bicycle," Dance said. "That's what made me raise an eyebrow. To begin with, that type of bike had no business being on Antelope Island. And if you were going to be dumb-skulled enough to use it, you'd know to stay on the flat trails. You'd be loco to be going over Frary Peak in a bike like that."

"And if he had stayed on the trails, there wouldn't have been so much damage," Jacobus said, finishing the thought.

"That's right. And just looking at the wreck of the bike outside the tent and hearing Callier—I mean Kuypers—at the same time insisting he was fine, well, it didn't add up. He had to've been lying, or at least stretching the truth. And if someone's in distress and won't admit it, that made me scratch my head. That's when I had one of the gals working for me keep an eye on him. Lucky for him, too. He'd just done a somersault into the lake. She came close to having to fish him out." Dance chuckled at the memory. "So I knew he was up to something. I just didn't know what."

"But if you suspected right away," Yumi asked Dance, "why didn't you say anything to the police?"

"I needed to see things play out. I hadn't made the connection that Kuypers, aka Callier, was a murderer, and I sensed Mr. Jacobus had a better handle on what was going on than the police did. They were coming in cold, and it was clear that they knew nothing about the island, the people involved, or the music profession. So I just thought it would better serve the course of justice if I let them take a bit of a detour toward it."

"Which is why you kept your mouth shut about Hocus," Jacobus said.

Dance snickered. "Hocus. Yes, Hocus."

Their meals arrived. Nathaniel handed Jacobus a roll of paper towels that was on the table.

"This'll be better than your sleeve, if you don't mind," he said.

"Doesn't anyone feel bad for Edo?" Yumi asked. "He didn't deserve to be fired for his Uncle Tom comment."

"I think we can all agree on that," Jacobus said. "But you can't blame everyone else for your own misfortune. You make yourself into what you are. And in any event, you don't kill people because of it."

"Didn't you know he was such a lost soul?" Yumi asked Renfro.

"I should have. After he dropped out of the concert scene, he'd show up like a phantom at concerts and festivals, lurking around on the periphery."

"Could they have been places Talbot or Flox could've been?" Dance asked.

"Now that I think about it, it's very possible."

"Do you think he could have been stalking them all along?" Yumi asked Renfro.

"I never thought of that, but that's possible, too."

"Maybe we should let the police investigate that," Nathaniel said, helping himself to more slaw.

"I should never have phoned him when Anita sent the 'bitches in heat' comment to Sunny," Renfro said.

"Yes, that was pretty damn stupid," Jacobus said. "What were you thinking?"

"I don't know. I suppose I wanted to make him feel better. To let him know that it wasn't only him who'd been singled out. That everyone—even someone as popular as Jamie Barov—takes their lumps sooner or later. Commiserating. I didn't mean to incite him. I really didn't. And then when he told me he was coming to the island...I tried to stop him. I told him not to. But he didn't listen. And then, when I saw him in the Big Top, before it collapsed..."

"What?" Jacobus asked. He almost choked on a hushpuppy. "You knew he was going to kill Anita?"

"No, I didn't know. But I guessed. I tried to get to him. I saw him go up to her. And then the lights went out. I couldn't see anything. No one could. But then, it was too late. And then...I knew I should have stopped him right there. But I couldn't."

"And then you remembered about Flox," Jacobus prompted.

"Yeah. That's when I left the group. When we were talking in the barn. I ran off to tell Sunny that Edo might be after him. But I was too late again. I couldn't believe it. Sunny was a good guy. Not that anyone deserves to be killed, but Sunny?"

"And you still allowed Kuypers to hightail it?" Dance asked. "No wonder Guzman wasn't happy to release you."

"Edo was already gone by the time I got there. I didn't know where he went. I didn't know he was on the other side of the island. I didn't know whether he was even still on the island at all. I looked all over the place. For all I knew, he was gone for good."

"And, still, you were willing to take the blame," Yumi said.

"If it came to that, yeah. If the police found him, I wouldn't have stood in their way. But I couldn't..."

"What changed your mind, Marcus?" Yumi asked.

"When Mr. Jacobus told us about the phone calls you had gotten. 'Don't go there.' 'Leave. Now.' There's only one reason he would go after you. He was crazy. He had to be stopped."

"I gotta say one thing," Nathaniel said, with a somber face. "I recently said to Yumi that I thought you were a little holier-than-thou. I'm just gonna take that one back."

"I appreciate that, Nathaniel," Renfro said.

"But I'm still not so sure about your Elgar concerto," Nathaniel said. He was so pleased with his barb that he slapped his thigh.

"There's more than one right way to play music," Renfro replied, with a little edge.

"And an infinite number of wrong ways," Jacobus rebutted.

"Ho, ho, ho!" Yumi said.

Everyone laughed, though Renfro not as much.

"Just like there're an infinite number of wrong ways to piece together a murder?" Dance postulated. "Until you get the right way, that is."

"You get the gist," Jacobus said. "But now I've got a question for you, Dance. How the hell did you know to tail us to the campground, and on your horse no less?"

"'Cause you remind me of my horse."

"Jake smell that bad?" Nathaniel asked.

"Don't answer that," Jacobus said.

Dance laughed.

"You're right. I'm not touching that one. It might incriminate me. But what I will say is that when we talked about the name Callier, you stiffened for a second, just like my mare does when she senses a rattler in the grass. I knew you were on to something. Then, after you sent me off to the G-men, I just bided my time, figuring there was a reason you wanted me out of your way. So I just hung back and watched the show. I saw you take off with the D'Angelo girl and figured where you were headed. My horse might not be as fast on the roads as the van, but she does do a better job going overland. I managed to get there before you did and just kept an eye out for the goings-on."

"Your nag have a name?" Jacobus asked.

"Sage."

"Figures."

It was time to head for the airport. To put Nathaniel at ease, Jacobus used a paper towel, and not his sleeve, to wipe barbecue sauce off his face. They all stood up and shook hands. Nathaniel called for a taxi.

"I've got one more question," Jacobus said to Dance. "I understand from

269

Yumi that you've got a patch over one eye. That true?"

"It is."

"Good. Means you're halfway there!" Jacobus went into a spasm of wheezing laughter.

"Well, Mr. Jacobus," Dance said, with a poker face, after Jacobus had recovered. "And I've got just one thing more to say. When it comes to solving musicians' name puzzles, you certainly un-Ravel-ed the mystery about Leclair."

"Oh, mercy!" Nathaniel said. "It's contagious!"

"I'll say my fare-thee-wells here, then," Dance said.

"Where are you off to now?" Jacobus asked. "Back to the ranch?"

"No, I think I'll be heading home to listen to Miss Shinagawa's recording of *Summer* in the comfort of my own living room. It should be safer there."

A Note from the Author

For three out of four seasons, majestic, mountainous, mysterious Antelope Island, in the middle of Utah's Great Salt Lake, is one of my favorite places on earth. Like most people, I stay away during the fourth season, summer, which is also locally and infamously known as "fly season," because that's when you're assaulted by swarms of little, biting flies. They're a much worse adversary than the free-range bison herds, who are more content to chomp on grass and than on human flesh.

I hope the readers are willing to suspend their disbelief that in *Cloudy With a Chance of Murder* I totally ignore the insect issue. I also hope they'll suspend it regarding the music festival on Antelope Island. I confess, there is none, nor has there ever been. But, I have to say, I've often thought about the possibility while hiking on one of the island trails or having lunch at the picnic area at the Fielding Garr Ranch. Bach, Beethoven, and Bison? Hmm.

The scenery, not only of the island but also the Great Salt Lake itself and the surrounding mountain ranges, is stunning and otherworldly. One quickly gets the sense that there is no "other world" out there, beyond the horizon. It's a scene that is at once tranquil and disquieting. What better setting for a murder mystery?

Cloudy with a Chance of Murder is based upon two real-life events. The first, an icy tent collapse at a Utah Symphony concert with the folk-singing ensemble, The Lettermen, occurred on August 4, 1991 at the Snowbird Ski Resort, one of the orchestra's standard summer venues. I was onstage as associate concertmaster.

It isn't particularly rare on a Utah summer day for a strong weather front to pass through, bringing a sudden drop in temperature, followed by torrential, fast-moving thunderstorms. In the mountains, the change in weather can be extreme. Such was the case on August 4. The mercury plummeted so precipitously, that rather than rain, we were assailed by an intense hailstorm.

The massive tent, under which the orchestra performed and the audience of 1,400 sat, had been designed—or so I was told—for a big wedding in Saudi Arabia. I don't imagine they had planned for hailstorms. Our prescient orchestra manager, Cecil Cole, stopped the performance and took the musicians off the stage because the noise of the wind, thunder, and hail made it impossible for anyone to hear the music.

It was a blessing in disguise. Bobby Poynton of the Lettermen left the stage just as a support pole behind him "exploded." "They went like dominoes after that," he said later. Within seconds, the tent crumpled under the weight of the ice. If we had waited another two minutes, the orchestra, which was sitting on an elevated stage, would have been demolished. The piano, next to where I had sat just moments earlier, was pushed through the stage floor under the weight of the ice, and was destroyed.

EMTs, Snowbird and orchestra staff and musicians came to the assistance of the audience trapped under the tent. Though several dozen people required medical attention in local hospitals, it was miraculous that no one was killed or seriously injured.

The second event was a race-based scandal at the Oregon Bach Festival in 2017, resulting in the firing of its music director, the English conductor Matthew Halls. During the summer, Halls had made a racially insensitive remark to Reginald Mobley, an African American singer raised in Florida, who appeared at the festival.

The two men were close enough friends for them to tease each other's ethnicity and race: "We always get into these little bits which we have," Mobley said. "He'll start speaking in this terrible Southern drawl, and I'll mock his British accent on occasion."

One of those occasions was at a post-concert reception. After Mobley told Halls about an uncomfortable recital he had recently given in London, which included an antebellum-South setting, Halls affected a Southern drawl. The two thought no more of it.

Apparently, however, the comment was overheard. A few days later, Mobley received an email from the festival's executive director, Janelle McCoy, stating that "These insensitivities should not be tolerated."

Mobley came to his friend's defense. "Trust me," he said, "it's been a couple patrons and audience members who've unknowingly said pretty insensitive things. Not Matt." Nevertheless, Halls was fired and was paid a $90,000 severance as part of a nondisparagement agreement. The festival claimed that the firing was related to artistic issues, but Halls had signed a new four-year contract only a few months earlier. Happily, his career was not ruined and he has gone on to conduct major orchestras around the world.

Tents collapsing. Professional misunderstandings and discontent. Life in the classical music world is fraught with such pitfalls, both natural and manmade. Perhaps that's why writing murder mysteries in that world flows so easily off the pen.

Acknowledgements

Writing a book is an individual effort, but getting it from the author's desk to the book store shelf takes a team of professionals. Like Daniel Jacobus himself, the mystery series of which he is the persnickety protagonist somehow manages to endure against all odds. I would like to express my heartfelt gratitude to Josh Getzler, my agent at HG Literary, Meredith Phillips, who patiently proofread my early draft, and Shawn Simmons, my editor at Level Best Books, for helping breathe new life into the series.

About the Author

Gerald Elias leads a double life as a world-class musician and critically acclaimed author.

Devil's Trill, the debut novel of his award-winning Daniel Jacobus mystery series that takes place in the dark corners of the classical music world, was a Barnes & Noble Discover: Great New Writers selection. In 2020 he penned *The Beethoven Sequence*, a chilling psycho-political thriller. Elias's prize-winning essay, "War & Peace. And Music," excerpted from his insightful memoir, *Symphonies & Scorpions*, was the subject of his 2019 TEDx presentation. His short stories and essays have appeared in prestigious journals ranging from *Ellery Queen Mystery Magazine* to *The Strad*.

A former violinist with the Boston Symphony and associate concertmaster of the Utah Symphony, Elias has performed on five continents and has been the conductor of Salt Lake City's popular Vivaldi by Candlelight chamber orchestra series since 2004. He maintains a vibrant concert career while continuing to expand his literary horizons.

AUTHOR WEBSITE:

geraldeliasmanofmystery.wordpress.com

SOCIAL MEDIA HANDLES:
https://www.facebook.com/gerald.elias
https://www.facebook.com/EliasBooks/
https://twitter.com/GeraldEliasSays
https://www.instagram.com/geraldelias504/

Also by Gerald Elias

The Daniel Jacobus series:
Devil's Trill (also an audiobook)
Danse Macabre (also an audiobook)
Death and the Maiden
Death and Transfiguration
Playing With Fire
Spring Break

The Beethoven Sequence (political thriller)

Coming Up:
Roundtree Days
Murder at the Royal Albert

Self-published:
Symphonies & Scorpions
"...*an eclectic anthology of 28 short mysteries to chill the warmest heart*"
Maestro the Potbellied Pig (children's book, also an audiobook)